I0658289

I dedicate this book to myself.

The Book of Ferret

Madison Doll

©Madison Doll 2014

This edition printed by Draft2Digital 2023

Episode One

Ferret and the Pheromones

'And another fucken' thing,' bellowed Ferret, his little yellow tuft of hair reeling from the shock, 'your pub smells like stale shit!' He sneered and stood, one leg forward, as if anticipating a brawl. The publican was having none of it. It was late and he was tired.

'Thanks for that,' he replied wearily. He knew the little ferret-faced upstart all too well. He was a regular and full of shit. 'Now if you could just leave?'

''n' I fingered your wife upstairs just before.'

The publican stared morosely at the wall, 'That's more than I've managed for a long time.'

'Did ya hear what I said?' Ferret fired again. 'I just had me index finger and pointy man right up ya wife's coit! I could a gone right frough to the pinkie, but I need somethin' to pick me teeth wif on the way 'ome.'

'Yeah, I hear ya.'

'Well, what are ya gunna do about it! You gunna defend your wife's honour, or what?'

The publican, whose name was Steve, sighed heavily and looked down at Ferret. What a dick, he was thinking. For one thing his wife had no honour left. She'd ridden everything in Windsor from the horse drawn diner, to his brother. And for another thing, this little prick was five foot, when kicked up the arse and wearing high-heeled shoes. Who was he kidding? Every Friday night it was the same – Ferret Cutler, first-class, unemployed loser would spend his entire dole cheque in 'The Imperial Hotel', pick a fight and get his head smacked in. Tonight he was picking on Steve himself because everyone else had gone. Steve knew that Tai, the bouncer, was listening outside the window and was ready to respond as soon as Ferret started the usual ruckus. Tai was a big Māori boy and would put a porthole through the little twit. Steve was basically a nice Aussie guy. He had no desire to have the diminutive dickhead beaten up but he was tired and he had to get rid of him.

'Listen, Ferret,' he replied, 'I got a proposition for ya. 'If you fuck off right now, no questions asked, you can have a freebie on me tomorrow night. What do ya say?'

Ferret hesitated. His single tuft of hair drooped down enquiringly over his brow to see what his decision might be. He relaxed his stance and his track pants lowered slightly and rested on his old sandshoes. 'Two beers,' he said.

'Alright, two beers. Now fuck off.'

'You're lucky I'm feelin' in a generous mood,' Ferret sneered. And he sauntered out with a drunken swagger, taking a small sideways detour into the furniture on the way out.

Tai looked at Steve. Steve shook his head and Tai let Ferret pass.

Ferret, for his part, didn't notice the big man, otherwise he would probably have picked him too. But he was bleary-eyed, and tired himself, now that the excitement of the pool table, the pokies and the drinking was over. So he stumbled home, yelling obscenities down Macquarie Street to no-one in particular, about nothing in particular. Several people yelled back for him to shut up which only inspired him to greater heights. His voice echoed down the early morning street. He was so busy raising his head to make the loudest possible noise his drunken tonsils could muster, that he slipped and fell into the gutter. It had been raining and his sock got soaked.

'Fuck!' he hollered.

He attempted to pick himself up. Then, he attempted to pull up his soggy sock, which threw him off balance and sent him hopping haphazardly into the street, where he fell and ended up on his back, looking up at the stars.

He was still in this position when the frame, within which the stars dizzily tumbled, was filled with a closer object; a much closer object; two much closer objects, in fact. These were two very angry faces. They looked down upon him as his mother used to when he was a baby - with complete disgust and simmering contempt.

'It's that fucken' idiot again,' said one.

'Let's kick 'is arse,' replied the other.

So they did and Ferret crawled home to his single-bed apartment above the local brothel, bleeding heavily from the mouth but feeling at least satisfied that he'd managed to get his face smacked in on a Friday night.

Everybody likes routine.

*

Ferret was on a tropical island. A beautiful dark-haired Hawaiian girl was licking his arse. Just then, her huge and furious husband ripped off the grass door of the hut and made a beeline for Ferret. 'Oh shit!' he yelled disengaging from the woman's waggling tongue, which now found only air, where previously there had been a fleshy, hairy orifice. The hulk pushed Ferret in the upper shoulder while Ferret grabbed for his trousers. The massive, snarling man shoved Ferret again. Ferret knew, from bruised experience, that this was a certain prelude to a beating.

Then Ferret woke up.

A large man was poking him on the shoulder.

Ferret, his heart in palpitation and his hands upon his genitals, yelped involuntarily and sat bolt upright in his bed.

Before him, stood a man of irresistible proportions. He was approaching six and a half feet on the old imperial scale and would have no doubt tipped those scales at several hundred pounds. He was sandy-haired and his facial features were most child-like. He was quite handsome in a boyish way: orbicular face; large blue eyes that drooped like a puppy's when seeking attention; generous large lips; a well-proportioned pug nose; large facial features and a matching, solid frame. In all, he was a study in 'big', and a physical juxtaposition to the small, scrawny Ferret who was now eyeing him suspiciously, having finally broken through the miasma of hangover clouding his mind.

'Who are you?' asked Ferret with characteristic grace.

'Are you Ferris Cutler?' asked the man politely. His voice was soft and sonorous. He bore the unmistakable scars of a British public-school education.

'Who's askin'?'

The man did not reply but instead delved deeply into his coat pocket and withdrew a jaded photograph, at which he looked for a moment, and then presented to Ferret.

'It *is* you,' confirmed the man, pointing at the photograph.

Ferret looked down at the photo and reeled his head back with surprise. It showed three boys - an oversized baby-faced boy of perhaps four, and next to him, identical twins in a large cradle. Both were swathed in huge bibs and both had a small tuft of yellow hair above a crinkled forehead. Apart from the tuft, both heads were as bald as a khaki-wearing lesbian. One of the babies sported an angry scowl whilst the other beamed a large and optimistic smile. It was as if Ferret had been shrunk by some sort of Bugs Bunny potion to an infantile version of his present self and then doubled. The large, older child stood proudly, smiling at the camera and bracing a protective arm around the cradle.

'My long-lost brother!' exclaimed the newcomer and he tried, in vain, to replicate the photo by embracing Ferret.

'Hold your horses!' Ferret replied in kind. 'I ain't no poof and I ain't got no brother.'

'But look! You have! Two of them!' remonstrated the large man. 'Surely you see it? That's you! That's me! And that's Horatio!'

'Who the fuck is Horatio?'

'Your twin brother. Mumsy took that photo on my fourth birthday. Pater was taken ill not long after this and that's when you went missing. But I've finally found you!'

He tried to hug Ferret again.

By this time Ferret was on his feet and pushing the hulk away. 'What the fuck are you crappin' on about?' he yelled. 'And who the hell is Mumsy?'

'You wandered off. Mumsy blamed herself. She's never got over it. For years she's carried the guilt and just recently she's become gravely ill herself. We promised her we'd find you and take you home to see her before she dies. Oh Mumsy!' And he began to cry.

Ferret had had enough. 'Alright. Fuck off!' he yelled.

'And she's leaving us a fortune.'

'Poor Mumsy,' consoled Ferret. He hugged the distraught man.

The large intruder blubbered like a preschooler. Tears fell onto Ferret's head with the intensity of a rich Eastern Suburbs girl's piss on the turf at the end of Melbourne Cup Day. Ferret's face was buried into the man's stomach but his facial expression, could anyone have seen it, resembled that of one who has smelled something bad in the fridge.

'So, what did you say your name was . . . bro?'

'Oh, I'm sorry,' the man replied, wiping away an offending tear. 'Bernard. I'm Bernard Cutler, your long-lost brother.'

'Yeah. Right,' said Ferret. He tried a disingenuous back pat, but due to their relative sizes, it ended up being a bum pat and Ferret pushed Bernard away on homophobic impulse.

'A fortune, you say?' he asked, wiping his hand on his track pants and trying not to seem too interested. 'Come 'n' 'ave a beer 'n' we'll talk this over.'

Bernard wiped another tear away. 'Oh, but you haven't met Horatio yet.'

'Is that the little cun... I mean, is that darling Horatio in the photograph?'

'Yes, he's run off to buy you a present. He knew it was you as soon as he saw you there sleeping. I wasn't so sure, but now I see it really is you.'

He went to hug Ferret again, but Ferret was having none of it. 'Alright. Alright. Just fucken' settle,' he warned. One sentence of polite conversation at a time was about his limit. He pushed the unwanted affection away.

Bernard stepped back towards the door and someone bellowed. Bernard stood to one side and revealed Ferret's double, jumping around in pain.

'Oh, sorry, Horatio. I always step on him,' explained Bernard, 'accidentally, of course.'

'Oh that's okay, Bernie,' replied the runt, in a strangled falsetto, as he hopped around in pain. Eventually, he stopped hopping, regained his composure and looked up at Ferret.

Ferret was stunned. 'Well fuck me with a greasy light pole,' he whispered. 'It's like looking in a mirror.'

The two young men were indeed identical. They had even chosen to wear the same colour t-shirt, except Ferret's had a picture of Black Sabbath and was somewhat soiled with beer and blood from the night before. Horatio's t-shirt had a drawing of Pokémon.

'Ferris!' yelled Horatio and he ran towards Ferret with his arms spread wide, like a lover on a beach in a

Hollywood flick. Ferret, however, would not have passed the audition, because rather than returning the wild embrace, he chose to sidestep the oncoming love machine and purposely tripped him up and shoved him onward as he passed. Horatio sprawled forward and cracked his forehead into the wall.

'Oh sorry, mate,' said Ferret as he helped Horatio up. 'Oh, and you bought me a present too.' Ferret took a quick look at the photo frame and tossed it on to the floor.

'Oh, no worries Fezza,' replied Horatio, in a high-pitched whining voice, shaking his head to regain his senses. A lump the size of a small golf ball was growing there by the second. 'Accidents happen, eh?'

Yeah they do, thought Ferret and there might by another big one, depending on the size of the inheritance. A two-way split sounded better than a three way split and a one way split sounded best of all. He wasn't sure he could take on Bernard but he could certainly handle this little shit head.

'Well I'll be damned. It's really you,' mused Horatio, now fully recovered from the blow and smiling at Ferret. 'Oops, sorry. Shouldn't swear. That's five cents in the swear jar, eh, Bernster?'

'Pater will be watching from Heaven,' replied Bernard solemnly.

Ferret looked from one to the other with his eyes wide and his upper lip curled up in amazement.

'Let's get the fuck out of here,' he said.

*

Ferret strutted down the Windsor Corso with has arse as tight as a Jewish landlord. When he walked, his whole body was clenched. His shoulders pumped forward alternately at almost forty-five degrees and his upper body followed in a tense macho dance propelled forward by his arms. These were held fast at the shoulders and formed two scythe-like arcs from shoulder to dangling fingertips, so that when observed from the front, the strutting figure looked like an aggressive, advancing trophy cup.

Ferret's face, as he strutted, was held in one grotesque visage of sneering disgust. His upper lip was raised slightly in an ugly version of the Elvis sneer, his beady Ferret eyes were semi-closed like Clint Eastwood's just before the kill and his yellow tuft of hair bounced from side to side like a drunken ballerina.

By contrast, Horatio skipped along, grinning at everyone like the kid in the playground in junior high school who often ate alone and Bernard, the giant, lumbered beside him like some monstrous, handsome Shrek, with his legs bowed slightly in his suit trousers from the weight of the chassis above.

It was after midday and in the pub the Saturday crowd was in full swing. The pool tables were taken by a group of local girls who had fat arses, bleached white hair, more tattoos than a Brooklyn hooker and who said 'fuck' a lot. The fellas looking on didn't seem to mind. This was a collective of fine Aussie males who urged the girls, through toothless grins, to pot any ball that would reveal the girls' cleavage. They rested their beers on their bellies, laughed uproariously and congratulated one another each time a tit was revealed. And they said 'fuck' a lot.

There were a couple of families in for an early lunch and a clever little girl of about five, who had evidently learned to read early, had looked at the cocktail menu and, just as Ferret passed, was asking her dad what a 'Cocksucking Cowboy' was.

'Three quarters shot of Butternut Schnapps and a quarter shot of Baileys,' he threw in. 'And if ya want a Wet Pussy, that's a half shot of Canadian Royal Crown whiskey, half a shot of Amaretto and Red Bull for a mixer.

Though lookin' at you, you're a bit young for a wet pussy.'

'Hey,' replied the father, 'watch ya mouth!'

'Settle down,' replied Ferret. 'They're both on the menu.'

The father was deciding whether to make something of it when Bernard's shadow fell upon him. So he shut his mouth.

Ferret, who was always looking for a stoush, was disappointed at the father's lack of action. He hadn't realised the impression his new brother was making, not just on the father, but also on the whole bar and he was surprised not to be already amongst the flying furniture. So for good measure he added, 'Or if you'd prefer me to be more educational about it,' and he swung the little girl around so that they were eye to eye, 'it's when one homosexual man who wears a big fucken' hat puts 'is mouth on another man's dick.' And he grabbed his own dick to illustrate the point.

'Right. That's it!' shouted the father, and he rose from the table like a genie from a bottle.

Just in time, Steve, the publican arrived. 'Alright. Enough!' he shouted. 'Ferret take your mates and piss off down the back. I'll get you the beer I promised ya. Go on. Git!'

Ferret gave the man one last withering 'I'll be back' look and withdrew, followed by his brothers.

'Sorry, mate,' Steve apologised to the father, 'he's a dickhead.'

'What's a dickhead,' asked the little girl?

'I'll get you extra fries,' Steve apologised again and left the father to his explanations.

Ferret settled himself at a large wooden trestle. He nodded towards the little girl in the distance. 'She'll 'ave the Windsor Waddle within ten years, no worries.'

'What's the Windsor Waddle,' asked Bernard, sitting

on one end of the trestle and rapidly elevating the other, so that Horatio was catapulted like a blur between him and Ferret and across the room. He landed on his back on a neighbouring table, which fortunately was unattended. 'Oops. Sorry, old man,' said Bernard.

'That's okay Bernie Boy,' croaked Horatio as he picked himself off the table and grimaced with the pain of a bruised lower back.

'The Windsor Waddle,' Ferret replied, ' is so named because the chicks in this town eat so much shit that by the time they get to senior high their arses swing from side to side. You gotta give 'em a metre each side or they knock you out. They need lanes for pedestrians in the Hawkesbury.'

'Hey, Ferris . . .' said Horatio, as he took up his seat.

'The name's Ferret.'

'Why do you have to swear so much, mate?'

Horatio had a musical falsetto twang for a speaking voice. It was a whining drone that grew higher pitched and more strained towards the end of his sentences where the 'mate' was invariably placed. It was a combination between Essex and Aussie and it was annoying the hell out of Ferret.

'Hey, listen,' Ferret said loudly, 'this is my fucken' pub, right? This is my fucken' world. So don't you think you can fucken' come in 'ere and tell me how to handle it, alright?

But Horatio was unperturbed and as whining and annoying as ever, 'Sorry, mate. No offence meant, eh' Bern?'

'Mumsy doesn't like swearing,' Bernard concurred.

'Speakin' of Mumsy,' said Ferret, suddenly polite with the memory of riches, 'what was that you were sayin' earlier about an inheritance?'

'There's heaps of it, isn't there, Bernster?' Horatio prattled out. He looked up at his big brother like a doughy-eyed antelope.

'You look like fucken' Bambi,' said Ferret.

'No need to swear, mate,' Horatio replied with a smile. With one hand he held his lower back and with the other, the egg on his forehead.

'Mumsy and pater were awfully rich,' Bernard began in his thoroughly upper-class British voice. 'Pater was in the Lords and mater, that's Mumsy, was originally his maid. You see, Mumsy flew out from Australia especially for the job of minding the three of us. She was originally from New Zealand, I believe, but she grew up in Australia. She lived with Pater for a year or so . . . I should explain that pater and was already married at the time and, well . . .'

'A bit of hanky-panky ensued,' Ferret guessed.

'To put it somewhat indelicately, yes.'

'One for the southern hemisphere, eh?'

'Well, yes I . . .'

'It woulda been less than a day before she hopped on. They're randy bitches those New Zealand girls. She woulda been blowin' the old fella faster than a Redfern Abo on a ring-pull bong.'

Bernard was about to continue when he stopped for a moment and thought about that. Then he did a short double take and said, 'I have no idea what you just said.' But continued. 'So Mumsy is really the only Mumsy I remember and, of course, you two, being younger, knew absolutely nothing of the first Mumsy at all.'

'So what happened to first Mumsy?' asked Ferret, becoming interested.

'Oh, real Mumsy died tragically on a visit to Australia.'

'How?'

'Terrible accident. Bitten by a funnel web under the golden arches . . .'

'Painful there.'

'. . . in Lithgow, I think it was.'

'Was second Mumsy on that particular trip?' asked Ferret with a glint in his eye.

'Funny you should mention that. Yes. She was. Pater had insisted on her coming, for some reason.'

'Can't think why,' said Ferret, scratching his balls.

'No. But everything turned out well in the end though. Pater was grief-stricken at first . . .'

'Naturally . . .'

'But he recovered quickly . . .'

'Of course . . .'

'. . . and soon after, married Mumsy two, who is of course, Mumsy. They remained in Australia for some time. Pater was president of the Windsor Polo Club and Mumsy used to service the local horses.'

'And their owners too, I'll bet,' mumbled Ferret.

'What was that?' asked Bernard.

'Nothin'. So what happened to me?' asked Ferret, who got the picture, but in spite of his usual lack of decorum, figured there was no need to unnecessarily disrupt the equilibrium of these two naïve little shits.

'Mumsy took you for a toddle by the Hawkesbury River, to see the ducks, but mysteriously, you went missing. They dragged the river but there was no sign of you.'

'Any reason why Mumsy would want me off the scene?' asked Ferret, with the faintest twinge of a soggy memory.

'That's a strange question,' replied Bernard. 'But I suppose you did bite off one of her nipples during breast feeding and you did used to spit at her.'

'And you used to head butt her knee as soon as you could toddle,' added Horatio, 'You broke her kneecap once, but she loved you dearly.'

'Yeah, I'll bet she did,' murmured Ferret, fitting jigsaw pieces together in his streetwise mind. He turned on Horatio. 'But how come you speak like some sort of apologetic, semi-Aussie poofter and the big guy talks all posh like?'

Horatio shrugged. 'Just lucky, I guess.'

Bernard chipped in, 'The doctors were puzzled by that too. They ended up thinking it was genetic: some sort of aberrant throwback to the convict days. Mumsy married into aristocracy but let's not forget she is from inferior antipodean stock. I mean, I think even you would agree that it is generally recognised world-wide that Australians are vulgar, fly-ridden scum, with mediocre minds and nasal intonation. No offence, of course.'

'None taken,' Ferret replied, staring at the wall in thought. 'So, how much?'

'Somewhere between five and six hundred, we think,' Bernard replied.

'Thousand?' asked Ferret, impressed.

'No, million,' replied Bernard.

'Fuck me!' replied Ferret. And he got an instant hard on.

'Five cents for the swear jar,' said Horatio.

'Fuck off,' said Ferret.

'No need to swear, mate,' replied Horatio with a broad, idiotic grin.

'Bloody right,' added Steve, placing three beers on the table. 'Mind your mouth. Here's three beers and that's one more than I promised. Who are your mates?'

Bernard stood and shook Steve's hand. 'I'm Bernard and this is Horatio. We're Ferris' brothers and we're here to take him home to Japan to be at Mumsy's side when she passes.'

Ferret was gulping down the VB and spat it out all over the table. 'What the fuck!' he blurted.

'Mind your manners,' Steve chided. 'Your brother's a gentleman. Take a leaf out of his book. And stop swearin' in my joint.'

Just then a fat, overly made up forty-something woman, wearing tights for pants and a loose t-shirt for a top, stuck her head around the corner. 'Steve!' she bellowed, 'stop talking to that little cunt and get your fucken' arse in 'ere! There's more customers at the bar than fucken' flies under an Abo's armpit!' Her head disappeared around the corner as quickly as it had appeared.

'Alright, I'm comin'!' he yelled at the blank wall.

'Your wife?' asked Bernard.

Steve nodded.

'She seems nice,' Bernard said with a smile.

Steve left.

Bernard resat, which sent Horatio skyward again. This time he was thrust vertically and he landed with a crunch on his backside, right on the edge of the trestle.

'What's this shit about me goin' to Japan?' asked Ferret. 'I ain't goin' there. 'Everyone's Asian and it's full of fucken' radiation.'

'But it's all arranged and paid for, Ferrisimo,' said Horatio, rubbing his bottom, stretching his back and feeling the egg on his forehead.

'What the fuck is she doin' in Japan? I thought she was in England.'

'She was,' explained Bernard, 'she and pater returned after a year or two but they went via Japan where Mumsy was lucky enough to discover she had three long lost brothers. They were in a pop band and if my memory serves me correctly two of them worked as male models as well. It was such a stroke of luck finding them. Mumsy seemed so fond of them. She admired their tattoos constantly. They would often kiss her extremely affectionately and playfully fondle her breasts and buttocks, as brothers do.'

Maybe in England and Japan, thought Ferret.

'At any rate,' Bernard continued, 'she stayed there

for several months after Pater decided to return to England. She lived with her brothers and we were put into a boarding school, even though Horatio was only a baby, really. Mumsy felt we needed to learn self-reliance. She was always thinking of us.'

'Tell 'im how I nearly died, Bernie Boy,' Horatio piped in.

'What? asked Ferret, back from his mental calculations.

'Oh yes. Just before Mumsy decided it was time to return to England, she took out Horatio for a day trip to Mount Fuji. I can't remember why I didn't go, but the strangest accident occurred. Somehow, Horatio here, managed to fall into the caldera and it was only by sheer luck that his nappy caught on a rock about thirty metres down or he would surely have perished. You were very lucky, young man.' He waved an admonishing finger at Horatio who beamed back at him, proudly. 'Mumsy cried for days after that.'

'No doubt,' muttered Ferret.

'So, to cut a short story long, Mumsy returned with us to England where a few years later pater died from a freak accident.'

'Freak accident?' parroted Ferret.

'Yes, there was nothing Mumsy and Renaldo could do.'

'Who the fuck is Renaldo?' asked Ferret.

'Oh, Renaldo was Mumsy's fiery Latin pool keeper. Lovely chap. Used to walk about with his shirt off all the time, even in winter. But I have to say he did keep that pool crystal clear in every season, didn't he Horatio?'

'Beautiful. And Mumsy appreciated it, didn't she, the Bernmeister?'

'Oh God yes. She was always very affectionate towards him. She used to rub oil onto his chest to keep him moist and supple and often, when pater was away on business, she would invite him in for dinner and they would have toad in the hole. Mumsy said it was a divine meal comprising of sausage enclosed in batter. We never ate with them, of course. We were put to bed by that time. Mumsy made sure we got our rest.'

'She was always thinking of us,' added Horatio.

'Unfortunately, one night pater ventured too near the pool filter and it severed his jugular vein. Poor old Renaldo. The police didn't know him like we did. They questioned him for days. Eventually he was charged. I have no doubt of his innocence.'

'Is he still in jail?'

'Oh, heavens no. He was accidentally beaten to death by a guard shortly after going to jail. I know Mumsy tried to protect him because the guard came over to our house on several occasions prior to Renaldo's death, but it was no use. The guard's truncheon accidently slipped a dozen times and poor Renaldo was gone. It was about that time that Mumsy disappeared.'

'Didn't she take yous?' asked Ferret, who couldn't believe what he was hearing.

'No, she just forgot, apparently. Silly Mumsy; always forgetful.'

Horatio laughed fondly.

'So we were brought up in an orphanage and beaten mercilessly, but it made us all the stronger for it. Then, out of the blue, we received a message a few days ago telling us that Mumsy was gravely ill, that she didn't have long to live, that she had quite by chance learned of your whereabouts and that we must find you and come to Japan immediately. And so, here we are.'

Ferret rested the back of his head against the wall of the pub. 'Japan?' he whispered to himself. 'I ain't never been out of Australia, as far as I can remember. Japan, eh? For how long?'

'Only until Mumsy passes, then you're free to do as

you please.'

Ferret's mind was alive with possibilities. '''n' I get a third of the treasure?'

Bernard and Horatio nodded.

Apart from the riches, he figured these two innocent little turds needed some protection from 'dear old Mumsy', near death or not. 'Alright. Fuck it!' he exclaimed. 'I'll go.'

'Excellent,' replied Bernard. 'We leave tomorrow. We'll arrange some new clothes for you.'

'I gotta take a piss first,' said Ferret.

He quaffed the remainder of his beer and headed for the toilet.

After he left, Bernard said, 'He seems awfully nice.'

'Mumsy will be so pleased to see him and so proud of us for finding him,' Horatio replied.

'Yes, it's funny that she never thought of looking in the telephone book before.'

'Oh well,' replied Horatio, 'all's well that ends well.'

He took a sip of beer just as Bernard slapped him on the back in congratulation. Horatio knocked out an incisor, which he accidentally swallowed.

'I say, sorry old boy,' said Bernard.

'No worries, Bernmobile,' replied Horatio and he smiled with a new gap.

Ferret was in the toilet, pissing into the troth, when he looked to his left.

On the wall were two dispensers. One was for condoms, he had seen that a million times before, but next to it was a brand-new machine. It was for some weird thing he couldn't quite read. So when he finished peeing, he approached the dispenser and looked at it more closely.

Printed on it was: 'Wannaroot?. The Aussie Pheremone Sex Wipe. Warning. Drives women wild. Apply with caution.'

'Bullshit,' said Ferret but he fished in his pocket for two bucks anyway. He put in his dough, pulled out a tray from the machine and took out a small blue box. 'But if I get a root out of it . . .'

He opened the packet and rubbed the scented moist wipe onto the back of his neck and onto his wrists, just like the packet said. Then he pushed out through the toilet door and went up to the bar.

'Give us another VB,' he ordered.

'Whatever happened to 'please'?' asked Raylene, Steve's wife, as she poured him a beer.

'How long you had the new machine?'

'What new machine?'

'The dispenser in the shitter.'

'I dunno. Steve, how long we had the new dispenser in the shitter?'

'Come in yesterday!' he yelled back from the pool table where he was devotedly leaning behind and into a young tart to show her how to line up the ball. 'I told the tall poofta bastard who brung it that pheromone was spelled wrong, but 'e wouldn't fucken' listen!' Steve played the shot with an exaggerated pelvis thrust and the young bleach-haired girl laughed a hoarse laugh and slapped him for his trouble. 'You cheeky fucker,' she said.

'Looks like your old man's not sure whether to pot the pink or the brown,' suggested Ferret with a dirty smile.

'So long as he leaves me alone, I don't give a fuck,' Raylene replied. But as she leaned forward towards Ferret to place his beer on the counter, she looked up at him with the strangest expression on her face.

'What?' he asked with some alarm, turning his head both ways to look behind him, unsure of what the look meant.

Raylene's eyes widened; the pupils dilated and her cheeks grew rosy.

'What?' he repeated, somewhat urgently.

'Jenny!' Raylene yelled to a nearby barmaid who was having a fag outside. 'Take over the bar for a minute!' To Ferret, from whom she had not taken her eyes, she said in a strangled voice, 'You come wif me.'

She grabbed him roughly by the t-shirt and hauled him in one swift movement over the counter. Within several seconds Ferret found himself down in a small cellar, with the door shut firmly behind him. Before he knew what was happening, the amorous woman had ripped off her tights and undies and was rubbing her vagina on his leg like a randy dog.

'What the fuck are you . . .'

But he had no time to finish the sentence. Raylene was on to him quicker than an Indian into a food queue. She ripped open his fly, sucked his cock to achieve firmness and rode him like an electronic bull stuck on ten. Metal barrels flew and unearthly moans of orgasm penetrated the hollow cellar.

Several minutes later, her torrid passion sated, Raylene quickly hitched up her tights and said, 'See ya next time.' And she was gone, leaving the defiled Ferret alone and breathing heavily into the gloomy den.

'Fuck me,' he gasped. 'It works.'

'We were wondering where you got to, Fezza boy,' said Horatio as the somewhat dishevelled Ferret approached them.

'Give us some money,' said Ferret with urgency.

'I say, are you alright?' asked Bernard, producing his wallet.

'I'll pay ya back,' replied Ferret, grabbing the wallet and disappearing as quickly as he had arrived and then returning as quickly again with a full plastic bag full of bumps. 'Let's get out of 'ere,' he said and several seconds later the three of them were marching back towards Ferret's apartment.

Later that night Steve went to check the pheromone dispenser. 'Hey Raylene!' he yelled, 'You won't fucken' believe it. Those stupid bastards've already emptied the pheromone dispenser!' He chuckled to himself. 'Silly pricks wouldn't know the truth if they fell over it.'

At about that same time, Ferret was lying awake in bed, thinking. From the next room came the snores of Bernard and the occasional yelp from Horatio who was apparently an unsettled sleeper. He kept yelling out: 'Not the face!' and then laughing uproariously and muttering, 'Nice one, Bernie.' before descending into sleep for a short while and then repeating the process.

It had been a big day. Ferret had gained two brothers and an inheritance and become a stud. In terms of significance, the brothers were obviously of least importance and the money, well, he'd believe that when he saw it, but the pheromone wipes: they seemed to work. Or was that coincidence? Fuck, could it be? Raylene had never paid him any attention before, except to turf him out of the pub on the odd occasion Steve was away. So surely . . . But fuck, he'd better be right. He'd just spent a hundred bucks on a dispenser full of the stuff. If it was bullshit . . .

He turned on the light, grabbed one of the little blue boxes beside him and squinted at it until his eyes adjusted and he could read the packet clearly. It read: WANNAROOT PHEREMONES AFFECT SEXUAL URGES IN THE ANIMAL KINGDOM. THEY DO THE SAME IN HUMANS. Ferret considered that. I thought we *were* a part of the animal kingdom. He shrugged and continued. THE PHEREMONE AROMA DRIVES WOMEN WILD. FOR EXTERNAL USE ONLY. Thank fuck for that, thought Ferret. THIS PRODUCT HAS NOT BEEN TESTED ON ANIMALS. What the fuck did they test it on, Ferret wondered - whitegoods? A HIGH QUALITY WIPE. So presumably there were lower quality wipes out there. If so, why would anyone produce a low-quality pheromone wipe? It was all so confusing. But so long as it worked.

He couldn't sleep so he rifled through the clothes the boys had bought him earlier in the day. They had tried to get him to buy all sorts of poofy stuff like suits and ties but he was having none of it. He went straight into Lowes and bought up a storm. Quality? Talk about quality? He sifted through the glorious collection of stubbies, t-shirts and thongs he had purchased for a song. And those Viking Jeans – beautiful. Fuck those expensive Levis. Who needed two pockets at the back?

He kicked around his room for a bit, bored and looking for action. He was supposed to be asleep, so he was rested for the flight tomorrow morning early, but he was too excited. He just couldn't sleep. Instead, he pocketed a pheromone wipe and he took a trip down the stairs to see what Cheryl and the girls were up to. It was Saturday night so they were probably all on the job but he thought he'd check and see anyway.

Out the front stood Cheryl and Danielle. Cheryl was the older of the two at twenty-one. Danielle was only eighteen. They were both good lookers and built for action. Cheryl was a blonde dyed black and Danielle was a black dyed blonde. Cheryl had bigger tits but they both had plenty and they both wore short skirts, fishnets and high heels to attract customers. Unfortunately for them, it was a slow night in Windsor. The pubs had been closed for an hour and there was little prospect of work.

'G'Day Ferret,' said Cheryl, as he appeared down the stairs.

'G'Day Shezza. G'Day Danny.'

'G'Day,' Danielle replied without much interest.

'Bit quiet?' asked Ferret.

'Whadda you reckon?' Cheryl replied, nodding towards the empty street. 'If you was a fucken' terrorist and you could let off a bomb in this shit 'ole 'n' you'd only kill yourself.'

'What about a threesome then?' asked Ferret. 'On the house? I won't charge yous.' He smiled hopefully.

'You like sex 'n' travel?' asked Danny.

'Yeah,' he replied.

'Then get in your car and fuck off.'

Ferret fingered the tiny box in his pocket. He took it out and began to open it as he listened to the girls talk.

'What 'appened to Mark Hogan 'n' his mob? They was always good for business on a Sat'dy night,' said Cheryl.

Ferret took out the pheromone wipe.

'He got married,' replied Danny, 'so we won't see 'im for a few weeks.'

'Pisser,' replied Cheryl.

Ferret dabbed the moist wipe onto his wrists and onto the back of his neck.

'Did 'e end up marryin' Debbie Hindmarsh?'

'Nah, some Asian bitch. He wanted his kids to play the piano.'

'Oh, right.'

'And do their homework.'

'Right.'

Ferret moved closer to the girls to see if the pheromone wipe had any effect. The girls didn't pay him any attention.

'They moved to Dundas,' said Raylene.

'Dundas? asked Cheryl. 'Where's that?'

'Parramatta way.'

'Right.'

'Why'd he move there?'

'To be close to James Ruse Selective High School.'

'Fuck me,' replied Cheryl, 'that's what I call plannin' ahead.'

'You know them Asians,' said Danielle, flicking the

G-string out of her arse. 'That'd be an interestin' country to visit, but.'

'Where.'

'Asia.'

'Yeah,' Cheryl nodded. 'Isn't that near Vietnam?'

Ferret was right between them now.

'Nah, it's . . .' Danielle began, but she stopped just as quickly and turned abruptly towards Ferret.

Simultaneously, Cheryl did the same.

Ferret smiled.

'Fuck me,' whispered Cheryl.

'Fuck me,' whispered Danielle.

And they pulled Ferret's trackies down there and then.

Both girls ripped in abandoned frenzy at their fishnets. Hosiery flew like black snow across the street. Cheryl rubbed her twat with such gusto upon Ferret's upturned mouth and nose that he could only breath on the upbeat. At one point the friction threatened to catch his snout ablaze. Meanwhile, Danielle stood above his nether regions and pulled him up by the tracksuit pants that hung limp around his shoes. She pulled him up towards her like she was on ice and working with hand weights.

Ferret wasn't sure whether he was coming or going. In the end it turned out he was cumming. And the three of them lay for a brief while, panting and regaining their breath on the footpath.

After a while Ferret pulled up his trackies. 'Thanks girls,' he said and disappeared back up the stairs.

Cheryl looked at Danielle. 'What the fuck was that all about?' she asked.

Danny shook her head. 'I dunno. But I was suddenly randier than an Eskimo in a sauna.'

א

The trip to Narita Airport was uneventful, except for the fist-fight Ferret had in the transit lounge in Cairns. There was only one place to eat and Ferret lost his temper after waiting in a food queue for an hour and a half only to be told he had to board when he was three customers away from finally being served. He was so frustrated by then that he left the line and hit the first staff member he came to. Fortunately, he managed to get on board and fly away before the authorities could catch up with him.

You could also count the ruckus he caused by lighting a joint in the aeroplane toilet and setting off the alarms. He wouldn't come out for an hour and when he did, he couldn't stop laughing and then he tried to touch the hostie on the bum and was strapped down for the rest of the flight.

And I suppose you could also count the offence he would have caused the Japanese Youth Choir had they spoken English. Ferret was tied down to his seat in business class. His language was colourful and at the end of the flight one small soprano, who thought that Ferret was western and cool, saluted his family on arrival at Narita and greeted them with the words: 'G'Day you bunch of cunts!' and was thoroughly boxed about the ears by his bilingual father.

But apart from these minor indiscretions, all went well. Bernard and Horatio read or slept at the back of the plane for the great portion of the journey and were only reacquainted with Ferret when they arrived at Tokyo's airport.

'Where did you get to, old boy?' asked Bernard, as he joined Ferret in the custom's queue.

'They put me in business class,' he replied.

'Well done, the Fezz monster,' said Horatio.

'Will you shut the fuck up?'

'Oops. That's another six yen for the swear jar.'

'Anything to declare?' asked the small Japanese

woman behind the custom's desk. She was petite and middle-aged; superbly presented in a brown uniform and she looked tired after a long day.

'Fuck off,' replied Ferret.

'Back pack, prease,' asked the woman with a perfunctory upturned palm. Under normal circumstances she would not have bothered, but Ferret's infamy had preceded him and his current recalcitrance wasn't helping.

'Let them have your backpack, old boy,' whispered Bernard who was conscious of several uniformed guards standing nearby, taking an interest in Ferret's belligerent attitude. He nodded towards them and Ferret got the message. Reluctantly, he pushed the bag towards the woman.

She opened it and stopped momentarily with surprise. She delved her hand into the contents of the bag and pulled out a handful of small blue boxes. She held them up, quizzically. 'What dese, prease?'

'That's personal,' Ferret replied.

This was far too cryptic-a-response for the guards who stiffened in preparation for trouble. Ferret, who was an expert on conflict situations, saw the problem. One of the guards was certainly invading Ferret's personal space.

'Hold on. Hold on,' he said, waving his arms about. 'Look. I'll show yous.'

He opened one of the packets and rubbed the contents onto his wrists and neck. 'See? It's a wipe. It's nothin'.'

For a moment nothing happened. The guards looked at each other, then to the customs agent and then back again to Ferret.

Then, suddenly, as if a sudden wind had blasted him, the guard nearest Ferret, who was an effeminate little fellow in an immaculately pressed uniform, threw himself upon Ferret from behind and began to hump his buttocks.

'What the fuck!' bellowed Ferret, trying to remove

the offending agent from his back. All he could feel was a stiff probing penis searching for a way through his track pants. And they were loose and giving way. Ferret had the feeling that he was being dry rooted by a cotton condom.

It took several seconds for the other guards to react, by which time Ferret was on the floor, pinned down and flailing beneath a Japanese nancy boy.

There was much screaming and chaos as the men were pulled apart followed but much bowing and apologies and sincere hopes that Mr Cutler would not report the unfortunate incident to the authorities. Ferret agreed and with much further bowing he was given back his bag and escorted out of the airport and down to the train station below.

Horatio and Bernard had stood wide-eyed at the encounter and were now glancing back towards the guards who were splashing water on the offending guard's face. He was shaking his head as if awaking from a nightmare.

And Ferret was free in Japan, along with his pheromones.

*

'Fuck me!' blurted Ferret, as he stepped off the platform in Shinjuku. There were people everywhere and not an inch between them. He, Horatio and Bernard were swept down the stairs. 'It's like bein' an ant trapped in a giant turd.'

'A very clean turd,' added Bernard.

They emerged from the controlled chaos of the train station up into an ocean of neon and a river of dark hair.

'Fuck! Everyone's Japanese!' Ferret shouted.

'Of course,' replied Bernard, 'we're in Japan.'

'No, I mean *everyone's* Japanese. Back 'ome there's wogs 'n' slant-eyes 'n' fucken' Muslims 'n' shit, but these are all fucken' Japs.'

'Swear jar,' Horatio chipped in with a smile but Ferret shoved him sideways without even looking and Horatio skinned his knee on a pole.

'It's a monoculture, Ferris,' Bernard explained. 'Japan has maintained its original traditions and kept its unique flavour by largely limiting intake.'

'They're fucken' on to somethin',' said Ferris, nodding his head towards the swarming, Sunday night crowd. 'The only advantage I can see for multiculturalism is food. People hate their own race enough without complicatin' matters. These people look like they got their shit together, 'specially the chicks.' He stopped to ogle a beautiful young woman in high leather boots, a mini-skirt and a fur-lined jacket.

'Harro baby!' he yelled, but the woman ignored him.

'I say, old boy, steady on,' said Bernard with a hand upon Ferret's arm.

'The sun won't be the only thing risin' over 'ere, I'll tell ya that for free, Bernie boy.'

'I'd settle down a little if I were you, Ferris.' He nodded more emphatically towards a small group of Japanese men watching them from across the road. 'The Japanese are a respectful people and they're not too tolerant of inappropriate behaviour.'

The small group of men were definitely looking over in their direction.

'Bernsickle,' Horatio's tiny voice came from behind them as he hobbled up the rear. They stopped. 'Those people over there have been following us. I saw them at the airport and on the train.'

But as he said this, the group across the road broke up and went their separate ways.

'I think you've been into the rice wine, pal,' said Ferret. 'Why would anyone be following' us? Come on let's get a feed.'

Even though it was a Sunday night, Shinjuku was jumping and spruikers soon had our three boys down into a packed, smoky bar. Ferret and Bernard slid into a cramped cubicle by the wall.

'So what now?' Ferret asked Bernard as they waited for Horatio to return with the beers.

'We have to find Mumsy.'

'Which hospital is she in?'

'Well, that's the problem. I'm not sure.'

'What?' replied Ferret, so loudly that a few people turned in his direction. 'You mean to tell me that we've come all the way to fucken' Nippon and you don't know where the fuck Mumsy is?'

'Settle down, Ferris. She said we'd find her.'

'Well that's a bit fucken' cryptic, isn't it? In a city of twenty-three fucken' million people?'

'Ferris,' replied Bernard quietly, almost hissing, 'some of these people can speak English.'

'Not many.'

'Many understand more than they can speak.' Bernard nodded towards a nearby table of businessmen who were shaking their heads in disapproval and leaving.

Horatio arrived with the beers and placed them on the table.

Ferret picked his up and held it up with the majority of his fingers away from the glass, as if it was a dog turd.

He puffed out the syllables independently in disbelief. 'What-the-fuck-do-you-call-that?'

'It's a beer,' replied Horatio with a smile. He added, 'Swear Jar.'

Ferret clipped him around the back of the head and made his nose bleed.

'This thing's got an uglier head than my ex. Who poured this piece a shit?'

'One of my brothers,' a voice interjected from the recently vacated table. Three men now occupied it. All were Japanese; all were casually dressed and all were heavily tattooed.

'Well tell ya brother he can't fucken' pour a beer for shit. This glass has got more head in it than my sister on a Frid'y night.'

The Japanese man was still processing what Ferret had just said. Bernard sat urgently forward and whispered quickly to Ferret. 'Ferris, for God's sake tone it down.'

'Why should I?' Ferret replied, syphoning off a large portion of head from the beer and spitting it defiantly onto the floor.

'Because,' Bernard replied, 'those people are not ordinary folk. They're Yakuza.'

'What?'

'They're Yakuza. They're Japanese mafia; gangsters. You can tell by the tattoos. Haven't you noticed? Japanese don't have them in general.'

'They're the ones I told you are following us,' added Horatio.

The Japanese man had apparently translated what Ferret had said. They all laughed uproariously.

'What's up with yous?' asked Ferret belligerently.

'Ferris!' Bernard implored.

But the three men were approaching. Their spokesman was a small man with a savage scar down the left side of his face. Otherwise, he was quiet good looking. He was fit and in his forties, 'You say funny thing,' he said.

Ferret hadn't been in a knuckle since Cairns and he was sizing up the three men. The leader looked easy enough. In fact, they all did. They were just scrawny guys and they were all heaps older than him. He figured he could take them.

'Fuck off,' he said and downed the beer. 'Japanese beer tastes like shit.' He put the empty glass down heavily on the table and looked up defiantly towards the men who now stood above him.

'Swear jar,' chipped in Horatio with a smile. Ferret clipped him behind the ear again.

The leader explained what Horatio had said and again the three of them laughed aloud.

'What the fuck are yous laughin' at?' Ferret asked. He began to rise but the leader, still smiling, gently pushed him back down. He was relaxed and he spoke quietly. 'You come with us,' he said.

'Like fuck I will!' Ferret replied. He stood up suddenly, but before he could say another word, a hand wrapped across his mouth and he briefly smelled something like nail polish remover.

Ferret fell unconscious.

*

He dreamed he was rooting a beautiful Japanese girl. She was squealing and naked and making little chipmunk noises as he banged her on the massage table. She was as tight as an altar boy's arsehole and as hot as the Catholic priest engaging with aforementioned arsehole. She was covered in oil and squirming around and she was gobbling his Jatz crackers. He became aware of laughter and he woke up, tied up and naked, in a smoky room full of men in suits, with a poodle licking off the honey that had been poured all over his dick.

'What the fuck!' he bellowed. He tried to ward off the dog's affection by banging its snout with his hard on.

'Time you woke up,' said the same man from the bar.

Beside him, Bernard and Horatio were still out cold.

'Where am I?'

'That not important.' He motioned to two huge men beside him. 'Untie him. Get his clothes and clean his dick.'

'You touch my dick and I'll fucken' scone ya!' Ferret threatened.

The men had no idea what he had said, but they understood what he meant. They laughed and spoke to one another as they untied him and gave him his clothes. Ferret found a tap to one side of the room, which he used to wash off the honey. As he stood on his tiptoes hanging his old fella over the sink, the dog trotted back to him and licked at his leg.

The men found this hilarious.

'He likes you,' said the leader and again there was mirth at Ferret's plight.

'Fuck off,' he whispered to the dog but the dog was persistent, so Ferret kicked it in the head. The men laughed again.

'How do you say? This as good as circus?' He stood. 'Come. You see Mumsy.'

'What about them?' asked Ferret, nodding towards his unconscious companions.

'No. Just you,' replied the man. And Ferret was lightly bustled through a doorway, down a wooden hallway and into a central courtyard full of small shrubs, fountains and pebbles. He could tell it was early morning by the light that filtered down into the open courtyard; light that fell upon a reclining figure, on a couch in the centre of the yard.

It was an imposing figure. 'Figure' is perhaps the wrong word for what it was. It was a round, female shape wearing sunglasses. Her long hair was dyed blonde and her orbicular face betrayed the ruins of an attractive woman but, like Troy, her features were now buried beneath the unforgiving sediment of time. The whale-like structure moulded over and around the long-suffering sofa whose wooden legs bent beneath the strain. She was perhaps forty, perhaps younger; it was impossible to tell because fat had robbed her entirely of wrinkles. To Ferret she looked like an unpricked sausage on the barbeque that was about to burst at the seams. She wore a bikini and was covered from neck to toes in tattoos. She threw down a neat scotch as she watched Ferret approach.

'Well I'll be fucked by a black fella.' She laughed and her body rippled like the San Andreas Fault on Judgement Day. 'If it isn't pater's little poofta!'

'Well, fuck you,' replied Ferret.

'That's my boy.' She laughed again and attempted to sit up, which proved impossible. 'Kanji. Lift.'

The Japanese man, who had escorted Ferret to the corpulent woman, rushed to her aid. Ferret thought he looked like an ant trying to roll a large breadcrumb, but the man was strong for his size and after several attempts, Mumsy was upright.

'Kanji's my right-hand man,' she explained. She mopped her brow with the exertion of sitting. 'But be careful, Ferret, 'e may be small but e's well versed in the martial arts and I know you like to fight. I've been followin' your progress pretty closely, my boy, and I'd think twice before I picked any fights around 'ere.'

'I thought you only just found me,' Ferret replied with a suspicious scowl. 'Your stepsons think you're about to fucken' cark it.'

'Oh come on Ferret, whose jerkin' off who? You 'n' me both know those little cunts wouldn't know shit from shampoo.'

'Fuck it! I knew there wouldn't be no inheritance.'

'Oh there's an inheritance, alright. We've just gotta get our hands on it.'

'What does that mean?'

'Hang on a tick.' She motioned to Kanji. 'Hey sweetie, fuck off will ya? I gotta talk to my boy in private.'

Kanji bowed and was about to leave but as he passed, Mumsy grabbed him with her enormous mitt. She dragged him down towards her ripe lips and planted a huge kiss onto his. She whispered, 'And for being such a good, obedient boy, I'll let ya fuck me later.'

Kanji smiled and left.

'Likes 'em big,' Mumsy explained. 'Reckons gravity makes 'em tighter. All I know is that he went down on me once and got his head stuck for half an hour. Took all the strength of two fucken' great sumos to pull the bastard out. He come up smilin', but. Now, what was I sayin'?'

'Inheritance,' prompted Ferret.

'Oh yeah. So here's the deal. Reginald, that was pater's real name, didn't exactly trust me.'

'I wonder fucken' why,' Ferret interrupted.

'Let me finish, shit head. Fair dinkum you're more impatient than a Year Seven student before his first tit-off-under-the-bra. Speakin' of which.' She pulled down one side of her bikini top to reveal an enormous drooping boob with scar tissue where the nipple should have been.

Ferret instinctively recoiled.

'Don't fucken' look away, China. You fucken' done it. Anyway . . . where was I?'

'Reginald.'

' . . . never trusted me after he caught me rootin' a horse, but that's another story. 'Course we was married by then and I had 'im by the balls. He didn't want to lose half 'is fortune, so 'e was stuck wif me. I tell ya Ferris, my boy, ya hear women complain about prostitution, but marryin' a man for money with the intention of divorce, is the biggest form of prostitution there is. Trouble was, Reg was so rich he had his lawyers stitch everything up. So we come to a mutual understanding. He give me plenty of money and let me run me own race as long as I kept up appearances – which I did. I spent half the time in England and half the time wif me boys in Japan. They syphon off me money and I live real good. But now Reg is dead and the money's dried up.'

'*You* killed 'im!'

'I never killed him, ya dick. Why would I fucken' do that? Why take a shit on the golden goose? Fucken' shit for-brains Renaldo killed him. Reg was gunna sack 'im for rootin' me. Renaldo was a very passionate man.'

Ferret regarded the flaccid vision before him. 'He musta been,' he muttered.

Mumsy ignored him. 'He knew too many bedroom secrets, so I had 'im seen to. I got away wif that but I still got no income.'

'He left it to his sons?'

'Right. And I can't fucken' get to it unless you three little fuckers sign it over to me.'

'Why the fuck would we do that?' asked Ferret. 'You tried to fucken' drown me!'

'Jesus, Ferret. Talk about holdin' grudges.'

'And you threw Horatio into a volcano.'

'He fucken' deserves it.'

Ferret didn't argue that one. 'The only one you spared was Bernard.'

'I poisoned him for six months but he was too fucken' stupid to die. It was easier to keep tabs on you three dickheads until I needed yous. And now I do. The papers are all drawn up all you boys've gotta do is sign 'em.'

'And what if we don't?'

Mumsy smiled slightly and leaned back. The air wheezed out of the cushion behind her. She spoke quietly. 'Ferret, you know and I know that those two drop kicks love me. They'll do anything for me. They're as naïve as a sixth-grade girl asked to do cartwheels. They'll sign. You, my boy, are my only stumbling block.'

Something in Mumsy's tone and in the fact that she was heavily connected with the Yakuza told Ferret to tread carefully. 'They're naïve,' he said, 'but I ain't.'

'Now you're talkin',' Mumsy replied. She sat forward, 'n I got somefin' in mind.' . . .

*

Mumsy sat on a chair by a table. She had her right arm around Bernard and her left around Horatio. They had snuggled into her large, maternal frame and both beamed with reclamation of lost childhood. Opposite them sat Ferret with a faraway expression on his face and on the table, between them, sat the inheritance papers bearing the signatures of each party present. In the corner of the smoky room sat three Yakuza, playing blackjack, stripped to the waist to reveal their tattoos.

'Oh, Mumsy,' Bernard whispered, 'it's so good to see you again.'

'Yes it is,' Horatio agreed. He sighed with contentedness.

Mumsy looked meaningfully at Ferret. Between them they had just disinherited the two men of over half a billion dollars.

'Kanji,' Mumsy called across the room, 'take these two boys downstairs and have Yoshi and Mario, or whatever their fucken' names are, take 'em to the airport.'

'Oh no, Mumsy,' replied Bernard, 'we just want to stay with you.'

'Yes, Mumsy,' iterated Horatio. 'It's so lovely and warm, isn't it Bernomagic?'

'Yes, indeed.'

Mumsy gave the two boys a quick love squeeze, which momentarily cut off Horatio's airway. He was still coughing and spluttering when Kanji and two other men tore them away from their mother.

'But we only just got to see you,' Bernard protested as he and his brother were marched towards the door. Mumsy wasn't even listening. She was admiring the signed document, almost salivating over the signatures.

'You fucken' beauty,' she whispered. 'I'm rich.'

'Don't forget our deal,' said Ferret.

'What deal,' she replied.

'The fifty million.'

Mumsy laughed so hard she pissed herself. 'Oops. Hey, Yamaha San, get the towel!' And while Ferret squinted suspiciously at the laughing giant, Yamaha San, a tiny slip of Japanese nothing, smiled and bowed as he mopped up the urine.

After he had departed and Mumsy had calmed down she said, 'Oh, Ferret, you're a fucken' beauty, you know that? As if I was ever gunna honour that agreement. You can fuck off.'

'Hey, now you wait a ...'

'No!' interrupted Mumsy, smashing her fist down hard upon the table, '*you* wait a fucken' minute! All I needed was your signature on this document and I got it. I got no more need for ya. Get it? And before you play holier than thou with me, cockbreath, just remember that you were prepared to betray those two stupid motherfuckers. You just got fucked over by a bigger fish.'

'Bigger fish is right,' Ferret quipped.

'Oh, fuck off. You're no better than me; you're just not as smart. I'm payin' for those other fuckwits to get home. You can fucken' find your own way back. Or you can die in the streets of Kobe for all I care.' She grabbed Ferret's bag of wipes and threw it across the table. 'There. Take whatever the shit is you've got in that bag and hit the road, mate. I got crimes to commit.'

She leaned back onto her chair and grinned a self-satisfied, condescending toothless grin. 'Bye. Bye,' she said with a dismissive wave of her hand. She returned her eyes to the signatures.

Ferret's thoughts swam. He looked from Mumsy to the bag of wipes and back again.

She looked up. 'Why are you still here, fuckface? Fuck off, I said.' And she called in two small, hard-faced men. She was about to get them to forcibly remove Ferret but he raised his hand.

'What?' she asked in a manner both bored and

impatient.

'Wanna see somethin' real funny before I go?'

'Make it quick, dickhead.'

Ferret delved into the bag and pulled out two of the pheromone wipes. He offered one to each of the henchmen. They looked towards Mumsy for orders. She nodded and they took them.

'Wipe it on yourselves, boys, and then go over and give Mumsy a big sniff.'

As the men applied the wipes Mumsy said, 'This better be fucken' funny, mate. 'coz if this stuff smells like shit or some such thing, you're a dead man.'

'No, no, trust me, this is gunna be a fucken' scream.'

The two men had finished applying the pheromone and were approaching Mumsy. Ferret clutched the bag with the remaining wipes and watched on with interest.

The men approached Mumsy and stood close beside her.

'What's the joke?' she asked.

'Just take a whiff,' prompted Ferret.

Mumsy did so. She sat back. There was silence for a moment. Mumsy smacked her lips in contemplation. The men looked on, awaiting new instruction.

Suddenly, Mumsy's eyes popped open wide. 'Fuck,' she whispered and she looked at the two men.

They looked at each other and back to Mumsy.

As she stared at them a deep guttural sound became audible. It wended its way upward from the depths of the large woman's gut and surfaced through her opened mouth like a primeval, Ginsbergian howl. She raised her mouth to the ceiling and screamed and the two guards took a step backward in fear. She shook with increasing tremor until the ripples ran across the entire surface of her body. She jolted in convulsion, but through all the violent spasm, she did not take her eyes from the men.

'Aaaah!!!' she screamed in mounting falsetto. She

stood and the table cracked in two across her lap. 'Come 'ere!'

She grabbed for the men but they were too nimble and avoided her rugged embrace. They backed off. When it became evident that she was still advancing, they took off in the direction of the door.

Mumsy was incensed as she raced after them. 'Come her! Come back!' she screamed.

Ferret quickly pocketed the legal documents that he and his stepbrothers had signed and followed.

Mumsy chased the henchmen through the door, her huge body bouncing and her boobs slamming holes in the gyprock as they swung from side to side. She chased them down the stairs and into the street. The two men ran close together in frenzied escape but one of the men tripped over the gutter and onto the road. The other man tripped over him. Before either could get up, Mumsy was upon them.

Several hundred people stopped to watch.

Mumsy was still roaring loudly like a lioness on heat as she pinned down the two men. She held one down with her knee and the other with one arm. With the other arm she disengaged her underpants and hitched up her dress, which was the size of a small tent. To the horror of the onlookers, Mumsy straddled one of the men and, still howling loudly, began to drop her full weight downward onto his face. The poor soul didn't stand a chance. The weight of her vagina smashed his head repeatedly into the road. The last he knew was a ferocious muckhole enveloping him like krill into the gut of a whale. His entire head disappeared and reappeared into the vaginal tunnel until, at last, he was suffocated in the warm stench.

The second man, who had managed to break free, ran, trouserless, up into the Kobe Tower, but Mumsy, still unsatisfied, pursued him upward towards its apex. Here she cornered him. Battering his head against the viewing-window with one hand, she attacked his cock with the other. But the man was in no mood for an erection and, tug though she may, the penis would not stiffen. Finally, in desperation, she went for 'the hoover', a manoeuvre that she had used many times and one which had earned her some fame in the Yakuza. But to no avail. The man could not be aroused. Mumsy howled and raged and in retribution and in her sex-crazed frenzy, bit off the man's cock and spat it onto the deck of the observatory.

Two schoolboys licked their ice-creams and looked on with interest.

Mumsy rose like Godzilla, blood in her mouth and fury in her eyes and smashed the man's head through the fortified glass. She thrust it with such force that both his body and hers fell through the cavity made by the splintering glass. Down, down they plummeted, the man already unconscious, Mumsy flailing and screaming, onto the road below.

All that remained of Mumsy was a bloody, fleshy ball and a great dent in the road. A handful of passing schoolgirls were splattered with the blood. They screamed in terrified unison.

From the side of the road Ferret watched the chaos. He stayed out of sight. He saw Kanji and several other men approach the shattered corpses.

They did not look happy.

*

Ferret jumped out of the cab and ran into Osaka Airport. He was counting on one thing – that the Yakuza realised how stupid Bernard and Horatio were and would therefore not worry about leaving them unattended at the airport. He was right. There they were, standing in line to get their boarding passes, smiling and chatting away like a couple of kids on summer camp. But Ferret also realised that he must nab them quickly. The Yakuza would not be far away.

'Quick. Come wif me,' he puffed. He grabbed them by an arm each. Horatio's shoulder popped momentarily out of its socket. He smiled.

'Hello, Ferris. Fancy seeing you here,' said Bernard as Ferret pulled him through the crowd.

'Quick. Over here,' said Ferret, pushing the two men down into a shielded corner and just in time too. Kanji and two large henchmen were scouring the check-in line. They were enraged hornets ready to sting.

'I say, old boy . . .'

'Sssh,' replied Ferret. He knew the stakes, even if his bovine friend didn't.

Soon, Kanji and the other men passed out of sight.

Ferret was sweating. 'Have you got access to any money,' he asked Bernard.

'Oh yes, pater puts pocket money in my account every week.'

'How fucken' old are you?'

'I'm . . .'

'It was rhetorical, dickhead. We need more than pocket money. We gotta leave the country but we can't leave here and now. We gotta get to England and sort this shit out.'

'That's lucky,' replied Horatio, 'that's where we're going.'

'Not today, dickbrain. They'll be watching.'

'Who?' asked Bernard.

'The Yakuza.'

'What, those lovely chaps who gave us a lift here?'

'Listen to me, you two thickheads - if they catch us they'll torture us. They'll find a way to get at our money and then they'll kill us.'

'Oh come on, Ferris,' replied Bernard with a jocular guffaw and a pat on the back, which sent Ferret a pace forward, 'those lovely chaps wouldn't hurt a fly. Anyway, they're Mumsy's friends and Mumsy loves us.'

Wrong notion: wrong tense, thought Ferret, but he saw no need to inflict grief upon the poor blighters. They were never going to see Mumsy again anyway, regardless of whether she was dead or alive.

'Look, boys, I haven't got time to argue wif yous. But we need money to get up to Narita and over to England.'

'I told you,' Bernard repeated, 'I have some pocket money. That should cover it.'

'How much've ya got?' asked Ferret, who used to get fifty bucks a week, before his old man turfed him out of home.

'Six or seven million dollars, I think,' replied Bernard.

'What?'

'Me too,' added Horatio.

'You lucky shits,' muttered Ferret.

Then something caught Horatio's eye. 'Oh look, Bernywerny. There's one of Mumsy's friends now.' He nodded over to the check-in line. He stood up and waved but fortunately none of the gangsters were looking in his direction at that particular second. Ferret's paw dragged him back down.

'Stay hidden in this corner until I tell yous to,' Ferret whispered through clenched teeth.

It was over half an hour before the coast was clear and Ferret felt safe enough to drag the boys out of the airport, into a cab and towards the Shinkansen. Soon they were racing at 300 kilometres an hour back towards Tokyo.

Ferret stared morosely out of the window. Doesn't this country have any space between cities? he was thinking. He'd never valued space so much before. He'd lived a secluded, horizontal life; now he found himself in a vertical world. Danger lurked on every storey. How was he going to get out of the country without being caught? It was bad enough trying to evade a well-organised group like the Yakuza without encumbrance - and he had plenty of that. They would have contacts and informants everywhere and one of his two dumbo brothers was just as likely to walk into their headquarters in Tokyo and ask for their old mate, Kanji. He had seen the expression on Kanji's face back at the Kobe Tower and for the first time in his life, he was scared. Really scared. He'd led his whole life in the Hawkesbury picking fights with fellow losers, he saw that now. Here, he was a minnow in a very big pond and that pond was full of piranhas.

'Wonderful architecture,' he heard Bernard say. He raised his hands to point at some passing attraction and accidentally thumped Horatio in the jaw. 'I say, sorry old man.'

'No problem,' replied Horatio, caressing his mandible.

Ferret was angry. He shook his head. 'You dickheads have got no fucken' idea, have yous?' Horatio was about to remove his hand from his jaw in order to speak but Ferret waved a warning finger towards him. 'You say 'swear jar' and I'll fucken' scone ya!'

A few people in the carriage looked around.

Horatio beamed. 'I *was* going to say that too. How clever you are Ferris wheel.'

'And don't fucken' call me stupid fucken' things! Wake up to yourselves! Both of yous! Don't you stupid bastards realise we're in trouble?'

Bernard and Horatio looked dumbly back at him.

'These people fucken' invented torture.'

'Oh no, I doubt that,' Bernard replied thoughtfully. 'The earliest torture probably predates the Japans by centuries. I mean you only have to look at the Babylonians who . . .'

'Shut the fuck up!' Ferret screamed. This definitely

got the carriage's attention and also the attention of one passing guard. 'Don't you get it? The Yakuza have lost their cash cow and they're going to milk us to get it back.'

'Marvellous extended metaphor,' said Bernard, shaking his head with admiration.

'Lovely,' agreed Horatio.

Ferret stared back at them in disbelief. It was hopeless. 'How can a person talk about Babylonian torture and metaphors and be so stupid?'

'Oh, that's easy to explain,' replied Bernard.

'It was fucken' rhetorical!' Ferret screamed so loudly that his face went three stages of red and the guard came scurrying over.

'Prease, sir, 'he said with a bow, 'but bad language understood by many. Might be Australian custom, but not in Japan. Prease.' He bowed again.

Ferret looked and listened around the cabin. Not a sound. He looked at the windows and the floor. Not a mark. He thought about the passing cities. No graffiti: no litter. He thought about the western suburbs of Sydney. And he suddenly got it.

'Sorry,' he replied. And for once in Ferret's life, he shut up.

*

Ferret dragged Bernard and Horatio through Tokyo Station and straight up into the multitudes. In the flood of Japanese people on the crowded streets there were virtually no white fellas, but Ferret and Horatio were difficult to spot, since they were short even by Japanese standards. Unfortunately, the immense, ursine Bernard stuck out like a huge, sore, white thumb, head and shoulders above every crowd he mingled through.

Not far from the station, Bernard and Horatio withdrew a half a million yen in travel money and gave it to Ferret. Soon the three men found themselves sitting on a small wall looking at the Emperor's Castle.

'Beautiful isn't it, Horatio?' Bernard asked.

'Beautiful,' Horatio agreed.

'Did you know, Horatio, that some estimates put the value of the Imperial Castle as more than the entire real estate of California?'

'Never,' replied Horatio, aghast and shaking his head.

Ferret sat eating a sandwich.

'Oh yes,' Bernard assured his diminutive brother, 'due to the Japanese economic bubble of the 1980's.'

'Well I never,' replied Horatio.

'I have two things to say,' said Ferret, after a while of mastication, 'first, this bread tastes like fucken' dessert and second, how the fuck do you know this stuff?'

'Oh Berneble's a computer whiz, aren't you?'

'Oh, one doesn't like to boast,' replied the timid giant.

'Yeah?' said Ferret, the wheels of his mind seeking possible advantage.

'Oh, yes,' Horatio continued, 'he looks up Google.'

'What?' said Ferret, the wheels of his mind abruptly clanging to a halt.

'It's true,' Bernard confirmed, 'but the trick is I never forget anything.'

'You're an idiot,' replied Ferret, looking distastefully at his sweet sandwich.

'Oh no,' Bernard replied, 'an idiot is generally under 25 I.Q. points, an imbecile at approximately 25 to 49 and a moron, 50 to 69. Generally speaking anyone under 70 is considered to have some mental deficiency. But Horatio and I score much higher than that. Pater had us tested.'

'We're actually quite clever,' Horatio proclaimed proudly, but he shifted too suddenly in his seat, overbalanced and fell off.

'I'll take your word for it,' replied Ferret, looking at both men as if they were lucky to have made it this far in life, 'but now we gotta find a place to stay the night.'

In front of the seated trio, not far away, was a bus visiting the palace. The bus had spilled its passengers out on the main thoroughfare where they were clicking away madly with their cameras at anything that moved. From the look of them they were women from a Japanese old-age care home. On closer inspection they could have been dug up from the cemetery. The bus was labelled: 'Centenarian City for Women'.

Bernard nodded towards them. 'Did you know that there were 200,000 Japanese people older than one hundred years in the early 2000's?' Bernard had been inspired by Horatio's vote of confidence. 'Many actually have little robots that can make them tea and have basic conversations . . .'

Ferret suddenly thrust his arm across the big man's chest and stopped him.

'What is it, old man?' asked Bernard.

Ferret didn't speak. He nodded to a group of men well beyond the bus. As far as Ferret could make out, they were speaking to a small group of other men who had earpieces and walkie-talkies. They were not looking towards them but they were animated, and Ferret, who prided himself on good eyesight, was almost certain that one of the men was Kanji.

He looked back in the direction of the train station. 'Fuck,' he muttered. He was in one of the most open areas that he had seen in all of Japan. If he and his two foolish friends were to retrace their steps they would be badly exposed and almost certainly spotted by the group. There was only one thing for it.

'Listen to me carefully,' he half-whispered. 'Don't say nothin', just listen.' To his amazement, both men remained silent. 'There's a bunch of men over there. Don't look.' They both looked. '. . . who will kill us if we don't get out of here. My guess is that they're gunna scour this area in a minute and we've only got one chance. Will you follow me?'

Bernard and Horatio sat quietly, looking back at him.

Fuck, he thought, it's like talking to a couple of kindergarten kids. 'Alright, now, see them people over there?'

Bernard and Horatio watched as the tour guide beckoned for the Japanese centenarians to reboard the bus.

They nodded.

'We are gunna join that group and get on that bus.'

'But we have no ticket,' remonstrated Bernard.

'Bernard,' said Ferret quietly, taking the large man by the forearm. 'If we don't, we're gunna die. Do you get it?'

Bernard thought about that for a moment, and then he nodded. 'Come on Horatio,' he said, 'let's go over to the bus.' He looked at Ferret and for just the briefest of seconds Ferret caught a glimpse of something. It was startling and new. It was 'understanding', certainly, but it was more than that. Could it be respect?

Ferret stood, pulsing with adrenaline, but also full to the brim with clarity as he, and his two brothers made their way towards the bus.

The last of the hobbling, old-aged crew were scaling the ramps especially designed for the elderly and securing themselves in the bus. Many were in wheelchairs and many had walking fames but there were also a number of able-bodied women attendants attached to the tour. There was much business to attend to before the bus could leave. While this activity was going on, Ferret, Bernard and Horatio sneaked up the front steps. Bernard and Horatio stepped straight past the driver.

'No wait, preas . . .' he began, but they passed him with a wave and a 'Hello, old man,' from Bernard and sat themselves down in the front seats to his left.

Ferret checked to see if they had been noticed by the ominous gathering. He could see them more clearly now. Damn it! It was Kanji and he looked agitated.

'This not pubric bus,' the driver suggested politely.

Ferret turned to him. 'I got a hundred thousand yen says that it is.'

He waved the notes under the driver's nose.

He was a small, middle-aged man, reasonably stout by Japanese standards, but well undernourished by those of the Hawkesbury. He licked his lips. 'Where you go?'

'Narita Airport.'

'That out of way,' replied the man, maintaining eye contact with the tempting notes that waved before him like glorious pines in the raging wind.

Under normal circumstances Yoshika, for that was the man's name, would never consider such a bribe. He, like nearly all Japanese people, was always a law-abiding citizen, but just recently he had run into some bad luck. His teenage son had contracted gonorrhoea from a whore in Roppongi and spread it all over Nishi-Nippori where he and his family lived. As a consequence several of the local fathers had banded together and were seeking damages for the insult to their reputation. As a driver his wage was only meagre and to make matters worse . . . but this isn't his story, so fuck him.

'Two hundred thousand,' he whispered.

'Done,' replied Ferret, handing over the wad of cash, which the man greedily and guiltily pocketed. 'But step on it. We're in a hurry.'

Yoshika nodded and immediately pulled from the curb before all of the occupants were fully strapped in. A feeble roar of surprise arose from the elderly women as the bus screeched out into the traffic.

The noise of the tyres drew the attention of Kanji and his henchmen. The boys would have gone unnoticed except for the fact that Horatio, who had taken the window seat, was looking out at Kanji and waving like one of the little maids from school in the Mikado. Kanji did a double take as he watched the bus dodge out into the thoroughfare.

'Come,' he ordered his men. They raced for their car, which was parked nearby, and though the bus was well up the road before they pulled away from the curb, still they had it in their sights. 'They will pay,' Kanji muttered to himself. He held his hands together and nursed the fresh bloodied bandages that were wrapped around the tips of three fingers on his right hand.

Ferret sat looking nervously from front window to back window to side windows. Upon his lap sat his bag full of wipes; to his left sat his two affable, idiotic brothers.

The bus stopped. Horatio was looking sideways and down upon the roof of the dark car within which Kanji and his men were now looking up at him. Kanji held up his bloodied fingers and Horatio took this as a good sign. He waved back.

'Who the fuck are ya wavin' to?' asked Ferret.

'Kanji,' he replied simply.

These words had a huge effect on Ferret.

'Kanji!' he screeched. He looked out over Horatio's shoulder and there he was: Kanji - mean motherfucker with a licence to kill, smiling up at him with a look of unimaginable violence, clutching his bloody hand and then holding it up so that Ferret could see. He snarled through the two panes of intervening glass and then the traffic was moving again.

'Great to see them,' said Bernard.

Ferret head butted him.

'What was that for?' Bernard asked when he recovered.

'Maybe it's a sign of respect in the colonies,' suggested Horatio.

'For being a smart, stupid bastard,' Ferret replied.

Bernard had to think about that one.

'Can I have one too?' asked Horatio with a goofy, toothy smile. So Ferret obliged him.

Ferret stared for a moment at his two inept friends and was seized by two things: almighty panic and a great desire to live. He saw the devil coming in the form of Kanji and he imagined his two twittish friends smiling on genially, as they watched Kanji string him up and kill him slowly by the death of a thousand paper cuts.

He must act. He looked around. The bus looked old. There was oldness dripping everywhere: that indescribable blue cheese maturity of a photograph indebted to the years. But here; even here in this musky den of moribundity there was opportunity. Something clicked in Ferret's head and suddenly, he saw a possible advantage. He was not certain it would work but he had to try. It was his only hope. He asked the driver how long until they reached the airport.

'Ten minute,' was the reply.

The next five minutes were the longest in Ferret's life. He sat, looking forward in silence considering the possibilities. Would it work? Even if it did, his timing would have to be perfect. Finally, he clutched his bag full of wipes and stood up.

'Ladies,' he announced. His nasal, twangy delivery was far from impressive but it hardly mattered: only a handful of people in the bus could speak English. As he spoke, he began to give a packet of wipes to each person on board. 'My name is Ferris. I'm from Australia.'

Many of the women turned up their hearing aids and were muttering to one another. Some, who could speak a little English, were translating for those who could not. Each woman accepted the wipe as it was handed to them and they all nodded their heads in recognition of the word 'Australian'. Many smiled and all bowed to Ferret as he made his way down the bus, most seemed to think that this was some sort of promotion. They looked at the small blue packets with interest.

'At your age,' said Ferret, shuffling awkwardly down the centre aisle, 'you sometimes need a refresher towel to keep yourself moist. After all, you're a bunch of dried-up old cunts.'

The translators let that one go.

'But if, when I tell you, you apply this moist wipe to the back of your neck and hands, you will immediately be rejuvenated. This is the best moisturiser in the world.'

More translations: more vigorous head nodding.

Ferret had handed out all but three of his wipes, which he pocketed. He was now at the very rear of the bus. All of the old women listened, but few could find the elasticity of neck to turn around and see him. Very quickly he felt the rim surrounding the back window and made a mental note. He moved back towards the front of the bus. 'Now don't open 'em yet. I'll tell yous when. Okay?' He held his hands forward, palms towards them in the 'hold on' position and then in pantomime pointed to his watch. Everybody seemed to understand.

'Narita,' proclaimed the driver and with a hiss, the bus came to a stop.

Beside the bus, so too did a dark sedan.

Ferret looked down upon the blazing eyes of Kanji and the great bulk of his two henchmen. They did not even try to conceal their weapons. As they stepped from the car they loaded their pistols with angry resolve and, in broad daylight, Kanji pulled a samurai sword out from the car. He looked straight up at Ferret.

Ferret gulped.

He had returned to the front of the bus by now. He stood beside Bernard and Horatio who were completely unaware of the impending danger. They smiled affably back at him. Horatio more or less winked.

'Hey driver,' Ferret whispered, 'three blokes are gunna get on this bus in a sec and if I were you, I'd wait 'til they came in and then I'd piss off, pronto.'

'Wakarimasen,' Yoshika replied.

'Fucken' oath,' said Ferret. Then, still in his announcer's voice he said, "Bernard, Horatio if you would kindly walk towards the rear of the vehicle.'

Bernard and Horatio, hearing the tour-guide tone of voice, immediately reacted and headed for the rear.

'Alright, ladies, open packages.' He did a rough pantomime and the ladies obeyed. Ferret moved purposefully towards the rear of the bus where his two brothers stood together in happy compliance. 'Now, apply the wipes.'

The sound of ripping paper followed and after this, a silence as fifty-two female centenarians applied the pheromone to their aged, wrinkled necks and to their sun spotted hands.

Ferret reached the back of the bus just as one of Kanji's sumos kicked the door of the bus in. It caved in with the crash of splintering glass. A ripple of shock ran through the bus, at least through those who had turned up their hearing aids. On stepped Kanji and his two big hit men.

Kanji smiled evilly at Ferret. He slowly and theatrically slid the katana from its sheath. Down the long line of the bus he pointed the sword directly at Ferret, moving gracefully towards him as he did so. The bus was deathly silent. He and his companions were at the centre point now, slowly homing in on their prey when . . .

The last of the advancing trio, a thug of six foot four, with no neck and a face like an overinflated football, suddenly noticed one of the women smile at him. There was a glimpse of denture there that he found utterly irresistible. He faltered for a moment. At the same time his doppelganger, henchman number two, became distracted by a glimpse of unshaven leg. The two men stopped. Kanji noted the unscheduled behaviour and turned momentarily to find its cause. At that precise moment, henchman number two, unable to restrain his unbridled lust, dived upon the elderly woman and ran his hand all the way up her floppy legs, until he found her floppy vagina. He pushed his whole fist in there and the old lady's dark eyes widened; whether with shock, or pleasure, or both, it was impossible to tell. This ruckus was followed by another, as henchman number one ripped the dentures out of the mouth of his centenarian, pulled out his cock and began shafting her gums with gusto.

'What are you..?' yelled the bewildered Kanji.

It was no use. His henchmen were mad raging volcanoes of passion. As he tried to pull them back he was knocked sideways and into the lap of an extremely attractive women who was no more than a hundred and five. He breathed in deeply the alluring scent of stale urine. With one deft flick of his katana he cut away her witches britches and he was up 'er. He thumped away like old puffing billy. The woman screamed. Some of the able-bodied woman tried to help but they too became victims of the sex-crazed loon who kissed all that was presented before him and thrust his penis at every passing orifice. Elderly woman swooned and fell from wheelchairs; cripples took up arms and hit Kanji and his accomplishes about the head with walking frames; some arms and legs flailed in uncontained rage, others in libidinous excess; wild screams of pain, pleasure and panic rent the air. To add to the confusion, Yoshika, who had stayed on the bus, was down the front savagely fisting a buck-toothed woman whose thick glasses had fogged up with pleasure and exertion. Other women hit him and tried to get him off her but the woman kept pushing them away saying, 'Reave him! Reave him! Oh, it has been so rong!'

While the writing bodies heaped up in an ungainly mountain of erupting lust and violence, Ferret pushed out the rear window of the bus and, together with Bernard and Horatio, disappeared into the airport.

A crowd had gathered around the bus but no one was game to enter the dangerous arena. Instead, all watched in astonished silence as the macabre spectacle played out like some hallucinogenic puppet show. Every so often an object would appear above the window sill: here a hundred-year-old arsehole; there an arm with a cane crashing down upon something or someone out of eyesight; and occasionally a man's face, beetroot-red with exertion would pop in and out of frame. The final shot, before the puppet show ended, was a close up of Kanji, his mouth filled with grey pubic hair, his head bloodied and battered, slowly falling beneath a sea of abuse and thumping walking sticks.

Finally, silence consumed the bus, the crowd buzzed with confusion and the sound of police sirens grew.

Ferret turned over the pheromone packet in search of information. He read intently for a minute. Eventually he stammered, 'I don't fucken' believe it.' He looked up at the departures list. 'There's a plane leavin' for Sydney in forty-five minutes,' he said. 'And we're gunna be on it.'

'I thought we were going to Heathrow,' said Bernard.

'We can't for two reasons,' Ferret replied. 'The Yakuza think that's where we're goin'. Come on. Let's go.'

'What's the second . . .?'

But Ferret ripped Bernard along.

During the trip to Sydney, Bernard and Horatio slept like babies and Ferret was as bored as a man with no arms at a wanking competition. He was angry that he had used up nearly all of his pheromones on a bus full of geriatrics. He fingered the blue packet. Only three packets left, he was thinking. But he was also thinking about the glorious bottom of the golden-haired, firm-breasted QANTAS hostie with the slight overbite and the face of a mischievous angel. She hadn't taken any notice of him of course, but he could change that.

'Fuck it,' he said to himself. 'You only live once.' And several minutes later he was down amongst the baggage bonking her brains out and watching her eyes roll up into the back of her head.

An hour later he was back in his seat. The hostie walked past him and he winked. She raised her hand to her mouth and headed for the toilet. The effect of those things might not last long, he thought to himself, but then again, neither do I.

On arrival at Mascot Bernard and Horatio woke up.

'Did we miss anything?' asked Bernard.

'Not a fucken' thing,' Ferret replied. He looked up at the hostie as he passed her.

And she did look ill.

*

'Ah, here we are back in the Hawkesbury.' Ferret breathed in. 'Cow shit 'n' bullshit.'

'That just about covers everything,' said Bernard.

'I ain't never appreciated space so much,' Ferret confessed, as he watched the green fields roll past, 'but I never realised what a bunch of disorganised backwater pricks we were neither.'

'Yes,' replied Bernard, 'but *we've* always known that, haven't we, Horatio?'

Horatio nodded with a grin. 'You're colonial scum.'

'The vulgarity of the Australians has often been noted in England. When God invented flies he had Australians in mind.'

'Yeah, alright,' said Ferret.'

'And they're stupid too. Educating an Australian is

like fine tuning a mini-minor.'

'Alright, I said!' shouted Ferret.

'Sorry, old boy,' Bernard apologised, 'it's just that it's generally felt in England that Sydney, in particular, has never ascended from the murk of a convict settlement, whereas Melbourne, being Victorian England transplanted, has at least a more genteel society, populated by Australians, though it is. Although it is fair to say that Sydney's multiculturalism has at least diluted the stupidity.'

Ferret hit Horatio in the face.

'What was that for?'

'Being related to him.'

Bernard continued, 'I mean, let's take this train as an example. It was late; we had to catch a bus for one section due to track work; it's filthy, not air-conditioned; there are scratches all over every window and there's graffiti everywhere. You can forget centrally heated seats; they'd be ripped out in no time by the local rabble.'

Ferret hit Horatio.

'And the service is appalling in this country,

'Rivalled only by British, hey, B.B.?' chimed in Horatio, wiping the blood from his nose.

'Yes, that is true. Australia inherited the English trait for poor service. In both countries you'd swear the attendants were doing you a favour. I mean, compare that to the superb service of the Japanese, or the Americans for that matter. Australian service is about as good as its public transport.'

Ferret hit Horatio.

'Never on time; nobody cares; this is a country full of indolent dole bludgers, many of them imported. They should have a sign: 'Come to Australia and do nothing.' Every race that comes to infect it has its own little knowledge trail freebies. Did you know that there are some communities in Sydney where virtually no-one works? The Bankstown, Liverpool area, for example.'

Ferret hit Horatio.

'The residuum of the trade union rights-for-losers mentality, largely imported from the British Isles, I'm sad to say, still lingers across this barren continent like a crusty vomit.'

'What about the ANZACS!' Ferret yelled, in frustration.

'Oh yes, I'm not saying it wasn't once a great country in some respects but now the place is run by minority groups. The Filipinos have your post offices; the Asians have your selective schools and the Aborigines have you on a guilt trip. It's pretty well: 'Land Rights for Gay Whales' over here in Oz.'

Ferret hit Horatio.

'And as for government, well your politicians are even worse than ours. Many of them would be well served to avoid I.Q. tests and most behave like spoilt brats. You've OH and S'd your small businesses out of existence, battered them with BAS statements and indemnity insurance. It's a wonder anything happens at all in this county.'

Ferret hit Horatio.

'At the same time, your government panders to the whim of every religious group it can find. Mosques springing up everywhere; businesses not having Christmas functions any more but having 'Happy Holidays' so as not to offend non-Christians. You're so permeated with guilt you thank the Aborigines every time there's a public function, as if they owned the land any more than you do. You'd be better off to thank the poor sods who built the buildings you're congregating in. You seem to spend your entire time taking it up the rectum, as if the same courtesy would be extended to you in any other country. I mean, you try building a Christian church in Saudi Arabia. All you seem to do is apologise about the past and worry about the distant future. People run around screaming the sky is falling and masturbate about global warming - saving the planet, when the planet is fine: it's you that needs saving, right here and now.'

'Finished?' asked Ferret.

'I could go on,' replied Bernard.

'Please don't,' said Horatio.

Bernard nodded.

'Good,' replied Ferret and he kicked Horatio in the shins. 'This is the end of the line.'

The three disembarked at Richmond and Ferret couldn't help comparing the people with those in Japan. Bernard may be a pain in the arse but he was right. In Japan there was sophistication and class. There were no public displays of disrespect, no unbridled excessive frustration bubbling over into anger, no hotheads swearing and filling the air with their noisy stupidity.

No, here a quick glance showed a culture ripe for subjugation. A tattoo-stained mob of swearing degenerates graced the platform – and these were just the teenagers. A toothless, dull-eyed pathetic procession of parents shuffled past. A bleached-haired, spindly bitch lugged her squealing spawn behind her and yelled towards the back of an arseless, appallingly thin man, who sauntered ten metres ahead of her like a self-assured moron.

'Wayne! Fucken' Wayne! Get back 'ere 'n' fix your fucken' kid. He fucken' stinks!' she bellowed.

'Fuck off,' he replied casually, ashing his cigarette onto the pavement and spitting after it in an impressive display of virility.

'Wayne! Fucken' Wayne!' she continued to scream as the couple disappeared around the corner to continue their sordid little lives.

'That kid'll probably think his Dad's name *is* 'Fucken' Wayne' until he hits high school,' Ferret said, sadly.

He'd never seen things quite the same way before. The Hawkesbury had been his world. He had known no other and so had nothing to compare it to. But a quick visit abroad had changed that. Now he saw with new eyes - and he didn't like what he saw. As yet he still did not clearly see how well he fitted its mould, but the realisation was beginning to dawn.

'Sad isn't it,' Bernard remarked.

'And they call this the greatest country in the world,' added Horatio, shaking his head.

'There's two things to be said about that,' replied Bernard, 'One, only Australians say that and two, it may well be the greatest country in the world but that does not necessarily imply the greatest people.'

'I hear ya,' muttered Ferret. Then more firmly he said, 'Come on. We got someone to visit.'

They passed a beautiful oval with a dilapidated grandstand and the mandatory graffiti, past two pubs and two bottle shops and entered a mall. Through a narrow passageway they went and then up a narrow stairway. Eventually, they reached a sign that read: Aphrodite Adult Books – from Anal to Zoophilia.

'I see they don't have aardvark fucking,' noted Ferret.

'That would be under 'Zoophilia',' suggested Bernard.

'And I'm telling you, I won't,' they heard one muffled voice say from within. There was a pause and then the same voice continued. 'If that's the way you feel, then do it.' There was a slamming door and then silence.

The boys entered.

The room was small and cluttered. It was disorganised, dusty and ill kept. Discs with lewd covers and sex toys with rubbery bits dangling were spread about in disarray like the legs of a Windsor female ninth grader. Hanging from the ceiling, with no particular nomenclature discernible, were rigid dildos and malleable vaginas and in the middle of the room was a plinth upon which stood, in a glass case, a bedraggled, second-hand, life-size sex doll, with stained undies. Its lifeless eyes appeared to watch the three men as they passed.

Horatio said hello.

Standing behind a counter, beyond all of this raunchy detritus, was an amazingly tall, thin man. He must have been closing on seven feet tall but could have weighed no more than seventy or eighty kilos. He had his back to Ferret, Bernard and Horatio as they approached. Ferret noted his brown hair tied back in a ponytail and the large bald spot that sat smirking above the mane. He wore a garish paisley shirt and tight-fitting jeans. He also heard the man muttering to himself as they reached him – probably about the altercation Ferret had just inadvertently eavesdropped upon.

'Hey, mate,' said Ferret unnecessarily loudly, 'got a question for ya!'

The man, who must have been preoccupied with his own thoughts and who had not heard Ferret's approach, turned suddenly in a surge of adrenaline and thumped his head on a light fitting, which was in the shape of a spread vulva. The clitoris got him in the eye. He unintentionally threw skyward the metal box he had been holding and, from a great altitude, it plummeted onto Horatio's forehead. Horatio fell backwards into a stand full of spermicide.

The contents of the box spilled everywhere. Four gerbils, stunned by their descent and jarring impact, nonetheless regrouped and scurried off in various directions, through the sexual accoutrements, and to freedom.

'Oh no!' the man whined in a high-pitched, feminine whine, 'they were for the Mardi-Gras!' He held his weeping eye. 'Oh, shit! Shit! Shit!'

'I say,' Bernard enquired with concern, 'are you alright?'

'Alright? Alright?' stammered the man. 'Of course I'm not bloody alright.' He looked like he might cry. 'I've poked meself in the eye with a clitoris and I've lost me gerbils.' He put a tissue to his watering eye. 'Now what am I gunna do with all the gaffer tape?'

'Are you the bloke who makes the sex wipes?' asked Ferret.

The man paused, took the tissue from his eye, bent one leg slightly, leaned his weight upon on the counter, scanned Ferret from top to toe, took a quick reconnaissance of Bernard and Horatio and said, with a sniff, 'Who's asking?'

'My name's Ferret 'n' I'm askin' you if you make them wipes?'

'What if I do?' the man replied, guardedly.

'I wanna buy some.'

The man did not reply. Instead, he fiddled thoughtfully with the gold chain that dangled around his neck and sat upon his exposed hairy chest. Ferret looked at the chain and beyond, into the hair. He noticed a tattoo of an attacking tiger, growling there, claws bared.

'Looks like 'es caught in the thicket,' suggested Ferret with a grin.

The man did not think this was funny. 'Oh very good,' he returned languidly, mock clapping his hands, 'like, I've never heard that one before.'

Then he closed his eyes, as if exasperated and bit his lip, as if listening to a complaint. He tilted his head downward, towards the rear of the shop and said, 'I heard you the first time.'

'Heard what the first time?' Ferret asked.

'I wasn't talking to you,' replied the man, curtly.

'Who were ya talkin' to?

'I am quite aware that I have not told him my name, thank you,' the man said with a flick of hair and a petulant tone that rose towards the last syllable of the sentence. There was a pause. 'Alright, I'll tell him. I'll tell him. Don't get your knickers in a knot.'

Ferret looked at the man and then to Bernard who was standing there, smiling like a half-wit and then to Horatio who was wiping spermicide from his arse from a squashed tube he had fallen on and then around him at the ribald chaos and he began to wonder if all of this was worth it and then he thought of a boundless ocean of smooth moist twat that he could navigate if things went well and he waited patiently for the man to finish whatever the fuck he was going on about.

'My name is Saliva,' the man pronounced with courtly affectation, bowing and performing an ill-executed gavotte. 'Saliva Misogyny Rastus Poofta Dungeon Chains O'Donnell.' He rose to his full height and held out the palms of both hands, as if he was being robbed, 'And before you say anything, I didn't name myself. My father was a sexist, racist, homophobic, sadistic Irishman.'

'At least he wasn't short of opinions,' Bernard interjected.

'And who are you?' asked Saliva.

'I'm Bernard and this is my brother, Horatio.'

'Hello,' chirped Horatio, cheerily. 'Nice place you've got here.'

'Thanks,' replied Saliva, with a sniff.

'You don't sound Irish,' said Bernard.

'Darling,' replied the effete tall man, 'once you realise you're gay and you get the voice down, accent doesn't come into it. All you need is a lisp and a perennial sense of outrage.'

'How the fuck did you survive in this town?' asked Ferret, who was less revulsed, than impressed.

'I did ballet and boxing from a young age. The ballet

helped me with the boxing and the boxing kept me alive in this God-forsaken red-neck shire.'

'Okay, Sal . . .' Ferret began.

'Sally, please. That's what all my friends call me.' He was about to speak again but paused, as if rudely interrupted. 'What do you mean I don't have any friends?'

Ferret stopped short. 'I never said you never had no friends.'

'I wasn't speaking to you. I was talking to Jesus.'

'Jesus?'

'He's my Pooka.'

'What the fuck are you . . .'

'Really?' Bernard interrupted. 'What form does he take?'

'He's a goblin. I would have preferred a rabbit, but still .'

'Where did you find him?'

'Up in the Kurrajong Hills. Well, actually, he found me.'

'Really. What happened?'

Ferret was watching the discussion like a drunkard at a tennis match. Each time he looked at one man, the other spoke. He thought he was going mad. 'What the fuck are you two talking about?' he blurted.

'His Pooka, old boy. His Pooka. Pookas are old Irish mythical spirits that sometimes reveal themselves to people and then befriend them. They can perform magic and even stop time.'

'If befriend is the word,' said Saliva, rolling his eyes. 'He looked immediately down behind him and added, 'I'm joking. I'm joking. For Christ's sake.' He turned back to Bernard and rolled his eyes again.

Bernard smiled in collusion.

Ferret stared at him. 'What the fuck are *you* smilin' at?'

'Just enjoying the moment,' Bernard replied, still

grinning affably from ear to ear, full of good will and bon ami.

'I think you're *having* a moment,' Ferret snapped. 'You mean to tell me this blokes got an invisible friend called Jesus?'

'Never seen the movie 'Harvey', F Major?' asked Horatio.

'Don't call me F Major and no, I 'aven't,' Ferret replied curtly, 'and I don't think I ever fucken' will, neither.'

'Pity,' replied Bernard. 'James Stewart is superb. Did he win the Oscar, Sally?'

Saliva nodded, '1950.'

'Fantastic.'

'What's fantastic,' said Ferret, 'is that you two bastards are still fucken' alive in Western Sydney. Now before any of yous start crappin' on again, invisible friend, or no fucken' invisible friend, Saliva, do you make these?' He held up a little blue packet.'

Saliva raised his hands to his face as if he had just won a beauty pageant. 'Oh my God!' he screeched. 'Jesus, we're saved.' He started dancing like a madman with his invisible friend and, what was more, his invisible friend knocked over a chair full of vibrators and eventually fell backwards onto Horatio who full back in amongst the spermicide. An invisible hand helped him up.

'Thanks,' said Horatio. 'Jesus is really very nice.'

'Oh, he's nice at the moment because we've relocated the treasure but you should see him when he's angry – terrible temper. (pause) Well you *have*, I'm sorry. (pause) I'm just telling the truth and anyway, don't be in a bad mood. We're back!' Saliva recommenced his jig.

'What the fuck are you on about?' shouted Ferret, stopping the gaiety.

'Don't you realise what that means?' He pointed at the packet of wipes in Ferret's hand.

Ferret blinked. 'It means I wanna buy more of 'em.'

'No you don't understand,' said Saliva, doing a glorious pirouette, which was applauded by Bernard and Horatio, 'we'd lost the formulae (pause) Oh alright, alright, *I* lost the formulae somewhere and we couldn't remember the secret ingredient. But now we have a wipe we can analyse it and (pause) Oh alright *Jesus* can analyse it and we can make more.'

'Are you sayin',' said Ferret, 'you don't 'ave no more?'

'No. I told you. I lost the formulae. I wasn't worried at first, I simply went down to 'The Imperial', but the dispenser was empty. I would have traded a thousand times the money in the dispenser for one of those little beauties. May I have it?' He smiled sweetly.

Ferret put the packet back in his pocket. 'I've only got two left.'

'Ooh you randy little fucker,' replied Saliva. He pushed Ferret on the shoulder like a flirtatious little girl.

'No, dickhead, I gave 'em to a bus full of geriatrics.'

'That was an odd thing to do. Still, to each his own. I *have* seen pictures.'

'No, I mean . . . look it doesn't matter. I'm nearly out, so I'm keepin' it,' he added cagily, 'unless you got a better offer?'

'Cheeky,' said Saliva with a salacious grin. He sidled up to Ferret. Ferret tensed. 'Ooh look at you, all nervous. How cute.'

And Ferret was nervous, given the relative sizes of the two. Saliva's Jatz crackers were at his nose level.

'You're not gay are you?'

'Fuck off!' replied Ferret.

There was a sudden movement nearby.

'No, it's alright, Jesus. No need to get upset. That's just Hawkesbury for 'no'.' Saliva bent down and whispered to Ferret, 'Also, he's a bit jealous. You two are about the same size and he thinks you might take his job.'

'What job?'

'The head job of course!' Saliva thought this hilarious. He pushed the bemused Ferret on the shoulder and giggled like a first-time stoner. 'Oh, I laugh at that every time,' he said, wiping a small tear from the corner of his eye.

Bernard and Horatio were also laughing loudly.

Bernard added, in witty persiflage, 'A goblin' from a Goblin.'

This brought further hilarity.

'You get head jobs from an invisible Goblin?' asked Ferret. He was looking around the room for a weapon, if required. There was a pretty fierce looking anal ring toss to his right and over to his left was an auto suck already plugged in and ready to go. 'You're fucken' crazy!'

No sooner had Ferret bellowed these words than an invisible fist hit him in the nose. He fell, but quickly recovered. He swung at the air and hit nothing. Another invisible punch to the gut, followed by a right to the cheek, sent him down for the count. He felt a small rough hand rummage in his pocket and by the time he was sitting up, Saliva had the packet of 'Wannaroot? Sex Appeal' in his hand.

He looked down from the heights of Heaven upon Ferret. 'So,' he lisped smugly, 'looks like we don't have to make a deal after all.'

'Wait,' said Ferret getting warily to his feet, lest the invisible goblin be in the vicinity. 'We can work as a team.'

'Listen, darl, I have a product so desirable men and women worldwide will clamour for it. This little beauty works and you know it. Once we remember the missing ingredient we'll market this and Jesus and I will be rich. What have you got to offer us?'

'Are you telling me that the dispenser full of wipes was the first load ever made?'

'The first and the only, so far.'

'So no one else knows about this?'

'Well, they would have if you hadn't been greedy and taken them all. But no, no one does, yet.'

'Okay,' replied Ferret, thinking aloud and rubbing his cheek, 'then I *have* got an offer for you.'

'We're listening.'

'Hear me out.' He wandered over to a nearby saddle-shaped contraption and sat. As he did he accidentally turned it on. He had the immediate sensation of a vibrator up his arse. 'Jesus!' he yelled and then quickly added, 'No offence!' before turning the machine off and reseating himself.

'You have to love the Sybian,' said Saliva, gazing lovingly at the appliance upon which Ferret now sat. 'Ooh and look, he's riding side-saddle.'

Ferret shuffled in his saddle and began, 'If you go into mass production wif this stuff you'll be rich, for sure, *but* every bastard in the world will be onto it within weeks and that means that pussy - or in your case, arsehole - will be difficult to obtain without competition. Are ya wif me?'

'Go on,' replied Saliva.

'So here's my plan. We work together, all four . . .'

Saliva coughed.

'. . . five of us and manufacture the wipes, but we keep 'em entirely for ourselves.'

'No, don't hit him Jesus. Let's hear him out.' Saliva turned back to Ferret. 'Why on Earth would we consider that? I mean, yes it would be great to have sole control of the pheromones, but what will you three bring to the table?'

Ferret grinned, 'How does three hundred million dollars sound?'

'Sounds great,' replied Saliva. He scanned Ferret up and down with a look of contained contempt, 'but you don't look like you even have a penny for the ferry man.'

'If you don't believe me, ask *them*,' said Ferret, nodding towards Bernard and Horatio. 'Hey boys! You don't mind givin' half our inheritance to this bloke so he can poof himself stupid do yous?'

'No, that's fine,' replied Bernard with a rakish grin.

'No worries, the F word,' added Horatio with a boyish wink.

Saliva looked from them and back to Ferret, then back again, 'You're serious? You really do have the money?'

'Oh yes,' replied Bernard. 'It may even be considerably more.'

Saliva half closed one eye with suspicion. 'I'd have to check and see it for myself.'

'Why don't you come home to England with us?' Horatio suggested with enthusiasm. 'We could be like 'The Famous Five.'

'What do you think?' asked Saliva (pause) 'Yes, well it's alright for you, you're invisible, you can get as much hanky-panky as you like *and* you bat for both teams which increases your odds of success by fifty per cent before you even get you're dick out. (pause) Yes, well I'd rather be rich and have the unfair advantage of nature's pheromones.' He turned back to the others. 'Three hundred million did you say?'

Ferret, Bernard and Horatio nodded.

'Very well, we're a team.' He shook hands with each of them. So did Jesus, which caused some confusion.

'Oh, and Ferret,' whispered Saliva confidentially, 'Jesus says he's sorry.'

'Tell him he's got a good right,' said Ferret, moving his jaw from side to side.

'Oh this is going to be so much fun,' said Bernard.

'Back to England,' Horatio trumpeted.

'But first we have to analyse the wipe and make a list of ingredients.'

'How long will that take?' asked Ferret.

'Only a few hours,' Saliva replied. 'Jesus and I will get to it.'

'I'll take these blokes 'ome. Well get some clothes 'n' I'll book the flights. Five for Heathrow.'

*

Twenty minutes later Ferret was on the phone in his apartment scribbling out flight details, watched with admiration by his two siblings. An hour after that he was in Kentucky Fried Chicken, arguing with the girl behind the counter that his fries were cold, watched with admiration by his two siblings. Then he went to River Music and tried out a cool 'Reynold's' amp, watched with admiration by his two siblings, until he was asked to leave for being a fucking awful guitarist and then, when he went to the loo in The Macquarie Arms Hotel, and his two siblings tried to follow him into the cubicle, he had to tell his admiring two siblings to piss off.

Eventually the trio walked back into 'The Imperial'.

Steve was serving alone. 'So, I heard you fellas went to Japan. Any good?'

'Fucken' unreal,' Ferret replied, after he wiped the VB from his chin. 'Those cunts've got their shit together; don't you worry about that. Listen to this, ya can't find a garbage bin for love or fucken' money, but there's no litter anywhere. Now, fucken' riddle me that?'

'Beats me,' replied Steve.

'And, there's virtually no fucken' street crime - in a country of a hundred and twenty-five million people.'

'Fuck off.'

'No, I'm fucken' serious. In some places they leave construction machines - fucken' hundred-thousand-dollar machines, thank you very much, on a construction site unattended without a fucken' fence or nothin' and no one even thinks've stealin' 'em.'

'Fuck off.'

'No. I'm fucken' serious. In some places ya see shops with fucken' . . . what's that shit called? Nettin', that's all, just like fishin' net hangin' loose across the shop front, like in an open mall where anyone could nick it, and no one does.'

'Well, I'll be fucked.'

'It's fucken' unbelievable. If ya did that shit in Windsor or Richmond, mate, I'd last how long?'

'Five minutes and it's on Ebay,' replied Steve.

'Ken'oath,' Ferret agreed. 'And because they got respect they can have nice stuff, like central heatin' on the trains.'

'Fuck off.'

'I'm fucken' serious. It's getting' cold right? 'coz it's getting' towards winter over there, it's all backwards right?'

'Yeah, right.'

'So, ya sit on your arse and it's as warm as piss from a virgin. Now, how long do ya reckon that central heatin' tubin' or whatever it fucken' is runnin' under them seats would last out in these parts?'

'About five minutes, I reckon.'

'If that,' stated Ferret with authority, 'before one of them dumb tattooed cunts wif no fucken' brains, a chip on their shoulder and smack addicted parents ripped the guts out of it.'

'Hey,' whispered Steve, 'easy on the tats. The missus just got a tramp stamp.'

'Oh, sorry,' replied Ferret. 'Speak a the devil.'

Raylene entered the bar from the back, took one look at Ferret and busied herself with some bottles that needed cleaning.

'G'Day Raylene,' said Ferret. 'Hear ya got a tat.'

'Yeah,' she mumbled. 'Hey Steve, I'm orderin' some

chong chow. Ya want some?'

'Yeah, alright,' he replied.

She took one brief darting glance at Ferret. He smiled. She left.

Steve clicked his fingers. 'Speakin' about Japan and tats there was a bloke in here earlier askin' after you.'

Ferret froze mid gulp.

'Said you'd know 'im. Sends 'is regards. Now what was his fucken' name?'

'Kanji?'

'Yeah, that was it, Kanji. He said 'ed see you real soon.'

'Oh good - Kanji,' said Horatio.

'Did 'e ask you anything?' asked Ferret quietly.

'Oh, just where you lived. I told 'im you weren't back from Japan yet.'

'Was he alone?'

'No, he had a couple of Sumo guys with 'im. He said he was a promoter. Seemed nice enough.' Steve wiped the bar and did a double take at Ferret. 'It was okay to tell 'im where ya lived, wasn't it? I mean 'e said 'e was your friend 'n' he seemed nice enough.'

'No. No, that's alright, Steve. No worries.'

'Except that . . .' Bernard began.

'No, it's fine.' Ferret looked at his watch. 'Well, we better go, boys. See ya, Steve.'

The three of them finished their beers and stood up to leave.

Steve grabbed Ferret lightly by the arm. 'Hey Ferret, everything alright?'

'Yeah, thanks,' he replied softly.

'Somethin' happen to you over there?'

'What do ya mean?'

'Well ya seem kinda different. Kinda . . . improved, or somethin.'

Ferret laughed, 'Mate,' he said, 'if I get through this,

things are certainly gunna look up. And in some ways, I got you to thank for it.'

'What do ya mean?'

Ferret looked at Steve for a few seconds, as if weighing up whether to tell him something. 'It doesn't matter right now. I might tell you an interestin' story one day. A true one this time.'

'Yeah, well, take it easy mate. You're worryin' me a bit. It's nothing' to do with that bloke is it? 'coz I'd hate to think. ..'

'Hey, Steve,' Ferret put his hand on Steve's shoulder, 'don't beat yourself up, mate. I'm just the boy who played in the wadin' pool with 'is floaties on and 'is mum watchin', 'n' then one day 'is mum was gone so he jumped into the divin' pool and ended up at the bottom lookin' up. 'N' let me tell ya mate, it's a fuckin' shock to ya system when ya realise how deep shit can get.'

Ferret smiled weakly and hurried away.

Steve watched him go. He kept wiping the bar calmly, but his thoughts were jangling.

'Don't look like no-one's bin 'ere,' said Ferret as he sifted through his apartment. 'Everything's exactly like I left it.'

'Except for the notepad,' noted Bernard, with a smile.

'What about the notepad?'

'The page you scribbled on is separate to the pad,' replied Horatio with an equally broad smile.

'Look, will you cunts stop fucken' smilin'? For fuck's sake, this is serious. What?'

'It's obvious isn't it, Horatio?'

Horatio nodded.

'You see, we both admire your work. You're ever so clever.'

'Even if you do swear too much.'

'And we loved the way you made those enquiries and reservations with so much aplomb and derring-do.'

'What the fuck is wrong with you?'

'But we did notice,' continued Bernard, 'that the notepad upon which you wrote the extensive details of our impending flight, most impressively, I might add . . .'

'Most impressively,' concurred Horatio.

'. . . was earlier attached to the aforementioned pad.'

'And now it isn't,' completed Horatio.

'So?'

'So, someone has been in your apartment.'

'And torn it off the pad.'

'My guess is that they were going to take it and then thought that if they did you might notice it . . .'

'So they put it back on the pad . . .'

'And they assumed that you probably wouldn't notice it.'

Ferret had a sense that he was in the presence of true dumb genius. They had solved a puzzle they had no idea existed.

Ferret sat back in his chair and ran through the ramifications. So, if Kanji knew what flight they were on, he'd be on it too. And if Kanji was on it too, when he got to London . . . shit. He didn't want to end up in the Thames. It wasn't even all that clean. Fuck. What to do? What to . . .

The phone rang.

'Fuck!' he yelled and he mopped some sweat from his brow.

'Hello? No, this is Bernard. Oh hello, Sally. How are you? (pause) Excellent. Excellent. No, just having a chat. (pause) Yes. (pause) Yes. (pause) Yes. (pause) No. Definitely not. When? (pause) Alright. You make the arrangements; we'll see you there. (pause) No, no. No problem. Just use the credit card I gave you. (pause) Yes, that's fine. Cheers and give my regards to Jesus. See you on the morrow.' He put the phone down. 'Lovely man.'

Ferret, his brow still bespangled with sweat, looked

towards Bernard for news.

Bernard looked back, smiling.

'What?'

'Oh, we're not going to London after all.'

'Why?'

'Oh something to do with the secret ingredient.'

'Well what the fuck did he say?'

'It sounds like quite a funny story actually.'

'Then fucken' tell it to me!'

'I seems that Jesus remembered the secret ingredient as soon as he looked into the microscope. It all came back to him, the silly duffer.'

Horatio and Bernard chuckled.

'Please fucken' tell me,' pleaded Ferret, looking from his watch to the window.

'Apparently the secret ingredient grows in only one place in the whole world.'

'Where?' asked Ferret, nervously standing and beginning to throw clothes into a small suitcase.

'You're never going to guess.'

'Where, for fuck's sake?' Ferret mopped his forehead with a pair of underpants.

'Guess.'

Ferret exploded. 'Fucken' tell me!' He jumped up on the bed and grabbed Bernard by the collar.

Bernard remained unfazed. 'Japan.' He smiled.

'I don't believe it,' said Horatio, laughing.

Ferret let go of the collar and crumpled onto the bed.

'Yes, apparently the only place this particular herb grows is in the Imperial Palace in Tokyo. Would you believe it? We were just there; right there the other day.'

Horatio shook his head. 'Incredible.'

Ferret stared at the wall.

'So, Sally is making the arrangements and we're all off tomorrow morning early. Better get a good night's sleep, Ferris.'

'Yes, good night, mate,' added Horatio.

They both headed for the bathroom to do their teeth, leaving Ferret trembling and furtively glancing out of the window. 'Shit!' he was thinking – 'back into the lion's mouth.'

He didn't sleep a wink and early the next morning, as he boarded the plane for Narita with his motley crew, he looked like a Barbie Doll after a feminists' convention.

*

Later that morning, Kanji stood, fuming, as he watched the last guests checking in for Flight QF 319 for Heathrow. He stood, fuming, as he watched the last passengers for Flight QF 319 for Heathrow go through the boarding gates. And he stood, fuming, as the last call for passengers Ferret, Bernard and Horatio Cutler and two other names he did not recognise fail to turn up for flight QF 319 for Heathrow. He did some quick legwork and he fumed still more as his Australian contact made some hurried calls to confirm the fact that Ferret had, in fact, boarded a plane for Narita earlier that morning.

He clasped his aching fingers against his heaving breast and he vowed, with silent anger, 'I will kill you, you dishonourable fool. I will kill you as soon as I catch you - you and every one of your friends.'

He made a booking for home on the first available flight and he fumed all the way back to Tokyo.

On Ferret's flight the hostess told him repeatedly that he could take the window seat if he liked since Jesus O'Toole hadn't turned up for the flight, which annoyed the hell out of Ferret, but of course any protest would have been met with a quick invisible kick in the balls, so he smiled as politely as he could and consistently declined, much to the endless surprise of the hostess.

Once back in Japan the five caught the Skyline into

Tokyo, jumped onto the city circle and within two hours were nestled in the dark outside the Imperial Palace.

'We have three choices,' Bernard suggested as the group stood in a children's playground looking at the palace grounds. 'One, we wait until December 23rd, the Emperor's Birthday, when it would be relatively easy to get the herb, since the garden is open to the public on that day, but unfortunately that's over a month away, or two, we could break in during the daylight hours, but that would be foolish, or three, we could go now.'

'Well thanks for the fucken' Mission Impossible spiel, shithead, but I think the course of action is pretty fucken' obvious don't you?'

'Emperor's Birthday?' suggested Horatio.

Jesus hit him.

'We play to our strengths,' stated Ferret. 'Sally, you're tall, Bernard, you're strong. Together you heave us over the wall then climb it yourselves. Once we're in we find the herb, grab as much of it as we can and we put it into this airline bag Jesus stole from the plane. Then we climb out the same way. There's a spot over there in the dark where we could jump over but none of us knows where the herb actually is in the garden.'

Bernard said, 'I do.'

'What?'

'Well, if I'm not mistaken the herb in question is called suckmydickusfuckanythingus and as you rightly say grows only here in the Imperial Garden of the Emperor. It should be about two hundred metres to our right if we scale the wall where you suggest.'

Ferret was amazed, 'How the fuck do ya know that?'

'Wikipornopedia.'

There was a rustle, followed by a smacking sound, followed by a sudden, startled reaction from Bernard, 'What was that?' he yelped.

'Jesus kissed you,' said Saliva, with an endearing

tone. 'Oh, isn't that nice – he likes you.'

One tall guy, one big guy, two small guys and one invisible guy sneaked across the lawn outside the palace and, under cover of darkness, made their way over the wall of the Imperial Palace. All knotted together for safety, they made their way around a small lake and into a beautiful garden, revealed under the pale, full moon.

'You do realise that there's a heavy jail penalty for this should we be caught?' Bernard said.

'No fucken' kiddin'?' whispered Ferret in response, as the five crept stealthily alongside a massive inner wall, towards their goal.

'Here it is!' stated Bernard. It was a rather loud proclamation.

'Will you fucken' shut up,' hissed Ferret. 'I don't wanna end up in a Jap jail being paid visits by the Yakuza, thank you very fucken' much.'

'We won't need much of it,' stated Bernard, again quite loudly. 'It's very powerful.'

'Quick everyone, grab as much as you can,' whispered Ferret, 'before this noisy prick gives us away.'

Saliva looked down upon the garden with disdain. He touched his chest with his long, spindly fingers and said, 'I'm not touching that stuff. It's got dirt on it.'

'Well it would have dirt on it – it's attached to the ground. See?' Bernard held up a handful of weed.

'Doesn't look like much,' said Horatio. 'What's it taste like?'

'Look. This is not a fucken' cooking show,' whispered Ferret loudly. 'Let's just . . .'

In the dim distance a whistle blew and several lights went on in the castle.

'Fuck a duck!' screamed Ferret as he imagined the gas chamber, or worse – the Yakuza's torture chamber. 'Quick! Grab everything you can and run!'

So the riotous group hurried towards the stone wall

at the exterior of the castle grounds. They were a bugs bunny cartoon-like mass of bodies all competing for limited space; a sort of mobile football scrum; a cloud of dust with arms and legs appearing here and there from the nebulae and moving as straight as a twister.

Behind them they could hear the increasing volume of approaching boots. Ferret looked back and he could see the first outlines of human shapes under the moonlight.

'I don't know why we just didn't send Jesus. He's invisible,' suggested Bernard as they ran past the small lake.

'Well why didn't ya fucken' suggest it?' asked Ferret, puffing like an asthmatic at a dance party.

Saliva climbed the wall with ease. He sat astride it like a cowboy on a steed. Bernard quickly handed up the two short arses and then scaled the wall himself. All were safe beyond it and about to skedaddle across the street when Saliva said, 'Oh my God.'

'What?' replied everybody.

'We've forgotten Jesus.'

As he spoke, a ruckus broke out on the far side of the wall. At first there were yells and then some sort of scuffle seemed to have broken out in the ranks of the soldiers. There were raised voices, angry tirades and screams. The furore rose and then there was a volley of gunfire.

Over the gunfire Saliva said with a smile, 'Oh, good. It's under control. Come on.' And he sashayed across the street.

The others soon followed and within minutes they were lost amongst the high-rise metropolis. It was relatively busy, even at this hour, which helped their cause, but they didn't need it. The Imperial Guard didn't seem to be on their trail.

They made their way down to the underground railway and they boarded a train. As the train pulled away from the station, in amongst the late-night multitudes, Horatio spotted someone and began to wave frantically to attract their attention. Ferret noticed the sudden gesticulation. He turned, and to his horror, saw a dishevelled Kanji alongside his two equally dishevelled thugs looking directly at him. Kanji's eyes burned like brimstone as he watched the train depart.

'Will you fucken' stop giving us away?' Ferret shouted, drawing everyone's attention in the carriage. Most had been asleep and blinked in confusion at the collection of white trash sitting beside the door.

'What's up, Fer's?' Horatio asked, with a baffled grin.

Ferret bit his lip and sat back in his seat, conscious of the watching eyes.

'Horatio, I think next time you see Kanji, you should hide, rather than wave,' Bernard suggested, patting his little brother on the head, but missing, and bringing his hand down rather hard across the bridge of Horatio's nose.

'Okay, Bernomatic,' Horatio replied, twitching his assaulted nostrils like Rowan Atkinson about to sneeze.

'So what about Jesus?' Ferret asked.

'He is your saviour, my son,' interjected the only other white man in the carriage.

'Fuck,' Ferret muttered, 'only one fuckwit on a train full of intelligent Buddhists and I have to sit next to the only cunt who knows everything.' He sat, silent, trying to be as invisible as possible. But the little conversion-from-logic had only just begun.

The wide-eyed man, who apparently knew exponentially more than any of those present what the meaning of life was, rabbited on about how one fella, out of the six major nuisances crucified by the Romans, the year of thirty something A.D., was, without a question of doubt, the indisputable son of God, because he had been told so by others, who had as little proof as he, that this was true. Through an infinite number of stations he extolled the virtues of this impressive middleman, who apparently on one occasion avoided a water dousing, on another saved money by turning water into physically addictive drugs and finally who defied all possible logic by returning from a permanent state of lifelessness (though the Jews suggested that the body may have been stolen), until Ferret, ducking beneath the barrage of learned, untested nonsense, skulked beneath the Christian arm to find succour and eternal peace upon the Harajuku Station.

As the doors to the train began to close and the man completed his unwanted sermon with, 'I know this to be true. He is the one true God.' Bernard replied, 'Only the fool is certain.' Which left the man belting his sermon at the closed doors of the train as it pulled away.

A carriage full of sane men and women looked upon him with either contempt or bemusement, depending upon their prejudice.

As they looked on, the faces of many passengers within appeared to think the Japanese superior to this savage white man, who like most white men appeared to know everything and was not backwards in coming forward in telling them so, but they were too polite to disturb the avid man's delicate sensibilities. Doubtless, he would not have listened anyway. There are none so blind . . .

Ferret watched the cancer retreat into the night. 'Back to my original question,' he said.

'Jesus will be fine,' answered Saliva as the four men stepped into the bustling night street. 'Trust me, he'll catch up with us. He always knows where I am.'

'How?' asked Horatio.

'Oh, sweetie, I don't know,' replied Saliva, grabbing Horatio under the chin and squeezing it, as one might a particularly cute child. 'He just does. He's a Pooka. He's magical.'

'We should be safe here,' said Ferret as he looked down the long, crowded street full of shops and stalls. He had grown weary from thought, concern and flight. He looked like he needed a good sleep.

'Now, pumpkins,' replied Saliva; he had suddenly become the boss, 'we find a hotel for the night and then we find a good pharmacy.'

'Do you need to buy something?' asked Bernard.

'Just a few household drugs and a mixing vat,' said Saliva, pouting and squinting as he looked at Bernard. 'My God, you're enormous aren't you?' He winked. Bernard smiled. Saliva clapped his hands. 'Right, so, first thing - mix up magic potion.' He clapped his hands again. 'Next thing – go to U.K. pick up vast quantity of money.' He looked around. 'Now, let's find a place to dilute this massive quantity of . . . what was it?'

'Suckmydickusfuckanythingus,' replied Bernard.

'Gawd, I can't even pronounce it,' said Saliva, laughing and slapping Horatio on the back.

Horatio fell over.

'Alright, let's get lost in that,' said Ferret. He pointed to the road down the hill from the station where at least a thousand people were funnelled down the narrow channel. The markets were alive on the banks, but the great flood of water was the people surging through the laneway. They moved in two directions like some drunken tide but one with absolute precision: hardly a bow required. 'We'll meet at the Hilton later. And we're gunna have to stay a few days too. Kanji and his boys are gunna be watching the airports like a randy sixth grade boy staring at a young female prac. teacher's arse.'

'It's settled then. Bernard, you and I will find a back street chemist and you boys,' Saliva pointed at Ferret and at Horatio who was unable to get up because a train had just come in and the exiting passengers were walking all over him, 'should go and get some rest.'

The men split up.

As Ferret and Horatio entered the foyer of the Hilton, Ferret said to Horatio, 'Wait here. Don't do anything. Don't go nowhere. I'll be back in a minute,' and he ducked off for a quick pee.

Horatio watched him go and then walked directly up to the counter.

'Yes, prease,' asked the well-attired attendant. He was in his middle years and he bore a large, welcoming smile.

'Anata no hohoemi wa hansamu desu,' Horatio remarked.

'Oh, thank you,' replied the man, his smile increasing. 'You speak good Japanese.'

'Arigato,' Horatio replied, 'Nihon no geijutsu ga suki desu.'

'Thank you. Thank you,' replied the man, bowing with pride. 'You are very kind and gracious man.'

'That's a lovely thing to say,' said Horatio. 'Oops. Back in a sec.' He retraced his footsteps and popped back around the corner to wait for his twin brother.

The fine-featured Japanese man straightened his tie with pride as he watched Horatio round the corner. Perhaps he had been wrong about foreigners. He had found them rude, arrogant and loud, in the main: especially Australians. But, well, he realised now that he shouldn't generalise.

Out of sight of the attendant Horatio stopped to buy a can of Calpis from a vending machine.

Ferret didn't see him as he passed. He approached the attendant.

'Ah, harro again.' The attendant beamed. ' Hoka ni nani ka?'

'What the fuck is wrong with you, China?' said Ferret. 'You look like someone just shoved a cock up your arse.'

The man froze for a moment as the words washed over him. His smile remained but it dimmed into professionalism.

'You have loom?'

'If I plan on doin' any weavin' I'll let ya know.'

'Ah, excuse prease?' asked the man.

'Never fucken' mind,' retorted Ferret. He was tired and irate. 'Two rooms.'

The attendant worked politely and earnestly, punching numbers into his computer. 'In name of?'

'Jesus,' replied Ferret. He had a private laugh to himself at the irony - Jesus was the only one not paying for a bed.

The transaction was soon completed.

Ferret said to the attendant, 'Give a key to the other pricks when they turn up,' then he muttered to himself, 'I suppose that stupid twin of mine got fucken' lost somewhere,' then he said to the attendant, 'I'm goin' to bed and I don't wanna be disturbed. Got it, Shogun?'

The attendant bowed as Ferret left. He watched him walk towards the elevator. No, he had been right all along about gaijins.

He ducked down behind his desk to retrieve a dropped piece of paper. When he reappeared Horatio was standing there.

'Hi,' said Horatio. 'I love your carpet. Anata no kaapetto ga daisuki desu.'

The man looked at Horatio, went to speak, went to bow, hesitated and stuttered uncertainly, '603 and 604.'

Horatio shook his head in wonderment. 'And I didn't even have to ask. How *do* you do it? This must be the best-organised country on the planet. Oyasumi nasai. Goodnight.'

With a wave and smile, he was gone.

The attendant shook his head. He was wrong.

Australians were neither good nor bad, they were strange. Perhaps it was something in the red soil down there. He went back to his typing.

'What is fucken' wrong with these people!' shouted Ferret. He threw his hot dog at the wall.

'What's the matter, the F'ter?'

'I swear,' replied Ferret, through gritted teeth, 'if you keep callin' me stupid fucken' things, one day I'm gunna fucken' belt ya.' He drew in a deep, unsteady breath. 'Everything tastes like fucken' dessert in this country. I ordered a fucken' hot dog, not a fucken' weirdo sausage buried in a weirdo fucken' cake!'

'Gotta love the Japanese cuisine though, 'eh, Fez Wez?'

Ferret drew in his breath again and quietly steadied himself. 'No, H- monster, the H-word, the H-machine or whatever your fucken' name is, I don't, okay? Just shut the fuck up. I need to sleep. I'm in a terrible fucken' mood and I just need to sleep. Got it?'

'I'll hold the fort, F'us majorus,' Horatio replied with a grin.

Ferret stared at him for a moment and went to his room.

*

When he awoke there was much activity in the main room.

'Ta da!' Saliva belted out like a retarded magician. 'Our first fifty pheromone wipes. Bring on the boys.'

'Or the babes,' muttered Ferret, wiping the morning mist from his eyes.

'Whatever's your poison,' Saliva replied, holding up a handful of sealed plastic bags. Inside of each was a single pheromone wipe. 'We'll worry about the packaging later. But these will do for now.'

Ferret scratched his arse and went to sit down, 'Did that little invisible cunt ever turn up?'

As his arse neared the seat, the seat magically withdrew, leaving Ferret strewn upon the floor.

'Yep, he showed up,' replied Saliva. He looked towards the heavens and then the nails on his fingers, which were curled back upon the palm of his hand like a comic player in a Gilbert and Sullivan operetta.

Bernard and Horatio laughed at his gay antics.

'Yeah, well I'm glad you fuckers think it's funny,' Ferret replied, picking himself up from the floor.

'You wouldn't be so dismissive of Jesus if you knew what I know.'

'And what do you know?' asked Ferret. He seemed in no better frame of mind for the eight hours sleep.

'Oh, nothing in particular, just a little information regarding a certain friend of ours. A certain Kanji.'

Now Ferret was listening.

'Yes, thought you might be interested.' He stopped and listened. 'Yes, Jesus, I know you were the one who found it out. I was going to tell him that. (pause) I realise that. I just don't know why you have to go and make such a big deal about it. (pause) I know that. (pause) Yes, I realise that we haven't had sex for over a week, but I've been rather busy, haven't I? (pause) Alright, so we've both been busy, granted but I can't fuck you on the JR Line now, can I? (pause) Well, yes, but they can see *my* cock, can't they?'

Ferret interrupted, 'Look, what the fuck has he found out?'

'Okay. Here's the lowdown,' said Saliva, going into espionage mode. 'Kanji knows we're here.'

'What the fuck? How do you . . ?'

Saliva cut him off with a feminine wave of his hand, 'Hear me out.'

Ferret shut up.

'He knows we're here. Jesus overheard a conversation at the station after we left. It seems that the Yakuza have friends all over Japan.'

'You think?' mocked Ferret.

'Now don't get all stroppy,' admonished Saliva. 'The least you can do is be courteous. Jesus beat the shit out of a dozen guards for us. And he got this information.'

'Sorry, Jesus,' said Ferret towards the nearest wall.

'He's over here,' replied Saliva, 'but never mind. The point is he knows we're here so there's no getting away stealthily. We must be bold instead.'

'Be bold?' Ferret iterated. He stood up. 'Be bold?' he reiterated. 'What the fuck does that mean? Listen, I'm being chased by the Yakuza, arguably the most well organised, most intelligent and most vicious crime organisation on the planet. I've killed their cash cow and they want revenge.'

'And money,' added Bernard, who had sat on the sideline and was thoroughly enjoying the discourse.

'So true, BB gun,' added Horatio.

Bernard and Horatio went to slap hands but Bernard missed and smacked Horatio in the ear.

'Before you say anything else, Negative Nancy,' said Saliva, (Bernard and Horatio laughed on cue), 'I have a plan. And this is it. Are you ready?'

Everyone apparently was because no one spoke.

'We become a famous rock band!' Saliva stood up. He looked towards the ceiling as if watching the reality unfold above him. Theatrically, he stalked the floor, watched admiringly by Bernard and Horatio, and watched incredulously by Ferret. Jesus' expression didn't change. 'Yes. I can see it now – 'Ferret and the Pheromones' playing live here tonight. We'll be so swamped by fans and media even the Yakuza won't dare touch us. Then, we'll wing our way to England, get our money and return to Australia. We can relocate so that the

Yakuza can't find us. Double bay, maybe?'

Ferret sat staring up at the tall man. 'What the fuck are you talkin' about?' he stated. 'I can play a bit of guitar but that's it.'

'Ahem.' Bernard coughed into his hand.

'What?'

'Well, not to put too fine-a-point on it but . . .'

'Tell him, Bernardus Aurelius,' urged Horatio.

'. . . but I'm a not-to-shabby bass player and Horatio here . . .'

Horatio winked and gave Ferret his best vaudevillian smile . . .

'. . . is a superb rhythm and lead guitarist.'

The two men high-fived again. Horatio caught that one on the shoulder.

'And I can play keyboards,' Saliva added, but it doesn't matter two hoots because I have this.' He produced a spray can. It was white, but scrawled upon it, in crude permanent marker was: 'Pheromone Spray'. He continued, dancing around with the can clenched to his chest like an unwilling lover. 'We spray this before we play, we all wipe ourselves down with copious quantities of wipes and before we've finished the first song, boys and girls, men and women will all be leaping out of their seats and onto the stage. It'll be 'The Beatles' all over again. We'll escape right under Kanji's nose. He daren't accost us for fear of the publicity and public scrutiny.'

'Genius,' said Bernard.

'Genius,' said Horatio.

'Fucken' stupid,' said Ferret. 'And what are we gunna do for a drummer?' But as he asked the question he was sorry he had.

'Why Jesus, of course,' proclaimed Saliva. 'He's been around, that cat. Haven't you, Jesus. (pause) It's an expression. Cat. (pause) Well, it may be passé, treasure, but it is true. (pause) Alright. Alright. No one's suggesting you're a homosexual. (pause) Alright. I'll tell them.' He drew in a breath. 'Jesus wants you all to understand that he is not a homosexual.'

'But doesn't he suck your cock and let you have intercourse with him?' asked Bernard with interest.

'Yes, he does, but that doesn't make him a homosexual.'

'Well what fucken' does?' asked Ferret, wide-eyed.

Jesus hit him.

'Being a homosexual,' Saliva explained. 'You see, he's not. He just engages in sex with men at times, that's all.'

'Perfectly understandable,' said Bernard.

'Perfectly,' Horatio echoed.

'Some of England's finest . . .' added Bernard.

Ferret had regained his seat. He knew when he was beaten. 'Fair enough,' he said, though it was far from 'fair enough' as far as Ferret was concerned. Back in the Hawkesbury you got your arse kicked in if you dared talk like that. But he said, 'If Kanji already knows we're here then where is 'e?'

'Oh he can't just waltz in here and kill us, petal,' replied Saliva with a practised roll of the eyes. 'Too many cameras. We're safe here for the time being.'

'Won't one of 'em climb the building and hide in the toilet until I shit and then thrust a sword up me arse like one of them ninjas?'

'Ninjas are defunct, darling and besides, you saw those two roly-poly beefcakes he has with him. They'd be lucky to climb the stairs. Mind you, I wouldn't mind hugging one. They are so strong and built for comfort.' Saliva shook his head and shivered his cheeks with the thought.

'We ain't got no choice then, do we?' murmured Ferret thoughtfully. 'But what'll we do?'

'Leave it to me,' announced Saliva with a great

theatrical flourish. 'I know the head of Sony. I'll get us a gig tomorrow night at the 'Rock Bar Mother Fucker'. We can rehearse tomorrow. Boys, we're going punk!'

There was much excitement as Bernard, Horatio, Saliva and Jesus stood and clapped hands in premature congratulation.

Ferret stared at the wall.

*

The following evening at the back of the smoky bar stood three, impassive Sony executives. Before them was a crowded room full of colourfully clad youngsters, pierced from arsehole to breakfast time with studs and chains. The three men were unmoved when the announcer thundered: 'Welcome Ferret and the Pheromones!' and they remained impassive as the drums began (obviously recorded, since the drums on the stage had no drummer behind them) but they shifted slightly and looked askance at one another as the cymbals and kick drum came to life as if by some magic. One of them twitched his nostrils and noted the unusual odour permeating the room.

Then, on came our lads, not to a cacophonous ovation, but to polite applause. Bernard wore a huge garbage bag, which became a plastic mini skirt upon his large frame; Horatio had painted himself white and wore speedos; all seven feet of Saliva was draped in a 1930's full length chiffon number, complemented by red high heels and Jesus was naked, but no one noticed. Then, on came Ferret. Against his better judgement he had allowed Horatio to pick out his costume. He had a symbolic brain piercing which ran through both sides of his temples, from ear to ear like a vertical halo, he had spiked his little yellow tuft to a fine point and he wore a suit of blue with the Union Jack emblazoned upon it with a fake tattoo of the Southern Cross sparkling upon his cheek. He wore stove-pipe trousers, a la the sixties, and his daring ensemble was completed by high rise Noddy Holder boots.

The crowd quietened. Ferret took up the mic.

'Here's one for fucken' Pearl Harbour!' he yelled and the band exploded into a version of 'Now I wanna be Your Dog', by Iggy Pop. The band was actually pretty good but Ferret was awful. He had to watch his fingers to make the two necessary chords but by the time he had formed the 'A' the band was already hitting the 'D'. He tried to sing but only managed an incoherent guttural gurgle. Then he tripped on the monitor and fell flat onto Horatio, who got a machine head in the eye.

If the Sony executives had any opportunity to widen their eyes and think 'What the fuck' in Japanese, the crowd suddenly erupted. People went wild. Young girls attacked the stage in droves far beyond the scope of the half a dozen security guards employed for that purpose. Bernard's glad bag was savagely ravaged by a group of milfs from Kyoto. He hadn't emptied the bag before donning it. Raw fish and chopsticks burst out like a supernovae much to the delight of the maddened crowd. Horatio had a high school girl wedge a finger up his arse and an emo rubbing her studded clitoris upon his ear. A fashion model was writhing in ecstasy upon the bass drum, thrashing about in wild orgasm, pummelled by invisible flesh, and Saliva had three young boys from the support band up his arse at the same time. He strode off the stage, waving all the time at the crazy audience who flooded upon the stage like a tsunami. Ferret was accosted from all angles by women of various dimensions. His eyes were his only visible feature as he lay prostrate upon the stage; each exposed, hyperventilating vagina competing for limited space upon his ravaged torso and appendages.

This was sufficient for the Sony executives. They knew money when they saw it. They left.

In the back corner, shielded behind the smoke of a short panatela, sat Kanji, staring at the chaos with a disengaged fury. He stared as the security guards pummelled the advancing crowd and did their best to stem the incoming tide. He stared as he watched Ferret crowd surf across the maniacal gathering and away into the dressing rooms beyond the stage. He flexed his bloodied fingers pensively once; twice. Then, he too left, followed by his hulking cronies.

Soon after, in the dressing room, to the accompaniment of riotous kids thumping wildly at the door, Saliva said to his fellow band members, who lay, strewn across the floor, heaving for breath, 'Well, that went rather well. Sony just called. We have two more gigs here. On Friday we play Earl's Court in London.'

The next two gigs were carbon copies of the first, except that Horatio got buggered by an ex-roadie from Aerosmith and Ferret copped a squirter from Hiroshima. He got a severe case of Mickey Juice Nose, which is not altogether unpleasant and certainly clears out the sinuses. One of the 'Rolling Stones' added Saliva on Facebook and the tweets went feral.

Of Kanji, there was no trace.

A quick trip to London; sirens blazing; a cavalcade of escort police cars and our boys were in the dressing room at Earls Court.

'Right,' said Saliva, brandishing a copy of 'The Times', 'listen to this. Headline. Ta da! – 'Ferret gets Mickey Juice Nose'. He stopped, 'Mickey Juice Nose. Hmmm. Not a bad name for a punk band,' then continued, 'And, again 'ta da' - all tickets sold out in .3 of a second. I think you'll find that's a record. We're on in thirty minutes.'

Ferret looked forlorn.

'What's up, FC?' asked Horatio as he applied the white Dulux.

'I'll tell ya what's fucken' wrong,' Ferret retorted. 'It's all very fucken' well to pheromone, or whatever the fucken' word is, a small room, but this is fucken' Earls Court. We can't drug all of 'em. They'll fucken' kill us.'

'Just leave that to me,' said Saliva with a sly grin. 'What? (pause) Oh, yes, alright. Sorry, oh magical one. Leave that to *us*.'

Soon after, Ferret listened to the crowd erupt for the support band. 'Fuck me,' he muttered to himself as he adjusted his vertical halo. 'Couldn't you organise a worse support act? Who the fuck is it anyway?'

'Now let's not get snippety,' replied Saliva with an extended bony finger pointed accusatorily at Ferret. 'It's only fair. Radiohead were booked for the gig and the tickets were already sold out.'

'Radiohead!' Ferret blurted. 'That's like goin' on after fucken' Zeppelin!'

But they did. To a cool reception. The British audience had just finished singing 'No Surprises' and they were ready to leave.

The air was tense with British expectation. The band struck up. So far, so good. Ferret played one revolting chord and dropped his pick. The crowd murmured. Within two bars, the 'boos' began. Ferret looked anxiously at Saliva who nodded towards some unseen roadie and from the great ceiling there dropped upon the crowd hundreds of large balloons. This proved a useful distraction as Ferret retrieved his pick and played a stunted bar chord. The crowd began bouncing the balls in the air. For a short while the amusement continued as massive balloons were hit skyward and battered about and above the audience like some slow-motion boiling treacle. But soon the 'boos' regained momentum. A walk out was imminent.

'Burst the balls!' Saliva shouted above the rising din.

So they did. With pocket knives, with lighters, with

fingernails. The sound of exploding balloons rent the air and a fine mist soon covered the auditorium like a fat woman, face-sitting.

For a moment, for perhaps two, the 'boos' continued but then subsided. And in their place grew the sound of a gathering force. At first it was a distant murmur and then a closer brook, then, the rising tumult of a running tributary, and within seconds it had become a raging flood enveloping the arena.

Years later, old men would place grandchildren upon their knee and tell them of the great riot of 2013. Elderly women would discuss in hushed tones the unbridled emotion of that night. And their grandchildren would listen, eyes wide with imagination at these censored tales from their elders - for on that night, grandma or grandpa would confide, history was made. There was nothing, and would be nothing, to rival it in the twenty first century, they would say, sagely shaking their heads at the enormity of the memory. It was the night London experienced 'Ferret Mania.' And their grandchildren could only imagine . . .

The number of dead was in the thousands; the badly injured and maimed, uncountable. But, when the pheromone mist cleared and the new day dawned, 'Ferret and the Pheromones' were the unassailed 'Kings of Rock', according to the tabloids.

When the news got out two days later that the band was taking a break due to extensive touring, no one gave a shit because the pheromones had worn off. Yet still, the magic lingered in the press. When would they return?

'Okay,' said Ferret. 'Let's go see our solicitor.'

So they did.

*

Saliva sat in the waiting room chatting away to his invisible Jesus, observed surreptitiously by a receptionist, called Beatrice, who had thrush, while the solicitor's door closed behind the three heirs to be.

Bernard sat beside Horatio and introduced Ferret to his solicitor.

His name was Matthew St. James. He was a large-featured, robust looking gentleman of perhaps fifty years. He wore a black suit and an MCC tie, possessed soft English pallid skin, spoke with the affectation of Eton or Harrow and had a nose that was more hooked than Arthur Wellesley's; a nose which bore, stoically, a pair of heavy horn-rimmed glasses.

He settled down behind his gigantic American Redwood table and nestled into his luxurious swivel chair. Ferret and the others sat opposite him and watched with silent interest as he shuffled the copious documents in front of him and adjusted his spectacles.

'Now, Bernard and Horatio, and . . .' he shuffled his documents, 'Ferris, is it?'

'G'Day,' said Ferret.

'Yes,' replied the man, looking over his glasses at Ferret as though he were encountering a new species. 'Now gentlemen, as I understand it there is no contest to the will in which you three equally share. Since the unfortunate demise of your mother, rest her soul . . .' he lowered his head slightly in respect for the dead and paused for a moment.

So did Ferret, but in that moment he was thinking, 'Thank God the fat cunt's dead.'

'. . . you three now stand to inherit a substantial fortune. Now, am I correct in understanding that you wish to give this gentleman . . . Saliva, is it?' He spoke the word with appropriate vigour.

'Call me Sally,' he replied. He held out his hand to be kissed.

'Yes,' muttered Matthew St. James, awkwardly turning the pages of his documents. 'The sum of $300 million.' He looked up from his papers, took the glasses from his ample nose and said, 'Are you sure, gentlemen?'

'K'noath,' replied Ferret.

'I beg your pardon?' said Matthew St. James.

'Yes,' Bernard assured him. 'These men have been of invaluable assistance to us.'

Matthew St. James allowed himself the luxury of a small smile as he listened to these words and the sonorous manner in which they were delivered. In this world there are few comforts, thought Mathew St James, but one that he treasured the most was the knowledge that there were still, upon this heathen planet, still men of refinement; of culture; of England. He had just heard one speak. Thank God. The bastard children of the colonies might still chatter like Eliot's apes but he knew that sanity and civility was a commodity that was forever England.

'Very well,' he said. 'So be it. I'll adjust the papers accordingly.' He began to rise.

''ang on a tick,' said Ferret, forcing the large man back down into his seat.

'Yes?' Matthew St. James' voice betrayed the condescension that for centuries has inspired English young men and been loathed by every other.

''Ow much are we gettin'?'

'Over two hundred million dollars apiece. Satisfied?' Again he went to stand, but again Ferret stopped him.

'Nothin' else?'

'Is that relevant, given the extent of the opulence?'

'I dunno what you fucken' just said, but yeah, I'd say it's pretty fucken' relevant since we're the cunts gettin' it.'

Matthew looked pained and embarrassed. 'Please Mister Cutler, I'll thank you not to use such profanities in my office.'

Ferret was in no mood for this man. 'Listen, you

pompous prick. I've 'eard you cunts speak to one another in your fucken' boys fucken' clubs 'n' you fuckers swear as bad or worse 'n' me, so don't give me that shit.'

'Mr Cutler,' Matthew St. James replied, sitting higher in his chair and returning the serve, 'Englishmen of my stature may swear but they are seldom vulgar.'

'Your class,' sniffed Ferret. He detested this man.

'Yes, my class, Mister Cutler,' retorted Matthew St. James, who reciprocated the sentiment.

'And what class is that?' asked Ferret.

'There are two types of Englishmen, Mister Cutler,' he spoke with apparent composure but there was an undercurrent - a wavering falsetto in his contained vocal cords, 'those of the working class who swear with abandon and those of the upper class, who eschew it, except for in the polite company of men.'

'As far as I'm concerned you and your upper-class men can get a shoe up your arses.'

'How dare you, you . . . Australian!' He threw the word as an insult. ' England is 90 per cent idiot and 10 per cent genius. These days, in a world unfortunately bereft of conscription, the 90 per cent have become rioting football hooligans. Fortunately, many of them have emigrated to Sydney, Australia, where they play Rugby League, I believe.'

'And the other 10 per cent?' asked Ferret, goading the large man, whose face was slowly reddening.

'Is me!' Matthew St. James almost shouted. Then, realising he had lost his composure, he straightened his tie, stretched his neck forward like a turtle and blinked without purpose several times. 'This is all of little relevance at any rate.'

''ow fucken' much?' Ferret persisted.

'Please, Ferris,' whispered Bernard.

'No, fuck 'im,' Ferret whispered back, but loud enough for Matthew St. James to hear. 'E's hidin' somfink.'

Matthew St. James licked his lips and cleared his throat, 'As a matter of fact there is one small caveat.'

'I don't want any fucken horse 'd oeuvres. What d'ya mean?' Ferret growled.

'A caveat is an addition, Mister Cutler,' he spoke with carefully veiled derision. 'This addition was added to your father's will.'

'And?'

'And,' he cleared his throat again, 'and, since you have *specifically* asked, I am *bound* to inform you, by the terms of your father's will, that an . . . allotment of shares is also yours to share.' He shuffled his papers in irate, contained fury. He went to stand.

''ang on. 'ang on,' Ferret pursued. 'Details?'

Mathew St. James fixed a stare upon Ferret that might have killed if it were a physical thing.

'I mean,' he replied in angry monosyllabic staccato, 'that you and your brothers also inherit an allotment of shares.'

'Well how come you never said nuffin'?' asked Ferret in staccato response.

'Because,' retorted Mathew St. James, 'under the conditions of the will I was not bound to, unless I was *specifically* asked.'

'See,' said Ferret to Bernard and Horatio, 'I knew 'e was hidin' somefink.'

'I have hid nothink . . .' he responded loudly and then corrected himself with stuttering poise, ' . . . nothing, from you, Mr Cutler. It was an express condition that the question be asked before it was answered.'

'So you never had to tell us unless you was asked? It was kinda like 'Owzat!' in cricket?'

'Precisely.'

'And I've asked?'

'Yes.'

'So you have to tell us?'

Matthew St' James bit his lip with frustration, took in a deep breath, and as steadily as he could, replied, 'Yes. That is correct.'

'So what 'appened to the shares if one of us never asked?'

Matthew St. James hesitated, 'They were to pass on to his financial advisor.'

'You?'

'Yes, me,' replied the besuited Englishman, glaring at Ferret as though he were the nemesis of everything England.

Ferret smiled. 'So there you go, boys,' he boomed, never taking his eyes from the simmering Matthew St. James, 'sometimes in this life, ya gotta ask. And I'll bet you one holy dump of the colony that my old man would've bet 'is life on the fact that my two brothers 'ere would never've asked that question. Am I right, Matty?'

Matthew St. James almost cracked a molar. His forehead exploded into a bright crimson.

'So you was tryin' to rip us off, the Matt monster?' Ferret smiled a toothless, infuriating grin.

Horatio laughed. 'Oh l'essie wasola,' he chuckled.

Matthew St. James had reached the end of his tether. He blasted, 'How dare you mock me, you . . . pathetic, low life, Australian scum!'

'Oooh,' Ferret responded like a high school reprobate pushing all the buttons of his riled teacher.

'Don't you dare 'oooh' me, you Philistine.' He stood up and his documents showered upon the polished floor. 'Yes, you're right, I would have inherited those shares, had you not asked, you . . . vulgar discourteous pig! You vile degenerate penal filth! And I deserved them too! My family has faithfully served the Cutler family for three generations! This was to be my reward!'

'So you were gunna take Bernard and Horatio's

money?' Ferret countered, himself rising from his seat. "coz they're too fucken' polite to ask?'

'You're damn right I was!' shouted Matthew St James, all propriety abandoned. 'Look at them!' He pointed at Bernard who showed no emotion at all and at Horatio, who smiled genially. 'They would never have asked for anything the . . . fools! It took a despicable Australian to do their dirty work for them!'

'The squeaky wheel, eh? See boys, it pays to have balls sometimes.'

'I tell you something, you Antipodean brat,' countered Matthew St. James, his jowls shaking like the later Elvis' mid-riff, 'I will have nothing to do with the Cutler family after this day. Do you hear me?'

'I hear ya,' Ferret replied quietly, but intensely. 'But I got one final question.'

Matthew St. James shook and his eyes blazed, 'And what is that?'

'What shares 'n' how many?'

A tear welled up in the corner of the large man's eye. It was a tear of expected opportunity lost. He could barely speak coherently, '10,000,000. Coca Cola.'

'Purchased?' asked Ferret, his eyes widening.

'1897,' replied Matthew St. James, crumpling upon his desk and dissolving into inconsolable tears.

'Worth?'

'At current share price,' blubbered the solicitor, barely audible because his face was buried into the desk, 'approximately four billion dollars.'

The enormity of the loss crashed upon him like a Riverstone burglar. He let out one ear-splitting howl, tore at his hair, ripping out great wads of it, stood like a man raised suddenly up the arse upon a wooden stake, wailed like a buggered clergyman and ran at the window. He screamed loudly as he hit it. Blood splattered onto shattering shards of glass as he fell through it and his hysterical yells could be heard as they disappeared down the long stories, where they suddenly ended in a distant thud, as if someone had just smacked a fish.

There was silence for a moment and then Horatio smiled and said, 'Well, that seemed to go pretty well.'

Bernard looked at Ferret, 'What now, old man?'

'Home,' he replied.

*

The homeward journey was uneventful, except that Ferret got caught wanking in first class over Anna Sophia Robb in 'The Bridge to Teribithia', (he only got caught because he yelled out his own name when he came) and two days later our boys were dining on the South Head of Sydney Harbour in Doyle's Seafood Restaurant.

The waiter was a small man who sniffed a lot and kept breaking pencils on his order pad. He was chaffed when the party wouldn't let him remove the fifth chair from the table, surprised when the food placed there disappeared, amazed when he peeked from the galley to see portions of the main meal rising above the table and disappearing into thin air and then in considerable pain when he tried to remove an unfinished course and felt a sharp kick in his shin for his troubles.

'Congrats all!' bellowed Saliva at the conclusion of the meal, as he raised his sauterne into the air above the cheese platter. 'Here's to being fabulously wealthy.'

'Too fucken' right!' Ferret replied and he hoed into his VB.

'Oh, that reminds me, the Fez Warrior. You owe sixteen thousand to the swear jar.'

'Put it on my tab,' Ferret replied. He laughed, as a man can when he has no trouble paying sixteen thousand dollars for a swear jar.

'What do you intend to do with the money, Ferris?'

asked Bernard.

'If you'd asked me a week ago,' replied Ferret, 'I'd 'ave said beer, women and shit loads of drugs, but, I gotta be honest wif ya, the last week has had a big effect on me. I've seen a few things and I've learned a few things. I've seen a foreign culture, superior to ours in some ways and I've seen two fat cunts fall from great heights.'

'Oh, and what have you taken from all that, Ferris?' asked Saliva, leaning his chin dreamily upon his knuckles.

'Well, Saliva, I've learned this: that life is wider than the Hawkesbury and that there are more things between heaven and Earth than tattoos, hookers and amyl nitrate.'

'I use it to clean my leather,' said Saliva.

'So what are ya gunna do with the money now, Fezcestakon?' asked Horatio, all wide-eyed and enthusiastic like a kid getting his first finger behind the wash shed.

'Now, Horatio, after all we've been through, all of us together . . .' he paused dramatically . . . 'I'm gunna spend it on beer and shitloads of drugs but I'm not gunna pay a cent on loose women 'coz all of us 'ave got a fucken' secret no one else in the world's got 'n' we can fuck any woman we want!'

'Or man,' Saliva interjected. He felt a sharp kick in the shins, 'Or goblin.'

'We are fucken horribly rich,' Ferret continued, standing almost to attention, the Australian flag fluttering behind him. 'We play in a rock band and we have an irresponsible control over women. Boys, it don't get no better than this! Nothing could possibly go wrong now.'

They all hurrahed and Saliva suggested they take a walk up to the lighthouse on the South Head to walk off lunch.

Ferret shouted everyone in the restaurant a free drink and the boys left.

There was one man in that restaurant who declined

the drink when it came. He was looking out of the window watching the casual perambulation of the small knot of men up the hill.

*

Our boys lounged casually beside the old lighthouse.

'The present lighthouse was built in 1883,' said Bernard, as he looked across the beginning of the Tasman Sea. 'But it's still called the Macquarie Lighthouse because it was built originally by Francis Greenway under Macquarie's rule.'

'Wikipedia?' asked Ferret, reclining and burping.

'Yes.'

'You're a fucken' wizard.' Ferret closed his eyes and let the sun beat down upon him. 'Billions and billions of fucken' dollars and more cunt than you can poke a stick at,' he whispered and he smiled with contentment. 'Every man's dream.'

'But now the dream is a nightmare!' The voice was strained with contained fury.

It was Kanji.

Ferret's eyes popped open like champagne corks. He stood and turned and there was his nemesis, sword in bloodied hand, his two huge accomplices immovable and impassive on either side of him.

'I'll give you a hundred million bucks to fuck off,' said Ferret.

Kanji laughed. 'You can give me billion dollars but can you give me back these?' He held up his right hand and adroitly unbound the bloodied rag wrapped across the three fingers furthest from his thumb. There, revealed, were three massacred fingers, the first joint of each had been savagely removed. Dried blood was congealed upon each of the three stumps.

'What the fuck!' Ferret burped.

'These were taken for my disgrace,' replied Kanji. In spite of the loss he still removed, with astonishing speed and agility, a short wakizashi sword from his loose-fitting trousers, though he winced as he manipulated the weapon in his bloodied fingers.

'Oh yes,' said Bernard, looking on with interest. 'The Yakuza take the first joint of the sword fingers when one of their members fails in some important task.'

'Not Yakuza,' replied Kanji, slowly; intensely. 'We are ninko dentai.'

'Traditionally it affected their ability and agility with a sword,' explained Bernard, apparently unaware, as Ferret was, of Kanji's quiet, mounting fury. 'Tell me, Mister Kanji, apart from those grotesque makings visible upon your upper body, is your penis also tattooed?'

'Ooh that must've hurt,' said Horatio, giggling.

'You think so?' added Saliva. He, like Ferret was looking from the three dangerous men and backwards towards The Gap; the sheer 80-metre drop directly behind them.

Kanji's eyes glowed like red coals as he spoke. The seething hatred incinerated the air between him and Ferret. 'I will be merciful to your friends,' he whispered. 'I will kill them quickly, but you,' he pointed his sword directly at Ferret, 'you I will save for rater. You I will save for ransom and berieve me you will wish that you had never seen rese eyes.'

'Isn't lallation a cruel word,' mused Bernard.

Kanji nodded and his two sumo accomplices moved slowly towards our boys.

'Shit. This looks like it,' whispered Ferret as he backed towards the precipice.

But just when all seemed lost, as if by magic, one of the sumos was suddenly pushed vigorously from behind by an invisible force. He yelped with surprise as he was furiously shunted past and beyond the shoulder of the smiling Horatio and sent screaming over the fatal edge of the cliff. The other sumo stopped in awe as he watched his flailing colleague disappear over the rocky ledge. Then he too, was assailed. But unlike his comrade, he managed to dig in his heals. He turned and grabbed at the apparently empty space, clutching in his powerful grip a writhing, invisible object. He looked towards Kanji with a bemused expression, squeezing the object against his chest.

With a roaring yell Kanji advanced upon the group with his sword raised for execution. The group of men screamed and backed to within metres of the drop. Bernard was scared, Ferret was petrified, Saliva squealed and Horatio smiled.

Kanji raised the razor-sharp blade and was about to hack into the group with one sweeping pass when . . .

Everything stopped. The planet stopped spinning and the sun stood still in the afternoon sky. The sumo was as frozen as a dud fuck. His arms, which had encircled an invisible something, soon encircled an invisible nothing. He turned, or rather was turned, by an invisible force and was kicked in the backside over the rocky outcrop and fell, uncomplaining and in rigid tableau, onto the rocks below.

Kanji, also in frozen pose, was dragged beyond the group, right up to the very edge of the escarpment. The invisible force turned him to face the backs of his enemies.

Then the world came back to life. Kanji swung his sword and found, to his astonishment, that he had hit nothing and that his intended targets were now turning, in equal astonishment, back towards him. He faltered.

'Bye. Bye,' said Saliva with a little feminine wave.

The invisible force shoved Kanji aggressively in the chest. He tried to regain his balance but couldn't and after several waves of his arms also fell over The Gap.

'Dear oh dear,' Saliva quipped to the incredulous bunch, 'three suicides in one day.'

'But . . .,' Ferret was agog.

'What happened, old boy?' asked Bernard.

'I thought you'd *seen* 'Harvey,'' replied Saliva with a look of self-satisfied, mock bewilderment.

'Well, yes,' replied Bernard.

'Well, you didn't listen very carefully, did you? In the movie, James Stewart specifically says that Pookas can stop time.'

'Oh I see,' replied Bernard. 'Marvellous.'

'What the fuck?' Ferret's eyes were still filled with fear.

'And before any of you say it was a deus ex machina it wasn't, it was a Chekhov's Gun. Remember? Bernard mentioned it when we first met.'

'What the fuck?' said Ferret.

'Marvellous,' said Horatio.

'Well done, Jesus,' muttered Ferret.

'You see,' said Saliva, pinching an invisible cheek, 'Jesus *does* save after all.'

The police were incredulous when Ferret and his boys explained the circumstances of the deaths, but after they looked into the records of the deceased and especially after Ferret pledged fifty million dollars to help fix up the Western Rail Link and a further ten million dollars contribution to the Policeman's Ball, they dropped all investigation and Ferret was free.

*

'The Imperial' was buzzing as Ferret took the stage to tumultuous applause. He looked around the room with satisfaction. Steve was there, holding up his beer in salute; Raylene stood beside him, flashing her tits when Steve wasn't watching; Raylene and Cheryl chewed gum and swivelled their hips in wonton display and all the other pub regulars cheered for the man they had never liked, but now because he was rich and famous, did.

Saliva, the invisible Jesus, Bernard and Horatio applauded as Ferret quelled the crowd.

'You CUNTS!' Ferret screamed into the microphone and riotous applause ensued. 'Alright, listen up, all of yous. As the first billionaire in Windsor . . .'

'Don't forget those polo fuckers!' Steve yelled.

Again, riotous applause.

'Yeah, yeah, alright, smart arse,' replied Ferret.

Laughter.

'As the second or third, or whatever it fucken' is billionaire in Windsor, hear this.'

Silence.

'I'm givin' each and every one of yous I've invited 'ere tonight, even some of you cunts who've beaten the shit out of me on past occasions, . . . 20,000 dollars!'

Murmurs. Surprise. Elation.

' . . . on one condition.'

Silence.

'That yous all take a holiday outside of the Hawkesbury and use some of the dough to wander far afield.'

'What d'ya mean,' asked Cheryl. 'Sydney?'

'No, fuck ya,' he paused for effect . . . 'and I have.'

Laughter.

'Who hasn't?' yelled Steve, and Raylene hit him.

More laughter.

'I want yous to go to Japan. Just fucken' go to Japan 'n' take a fucken' look at how those cunts run things. And take a look at how they behave. I won't say nuffin' more about it but go 'n' when ya come back you'll notice two fings. One, there's so much fucken' space over here and two, what yous already know . . . Australians are a bunch of cunts!'

There was tumultuous applause as Ferret left the stage and his back was smacked harder than a two-bit hooker.

He reached his mates.

'Well done, old man,' said Bernard.

'A few more dollars for the swear jar,' added Horatio.

Jesus hit him.

'All's well that ends well,' quipped Saliva. 'So, where do we go from here?'

'Well boys,' replied Ferret, raising a glass of Carlton Draught, because the VB was frothy off the tap, 'I'd like to tell yous that I'm donatin' half me money to charity.'

'Why, Ferret, that's fantastic,' said Saliva, clutching his chest like a Year 8 girl who's just seen her first hard on.

'Yeah, I'd like to tell yous that, but it ain't gunna happen. Instead, I'm gunna fuck meself stupid, I'm gunna gamble, I'm gunna get pissed and I'm gunna fight any cunt what'll fight me.'

'Ah, the Australian way?' said Bernard.

'Great,' said Horatio, shaking his head in admiration.

'Boys,' said Ferret, raising his glass in a toast, 'I'm buyin' a mansion in Kurrajong, I'm takin' guitar lessons wif the legendary guitarist Jason Garwood over at Blake's Music and we are gunna fucken' howl, boys! Cheers!'

And they all got horribly pissed.

Episode Two

Ferret Goes to High School

DAY 1 – THE MONDAY

'I'm fucken sick of it!' yelled Ferret, smashing his 1962 Telecaster against the wall of the rehearsal room and biting his plectrum in two with frustration.

'What's up, mate?' asked the ever-patient Jason Garwood, his long curls dancing about his face; his mountain-man beard tilted slightly with the angle of his enquiring face. Jason was in his middle years and resembled what Jesus might have hoped to look like if he had ever reached that age. In all probability Jesus would have had a few too many last suppers and ended up like Elvis and the rest of us – overweight and bloated with carbs. But not our Jas. He was a man of rare distinction and talent. At fifty he was the premier guitarist in the land: as fit as a poofter with a new boyfriend; as humble as a heterosexual whose been caught masturbating over shemales, and as patient as a uni student whose gotta wait for his parents to go to bed before he can pull a bong. When people heard the word 'Garwood' in the Hawkesbury, they instinctively kneeled on the spot and bowed with lustrous zealotry.

Jason Garwood was a man.

'I told ya!' squealed Ferret. 'I can't get me finger straight for any of those fucken' bar cords!' He kicked the wall in anger.

'It'll come,' soothed Jason, beaming with benevolence.

'So will the end of the fucken' universe!' retorted Ferret. His little yellow tuft of hair whipped around in

360-degree rotation, threatening his eyes.

'No, mate,' said Jason with perfect reasonableness, 'it'll come quicker than that, but ya gotta practice.'

'Listen,' replied Ferret, suddenly sane but still intense in his delivery, 'I am one of the fucken' richest cunts in Australia. Women fucken' love me. I could walk onto any stage in the world and they'd throw themselves at me and you're tellin' me I gotta practice?'

'Yep,' said Jason. 'If you wanna be a decent guitarist.'

Ferret was about to protest but he looked at the dent in his Telecaster and then back to the cool glance of Jason Garwood and he remembered Japan and he remembered control and he bit his lip and he stopped.

'Alright. I will.'

'Good,' said Jason.

'But not fucken' now,' stated Ferret decisively. 'I've had enough, Jas. I've had enough.'

'What of?' asked Jason.

'Of everythink. Of limousines; of pure cocaine and of head jobs from incredibly attractive eighteen-year-olds who have shown me their birth certificate. It's been six months since Kanji cashed in 'is chips 'n' you know what?'

'What, mate?'

'I need a break.'

'Mate,' replied Jason with measured tone. 'I can understand that. Many of my students, Hendrix among them, have felt the same way. But I've told all of them - come back when you're ready. The flow will return.'

'Jimi Hendrix?'

'No Peter Hendrix from Bligh Park. He's a shithouse guitarist but a good bloke.'

Ferret chewed over that one. 'Alright,' he replied, 'I'm gunna do somefink worfwhile. Then I'm gunna come back wif renewed passion.'

'Good man,' said Jason. He smiled and the sun glinted off his front teeth. 'What are you gunna do?'

'I dunno just yet. But me brothers and the other band members are away on tour, so I got time to think.'

'Did they go on tour without ya, mate?'

'Yeah, unlike me they can actually play their instruments. But it's okay. I'll get me head together 'n' when I re-join 'em, we'll be better than ever, by which I mean I'll at least be able to play me guitar.'

'That's the way.' Jason smiled. 'Oh, and Ferret, 'he added. 'Since we cut today short it'll only be $10,000.'

'Thanks, Jas,' replied Ferret.

*

Ferret walked from 'Blake's Music' down the hill towards McGoo's Hill. He dragged his guitar case behind him in dejected silence. He passed an intersection and stopped to take a quick look in the door of The Jolly Sprog.

The pub was in full swing. Ferret could see the punters, each with a beer in hand, looking up at the ubiquitous television screens where greyhounds, fake rabbits and odds dashed about like a Jew at a free lunch. He could see the stiff nipples of the topless waitresses, which reminded him that winter was coming on. And he thought about where he was heading in his life.

Thoughts had never bothered Ferret before. He had always been a solitary leecher; a lonely lecher; an island of contented ignorance. But things had changed. Now he was wealthy, he had power over women and everybody wanted to know him; everybody wanted a piece of him. There was talk of a tour in the upcoming months for 'The Pheromones' to coincide with the Northern summer, but right now he was bored, he was hassled and, for the first time in his life, he was looking for purpose. A Friday night stoush may have been sufficient before, but not now. His overall tastes hadn't changed: he still liked drinking, gambling, whoring and fighting – who didn't? But now he wanted more. Japan had showed him the possibility of appropriate behaviour, and though he was never going to fully embrace the silent efficiency and ant-like community spirit of the Japanese, yet still he had seen in Japanese customs and in their social rigour a hint of some otherness, of other possibilities beyond the scope of his hometown.

Along the flats he drifted, as if in a dream, and wandered up the hill towards McGoo's Hill. He was waiting at the lights and staring across the road towards an adjacent series of buildings. They rose, it seemed to him, like a glorious hard-on, towering above the hairless scrotum of the surrounding flat land. He admired the graffiti plastered along the front wall, which later turned out to be Aboriginal art – he always found it hard to tell the two apart - and he marvelled at the dilapidated basketball courts in the foreground, tattered reminders of his own high school days. He breathed in the heady combination of sewerage treatment works; slaughterhouse and freshly turned mushroom farm and he knew that he was home – McGoo's Hill High; his Alma Mata; his fostering mother.

Two young boys and a girl passed him as he stood there, transfixed. Once beyond him, one of the boys, who was a skinny runt of about fourteen, said to the others loudly enough for Ferret to hear: 'Look at that stupid cunt. He looks like a fucken' ferret.'

The others sniggered.

Ferret replied with his eyes still fixed upon the building, 'You might think that, cockbreath, but I notice ya never said nothin' 'til you was up the road. Come 'ere 'n' say it 'n' I'll rip your cock off and shove it up your arse.'

'Fuck off,' replied the boy loudly.

Ferret turned his gaze towards the overconfident little prick. 'Nice come- back, cunt face. Now either come 'ere 'n' back it up or go 'ome 'n' have a wank to YouTube. Just type in 'Boys' Gymnastics'.'

The boy's friends laughed at that. The boy became red-faced and angry. He stormed off.

Ferret was still thinking about the boy as he approached the school gate. He kicked at the cigarette butts in the gutter and he looked up at the school motto. 'Safety, Teamwork, Achievement, Respect'. When he wasn't wagging, that wasn't quite how he remembered high school. But, hey, things change. In this more enlightened age maybe the students were more respectful. Maybe the boy he had just encountered was an aberration. Maybe the joy of teaching had increased with the new tolerant society that Australia had become. Maybe all the new age fuzzy shit had paid off. Maybe now McGoo's Hill High was an egalitarian, non-sexist, non-racist environment in which teachers and students strove together for the betterment of humankind. And maybe . . . he began to think, just maybe . . . here was an opportunity. The brickwork was chipped and rundown, the grass uncut, the sign out the front graffitied and broken. Ferret imagined shabbily uniformed boys and girls standing to attention amidst the ruins of a poorly funded courtyard, striving with all of their tiny might, in ramshackle classrooms, against the scourge of publicly funded private education, willing-on their poorly paid teachers as they laboured with inefficient marker pens upon old whiteboards that where impossible to clean.

And, he had it.

He was going to give something back.

Ferret was going to be a teacher.

There was a solitary car in the car park and the gate was still open, so Ferret took the liberty of entering the school and walking up to the Administration Block. A battered, old motor scooter was parked outside the door.

He entered to find a small man of Mexican

appearance standing next to an interior wall, staring up close at a picture of some sort, furiously yanking at his dick.

'You right there?' asked Ferret.

The small man quickly whipped away the offending organ, did up his fly and turned to face Ferret. He was a little taller than our hero. He had a dark swarthy complexion, darker hair and a five o'clock shadow that had reached at least half past six. He wore track pants and a grubby old t-shirt. He was flustered and obsequious. He nodded his head in embarrassed apology as Ferret approached him.

'Don't let me stop ya,' said Ferret, gazing past the man to consider the picture on the wall of which the man had been so fond. 'Last year's staff photo. What's the inspiration?'

The man shuffled uneasily. He bowed his head. 'There is a woman, senor. A very beautiful woman. She is the principal. I love her, but I am but a lowly janitor. She does not even know that I exist.'

'Which one?'

The man pointed with trembling finger towards the picture. Ferret had a closer look. The man had identified what Ferret generally referred to as a 'bush pig'. The specimen in question sat in the front row and had the dubious distinction of requiring a seat and a half. If her arse had been a hat it would have been a fucking big sombrero. Her hair was red; her face was bloated; her skin was freckled; her nose was hooked; her ears were too big. She looked like the kid on the cover of Mad Magazine with a thyroid problem.

'The fat ranga?' said Ferret in disbelief. 'I'd fuck me dog before I'd give that one a slice of the old blue vein steak. And I haven't got a dog. She's a fucken' shocker.'

'Do you not find her beautiful, senor?' asked the man wringing his hands together in servile agitation.

'No, she's beautiful,' Ferret replied, sarcastically.

This seemed to please the man. He approached the photograph with renewed adulation. 'Yes, she is, isn't she?' he murmured and he smiled and he gazed at it, lovingly.

Ferret stared at the smiling post-masturbator and shook his head. 'So who the fuck is she and who the fuck are you?'

'I told you, senor, she is the principal. Her name is Pearl . . . Pearl Necklace, and that is what she is to me – a pearl. My name is Dirty Sanchez and I am just a poor but passionate janitor. I love nothing better than to eat tortillas in my hammock; ride my burro; say yeeha - and chillies? I can eat them whole. My barbacoa is out the back. You can share some goat's head soup with me if you wish. I am humble and servile and not at all the stereotypical Mexican of imperialistic penmen.' He sighed. 'Ah me. The pangs of unrequited love. She will never see me for my true worth.' He appeared as though he might burst into tears.

'Listen,' replied Ferret, trying to diffuse the Latin passion of the grubby little fellow, 'there's no reason why she couldn't fall for you. After all, there's no difference between a tortilla, a burrito and a taco except for the crispy crunch of the taco. They're pretty well all the same fucken' thing! Same goes for women. So you listen to me, Pedro . . .'

'Dirty,' the man corrected him.

'Pedro, I like you. You've got spunk. Or at least you would've had if I hadn't caught ya in time. So I'll give ya some advice, gratis.'

'Se, Senor?'

'Tell her how ya feel at the right time.'

'How will I know when that is, Senor?' asked Dirty, his eyes as wide as a centrefold spread.

'Don't you worry about that. Just play it cool until I

give ya the word. Work hard and do lots of jobs. Be about the place and make yourself accessible. When the time's right, I'll help ya.'

'Oh, thank you. Thank you, senor,' stammered the man, nodding and bowing with gratitude. He went to take Ferret by the hand but Ferret, remembering the man's previous occupation, declined.

'But who are you, senor?' asked Dirty, suddenly full of Mesoamerican curiosity.

'Me name's, Ferret. But to you, when we're in public, I'm Mister Cutler. And if things go the way I plan, Pedro, before you can say 'Shit, sorry I didn't mean to cum inside ya', I could be pretty fucken' important in this joint.'

'Oh thank you. Thank you, senor,' Dirty Sanchez repeated, and he bowed as he traced a path backward away from Ferret and exited thought the front door.

Ferret heard a noise coming toward the building from the schoolyard side. He waited with interest to see who, or what, appeared.

It wasn't the bush pig. It was a man.

He opened and closed the door. He hadn't noticed Ferret. He was lost in his own thoughts. He was a spindly man of about forty. His suit hung from him like shit from a constipated arsehole. His face was gaunt and full of concern. His eyes were dark-ringed and this punctuated his sallow complexion. The lines on his face betrayed a tortured soul. He was a thin man, withered and battered by anxiety. He mumbled to himself as he approached Ferret, still unaware that the intruder was present. He looked up and involuntarily recoiled with a feminine yelp when he finally did notice him.

'Oh. Who are you?' he asked in tremulous falsetto.

'Ferret. Who are you?'

'I'm Donald Meek, deputy principal,' he replied, and added, hesitantly ' . . . if that's alright?'

'It doesn't fucken' worry me, boss. You're the one

who's gotta live wif it.'

'Yes, that's true.' Donald fidgeted with his tie and stared at Ferret. For an eternity he stood there, fiddling, turning his tie this way and that and moistening his lips with his tongue. Ferret noted that the man had an occasional facial tick. Every so often his left eye would close suddenly and spring back open wide. It gave the impression he was winking. Ferret stood watching the nervous man's unwitting performance and waited with interest, to see how long it would take Donald to ask him the obvious question. Eventually Donald drew up his courage. 'Can I help you?' he asked.

'Yeah. I wanna teach.'

'Here?' replied Donald with a mixture of surprise and wonder all tossed together into the one syllable.

'K'noath. I feel like fuckin' a minor and it was either this or bein' one of Father Christmas' helpers in the mall.' Ferret smiled.

'Oh, I'm afraid you can't have sex with the students, Mister Ferret. Not even the executive can do that.'

'What's the point of bein' a teacher then?'

Donald almost yanked his tie off with anxiety before he detected the faintest of grins on Ferret's face.

Ferret laughed. 'Fucken' had ya goin' there, didn't I, boss? Of course I know ya can't fuck the kids. I ain't that fucken' stupid.'

Donald visibly relaxed.

'You can punch 'em out but?'

Donald tensed.

'I'm kiddin'. I'm kiddin'. Fuck me, boss, settle down. Jesus, you're about as much fun as haemorrhoids at a fisting fest.'

Donald almost smiled.

'Ah, I seen that. That's more like it. No, Don, I wanna teach. I'm ready to give somethin' back.'

'What've you taken,' asked the timorous man, on

edge once again.

'Fuck, mate,' said Ferret quietly, placing his arm around Donald like he had just escaped from a special unit, 'if you don't lighten up, you'll have a heart attack, pal. What are you so fucken' nervous about?'

Donald drew in a long, deep breath. When he exhaled, it was with an equally long, shuddering expulsion of air. He sat down and Ferret sat beside him.

'Many years ago, Mister Ferret, I joined the teaching profession because I wanted to make a difference. I wanted to imbue youth with the joy of learning and to give them an opportunity in this ever-increasingly dangerous world. But as time went on I discovered that the classroom was a battlefield; a war fought against belligerence where all artillery had been taken from the occupying forces. I found myself unequal to the task, Mister Ferret. I was battered by juvenile anger and apathy alike. Students mocked me; despised me; mistook kindness for weakness. In the end, I panicked. I got as far away from the classroom as I could.'

'You resigned?'

'No, I joined the executive. But the bullying didn't stop.'

'Kids still gave you the shits, eh?'

'No, the executive did. Affirmative Action saw me leapfrogged by hairy-legged females with knee problems. I pointed out that they could lose a few pounds only to be labelled as a sexist pig. So I bit my tongue and climbed the tree as high as I could to get away from the maniacs on the ground but there were many more monkeys half way up the tree.' He grabbed Ferret by the t-shirt. 'I was a man, Mister Ferret. A man! But now,' he slumped away from Ferret in dejected defeat, ' . . . now I am a *beaten* man; a sad, hollow relic of a man, thrashed into submission by time and the ungracious ineptitude of a department that seeks image rather than integrity; defeated by a bureaucracy that seeks to tick boxes rather than to educate; caught between the fangs of the communistic egalitarianism of the Teachers' Federation and the calculated penny pinching of the NSW Department of Education. I am an educated man, Mister Ferret; an educated man but . . .' he began to weep, 'I have become a no-man. I have become a lackey; a toadying sycophant; a pathetic, lacklustre shadow puppet, dancing to the tune of an obsessed and self-serving master. I spout educationalist jargon with the ease of a university student and at night, I am afraid to say, I cower in my lonely bedroom dreaming of a time where I have the guts to state my case. To say what I really think.'

'What do ya really think?' Ferret was impressed. This guy had turned from a dry creek into a raging river of words.

'That we should spend more time teaching and less time reading gobbledygook from those above us who seek only to further their own agendas. We are being used by CV addicts to fulfil their personal goals. And as for the students - we are too soft, Mister Ferret, too soft. We teach them bad lessons. We are not preparing them for the angry, the self-obsessed, the self-interested ways of the world. We do them no favours insulating them from responsibility. We do them great harm. They are sheltered behind the cotton wool of well-intentioned activists who incorrectly inform them that they cannot fail. When all the while the world waits for them, it's brilliant teeth smiling with carefully veiled indifference. And they have no idea, no notion of its self-interest until, at last, they leave school and it hits them, too early, too late, and they are shipwrecks upon the coast of a foreign world; confident in their ignorance, they stumble, half blind into its midst. They soon realise that attention and discipline is required for success, but they have acquired neither. They have sat in mixed-ability classrooms with an assortment of fools who have impeded their learning. The school system has failed them and a lifetime of packing shelves awaits them.' He began sobbing. 'I'm sorry . . . Mister Ferret . . . it's just that I love teaching but the further I progressed in this job . . . the less I was able to do it.'

While the man sobbed, Ferret sat back and thought.

So, it wasn't all wine and roses. And what this bloke had just said would explain the Hawkesbury rabble. The unwashed, tattooed, angry mob he saw every day was a result of a system so careful to protect them, it had unwittingly created an underclass of social misfits, ill prepared for the wider world. And then, right then, it crystallised. The lesson of Japan crystallised in his mind – he was one of them. He, himself, was a child of this well-intentioned-don't-ever-hit-your-kids-even-if-they-deserve-it mentality in the backwater of a country, itself a backwater of the world; a country too well protected from the truth. And the truth was – no-one really gives a shit, it's every man for himself and if you're not equal to it, you're fucked, mate. Get packing shelves. The world this broken man had uncovered for him was *his* world; the world of the Hawkesbury in which he fought and got pissed daily; a world where it was okay to bludge because no one had taught you otherwise; a world where there were no consequences for your actions; a world where you could tell a teacher to 'get fucked' have a three week holiday and return, no questions asked. Ferret knew. He had done it many times at this very school. In this world students misguidedly believed that it was okay to sup from the pot of the tribe's food without the tribe requiring them to at least put something in that pot occasionally. For the first time, he saw it clearly and he wanted, more than ever to contribute to that pot.

'Is that it?' asked Ferret.

'That's it, Mister Ferret. He hesitated, 'Well . . . it's almost everything.'

'Fuck, you mean there's more?'

'Unfortunately, yes, but I've told you more than I have ever told another soul already and you'll learn the rest soon enough. I don't know why, but I feel that I can trust you.' He slumped back in his seat, his eyes closed. A single tear trickled down his cheek, in close up.

'Can I come in tomorra?' asked Ferret. 'As a casual teacher?'

'Donald laughed as he wiped the tear from his haggard cheek. 'Of course,' he replied.

'You sure? Maybe no one'll be away sick.'

'Mister Ferret,' replied Donald, adjusting his tie and regaining his self-composure, 'someone is *always* away sick. Just bring your teaching number with you.'

Donald stood up and attempted a smile. 'Good day, Mister Ferret. We shall see you tomorrow.'

The two shook hands and Ferret followed the careworn man as he shuffled towards the main door. He stood thoughtfully as he watched Donald's car disappear up the road.

It seemed that his help was needed even more than he had imagined.

*

DAY TWO – THE TUESDAY

The following morning Ferret walked across the flats and up into McGoo's Hill High. His exaggerated strut had been toned down quite a bit in the course of the last few months. Success and wealth had tamed him in both his walking style and his behaviour. Some people actually looked up to him now. Certainly, the locals watched him more carefully, probably because many of them wanted some gain from him, but others, like Steve from The

Imperial Hotel, genuinely liked him. Either way, he was now a man about town and with that accolade came some responsibility. Consequently, he was trying to be good. He was trying to be a good role model. He was trying to control his temper.

He was about to be tested.

He wasn't sure where to sign on but he caught sight of two women with fat arses waddling towards one building, so he followed. He figured by their dress: the old thongs, the shabby shorts and the t-shirts that they were cleaners.

'G'Day,' he said, when he finally caught up with them in the common room.

'G'Day' they both replied.

On closer inspection they weren't identical. One was ample, the other was fucking huge; one was ugly, the other was gnaw-your-arm-off-material; one was old, the other was young. Both had teeth but in different positions; one had three at the front and seemingly no others, while the younger, gnaw-your-own-arm-off-material one had six, spread equidistantly about the lunar landscape of her gums. They were smiling, which was a good sign, but Ferret wished they wouldn't.

'I'm Ferret,' he said. 'Are yous the cleaners?'

'I'm Celeste and this is Chardonnay,' said the good-looking one. 'Chardonnay is a first year out and I'm the head of English.'

Good start thought Ferret. 'I'm lookin' for the principal.'

'She's sick,' replied Chardonnay. 'Won't be back 'til tommora.'

'Sick my arse,' Celeste chuckled. 'Meek's away too.'

The two women shared a cackle.

'Here's your sheet,' said Celeste. 'Looks like your with us today. Come on, I'll show ya up.'

Ferret followed the two animated arses through a

corridor and into the main playground. Tennis balls were flying and so was the language. The word 'cunt' was used as a term of endearment. The two women didn't seem to mind; didn't notice at all. They babbled together about Facebook and what a shame so and so was in a bad mood and how they must Facebook her and be good friends.

'Someone sick?' asked Ferret, as he looked up at the duo of formidable shitters lumbering up the stairway.

'It's just Alice,' replied Chardonnay, 'she's away again today 'coz she's struck a rough spot. Sometimes life throws shit at ya, eh? Hopefully, she'll be in tomorra.'

'What 'appened,' asked Ferret, then on his best behaviour he added, 'if ya don't mind me askin'?'

'Ah, she got Facebook stalked by some bloke in Hassle Grove,' Celeste replied. 'He reckons she led 'im on. I mean how ridiculous. She only gave 'im a head job and the guy goes 'n' gets all possessive.'

In defence of the stalker, Chardonnay replied, 'Yeah, 'but she did stick her finger up 'is arse and give 'im a quick hand job on that school excursion to the cinema.'

'It doesn't make it right, Chardonnay,' Celeste replied, shaking her head sagely. 'There's no excuse for stalking. She may have sent him naked webcams of herself and she may have snapped the odd erotic pic of her with Bruce, but that is no excuse for the man to stalk 'er.'

'Who's Bruce?' asked Ferret.

'Her dog,' Celeste replied.

Ferret followed the two large pots of flesh into a staffroom to find three people drinking coffee around a central table. He was introduced to Kim, who was tall, thin and about thirty. She had bleached blond hair, hair on her upper lip and a 'Heartbreaker' tattoo on her upper arm. He was introduced to Sally, who was in her twenties, had glasses, buck teeth and a lisp. And finally to Lucky Pierre who was fortyish, sported a beret, had a pencil thin moustache and spoke with a French accent that Ferret suspected might not be authentic.

'Just so ya know,' said Celeste, 'Kim's a long-term casual, in for Jenny, who's pregnant, Sally's a casual in for Regina, who's also a casual doin' a term for Skye while she's on stress leave and Lucky's doin' a block for a term while Angela's away on long service leave. Michelle's classes aren't covered so I'll send 'em out into the playground. That should keep the little bastards happy.'

'That reminds me,' said Chardonnay, 'I'll be droppin' another one in Term Three.'

'No worries,' replied Celeste. 'There ya go, Ferret. You can have Terms Three and Four if ya want it. What've ya got, Chards?'

'Two year 7's, a Year 9, and two Year 12s, all English except for the 12 Drama.'

Ferret was surprised and a little daunted. 'Don't you wanna see me teach first? Especially before I take the Year 12s?'

'Don't worry about teachin'. Just make sure they appear to be doin' somethin.'

'But don't they have prac. exams in Term Three?' asked Ferret, vaguely remembering his school days. 'Won't they need some help?'

'I don't give a fuck,' said Chardonnay. '*They* certainly don't.'

'Mate, just make sure they don't kill one another,' said Celeste, 'especially the Year 7s. Let's have a look at who you've got today.' She grabbed Ferret's work sheet. 'Let's see, you got Sue's classes. 7P first up. Is Gary Finlay in that class?'

'Yeth, unfortunately,' Sally replied.

'He got his cock out after lunch yesterday,' added Kim, as if it was a common everyday occurrence.

'Again?' asked Sally, confirming Ferret's fears. 'He wath waving it about in the corridor lathd week.'

'Yeah. It's actually quite big.'

Sally seemed quite enthusiastic. 'Yeth, isthn't it?'

'Did ya report it?' asked Celeste.

'Oh yeah, we both did.'

'Good,' said Celeste.

Ferret was pleased momentarily that some justice was being dealt out. But Celeste added, 'No one'll do nothin' about it. Probly won't even read it, but as long as it's on the system, our arses are covered.'

And that's a big job, thought Ferret.

She returned her gaze to the work sheet. 'Ya got a double with Year 11 Drama Periods 3 and 4 and 8E Music last period. That's a pretty cushy day, Ferret,' she noted, as she returned the sheet to him.

Ferret was relieved until Kim added, 'Except for that Year 8 class.'

'Who's in that one?' asked Celeste.

'Barry Underwood and Cheryl Tate.'

Everybody groaned.

'What?' asked Ferret, with concern.

Pierre finally chipped in. His accent was Pythonesque, 'Barry Underwood iz la petite turd and Cheryl Tate iz, 'ow you say? ze gross slut.'

'Knock it off, Pierre. You know we don't speak French,' replied Celeste.

'What part of France are ya from?' asked Ferret intrigued by the man's accent.

'He's from Newcastle,' interjected Chardonnay. 'He took a school group to Paris for two weeks in 2010 and he come back speakin' like that. He's a fucken' wanker.'

'Ze ladies love it,' Pierre replied, twiddling his moustache and winking at Ferret.

'Knock it off, Pierre, you sound like a cross between Pepe Le Pew and Adolf fucken' Hitler.'

'How come this Sue girls got a music class?'

'One of the many periods we have to teach out of area. Welcome to public education.'

The bell went.

'You wanna combine our classes for first two?' said Kim to Sally.

'What clasth do you have?'

'Year 11.'

'What are ya thtudying?'

'We're watching 'The Simpsons'.'

'Does that fit in with the curriculum?' Ferret asked.

'Yeah,' Celeste spoke for her, 'we used to do it under the umbrella of 'Change', then it was 'Journeys', then it was 'Belonging' and now it comes under the umbrella of 'Who Gives A Flying Fuck'. Come on, you lot, roll call. Ferret, the lessons are on my desk. Sue called 'em in to Chardonnay last night. You might have trouble decipherin' Chardonnay's handwritin' but.'

And she left.

Ferret approached an immaculate desk. This Sue girl was obviously very organised. Not a book or leaf of paper was out of place. Ferret took a quick glance around and was struck by the incongruity. The rest of the staffroom looked like a young white girl getting fucked up the arse by a large Negro: there was shit everywhere.

He found the note and this is what it said:

No role call.

Period 1 7P Keap reeding the indian in the cubbud do questions 3 too 6

Year 11 drama work on individul projex for dubble

Year 8 Music worksheats on my desk

Fuck me, thought Ferret. She must've gone to UWS.

Ten minutes later, he found himself standing in front of 7P. Of the twenty-six students present, only three young girls sitting down the front, pens and pencils lined up on the ready, noticed Ferret standing there. Everyone else was either talking or pushing each other off seats. The noise was cacophonous.

'Righto. Settle down,' said Ferret.

No change.

A little louder, 'I said settle down.'

No change.

'Hey, fucken' settle!' he yelled, and accidentally sprayed some spit into the eye of one of the three little girls.

This got the class's attention.

'You can't swear,' said one fat kid in the back row.

Ferret remembered his vow to be good. 'Sorry,' he apologised. 'Now listen up . . .'

But the class was already ignoring him again.

'Hey!' he bellowed.

They stopped.

'What sort of attention span is that? Yous are a pack a drongos! Look at yourselves!'

One boy, with a large head, shouted from the back, 'You look like a rat!'

'A ferret!' added the fat kid.

'Hey, listen 'ere, McDonalds,' growled Ferret, who was quickly forgetting his promise to be good, 'shut your mouth occasionally 'n' ya might lose some fucken' weight!'

'You swore again,' said McDonalds.

Ferret walked up to him and looked down menacingly. Looking down was a rarity for Ferret and he savoured the status. He whispered, 'Now listen up, McDonalds. I'm an angry cunt at the best of times but at the minute, I'm tryin' to behave, so think yourself lucky, shithead. Now I'm gunna set you some work and you're gunna do it. Got it?'

The boy stood up and even though he was only twelve, he was taller than Ferret. He pushed his face right into Ferret's personal space, so that their noses were almost touching and he whispered, 'You can't fucken' do nuffin' to me.' Then he smirked and lingered directly in front of Ferret's face, bobbing his head up and down like one of those fucken stupid jester puppets you can get at the Easter show.

Ferret watched the infuriating display with mounting fury. His lower lip was invisible and white from blood starvation denied it by his lower teeth, clenched as they were upon it.

The boy turned and smiled at his fellow students who grew loud in their appreciation. Whoops and yelps of infantile defiance rent the air. McDonalds pumped that air with celebratory zeal and turned back to Ferret with the biggest, most annoying facial expression of smugness ever imaginable to man. He tilted his head slightly to one side and widened his eyes in mockery.

One second later, McDonalds lost seven teeth.

In years to come it would be folklore, but it did actually happen. Ferret took one look at that 'I-dare-you-to-hit-me-'cos-I-know-you-can't face - and did. He drove his fist as hard as he could, directly into Macdonald's mouth. Teeth splintered and gums exploded everywhere. McDonalds went down like a sack of personal lubricant and the class stopped cheering.

Then Gary Finlay got his cock out.

*

Fuck me, she's a fucken' gorilla, thought Ferret as he watched Principal Pearl Necklace march up and down in front of him. She had hurried over, presumably from her sick bed, dragging Mister Meek out of it too. She had called Ferret into her office. He had sat down. She had said nothing but had marched up and down before him like some primal British Grenadier for at least a minute. She was thinking, and the process made her even more ugly than usual, if that was possible. Had a male orangutan been present he would have had a woody, for sure. She grunted on two occasions and she stamped, slightly bow-legged, hauling her great bulk with the strength in her tree-stump legs. The scowl upon her ugly face would have changed the Pope's mind about contraception and put forever to bed the argument against evolution.

Mr Meek sat silently in the corner; his head bowed, awaiting the inevitable tirade.

Pearl Necklace stopped, turned on the spot and faced Ferret. 'You,' she began, 'have been in my school for less than an hour. You were in the classroom for less than three minutes. In that time you have managed to physically assault a student . . .'

Right on cue two ambulance officers raced past the Principal's Office with McDonald's on a stretcher. One said to the other, 'Looks like the jaws gotta be wired.'

' . . . who is being taken to hospital as we speak.' Principal Necklace was still relatively calm but both Ferret and Donald Meek knew what was coming. 'Also, as we speak,' her voice began to rise in volume, 'Jeremy Sweetman's father is coming here, to this office, now! He is just minutes away!'

'Sweetman,' muttered Ferret, 'ironic name.'

'Shut up!' roared Pearl Necklace with such vehemence that the school sporting shield fell off the wall. Then, more calmly and with sinister tone she continued, 'I intend to throw you to the wolves, Mister Cutler. Mister Sweetman is a very big man; a *very* big man, and I intend to watch with pleasure as he smashes your face in. The media will certainly get wind of this and they can have you after he's finished. I wash my hands clean of this whole matter.' She pulled up her bulk to a full standing position, chin pushed prominently forward. 'Now, before he arrives, what have you got to say for yourself?'

'I think the media will enjoy this one,' replied Ferret with a glint in his eye. He knew how to handle bullies – he *was* one.

'And why is that?'

''coz they're gunna love the fact that you let a civilian beat up a kid in one of your classrooms. And you weren't even on the premises when it 'appened. I can see it now 'NSW Ship of Education – Rudderless.'

'What are you talking about?'

'I ain't even a teacher.'

'What!' she screeched! 'Then how did you get in?'

Mister Meek shot Ferret a concerned glance. His facial tick went into overdrive and his head began to shake like a dog with a snout full of pepper.

Ferret didn't even see him. He maintained eye contact with the lumbering behemoth in front of him. He could see the first cracks appearing in her composure. 'I just turned up. No one stopped me. Seems any bastard could walk into this place with a fucken' shotgun 'n' you wouldn't fucken' know. You're too busy forcin' Donald's limp dick up ya clacker. 'N I'll be tellin' the media all about that too, don't you fucken' worry, you fat slut.'

This was not exactly the response Pearl Necklace was expecting. Her face began to warp. She appeared, to Ferret, to become unsure whether to explode with anger, or to collapse with grief.

Before she could do either, a very angry face appeared at the door. Mister Sweetman was six foot five, built as sturdy as a 1970 Valiant, had tats all over his arms and a huge brown beard with dark, wild eyes above it. He was so large he filled the entire doorway. 'Where is 'e!' he bellowed in a gravelly voice, so low it seemed to come from his scrotum.

Ferret stood up to meet his advance. Mister Sweetman reached him, looked down and laughed. 'You're a puny little runt, ain't ya?'

Ferret assumed that was rhetorical.

'Well, I'm gunna do to you what you done to me boy,' and he pulled his elbow back, high into the air, with his fist tightly clenched. It was a pile driver about to send our hero into oblivion.

'I can solve this,' said Ferret as calmly as the situation would allow.

'There ain't nothin' you can say to save yourself,' replied the huge man, his forearm quivering with potential energy.

'I'm Ferris Cutler. I'll give ya 50,000 dollars.'

The man dropped his arm. 'Ferris Cutler?' he asked, suspicious but suddenly changed. 'The local bloke who ventured out of the Hawkesbury?'

'That's me,' replied Ferret. 'I'm as rich as they say and I'll give ya 50,000 dollars to forget the whole thing. No questions asked. No publicity. No come backs. What d'ya say?

Mister Sweetman mumbled to himself, '50,000 bucks,' then he looked sly and said, 'And what if I take the money and still tell the press? Who's gunna stop me?'

'Not me,' Ferret replied, 'but I'm so fucken' rich that I could pay a bloke, to pay a bloke, to pay a bloke who's never heard of me to pay you a visit and that bloke'll be a professional. You won't even know 'es comin' but 'ell be there. And he'll fuck you over so bad you'll have to push your fingers up your arse to pick your nose. Get it?'

Mister Sweetman thought about that for a moment, then nodded quiet assent.

'Good,' continued Ferret, 'and I'll throw in another 10,000 to fix your boy's teeth, but remember, not a word.' He pulled out a cheque book and scribbled out a cheque for 60,000 and handed it to the startled man. 'That's a lot a dole money, Sweetman. I wouldn't be mentioning too much to the others in the caravan park, or ya might get a few unwelcome visitors, if ya know what I mean.'

Sweetman, still shocked, nodded again and turned to leave.

'Oh, and Sweetman,' said Ferret.

Sweetman turned back.

'Your son's a cunt.'

'I'll wait 'til 'e gets betta, then I'll beat the shit out of 'im for bein' rude to ya.'

He left, shaking his head with excitement and staring at the cheque.

'How did you know he lived in a caravan park?' asked Donald Meek, who had spent the last few minutes cowering in the corner behind his principal's horrendous bulk.

'They always do,' replied Ferret,' that or commission houses. He'll 'ave six or seven kids . . .'

'Eight,' corrected Meek.

' . . . and he'll make more money every week from government handouts than good honest people do by workin' their rings off. That's fucken' Australia for ya. Why would ya bother workin' when ya can get more sittin' on your arse watchin' the tele?'

Pearl Necklace had said nothing for some time. She was trying to work out how all of this was going to play out. 'What do you want?' she asked Ferret.

'I wanna teach here for the rest of the week,' he replied. 'No teachin' certificate. No teacher number. No nuffin'. I don't want no money. I just wanna see what it's like. You cover for me for the next three days. I don't care how.'

'What's in it for me?' she asked warily.

'Well, for a start I won't go the police and tell 'em that you let cunts like me into your school wifout even checkin'.'

'You'd be in more trouble than me,' she countered. 'You attacked a student.'

'You're right there, fatso, but I can afford 20,000 a day for a top notch QC. Can you? Or maybe the Teachers' Federation can help ya out. I'm not a member so they'll fuck me over quick smart. I'm sure they'll lend you a quid.

After all, they can afford 20,000 for a fucken' float at the Gay Mardi Gras. Now there's teachers' money well spent.'

'And what are you going to do about the witnesses? The whole class saw you hit Sweetman.'

'If ya get any complaints, send 'em to me. I'll sort it out.'

'Very well,' Pearl replied after several seconds thought, 'but no more nonsense. Keep a low profile for the next four days and then go. Is that understood?'

'Yes, dear,' replied Ferret with a snarl.

He began to leave the office but turned at the doorway. 'Oh, and by the way, tell the fucken' Teachers' Federation to get a fucken' apostrophe after the 's', will ya? It's fucken' embarrassin', even for a lowlife like me.'

After he'd gone, Pearl Necklace closed the door and moved purposefully in the direction of Donald Meek who was trapped in the corner and unable to semi-circumnavigate her. 'All of this excitement has made me horny,' she whispered. 'Get your trousers off.'

Donald trembled as he watched a gob of dribble make its way down onto the chin of her advancing face.

*

Year 11 Drama was uneventful, certainly in terms of Drama, except for when Debbie Wilson flashed her tits at Bradley Major and Ferret copped an eyeful. And also worth a mention was when Ferret caught three of the students blowing a joint in the video room. He joined them and told them it was okay so long as they blew the smoke out of the window. And the only other thing worthy of note was when Joshua Day, a dwarfish boy with curly black hair, tried to light his own fart and caught his pubic hair alight and scorched his scrotum and ran around in wide circles under the strobe light and Ferret laughed so hard he followed through and had to flush his undies down the toilet.

At lunchtime, Ferret decided to avoid the English Staffroom and go straight to the Music Rooms to have a look around before he had 8E, but as he was passing, Lucky Pierre rushed out of the English Staffroom and walked along with him.

'Monsieur,' he panted, 'I 'ave a question pour vous.'

'What is it?' asked Ferret, who walked quickly, keen to avoid any probing questions from Celeste and her fellow gossips.

'Did you hit ze student today?'

'How the fuck do you know?'

'It iz all over ze Facebook.'

'Ah fuck. I shoulda known.' He stopped to have a quick think. 'I'm off next period. How can I find out where 7P are?'

'I will 'elp you, monsieur. I will find out. Leave it to Lucky.'

Lucky ran back towards the English staffroom.

Ferret walked into the Music Staffroom to find one man standing up, with his trousers down, while another man on his knees behind him, licked the standing man's arsehole, while reaching around and masturbating him.

'Fuck me!' blurted Ferret.

The men disengaged. The standing man was tall, thin and had a goatee. He did up his trousers. 'Sorry you had to see that. Don't be alarmed. We're not poofters or anything.'

'Nah, it didn't look like it,' Ferret replied.

'I'm Felch Seaman and this is Rusty Trombone.'

'G'day,' said Rusty, as he got up and wiped his mouth. He was fine-featured and had long, sandy hair.

'You got a bit on your upper lip,' said Ferret.

Rusty went to wipe it off and then realised that Ferret was taking the piss.

'We really aren't gay, well, I'm not, Rusty'll have an

each- way bet but I'm straight.'

'Then why was he lickin' your arse?' asked Ferret.

'I just told you: he is gay sometimes.'

'Why were you lettin' 'im?'

'Oh, because we're the horn section for 'Cannesten'. I play trumpet and Rusty was just practisin' his trombone.'

'I'd be takin' a closer look at my excuse list if I were you, Felch.'

'I'm not gay. He was practising.'

'I have heard of Cannesten, though,' said Ferret. 'You guys are supposed to be pretty good.'

'Thanks. You've probably heard of us since that YouTube clip went fungal.'

'I've also heard of denial, Felch, but I'm not the one to judge.'

'I'm not gay.'

'Are you the bloke who hit the kid?' asked Rusty after he had finished gargling Listerine.

'Yeah, that was me.' Ferret was becoming worried. If the T.V. reporters got a hold of it, his week of discovery was over.

'I wish I'd been there to see it. That kid's a prick.'

'I just come to take a look at the Music Rooms to see what I'm workin' wif,' Ferret explained.

'No worries,' said Felch. 'Across the hall. They're open.'

'Ain't ya worried stuff'll get stolen?' Ferret asked.

'You'll understand when you go in,' suggested Rusty.

'Nice to meet you, boys. You can go back to your practisin' if you like.' Ferret smiled and exited.

As he crossed the corridor he heard Felch yelling out from behind, 'We're not gay!'

The Music Room was underwhelming, to say the least. A sad old drum kit sat upon a raised platform. Every skin was torn and every cymbal damaged. A row of xylophones ran around the perimeter of the room. Keys were damaged, stands held up by string and splintered hammers were snapped and lying all over the room. Someone had kicked in the bass speaker and the shitty guitar lying in the corner only had three strings.

Ferret burst back into the Music Staffroom. He was angry. 'What am I supposed to do . . .'

Felch and Rusty were practising again.

'Fuck me!' shouted Ferret and he left.

Felch's yelled strains of, 'We're not gay!' reverberated around the walls of the corridors behind him.

Lucky Pierre caught up with him as he crossed the quad. 'Monsieur,' he panted, 'zey are in ze library.'

'Who's got 'em?'

'Ms Stenchbucket. But be careful, monsieur, zey call her ze angry dragon.'

'Alright, I'll stand warned. Thanks Pete. If there's ever anything I can do for ya . . .'

'Monsieur, zere is one sing.'

'Yeah, what's that?'

'I 'ave 'eard zat vous 'ave a way wiz ze ladies. I 'ave seen video of ze Tokyo gig.'

'And?'

'I, myself, am a raging sex machine. I am ze lover trapped 'ere in a battlefield of fat fucks.'

'I hear ya.'

'So, monsieur I ask only zis - zat when you tour again wiz ze pheromones, you consider me as a part of your team.'

'What can you do?'

'I believe zat you could benefit from a horn section. I myself am a saxophonist. Sometimes I sit in with Rusty and Felch.'

'Yeah, well I'd stay sittin' if I were you. I'll think about it, Pete. Maybe we could use a horn section. Cop ya later.'

The bell went as Ferret entered the library. He was met with a scowl from an undersized woman of about forty who wore a frumpy old dress that made her look like an old maid. She had red hair, the compulsory librarian glasses and a head that reminded him of his last home brew – the one that got a virus in the bucket and went sour.

'Where have you been?' she bellowed.

Ferret looked behind him and then back towards the angry dragon. 'You talkin' to me, you little ranga turd, or did someone let a dog loose in 'ere?'

The little ranga turd did not reply. Instead, she rose her cheeks and pulled her lips back into an infuriating, toothless, smug grin and motioned to 7P, already assembled. They were seated in an open area and behind each was an agitated parent. Standing to one side were Principal Necklace and the ever-present, ever-trembling Deputy Meek.

'Fuck,' Ferret mumbled.

'Yes, fuck,' whispered the angry dragon, loudly enough for Ferret to hear, 'Let's see you get out of this one.'

He whispered back as he passed her, 'Do I fucken' know you, fallopian face? Or are ya just a crabby old bitch? Jesus, with a charmer like you in charge I bet these kids love readin'.'

Into the lion's den he walked and as he did the angry shouts and accusations began. Ferret let them take their course.

'Alright, listen up,' he began, when at last the collective tirade died away. 'I understand why some of yous are angry.'

'Fucken' oath we're angry!' shouted out a morbidly obese housewife with B.O. and nicotine-stained teeth.

'Yeah, and I can understand that but listen, think

about your own kid and be honest – do you ever get so mad you could hit 'em?'

'*I* fucken' hit 'im all the time but that doesn't mean *you* can!'

Again the lynch mob sparked into animated verbal clichés.

Another bloke with wiry brown hair on the sides and nothing on top, piped up, 'I hit my kid too. That's why I had 'im.'

Several people agreed.

'Yeah, well it's nice to have a scapegoat. My dad used to smash me and look at the result.'

The crowd quietened, mainly because they didn't know what to make of the comment. Ferret took advantage of the short break in volume. 'Listen up, everyone, I have a proposal for yous.'

'It better be good!' yelled out a bleach blonde of thirty-five plus who wore a short skirt in spite of the cellulite.

'It is. Here's my plan. I won't hit any more kids. You won't mention any of this to the police or to the press or post anything about it on Facebook. And, in return, I'll give each of yous $30,000 to shut up.

'That's bribery!' shouted a small, fat woman with huge tits who would have been taller when she lay down. 'Make it $40,000.'

'Yeah!' shouted several others.

'Alright, $40,000 'n' that's me final offer. And there's one more thing. If ya take the money yous have to use some of it on an overseas holiday. Go 'n' take a look at the world.'

There was much rhubarb at this.

Principal Necklace broke through the noise. 'Everybody, Mister Cutler is very sorry for his actions. I think you should accept his generous offer.' She cast a harsh glance at Ferret, who ignored her.

'So, what d'ya say? If ya don't wanna accept the offer, leave now, but if ya stay, you get the doe on my terms. What's it to be?'

No one moved.

'Good. Kids go to class, parents and carers line up and I'll sign your cheques.' He moved over to the front desk. 'Fuck off out of the way dragon lady,' he whispered.

'You're not gunna get away with this,' she whispered back.

Ferret handed her the first cheque. She looked at it, drew in her breath, her eyes widened and she moved quietly away.

Ferret yelled after her, 'Hey, lady!'

She turned back.

'They call you the angry dragon behind your back. Look it up.'

Ferret finally made it to last period but it turned to be a bit of a washout. Barry Underwood and Cheryl Tate wagged the lesson and the rest of the class was okay, although a little uninspired. Ferret couldn't blame them. A few of them sat around plucking on $30 guitars with tuning pegs made of Taiwanese plastic and the rest chatted by the broken xylophones, occasionally playing a desultory note out of boredom.

*

'Much happen today, Ferret?' asked Steve as he poured Ferret a beer.

Ferret laughed. 'Nah, nothin' much, so long as the cops and the reporters stay away, I'll be right.'

'What 'appened?'

'It's a long story. I'll tell ya some time when the heat dies down.'

'Righto,' said Steve, mopping down the bar. 'Hey, by the way, I meant to tell ya, that tall poofter come 'n' took back 'is pheromone machine.'

'That doesn't surprise me,' mused Ferret. 'Those fucken' things never work anyway.'

'Yeah,' replied Steve. 'So, you knockin' around with anyone, now that you're rich and famous?'

'Nah, nothin's changed.'

'I seen a few of the local girls givin' ya the eye, but.'

'Money's an aphrodisiac. None of 'em looked at me before.'

'True,' Steve agreed. 'Still, if ya got it . . .'

'I'd like to have a woman who likes me for who I am, not for me money.'

'That's a big ask,' Steve replied with a smile.

'Ha, ha, fucken' ha,' said Ferret. Then a thought struck him. 'Hey, did you and Raylene ever use the money I gave yous to visit overseas?'

'Not yet, but we will. We been busy here.'

'Fair enough,' replied Ferret. He looked around the bar. There were several of his friends in there sitting, drinking, or playing pool. He noticed that Shaza had a new dress on and Jimbo had a new IPhone and he began to wonder if anyone of them had used the money to take a look around the world.

'Hey!' he yelled.

Everyone looked over.

'Did any of you cunts use the money I give yous to travel?'

'I will,' replied Billy.

'Not yet,' replied Nancy.

'Fuck me,' mumbled Ferret, turning back to Steve. 'These fuckers are good people but their minds are kept small by small town livin'. You can only see a rainstorm comin' from a distance. Once you're in it, you just get fucken' wet.'

Steve stopped cleaning the bar. 'You know what, Ferret, I reckon you're smarter than you think.'

'Ain't that a paradox?' replied Ferret.

'See,' said Steve.

*

DAY THREE – THE WEDNESDAY

The next morning, as he got ready for school, Steve's words haunted him. 'If you've got it . . .' and he did. He did have it. He had a bag full of pheromones, courtesy of Saliva, the tall poofter, so why wasn't he using them? It was something to do with self-satisfaction and the challenge of achieving something without external help. He tossed a pheromone packet up into the air and caught it. He examined it closely and considered its power. But no, he was going to resist the temptation. He was in enough trouble already. High school was probably not the best place for sex-crazed activity.

The cops hadn't called and the reporters had stayed away. So far, so good, he thought to himself as he walked through the car park and towards the Sign-on Block. It was only 8.30am so predictably there were very few cars. Celeste and her cronies would probably turn up 8.55am fully prepared and raring to go.

He looked at his day sheet. Who was Ms Walters? Whoever she was she was in English.

Just then Chardonnay rumbled in early.

'G'day Ferret. Who are ya today?'

'Ms Walters,' he replied.

'Oh yeah, that's right, I forgot. That's Celeste. She's got a specialist appointment today and she won't be in tomorra either.'

'How come?'

'She's gettin' her hair done. I told her to take off Friday too, 'coz you can 'ave up t'three days wifout a medical certificate, but she said she was comin' in.'

'How come?'

'She's dedicated.' She looked at the day sheet. 'I see Sue's back in today but. That'll help. Come on.'

Ferret tried to stay ahead of her arse as they climbed the stairs.

'I hear you caused a ruckus yesterday. I hope ya get away wif it. Everyone was cheerin' for ya at the staff meetin'.'

'When was that?'

'Yesterday arvo. Don't worry, casuals don't 'ave to go.'

As Chardonnay entered the staffroom, Lucky Pierre appeared from around a corner and beckoned to Ferret. Ferret followed him into the Drama Room.

'I 'ave talked to ze Fed. Rep. on your be'alf. I 'ope you don't mind? 'e is pretty sure zat 'e can hush up yesterday's incident.'

'Thanks, Pete.'

'Oh and I 'ave also talked to Rusty and Felch. Zey say zat ay are keen to join me in ze horn section of ze Pheromones, if you like?'

'Jesus, I can't understand that, Pete. Tour boring old Europe and leave all of this?' Ferret placed his hand on Pierre's shoulder. 'Listen, mate, don't nag me and I'll see what I can do.'

Pierre broke down. 'Oh sankyou. Sankyou. One chance is all I ask. I must get out of 'ere. I must . . .' he began sobbing uncontrollably.

Ferret left him to compose himself, which is polite talk for, 'He didn't really give a fuck' and he walked into the staffroom.

In all of his life Ferret had never heard the angels sing, but when Sue Hamilton, who was standing beside her desk, turned to face him, Gabriel's trumpet detonated his cochlea.

Sue was in her early twenties. She had dark tousled hair wildly framing her peaches and cream complexion. Her eyes were crystal blue; her mouth was full and sumptuous; her nose was small and cute; her face was heart-shaped and unblemished. She had the features of an angel. She was a little taller than Ferret, but not too tall. By his reckoning he could kiss her in a standing position if he got up on his toes. She wore a light floral dress, which was modest but alluring and showed off her shapely body. All in all she was a fucken' spunk and Ferret was momentarily stunned to find such superb beauty in amongst the detritus of McGoo's Hill.

'Hello, Mister Cutler,' she began, walking towards him with her hand outstretched. 'I'm Sue Hamilton. Nice to meet you.'

She had a sonorous, exquisite, educated voice. Ferret shook her hand in a daze.

'Thank you for taking my classes yesterday. I believe you had a bit of trouble with Jeremy Sweetman?'

Ferret tried to speak but the words stuck in his throat.

She smiled. 'Yes, I know what he can be like. He delights in making casual teachers cry. I think he might have bitten off more than he could chew on this occasion.'

'He won't be chewin' nothin' for a while, I reckon,' Ferret replied, distantly.

He had forgotten to let go of Sue's hand. She looked down to remind him.

'Oh shit, sorry. Sorry.'

'That's alright. It is Mister Cutler, isn't it?'

'Yeah. I mean Ferret. I mean Ferris.'

'Ferret's your nickname, they tell me, so that's what I'll call you - if that's okay?'

'Yeah. No. I mean yeah, no that's fine. I prefer it.'

She laughed like the summer wind and swept back to her desk. Ferret watched her tight little bottom swish away and he had to sit down. His heart was thumping away like a dwarf at a midget fucking contest.

Chardonnay burst in. 'Where's fucken' Lucky? Fucken' Sally and fucken' Kim phoned in fucken' late and they're not fucken' covered. Fucken' Michelle's away again and fucken' Celeste ain't 'ere. Lucky's gotta do Sally's fucken' roll call.'

'I got nuffin' on. I'll do it,' said Ferret. He wasn't usually the volunteering type but he thought Sue might be impressed. She was.

'Thanks, Ferret,' she said and she squeezed his hand as she passed him.

She may have well as squeezed his dick. It went as hard as a week old bagel.

Soon he was in roll call with 9E6. They kept asking him questions about what happened to Jeremy Sweetman and he kept avoiding the issue. Things were made worse by a constant flow of students from other roll calls whose opportunist parents had sent their children to seek out Mister Cutler. Most presented bits of paper upon which were written things like: 'I will accept $20,000 if you punch my daughter in the face' and '$10,000 per tooth – I don't want to be greedy'. One Year 8 boy turned up with a sign around his neck saying: 'Will have my testicles removed ($30,000 each)'.

'Fuck,' Ferret mumbled to himself as he left roll call. 'Some of these parents don't deserve children.'

The morning was uneventful. Celeste's Year 12 were working on their Group Work which meant Ferret drank coffee and flirted with two pretty girls whose third group member was away. After that he had to do something called Pastoral Care, which as far as Ferret could ascertain, meant wasting fifty minutes with his feet up while students made paper planes and farted.

Things got a little more interesting during sport. The dickhead who had called Ferret 'a ferret' two days before, was in his group for soccer.

'Oh, so it's you, fuckface,' Ferret whispered to the boy when other students couldn't hear him. 'I thought I might come across you sometime. How the fuck are ya?'

The boy was wary of Ferret. He valued his teeth, so he didn't reply.

'What's the matter, jackass? You had plenty to say the other day over at the intersection.'

'I was showin' off,' the boy replied. 'Sorry.'

Ferret was ready to verbally assault him, but there was something in the boy's tone that he pitied and even found endearing.

'Well, it's a big man who can apologise,' said Ferret. 'Let's start again. I'm Mister Cutler.'

'Danny Green,' replied the boy.

As they walked out towards the overgrown soccer field, Ferret asked Danny a few questions about his life and as he listened to the answers, he reflected on his own. Like him, Danny had been brought up around Windsor. His mum and dad argued a lot and his dad pissed off when he was in primary school. That left mum, who had never worked, seeking compensation from the government. Unlike Ferret's mum, Danny's mum had shacked up with loser after loser and dropped a kid to each, before they pissed off too.

'Has your mum ever worked?' asked Ferret.

'Nah,' replied Danny.

'So how do you make ends meet?'

'There's enough of us. I got three brothers 'n' two sisters.'

There you have it in a nutshell, Ferret thought to himself - the social welfare mentality. How do you break that cycle?

He was relaying the story to Sue at the end of the day.

'You're right,' she agreed. 'If you've never studied or

acquired skills you're only going to get the minimum wage and whatever that is, what is it, $20 an hour? You'll make more having babies and staying home.'

Exactly,' said Ferret, as if finally someone could see the sense in his argument. 'But what about you, Sue? You don't sound like you're from around here.'

'I live in Carlingford.'

'Carlingford,' Ferret echoed with a hint of wonder in his voice. He had heard of Carlingford. It was a mythical place to him. A far away world where little white kids and little Asian kids played in harmony in houses without backyards. Where people had spare cash and only swore when they needed to. 'Carlingford,' he repeated and his eyes grew glazed and distant like a politicians response to a thorny question.

'I drive in every day. It's okay though. It's against the traffic.' She looked at her phone. 'Sorry Ferret, I'd love to chat but I have to go.'

'No worries,' Ferret replied but he was obviously disappointed.

'I have a few things to get for tomorrow night. It's my anniversary.'

Ferret was crestfallen. 'You're married?'

'No,' replied Sue, laughing. She saw the disappointment on his face and she smiled sweetly. 'Just a boyfriend. You'll meet him tomorrow afternoon. He's picking me up.' She touched Ferret's cheek. 'You're cute,' she said. She gave him a kiss on the forehead and she went.

Ferret held his fingers to his forehead and he felt the drums beating in his skull. Ferret, you fool, he thought, of course she has a boyfriend. A beautiful girl like that will always have a boyfriend. And you're just an ugly little ferret face, in spite of all the money. Keep dreaming, boy.

He packed up his bag and left for the day. He'd managed to stay out of trouble and he'd managed to avoid the principal all day. He was proud of himself. All he had to try now was teaching.

Maybe tomorrow.

*

After a few cold ales at 'The Imperial', Ferret retired to his apartment above the brothel. He hadn't moved because he was determined that the money wasn't going to change his life style. However, he had noticed a large estate and a mansion up for sale for five million dollars in the Kurrajong Hills and he was beginning to think seriously of making an offer. Five million was nothing to him now and he was tiring of well-wishers who knew where he lived. Maybe it was better to move a little out of town. Bernard and Horatio were talking about doing that when they returned from the tour. He could always come in to town whenever he wanted. It would mean getting his driver's licence though.

These thoughts were still occupying his mind as he opened the door to his apartment and heard 'Ta Da!' at ludicrous volume. This was immediately followed by a vision of Saliva, all seven foot of him, completely naked but for a skimpy apron.

Once he had overcome the initial shock, Ferret exclaimed, 'What the fuck are you doin'?'

'Well, hello and welcome home, Sally. It's nice to see you too.' He smiled sweetly. 'Just a little house cleaning, Ferris. I know you don't look after your apartment or yourself, so I've made you some dinner too. It's in the oven. I'm not staying.'

'Why are you naked?'

'Oh, no reason really. It just adds a little spice to mundane activities.'

'Yeah, well could ya put your little spice away, mate? Otherwise it'll put me off me dinner.'

'Oh, very well,' Saliva replied with a sigh and a harrumph. He put his trousers on. 'The tour went well, thanks for asking.'

'Give me a fucken' chance, for Christ's sake. I've only been in the door two seconds and most of that time's been spent watchin' your dick wave about behind your fucken' apron.'

'Ooh you saucy boy,' replied Saliva, donning a polo shirt. 'Anyway, it was fabulous, darling.'

'Yeah, I heard it went well.'

'It went better than 'well', my dear. In layman's terms – it was fucking great. You should have seen us, pretzel . . .'

'Don't fucken' call me pretzel.'

' . . .we were fantabulous. I tell you, my dear, if there is a Heaven, it heard us. We were awfuckingsome.' He adjusted his bandana. 'Well. Of course the pheromone wipes helped, but honestly, I'm not sure they were necessary. You should have seen us, petal. They loved us.'

'Better wifout the guitar, eh?

'Ah, now,' Saliva mimicked Ferret's facial expression, 'I do believe you're pouting. Now stop it, Ferris, you're a grown man. You've left the Hawkesbury. You'll never be the same. I know it and you know it. So, what's happening? And don't try to fool your Uncle Saliva.'

'Uncle Saliva?' Ferret repeated, as if he'd just tasted it. 'Fucken' settle down.'

'Not married yet?'

'It's only been a few fucken' months.'

'I was hopeful.'

'Yeah, you just didn't want me to come on tour with yous. You think . . .' he hesitated, ' . . . you *know* that I'm not good enough and I accept that.'

'Oooh, look who's grown up all of a sudden. Alright, I'll tell you the truth. No, you weren't needed.'

'Thanks.'

'But yes, you were missed.'

Ferret considered that for a moment and it dawned on him that this was the greatest compliment he had ever been paid. For even though these men realised that musically he was more of a liability than an asset, they still preferred that, to not having him with them. He was choked up.

'Thanks, mate,' he said quietly.

'Now don't go all misty on me.' He flicked Ferret playfully with a feather duster. 'Ooh you are cute when you're teary. Pity you're not a poofter.'

'Fuck off.'

'Aha, the Hawkesbury reply to any intimation of homosexuality. Do they teach you that in school in these parts? Do you stand up in the morning and recite 'Fuck off!' as the standard reply when someone suggests anything to do with homosexuality? Is it like your times tables? You all rattle them off as a group. 'Are you a poof!' in unison 'Fuck off.'

In spite of himself Ferret smiled.

'I saw that. Now that's more like it. We're all heading off to Europe in June. How's the guitar playing coming?'

'Slow.'

'Well keep at it. Oh, and by the way, I'm considering putting in an offer for a place up in the hills. That way Jesus can see his rellos whenever he wants.'

'The place in Comleroy Road? The one they want $5 mill. for?'

'Yes. How did you know?'

'I was thinkin' of buyin it.'

'Oh my God!' shouted Saliva, throwing his hands to his mouth. Ferret turned abruptly and looked behind him. He was trying to locate the cause of the calamity. But there was none. When he turned back, Saliva still had his hands up to his mouth, as if he'd had the greatest epiphany possible to mankind. 'Of course! We can all live together. You, me, Jesus, Bernard and Horatio. It's a huge place. And we'd all have adventures and . . .'

'Hang on . . .'

'It'll be just like Tin Tin and Captain Haddock.'

'Who?'

'We'll all be in Marlinspike Hall. And we could have a butler and we could call him Nestor. I'll get a little white dog and I'll call him Snowy. No, I'll call him Milou, that will be more authentic and . . .'

'What in fuck's name are you on?'

'I'm high on life, Ferret! I'm high on life!' He did a small pirouette. He grabbed Ferret by the shirt and whispered with passion, 'You should have seen us at The O2 Arena. When we broke into 'The Granny Thriller' I thought the roof was going to come off.' He danced away and span in small delicate circles in the kitchen, 'Next stop - Europe' He stopped spinning and became business-like again. 'And you're coming, so practise that bloody guitar. I'm off.' And he headed for the door. Stopped when he got there and finished with, 'I'll organise the mansion. I think living together is a fabulous idea. And don't worry, I'll organise everything. Tat Ta.'

'Hold on a . . .' Ferret was speaking to a closed door. 'It wasn't my fucken' idea!'

*

DAY 4 – THE THURSDAY

The next morning, as Ferret signed on, he was feeling a little ashamed of himself. He had woken up as a randy as an airhostess and whilst he took his dick for its morning constitutional, all he could think about was Sue's pretty face. That was nothing to be ashamed of, but putting a pheromone wipe into his pocket was. He knew Sue was spoken for, but lustful imagination had made him do it. As he left his apartment he thought he might take her for a little excursion into the Drama Room where she would fall under the sway of his Wannaroot? but now his immediate lust had abated, he realised that it was simply the wrong thing to do.

He picked up his work sheet to find that he was Celeste again. He noticed also that Sue was going to be late. He hoped that she was okay.

Just then Deidre Gilmore came in. She booked the casuals, which was an irony, because she was such a formal character. She was an elegant looking woman of about forty with a huge bust and hair that was up, didn't move and looked like it had been sculpted out of Pears Soap.

'Good morning, Mister Cutler,' she said but her voice was tired and far from joyful.

'You alright?' he asked.

'The answer to that lies on the Day Sheet. Have a look at how many people are away today. And all my regular casuals are unavailable. I wish some of these teachers would phone in before 6am so I could get in first and hire the good ones. I'd prefer it if they told me the night before.'

That they're gunna be sick?'

'Yes.'

'What, before it happens?'

Deidre raised her eyebrows, 'You haven't been here on a Thursday before have you?' She left.

What happens on a Thursday? thought Ferret. He looked at the sheet. Holy shit! Whatever it was about Thursdays, it was certainly infectious. About half the staff was away. The principal was present, unfortunately, but even Deputy Meek was away. No one from his staffroom was present except for Lucky Pierre and Sue, when she turned up. For roll call it was just him and Pierre. That was gunna be fun.

He made his way across the quad. The students were beginning to get to know him. One boy yelled out; 'G'day, sir!' another, a little girl, squeaked out, 'Good morning, Mister Cutler.' And Ferret loved it. He'd never been paid any respect before. He realised now that he hadn't deserved it. He also realised that he probably still didn't, but he did love being called 'Mister Cutler' and 'sir'. These were terms he usually only encountered when the police called or when people asked him to leave restaurants.

He waved to Felch who was doing a morning playground duty. Felch waved back and yelled, 'I'm not gay!'

There was some sort of a ruckus in the playground. There was a barbecue on and the smell of pancakes washed across the yard. A bunch of smiling young people, probably in their early twenties, served them out to eager students.

Ferret entered the staffroom to find Lucky Pierre juggling rolls. He looked slightly panicked.

Ferret saw the problem. 'What d'ya say we do half each and hold the fort until Sue gets 'ere?' he suggested.

'Uncovered classes will 'ave to go to ze playground,' replied Lucky, still looking flustered.

'She'll be right. We'll get through. Slow 'n' steady.'

But Lucky looked far from both. He dropped the rolls and shouted, 'Merde!'

'Alright, take it easy, Frenchie,' said Ferret trying to calm him as he helped pick them up. 'Hey, tell me, what's so special about Thursdays and what are those people doin' out in the quad?'

'Oh it iz ze fucking Christians. Zey are here every Sursday bribing ze students with food so zey go to scripture.'

'Ain't this a public school?'

'You cannot stop zem if zey ask. Zey are a pain in ze derriere. Zey invade us every Sursday and we are not allowed to teach our classes when ze other students do ze scripture.'

'Why the fuck not?'

'Because zey say we are disadvantaging ze ones who go to scripture.'

'That's puttin' the cart before the horse, ain't it? The ones who do scripture should fucken' catch up.'

'Zat is too logical, monsieur and zese people are not too logical. Zey threaten ze children with the wrath of ze Devil. Zey are scary to overhear. Zey are more like a cult.'

'Who the fuck are these people?'

'Zey call zemselves ze Bilgewater Group.'

'So you tellin' me I don't get to teach much today because of this lot?'

Lucky nodded his head sadly. He stood up and handed half the rolls to Ferret, 'Yes, but it gets worse zan that, monsieur. At lunchtime zey play Christian Rock at 'igh volume in ze playground.'

'Christian Rock?' Ferret spat out the words with disdain. 'That's a fucken' oxymoron. Rock's about sex and drugs. It's about snortin' cocaine off a hooker's back while you're up 'er. It's about getting' pissed 'n' fallin' off ya drum kit. It's about filth and liberation and new ideas. These cunts ain't allowed to experience any of those things. They can't even 'ave sex before they're fucken' married. What would any of them know about fucken' life? They're married by twenty-one 'coz it's the only way they can score a fuck. The only time they travel is to build houses for little black cunts 'n' the only reason they fucken' do that is to convert the bastards to their fucken' stupid religion.'

'You are indeed eloquent, monsieur, but zere is nussing we can do.'

'Yeah, well I'll be fucked if I'll be governed by a

bunch of wide-eyed, holier than thou fucken' deadshits who know as much about what happens after ya die as I fucken' do – and that's fucken' nuffin'!'

Roll call was a disaster, of course, and many of the rolls weren't marked at all. For the next two periods Ferret had junior classes and he wasn't supposed to teach anything new. But as he watched the students wasting their time playing with the computers the government had given them, he thought to himself, I'll be fucked if I miss this opportunity.

'Alright, listen up,' he said and they did. This surprised him. 'What class is this?' he asked.

'9E1,' replied a small boy with oversized glasses.

'Is this the top class or somefink?'

'Yes,' replied the boy. 'All the other classes are mixed ability.'

'What does that mean?' asked Ferret.

'It means,' replied the boy, 'that there are at least ten troublemakers in each class, so no one can learn effectively.'

'Why the fuck would you have mixed classes then?'

'Educational theory. The idea is that the smart kids help bring up the slower kids.'

'Trouble is,' added a pretty little blonde girl from down the front, 'it usually works the other way around and the slower kids stop the smart kids from learning. In mixed ability classes the slower kids often have strong personalities and they tend to talk more than listen. It's okay for Drama but not for more serious subjects like English, Maths and Science.'

'So it's really important,' added the little boy with oversized glasses, 'that you don't fall out of the top thirty. 'coz if you do, you don't go down one grade, you drop straight into a class where it's hard to learn.'

Ferret struggled with an idea. He wasn't used to having them. 'So if you applied the same principle to sport, that'd mean that if ya played first grade at say, cricket, and you fell out of the first eleven, you wouldn't drop to second grade, you'd just get chucked in wif all the rest and some of 'em'd be fucken' 'opeless?'

'That's right,' suggested the little girl down the front, 'try bringing in mixed ability Saturday morning soccer for the kids and the parents would be outraged. But they don't seem to care about the consequences of mixed ability classrooms.'

'Exactly my point,' said the boy. 'White Australians value their sport above their education. Asian people know the value of education. If you go to a physician in the future they'll probably be either Asian or Indian. They work harder than us and they go to selective schools where you can learn something. The only trouble with selective schools is that they don't have selective teachers.'

'Bullshit,' replied Ferret.

'No, it's true,' one freckle-faced fat kid chimed in. 'Sometimes they even drop the dead wood teachers into selective schools 'coz they can't get rid of them anywhere else.'

'Bullshit,' said Ferret.

'So we all work hard to make sure we stay in the top class, or you're in trouble. But every Thursday we miss valuable school time because of scripture which, in my opinion, shouldn't even be allowed in secular schools.'

The rest of the class all seemed to agree.

'Look around,' said the blonde, 'this class is full. No one from this class even went to scripture but we're still not allowed to learn anything.'

Ferret had grown angrier by the minute. 'Yeah? Well that's a truck full a horse shit 'n' I'm gunna teach yous somefink. Wait 'ere.'

Ferret dashed out of the room and grabbed a bible that he'd noticed above Chardonnay's desk. He figured that was fair enough – she needed all the help she could get.

'Right,' he said, clearing his throat. 'Where are the Ten Commandments? I'm gunna explain 'em for yous.'

'Exodus 20,' someone said.

Ferret eventually found it. 'Ah, here we are. This is the bit where Moses reads out the word of God. Now bear in mind I'm putting it in everyday Windsor terms.'

The class listened on with interest.

'Okay, Number 1 – You can't have any other God but me. Sounds fair enough. Mind you, I dunno where you'd find another one, but still, 'e goes on to Commandment 2, which is: Thou shalt not make unto thee any graven image. What 'es sayin' here is - don't worship idols, which is right 'coz all you're doin' is bowing down to a fucken' piece of wood, or gold, or somefink but apparently no bastard told the Catholics. 'e backs it up by sayin' that 'es the jealous type and if you *do* 'ave any other God 'es gunna punish not only you, but your kids and their kids as well for three to four generations. So everyone in this room who didn't go to scripture is pretty well fucked.'

The class laughed.

'Number 3 – Don't take 'is name in vain or he'll fuck you up. So if you've ever said 'Jesus' or 'God' or 'Lord' he'll get ya. Angry cunt, ain't 'e?' Next, Number 4 – Remember the Sabbath and keep it holy. The trouble is that someone fucked it up along the way and they started worshippin' on a Sunday, when it should be the Saturday, but since that fucks up Saturday sport, they changed it. By the way not only are you forced to rest on the Sabbath but that goes for your maids and servants too. Even your cattle have to fucken' rest on the Sabbath. How the fuck do ya manage that? If your cow has a mind to work, how do you stop him? Next, Number 5 – Honour thy father and mother, which is fair enough, so long as 'es not your stepfather and 'es fucken' ya up the arse. The Catholics are strong in that area, probly 'coz the priests ain't allowed to fuck and it tends to pervert 'em. All in all I go along wif the sentiment, but my old man was a cunt so I ain't honourin' him. Remember that kids - old people don't deserve respect just because they're old. You have to earn respect. The old fuckwit who pushes into the queue in front of you was a young fuckwit once and he just got old. Don't cut that cunt any slack. Send 'im to the back of the queue.'

'Number 6- Thou shalt not kill. Pretty straight forward. Only applies to humans, but. You can murder anyfink else on the planet and God doesn't seem to give a shit. In fact, if I remember correctly, 'e put 'em there for us to murder in the first place. Also it should be noted that religious believers are the biggest mass murderers in history. The Nazis had nuffin' on the Tykes. Hitler only lasted a dozen years. Those Tyke fuckers have been killin' in God's name for fucken' centuries, but that's another story. Look up the Spanish Inquisition. I'd write it up on the board but I can't fucken' spell it.'

This was the most engaged Ferret had ever seen any class. So he continued. 'Number 7 - Thou shalt not commit adultery. That's pretty straight forward. That just means, boys, don't put ya dick where it don't belong and girls, don't open up ya vertical smile for anyone but your husband, even if he is a fat old prick who farts a lot and snores and you've looked after yourself and a good lookin' young bloke moves in next door and 'e comes over to borrow some sugar wif 'es shirt off and 'e comes in and ya desperately want 'im up ya – don't! Cos if ya do, the benevolent God'll fuck wif you.'

One fat boy up the back had to leave the room because he shat himself laughing. Ferret's irreverence was winning the day. Much of the class was howling with laughter, although there were a few goody two shoes kids who were unsure whether it was okay to listen to this stuff.

'Number 8 – Don't steal – unless you're absolutely certain that you won't get caught. Nah, I'm jokin' I made the last bit up. Don't steal, that's good advice. Number 9 – Thou shalt not bear false witness against your neighbour. Well, I dunno about yous but no-one's ever asked me to do that. I can't remember a time when I was ever asked to bear any fucken' witness against me neighbour. In fact, I wouldn't fucken' know who me fucken' neighbour is and I don't wanna fucken' know 'n' I reckon that'd go for the rest of yous too. Stay as far away from fucken' other people as ya can, I reckon. And last one, Number 10 – Don't covet your neighbour's stuff. Don't be envious. That goes for his wife, his manservant, his maidservant, his ox, or his ass. Don't ever get caught looking longingly at your neighbour's ass, or you're fucked. And that just about wraps it up.'

The class erupted into hilarious applause and Ferret took a bow but half way through his second bow, the class suddenly became deathly silent. Ferret looked up with a smile on his face but he immediately saw in the fearful eyes of the students that he had some reason for concern.

Principal Necklace was standing in the doorway.

'Bin there long?' asked Ferret.

'I've been listening around the corner since Commandment 3. Come with me please, Mister Cutler.'

Ferret whispered, 'Sorry kids. Gotta go.' And he left the room.

*

'What the fuck do you think you're doing?' bellowed the red-faced ranga, immediately after the door to the Principal's Office slammed behind her.

'Teachin',' replied Ferret.

'You call that teaching?'

'K'noath. I never said nuffin' that wasn't gospel.'

Above her furry upper lip, Pearl Necklace's eyes widened with fury. 'How dare you,' she began, but she got no further. Ferret mounted a counterattack.

'How dare you!' he shouted. 'How dare you let thirty kids, who are probably smarter than both of us, sit in a class room and do nuffin' for whole periods at a time! No wonder nuffin' happens in this fucken' country! The Department of Education's runnin' so scared of cults and minority groups our kids ain't learnin' nuffin!'

'You specifically disobeyed a directive. I wash my hands of you.'

'You're pretty fucken' good at washin' your fucken' hands, lady. Maybe you should try getting' 'em dirty occasionally.'

As he spoke, Ferret caught a glimpse of Dirty Sanchez loitering outside the principal's office – no doubt perving on Pearl, whackin' off in the bushes.

'I can abide this no longer. Go away, Mister Cutler. You are a disgrace to the teaching profession.'

'Well that may be so, cockbreath, but at least I'm here, which is more than I can say for half of your staff. Did you know that there's not one fucken' head teacher in at work today?'

'I was aware of that. Yes. But I'd prefer that, to the trouble you're causing.'

'Alright. I'll fuck off.'

'Good.'

'But I'll tell ya somefink before I go. People in this country pride themselves on bein' tolerant. I hear it all the time on the news. But I'll tell ya this for free – we're only tolerant in this country of selective opinions. So long as you toe the line 'n' don't knock the Abos, the religious groups, the foreigners and the poofs, you're okay. But if you dare speak out against 'em, even if you've got a logical gripe, you're either racist, or homophobic, or some fucken' thing, and that ain't tolerated. In this country we say we value free speech, but we practice censorship.'

'Good day, Mister Cutler,' replied Pearl, languidly. She settled herself behind her desk in a manoeuvre calculated to infuriate Ferret.

He watched her pretend to read a memo on her desk and he was appalled; appalled at her incompetence; appalled at the teachers who were absent and appalled at the Department of Education that allowed this cult to infiltrate schools and brainwash young minds. It was pointless speaking. Principal Pearl Necklace was not listening.

He stormed out of her office and thumped about in the administration area cursing to himself and scaring the office ladies. They quietly shut the door to their office as Ferret stomped about, kicking partitions and sending pictures of student sporting heroes spiralling into the air.

Several minutes later he had calmed down. He would get even with her but how? Dejectedly, he put his hands in his pockets as he mindlessly patrolled the room and there he found . . .

'Of course,' he whispered.

He ran outside to find Dirty Sanchez, cock in hand, lurking in the bushes.

'Pedro,' he said, which caused Dirty Sanchez to catch his balls on a rose thorn. The swarthy man did up his pants.

'Senor, I was just . . .'

'Never mind that. I think I've found your opportunity to pork the porker.'

'Oh, joy of joys,' Dirty replied. He went to hug Ferret, but Ferret evaded his embrace.

'I don't need gratitude. All *you* need is this.' He handed Dirty a pheromone wipe.'

'And what is this, senor?' he asked as he looked at the unmarked packet.

'It's a love potion. It'll make the object of your desire

rip off your jeans and fuck your brains out.'

'I see that you too are a romantic, senor. Oh, thank you, thank you.'

'Mister Meek is away today, so here's your chance. Just rub it on your neck and bust down the door. It won't work 'til ya get close to 'er. So be brave. Open the door wide, proclaim your love for 'er and take 'er in your arms. She'll be as willing as Year 8 girl if Harry Stiles got 'is cock out. You'd better hurry up, but, before she leaves 'er office.'

'I will. I will,' replied the excited Latin lover. 'I will never forget this, senor. Thank you.'

Dirty Sanchez raced away, ripping open the pheromone packet as he ran towards the Admin. Block.

Ferret watched from the bushes as the door to the principal's office was flung open. Ferret couldn't hear because the window was closed, but he smiled as he watched Pearl Necklace stand and no doubt scream some obscenity at the man. She advanced and the two met on the far side of Pearl's desk from Ferret's point of view. He clasped his hands with delight as he watched her hesitate momentarily. He knew that the potion was about to wreak its havoc.

And it did.

It was hard to tell whose passion was the more savage. She looked like she was trying to eat his face but he was eating back. Then she ripped a hole in her voluminous undies to allow him general access. He popped every button on his overalls with one rough tug of his hand. She lay back across her desk, opened her legs and raised them straight up into the air. She looked like a sunburnt whale with two hardons, landed on a ship. He needed no invitation. He jumped on the quarterdeck and was scaling the rigging in no time. Unearthly howls from both parties were audible even through the closed window and Ferret was further delighted when the office staff, suspecting murder, came barging into the room in time to see the desk collapse under the combined weight of the two flailing animals. There was no chance of pulling them apart, so half a dozen women stood, with their hands to their mouths, watching their flaccid leader on the floor, wood splinters all over her, humping the brains out of the janitor. He was so far up her arse Ferret thought he detected a throb in her throat. But the piece de résistance came after the climax when Dirty Sanchez was true to his name. At this point, two of the office ladies swooned and fell, adding to the confusion. Both Dirty and Pearl lay in a love embrace that could not be broken. They had both apparently fallen asleep as a result of the conflagration.

When the police arrived, they found them still locked in this position. An ambulance was called and the two were placed upon a king size stretcher and taken out the door. The police asked why the principal had a brown upper lip, but nobody was talking.

Ferret had won the day.

*

There was a hurried meeting in the common room twenty minutes later. The twenty-two teachers present all attended. The ship was without a captain, or a first mate, and the lure of gossip was strong. It fell to Ferret to explain the events of the morning. So he found himself in the limelight. Teachers settled down as he moved centre stage. He was savouring his new notoriety and he was a little disappointed that Sue had still not turned up in time to see his performance.

'Good mornin' everyone. I'm Ferris Cutler. Those of ya that know 'n' love me can call me Ferret. I'll make this short 'n' sweet. It seems ya principal has popped a tube or blown a ring or whatever metaphor ya might like to choose. Basically, she's cracked up and fucked the janitor until the poor bastard's cock was as sore as an altar boy's arsehole. This should come as no surprise 'coz as most of yous know already she's been terrorising poor old Don Meek for fuck knows how long. Seems she can't stuff enough fillin' in the old lasagne. I don't know what you'd usually do in this situation. I suppose it is a bit of a rarity. So, I'll leave it wif yous.'

He sat down.

A dishevelled, messy-haired bloke of about forty-odd stood up. He looked to Ferret like a fella who might blow the odd joint, in spite of school policy. He wore tattered jeans and a paint-spattered t-shirt. He began, 'I'm Pat Sinclair, Ferret. I'm in the Art Department.'

That figures, thought Ferret.

'And since Joyce, the union rep. isn't here today, and I know she won't be in tomorrow, 'coz I happen to know her dogs got a bowel complaint, in her absence and in the absence of any senior executive, it falls upon me, as 2IC in Federation matters, to make an executive decision. Now I know you're only a relieving teacher, Mister Cutler, and I know through the grapevine that you're not even a proper teacher, full stop, but I think most people in this room will agree with the proposal I'm about to put forward. Many of us here have been impressed by your brave talk and actions over the last couple of days. Now, given the circumstances, i.e. none of us wants to get our butts kicked, I propose that for the remainder of the day and for tomorrow, when I believe you're going anyway, you become acting principal of the school. I'd like a seconder.'

Twenty-odd hands went up and it was done. Just like that. Ferret had risen from nothing to principal in less than three days.

Who says promotion's difficult in the Education Department, thought Ferret.

He stood up. 'Thanks, comrades,' he said. 'And Pat, I know you're takin' a bit of a dangerous punt 'ere, so if there's any repercussions for ya, I'll see you right. As for the rest of yous, let's get back to teachin'. Leave the Christians to me.'

The meeting broke up and there was much back slapping of Ferret as teachers left the common room.

Ferret was feeling mighty proud of himself as he walked back up to the English Staffroom but his mood changed when he got there, because he found pretty Sue Hamilton sitting at her desk with tears streaming down her face.

'What's up, Sue?' he asked as he approached her.

'Oh, Ferret,' she replied, collapsing in grief into his arms, 'he's called it off.' And she bawled even more.

'What? Your boyfriend?'

She couldn't speak so she nodded into his chest.

'Well. I'll be fucked,' he muttered. 'Some blokes wouldn't know their dick from the dining room table. How could anyone leave a beautiful girl like you?'

'And on our anniversary too,' she blubbered.

'Why?'

She looked up into his eyes. 'He's got someone else.' She shattered into more tears.

Ferret held her as she shuddered into his chest with grief. As he felt her soft hair and felt her trembling beauty, he also felt an unaccustomed emotion. He couldn't place it at first. Usually Ferret's emotional depth was as shallow as a Special Unit class's poetical analysis. His relations with women were always without strings. He had always considered them merely as objects; as his no-hands-wanking-machines - but not this one. As he felt her next to him his heart was as soft as a fat chick's belly and his cock was as hard as an overcooked meringue.

Ferret was in love.

He took Sue by the cheeks and gently raised her face up so that her bright and lustrous dew-moistened eyes looked into his. 'I'll look after ya,' he said quietly.

And it happened. She kissed him long and lustily upon the lips. Him, little Ferris Cutler, no-hoper from Windsor, was being pashed-off by a beautiful young woman. And she meant it too. Ferret had to breathe through his nose to survive the onslaught. But it was worth it.

When she finally broke the embrace she whispered, 'Thank you, Ferret.'

Just then Lucky, Rusty and Felch came into the room.

'Why if it isn't Frenchie and the two poofs,' said Ferret.

'I'm not . . .'

'I know. I know.'

'What orders do you 'ave for us, ma capitan?'

'It's mon capitan, dickhead. Even *I* fucken' know that.'

'So what do we do?' asked Rusty.

'Well since you've put your trombone away, I'll tell ya. Call an assembly. Now.'

The three men scurried from the room like excited schoolboys.

'Oh, Ferret,' whispered Sue. 'I'm so proud of you.'

Ten minutes later Ferret addressed the school. They were a rag tag lot in general. Some in uniform, some not. But they appeared interested in what was going on. The grapevine had been climbing fast.

'Right, now listen up,' Ferret belted across the P.A. system but it cut out, so he had to wait. When it was finally restored he said, 'Now, for the rest of the day it's classes as usual.'

This announcement brought the expected collective moan.

'Yeah,' Ferret shot back at them, 'I know how fucken' devoted yous are to your religion. Well, fuck you. No more pancakes and bullshit. It's work time. Get your arses in there.'

He stood down from the small outside stage and the assembly broke up.

A longhaired young man came sauntering towards him. He was the elected Christian spokesman, apparently, because Ferret could see a bunch of other young people in the distance behind him. They had guitars and amps with them.

He dressed like he had heard rock 'n' roll regalia described but had never actually seen it. As he approached he high fived and slapped hands with two or three passing students and he said stuff like: 'Cool, bro.' and 'Sup?' and 'What's happening, man' in an attempt to sound cool and thus snare the poor little sods and then indoctrinate them into his God club.

He greeted Ferret with a 'Sup, man.'

'Your head's sup.'

'Huh?'

'Your head's sup your arse.'

'Hey, man, that's not cool,' the young man replied, nodding his head back and forward like a toy dog on a dashboard.

'Neither's tellin' kids the Devil's gunna get 'em. I hear you and your wide-eyed morons've been tellin' students that they're goin' to hell unless they accept Jesus as their Lord.'

'That's right, man. And it's the truth.'

'The truth is, pencil-dick, that you don't have a fucken' clue and it's not your fucken' place to say shit like that to kids. Right?'

'I *do* understand, man.' The boy was growing agitated. 'Jesus is our Lord and if you don't accept him into your heart then you're going to hell.'

'If that's where I'm goin' then you'll be comin' wif me.'

'I'm not going to hell. I accept Jesus.'

'Sorry, Tonto, but you are and so are all your creepy

mates.'

'How do you figure that?'

"coz my idea of hell is hangin' out wif a bunch a cunts like you!'

The young man was trying not to get angry but he was losing the battle. 'Listen, we came here to spread the word of God.'

'I got no problem wif the word of God,' Ferret replied, 'it's the shit your peddlin' I got a problem wif.'

'There are none so blind, man.'

'Exactly what I was thinkin'.'

Ferret was toying with the young man. He realised that the Christian rock brigade wanted to set up and he was waiting for the boy to ask, which he eventually did, to which Ferret replied, 'Fuck off'.

The boy was shocked. 'What?' he stammered.

'You 'eard me. Fuck off.'

'You can't do that.'

'I fucken' just did. I'm the principal.'

As Ferret walked away, followed by Pat, he heard the boy yelling behind him, 'You'll be hearing from us, man!'

'By tomorrow,' he said to Pat, there'll be some trouble to sought out wif parents, I reckon.'

'It's worse than that,' Pat replied. 'There's a morning assembly in the hall tomorrow. There'll be plenty of parents alright.'

'Fuck me,' Ferret replied.

*

DAY 5 – THE FRIDAY

The next morning Ferret was in early. He had never owned a suit before but he had taken advantage of late night shopping and bought one at Lowes. It wasn't a perfect fit. It was probably a size too big for him.

'How do I look?' he asked Lucky.

'Like a ferret in ze suit,' he replied with a smile.

'Fuck off,' said Ferret, but he smiled. He kinda liked Lucky, in spite of the bullshit accent, or maybe because of it.

He looked around the office. Someone had set up a makeshift desk. The splinters from Pearl's destroyed desk were still visible, swept into one corner. 'So, what does a principal do?'

'Zey shuffle paper and when zey 'ave finished zat, zey make speeches and go to conferences.'

'Don't they do any work?'

'Zey delegate to zere deputies and ze deputies put pressure on ze 'ead teachers to make sure zat zere teachers are getting ze good HSC results.'

'And do they?'

'Not 'ere.'

'How come?'

'Because 'alf of zese children would be better off getting a job. All zey need is basic literacy. Zey are not about to write ze novel. But zey are forced to stay by ze government until zey are seventeen and all zey do is disrupt ze uzzer students because zey 'ave no interest. What good is a knowledge of polysyndeton to a car mechanic?'

'Poly what?'

'And ze 'ead teachers get ze blame for bad results when ze real culprits are mixed ability classes and days lost to religious instruction.'

'So the teachers do the real work?'

Lucky nodded, 'When zey can, but zey are constantly 'ampered by paperwork from ze deputies who want ze promotion. So instead of doing what zey do - teach - zey spend hours writing about educational seory which zey know zey will never employ. Zen, ze deputies can tick zat box and ze principal is 'appy.'

'Which brings me back to my original question. What the fuck do I do?'

'You do nothing,' said Donald Meek as he entered the room. 'You give the speech, you get off, you avoid parents and you get out of Dodge.'

'Do ya mean Dodge City in South Windsor where all the trouble makers come from?'

'No, Dodge City, Kansas where Wyatt Earp came from.'

'Hey, Don,' Ferret commented, 'you look like a man on a mission. Not so submissive and scared.'

'The witch is dead, Mister Cutler. I heard this morning that she won't be here any longer and I must admit, I feel a certain freedom this morning I've not felt for many years.'

'So they've sacked 'er, eh?'

Donald laughed, 'Oh, Mister Cutler, if only it were that easy. No, in order to get sacked from the Department of Education in NSW you have to either fuck one of the kids or drop a shit in front of the assembly.' He hesitated. 'Actually, come to think of it, if you're a woman you have to fuck three kids but the shit should definitely do it, unless you claim you were stressed, in which case you'll get paid out until you return to light duties, which is unlikely since stress is a difficult thing to diagnose.'

'So what 'appened to 'er?'

'She's been moved on to a selective school. The union made sure of that.'

'Doesn't that disadvantage the students?'

'The Teachers' Federation represents the teachers, Mister Cutler. They're not concerned about the students. We're all comrades here, regardless of ability.'

'Yeah,' replied Ferret thoughtfully, 'I'm beginnin' to get the picture.'

'So, Mister Cutler, I suggest you do the three B's this

morning.'

'And what's that?'

'Be brief, be bright and be gone.'

'Yeah, righto, I get the message,' Ferret replied. He wasn't looking forward to it either.

An hour later Ferret peeked out of his window. There was an angry mob developing outside the hall. Men with Christian beards were speaking loudly about outrage and sacrilege. Angry believers thundered against those non-believers, including him, who were destined for the scrap heap in the afterlife because they didn't agree with them. Ferret waited until 9am when everyone had entered the hall before he joined the rest of the Official Party and walked into the hall.

There were four uninvited guests who joined the end of the Official Party queue and who entered quietly behind Ferret, Donald Meek, Danzer Slap, The Local Member, and the two school captains.

It was like a bear pit. There's nothing more vindictive, more cruel, more inhuman than a Christian whose been asked to turn the other cheek. The snarling hatred permeated the acoustically booming room. It sounded like a bunch of monkeys caught in a bass trap, if you can audiolise that.

'Wait 'til after this assembly!' belted out one Christian thug. 'I'll be praying for you in the playground!'

The power these people have, thought Ferret.

He sat down and then immediately had to stand up again for the National Anthem. That's the piece of shit melody that Bob Hawke decided we had to have before Paul Keating decided we had to have a recession as well. Nobody sang it of course because it's awful and also, many of today's crowd only knew the words to Kumbaya. Given the level of their thought process in general, thought Ferret, they're lucky to know the words to any songs at all.

'Before we start the assembly,' the girl captain began, 'our principal, Mister Cutler, will give the 'Welcome to Country'.'

This took Ferret by surprise. He'd heard the 'Welcome to Country' before, where you thank elders past and present for the land and everything, but he'd never paid it much heed before. Fortunately, the girl captain was a smart one. She had foreseen this possibility and had written it out for Ferret. He thanked her as he approached the podium.

The atmosphere was icy. There was a subdued rumble, like someone on a first date who wants to fart.

Ferret looked towards the angry sea of faces; looked at the paper, and he crumpled it up.

'Ladies, gentleman and Christians,' he began, 'We'd like to thank the Whydon'tyafuckmeoveragain people for leasing out land they claim no one owns 'n' not payin' any tax on the royalties. We'd like to thank 'em for holdin' as sacred all the land in the country worf fucken' havin' and for bein' a general pain in the arse. We'd like to thank 'em for survivin' for sixty fousand years or so in this hostile environment. They did know how to manage the land, but not one of 'em ever kicked over a log, saw it roll, and thought of inventin' the wheel, even though they were nomadic and you might 'ave thought that it might 'ave been occasionally useful.' He added as parenthetical, 'Ya can bet ya life they would've invented the wheel but, if there'd been a pub 100 k's up the road. I know I fucken' would.' He continued, 'I'd also like to thank the wombat and the Echidna and other Australian Fauna for achieving the same as the Australian Aborigines. They all survived wifout contributin' one iota to the sum total of human intellectual advancement. While Sir Isaac Newton was formulatin' the Laws of Gravity 'n' Optics, these cunts were fishin' and goin' walkabout. I guess ya can't blame 'em – there's fuck all to do in this shit hole of a country.

Lastly, I'd like to say that it's lucky this quaint tradition we 'ave in this country of apologisin' to the black bastards we invaded has grown momentum, at least amongst those too scared to speak out, and that's a few of yous, I'm sure. And it's lucky it doesn't 'appen in Iraq, say, 'coz them Arab bastards'd be apologisin' to the fucken' Assyrians and the Chal fucken Deans and every other fucken cunt who 'appened to find 'emselves hangin' about the place fru the course of 'istory.' He concluded, 'Ya might, instead, say thanks to Peter Johnson and 'is contractor, who I happen to know built this place a few years back.'

And he sat down.

For several moments there was stunned silence. This was followed by a growing murmur, which rapidly percolated in intensity. Soon the hall was in near riot.

Danza Slap, the local member whispered into Ferret's ear, 'I want you to know that I in no way endorse what you just said. It's racist and it's evil.'

'That's alright, Danza,' Ferret replied with a smile, 'I know you can't embrace any controversial ideas. You have to keep in power, mate.'

The two spoke no more.

The school captains stopped the pot from boiling over by retaking the stage. They did the whole 'Oscar' thing where they presented alternately and cracked poorly set up gags and the crowd simmered, close to boiling.

There was a musical item where Lucky, buoyed by Ferret's success, tried a punk song and it fell flat. Not surprising, thought Ferret. This was real Punk, not Christian Punk. Christian Punk was Johnny Not So Rotten minus the spit. In an attempt to impress Ferret, Lucky went for it. He started on his saxophone, and joined by Felch and Rusty, they blasted out their brass fury and at the end of the song threw their already battered school instruments out into the crowd. One girl in Year 7 was taken away with head injuries. The riot broke its banks.

Men stood. Women howled abuse. All seemed lost. The river was about to break its levee, when a large voice: impressive, stentorian and mellifluous threw a calming net upon the waters.

'Ladies and Gentlemen,' it said, 'let us not let our emotions get the better of us. Let us instead pay homage to this great man.'

It was Bernard. He had taken up the microphone. He turned and smiled at Ferret. Then turned back to the audience.

'Which man?' asked one particularly irate Christian with a rat's tail and a t-shirt that read: 'It's okay – I'm with the Lord.'

'Why, Ferret Cutler, of course,' replied Bernard with another generous smile.

This really set the house alight. But he calmed the swell. 'Hold on, ladies and gentlemen. Let me speak.'

The crowd simmered again, but there was only a thin wall of piss on the porcelain separating the current seated throng from a riot of maddened, maniacal hooligans.

'This man,' he pointed at Ferret, 'is a God.'

This didn't go down well. People began to scream and boo.

Bernard held out his hands and managed to quiet them again. He wore an immaculate suit and tie and his height, along with his impressive, educated voice, served to give him enough authority to do it. 'I didn't say he was *the* God, just *a* God. Think of him as a minor deity.'

'He punched a student in the face!' yelled out one fat, ugly woman from the midst of the crowd. Given their number, it was impossible to say which fat, ugly woman in particular.

A thin, toothless man with skin the colour of the Simpsons and squinty eyes added, ' 'n' he took the Lord's name in vain!'

This really got the crowd going.

'Alright. Granted,' replied Bernard, speaking loudly into the microphone, crushing, again the verbal dissent, 'but look at the good he has done.'

Shit, what good have I done? thought Ferret.

'What good has he done?' yelled out a young Christian male with a bandana that read: 'Jesus and me have an understanding'.

'You may not realise this, but Ferret Cutler, former dole recipient from Windsor, former drunk, former pub brawler . . .'

'I'm not sure I need your fucken' help, Bernie,' whispered Ferret.

' . . . has turned a new leaf. He has become a benevolent benefactor to the Hawkesbury.'

'How?' yelled out a small, bearded man with no hair.

'He intends to donate one hundred thousand dollars to this school . . .'

Do I? thought Ferret.

' . . . and make note, he has already donated money to various charities. Only the other day, Ferris donated fifty thousand dollars to help renovate the Windsor Brothel.'

'That's disgusting!' yelled out a woman who was so ugly that I refuse to describe her.

Ferret looked at her and did a double take. I know what's disgusting, he thought.

'Well, it was good enough for Mary Magdalene,' replied Bernard.

The crowd percolated again. Bernard turned to Ferret and shrugged. He sat down. There was going to be a riot. There seemed nothing surer.

Just then, right when it seemed all was lost, in the darkest hour of them all, when carnage seemed imminent, there came upon the stage a vision of beauty, in the form of Sue Hamilton, and seemingly floating behind her, like a man who walks on water because he knows where the stepping stones are, was Jason Garwood.

Sue did not need to speak. She simply smiled at the crowd and then at Jason. Then she ushered him to the microphone.

The hall was filled with instant silence. Those standing in anger, instead, sat in wonder as they gazed upon the legendary Garwood. He stood upon the stage, his glorious locks unfurled in exquisite and unruly splendour; his arms outstretched, his palms held skyward, his eyes shut in spiritual contemplation. The great stillness of his mind flooded the hall with omniscient love. And lo, Garwood's love flowed outward like a mighty river unfettered by banks. Christians kneeled and wept; normal people held their breath and Ferret scratched his cock 'coz it was itchy.

Thus, spake Garwood: 'Hear this, good people of the Hawkesbury. Exorcise the evil thoughts you have from your hearts. Hate not this flawed individual you see before you.' He pointed at Ferret. 'Let his harmartia be a warning to you all but also let his redemption be a shining beacon of his deliverance from evil. He has been a maverick; a stray from the herd; a little lamb who has gone astray but people,' he paused and the crowd's attention was as thick as the crust on an Envirocycle, 'he has come back to us. He has redeemed himself with good deeds and a fervent wish for his own self-improvement. He is, without doubt, the worst pupil I have ever had in my guitar tuition room . . .'

Thanks, thought Ferret.

' . . . but he refuses to give in. And, in his ludicrous enthusiasm; in his hopeless quest for quality; in his pathetic but enduring wish for improvement, can't we see a little of ourselves, good people?'

Christians nodded their heads throughout the hall so that from the stage it looked like soda pop bubbles popping upon the surface of a glass of cola.

'So I say unto you, verily, let this poor lamb be accepted back into the fold. Bring this sad and lonely pariah home. Wrap him in love, for it is only with love that any man will heal all men.'

Garwood took his seat to a thunderous ovation. Ferret sighed with trembling relief. Everything was going to be alright, thanks to Jason Garwood.

Up stood Saliva. He approached the microphone. In his hand he held downward what appeared to be a huge water pistol. 'Alright, listen up!' he yelled. His feminine voice and his tall spindly frame filled downstage. 'Call me Sally. I'm Ferris Cutler's good friend and I'm here to tell you that Garwood's good, for sure, but Ferret Cutler is flesh wrapped 'round a miracle. Remember, he has risen through the ranks of the education system from nothing to principal, in three days. He is moral perfection and intellectual integrity.'

'Settle down,' whispered Ferret.

'And you denounce him as once the Roman authorities denounced Jesus of Nazareth? I say unto you, you sinners, repent your evil ways and accept Ferret of Windsor as your true lord and the one true God!'

'I think you might be pushin' it a bit, Sal,' said Ferret, as he looked out across the increasingly angry, shifting sea of beards.

'Now, hang on,' whined Saliva, 'I said Garwood was really good.'

This did nothing to dampen the fire growing in the room.

'Sal,' whispered Ferret. 'Let it be. We were nearly home. You're stirrin' 'em up again.'

One lone voice from the Bilgewater Group screamed out: 'Poofters shouldn't be allowed to get married!'

And Saliva, incensed, replied: 'Yeah? Well fuck you!'

He raised his water pistol and aimed it high above

the crowd. In a few brief seconds he had pumped into the air a dozen rounds, evenly dispersed above the gathering. Each round exploded like a wet fireworks display and pheromone drizzle soaked everybody.

'Might I suggest,' said Saliva to Ferret, Bernard and the rest of the Official Party, as he quietly edged away from the microphone, 'that we all make an exit. He nodded towards backstage.

'Not before I speak,' stated Danza Slap, standing. He wasn't going to miss his opportunity for a few votes.

'Very well,' said Saliva. And he motioned towards the microphone, which Danza duly approached, coughing as he did so.

Saliva nodded his head in the direction of backstage again with some urgency. The Official Party responded quickly and soon was leaving the backstage area, as Danza settled himself before the crowd; a crowd that was twitching their nostrils and looking from one to the other in puzzlement. He was about to begin with a short introductory joke, something along the lines of: 'Well, I guess no matter whom you vote for, you get a politician,' when there was a stirring among the crowd. Bearded man looked in sudden surprise towards fat Windsor woman; fat Windsor woman looked with surprise towards shabbily dressed teacher and shabbily dressed teacher looked towards nearby attractive senior student in short skirt and knee high white socks when . . .

Years later the locals still talked about it in quiet corners. Sage intellectuals and streetwise thieves alike whispered of it in hushed tones.

The Penrith Women's Choir dived upon the Londonderry congregation of Latter Day Saints of Mother Mary Surgical Implants; the Year 7 boys ravaged the Year 11 SRC Representatives; the Science Staff, suddenly harmonious with the strains of Hallelujah, physically coupled with those who refused to listen to logic, in spite of the former's dedication to belief only in empirical evidence, and the teachers, aroused and unruly in their passion, made glorious and fulfilling love to the Support Staff, who regardless of their sexual orientation, moaned in orgasmal ecstasy as they tugged away mercilessly at engorged phalluses and licked wildly at throbbing vaginas. Heads and genitalia crashed erratically; bodices were stained and shirts torn away in an excess of libertine frenzy; bodies tumbled across the wanton landscape in unbridled chaos and Danza Slap kneeled upon the stage thumping a year 8 boy across the face with his old fella. 'Christian Carnage and Secular Shame' the local press called it later, but those who were there to witness it knew that it was much more than this. It was the day when those who believed in probable bullshit and those who believed in thinking, together joined and formed a common bond of humanity; a bond forged in the fire of a pheromone haze of love.

When the carnage subsided and the lovin' was done, several hundred bodies lay in wretched fulfilment, strewn across the school hall floor like a whole bunch of those really well-made sex dolls you can get from Japan or the U.S.A.

'Well,' said Saliva, as he listened to the thump and crunch slowly dwindle from inside the hall, 'the highest rate of pornographic downloads in America is in Utah. Come on, everyone, let's head over to the main quad. I've got a surprise for you, Ferris.'

As Ferret and his entourage made their way around the back of the hall and towards the main quad, a solitary figure, too small and inconsequential to have been noticed on the stage as a part of the Official party, limped gingerly behind them. He had been injured in a freak accident whilst getting off the plane, involving a bevy of heavily laden suitcases and a cargo forklift. Horatio, his little legs dragging beneath him like a skid mark down the bowl,

scaped his way across the school car park just as a car full
of Christians, who were running late, disembarked from
their well-documented, fish encrusted car, in front of him.

'That's him!' yelled one.

'Let's get 'im!' returned another.

'Hello, everyone,' beamed Horatio in salutation.

And they beat the living shit out of him.

Ferret entered the main quad and was amazed to see
a huge P.A. system suspended on the outside of the
gymnasium, a stage full of amps and five hundred seats
arranged in the quad.

'What's this?' he asked.

'If you build it, they will come,' replied Saliva with a
knowing grin.

And they did.

Christians and humans alike, in broken procession,
entered the quad, nursing their newfound guilt and
tattered genitalia. Within fifteen minutes the quad was
full.

'Ferret,' whispered Sue, as close into his ear as a scat
fiend on an arsehole, 'Horatio's been hurt. He has to go to
hospital.'

'No wuckers,' Ferret replied. 'He's a cunt anyway.'

'I love you,' replied Sue. She tried to finger his arse
but he resisted, being ambivalent about that particular
practice, in general, although he had experienced at least
one prostate orgasm and it was great . . . but that's another
story.

Felch, Rusty, Pierre, Bernard, Jason Garwood and the
invisible Jesus, who it turned out had been there the
whole time, took up their instruments.

'Where's me guitar?' Ferret asked.

'Just sing,' Bernard said.

'Use the force,' suggested Jason, adjusting his
distortion unit.

The ashamed crowd settled.

All eyes on Ferret.

'Students, teachers, supporting staff and local Windsor Christians. As a community we've come a long way in the course of this week. Together we've forged a mighty allegiance for the greater cause of the Hawkesbury. I know that I must leave yous now, for my destiny lies along another parfway, but I leave yous wif this; wif a song; a song that, in its magnitude, will reverberate fru the hallways 'n' corridors of history. 'n' I want yous all to know that I am gunna fuck the brains outta Miss Hamilton as soon as she'll let me. I'm gunna take it slow but fink of me in about two hours' time when I'm gunna be chockablock up 'a.'

Sue Hamilton smiled in wanton fashion back at our hero and swivelled on the spot with feminine allure.

No one in the crowd had the energy to respond, so they listened in exhausted unison as Ferret and the Pheromones played their latest single: 'Censorship is for Cunts.'

Episode Three

Ferret for P.M.

'And keep your fucken clothes on, ya randy cunts! You got no excuse! You're fucken landlocked!' Ferret screamed and the German crowd went wild. The stomping of feet for a third encore and the raucous cacophony was louder than a middle-aged man up a tight twenty year old.

Ferret, Bernard, Saliva and the Invisible Jesus left the stage for the final time in their whirlwind two-month 'Go Fuck Yourselves' world tour. Lucky Pierre, Felch Seaman and Rusty Trombone took the final accolades, along with Horatio, who collected a pair of women's undies in the face and ended up with a nose full of discharge.

'Well, that's it,' chirped Bernard, as they entered the change room. 'Ten million records sold in two months. Not a bad effort. And you didn't need to play a note, Ferris. Oh, and by the way, Germany's not landlocked.'

'You're a great front man, Fezzometre,' added Horatio as he cleared the off-white fluid from his nostrils. 'We sing well together.'

'You sing like Johnny Rotten, darling,' said Saliva to Horatio, 'and Ferris, you sound like, well . . . Ferris. But good.'

'Yeah, I just ain't no guitarist.'

'Don't worry, Fezzles. Garwood's magic will rub off on you one day.'

'Yeah? Well it'd better fucken' hurry up. I ain't getting' no younger.'

Saliva pushed past, threw himself onto a nearby sofa and grabbed a handful of chocolates. 'And was I right? Or was I right?' he chirruped. 'I was right. We didn't even have to use the pheromones.'

Ferret looked suddenly alarmed. 'Yous didn't tell the horn section, did yous?'

'Scouts' honour,' said Saliva, holding a chocolate wrapper to his heart.

Horatio and Bernard shook their heads.

'You're not just a little jealous of them are you, Ferris?' Saliva inquired with a glint of mischief in his eye.

'Why should I be jealous?'

'Well, we all know you've been a very good boy and you've saved yourself for pretty Sue Hamilton back home.'

'It's not 'coz of that, although me cock has been harder than tryin' to spell Kosciusko. It's 'coz it's our secret. And let me tell ya, that Fucken' Lucky Pierre ain't misnamed. I seen 'im doin' helicopters in the shower and the wind just about blew me off me fucken' feet. He don't need no pheromones. Neither do the others. All those poofters done alright wifout 'em.'

'I'm not gay,' remonstrated Felch as he entered the room.

'I wasn't talkin' about that, shit'ead. I was usin' it as a term of endearment.'

'But I'm not. Truly.'

'I believe ya but try tellin' that to the shemale you bonked in Detroit.'

'That was a woman. She just had a distended clitoris.'

'Which she distended up your arse, I believe.'

Before Felch could respond Saliva interjected. 'Oh come on, Felch. It's nothing to be ashamed of. These days it's celebrated. Back home in Sydney it's positively encouraged.' He stood up and did a little dance as he spoke. 'At the Mardi Gras thousands of people come to celebrate.'

'Yeah,' replied Ferret, 'dressed as fucken nurses and

cops they celebrate whackin' their old fellas up another man's arsehole. 'Look at me! Look at me! I regularly get shit on me old fella!'"

'Oh Ferret, you old fuddy-duddy. They're celebrating a lifestyle. Now don't be in a bad mood. You'll see Sue soon and you'll be happy again.'

'If she still loves me,' mumbled Ferret morosely. 'Two months is a long time to be away from a beautiful young woman. To make matters worse she's away wif her folks for a couple weeks over in Karratha.'

'Where the hell in Karratha?' asked Rusty, absent-mindedly polishing his trombone with his groin.

'Will you fucken' stop doin' that?' asked Ferret. 'We've talked about that, 'aven't we?'

Rusty put down the trombone and nodded solemnly.

'Karratha's not the arsehole of the world but it's close to the sphincter.'

'Red Dog territory,' added Felch.

'Run around in that dirt and you'd be fucken' red too.' Ferret grew pensive. 'I just hope Sue stays away from them miners.'

'Does she have a penchant for young boys?' asked Bernard.

'Not Minors, you dickhead – miners. Men who work in mines.'

'Oh, I see. Well, I shouldn't worry, old boy. She only has eyes for you.' Bernard clapped Ferret on the back. 'Cheer up, when we get home we'll all move into our new mansion in the Kurrajong Hills and we'll have a spiffing time of it. It's all set up apparently.'

'I ain't so sure about that,' muttered Ferret.

'Oh nonsense, Ferris,' Bernard assured him. 'You can't move back home into the middle of Windsor. You're famous now. You'd be swamped by admirers.'

'That's right, Ferry-Werry,' added Horatio, trying, with some difficulty, to remove a solid flake of greyish crust that had gravitated into his left eye. 'And I'll teach you to drive.'

'No fucken' thanks,' retorted Ferret. 'If I hop into a car wif you a telegraph pole'll jump out at us.'

Just then Lucky Pierre ran in. 'Oh my Got! My Got!' he bellowed. 'It was just on ze Sky News.'

'What is it?' everyone replied.

'The Commonwealth Government is going to build a by-pass right sru zat beautiful park in Windsor. Ze one next to ze Macquarie Arms 'otel.'

'But that's the oldest park in Australia. Built under Macquarie's rule,' said Saliva with his hand up to his mouth.

'Whatever happened to sacred fucken' sites?' muttered Ferret.

'That only applies to Aborigines,' Bernard replied.

'Yeah? Well we'll fucken see about that.'

'Ze rumour is zat ze government wants a bridge wiz more space between ze columns so it can dredge sand from furser up ze river. So it is a double catastrophe.'

'No,' Ferret replied thoughtfully. 'It's a triple catastrophe, 'coz puttin' the bridge through there'll kill off Blake's Tuition and River Music and if it kills off Blake's music, it kills off Jason Garwood's employment and let me tell ya boys, that ain't gunna happen.' He jumped up suddenly like a man on a mission. 'Come on. Let's phone ahead to have our private jet ready - the 767 with the private stage, the individual bedrooms, the personal Jacuzzis, the drop down joint rollers, the inbuilt cocaine arm rests and the Swedish girls' mud wrestling team - and let's get home.'

'What do you intend to do, Ferris?' asked Bernard.

'I'm gunna start by seein' the local member for Macquarie.'

And twenty hours later, they were landing at Mascot.

*

As it turned out, Ferret never did get to meet the local member for Macquarie but he did see her briefly on the six o'clock news the following evening. He was packing up his possessions, ready for the move up into the hills, when a story came on about a sudden by-election for the seat of Macquarie. Ferret stopped, mid underpants fold, and watched.

One announcer said: 'The standing member for the House of Representatives for the Hawkesbury area in Sydney's north-west has suddenly stood down from office. Edwina Crunt, member for Macquarie, has given a number of reasons for her snap decision.' Then the other newsreader took over because the first newsreader could apparently only manage two sentences: 'That's right, Serendipia. The forty seven year old Crunt has given a hurried and somewhat unusual potpourri of reasons for her decision.'

'She just fucken' said that!' Ferret yelled at the screen.

On that screen appeared a troubled looking woman who may well have recently been crying. 'It is with some regret that I am forced to stand down from my position,' she told the sensitively manipulated microphones jabbed into her upper lip, 'on the grounds that I have become too mentally unstable to carry on my duties and have subsequently neglected regular attendance in the lower house. I have also become bankrupt and as a result a petition of recall has been forwarded to me by many members of this great electorate and I am forced to resign my office.' After a barrage of noise from the press she held up her hands for calm. When it arrived she concluded: 'There is also some chance that I may become ennobled. A lesser-known royal from Lichtenstein has proposed marriage. This would further preclude me from office. I stand down with a heavy heart.'

'What the fuck?' yelped Ferret.

Back in the studio it was all squints and bafflement.

'Well Serendipia, that sounds just a tad confusing.'

'Ya think?' yelled Ferret.

'It certainly does, Hernandez. And with equal seats in the lower house shared by the Liberal and Labor parties, this is a vitally important by-election.'

'That's right, Serendipia. Whoever wins this seat will hold the balance of power in the House of Representatives. In other stories . . .'

With another expletive, Ferret turned off the set. But what did it mean? She was obviously a lying Crunt. She had listed every reason possible for betraying her office but why? Someone had pushed her. But who?

Ferret sat on his bed and thought. He thought and he thought. It took Ferret a long time to think but eventually, he stood up with inspiration, and finished packing.

*

The following morning was a cool but beautiful one. It was July and the early fog in Windsor and Richmond gave way to a clear sky as Ferret's taxi drove up above the haze and into the hills. The rest of his stuff was to follow in a van. He was too excited about his new idea to wait for it. He must tell his friends – especially since they were to be involved in his adventure.

He stepped out of the cab and looked, for the first time, at the enormous dwelling Saliva had purchased for them. At the end of a long, sinuous concrete driveway it sat overlooking the valley. It was a colonial style house – just one huge, rambling storey, encircled by a huge, low verandah, two steps up. It was a freshly cleaned sandstone beauty and to top it off there were horses in the paddock and fences as far as the eye could see.

'Fuck me,' muttered Ferret with surprise. Then he saw Saliva, Bernard and Horatio approaching. 'Fuck me,' he muttered again.

They were dressed as pirates.

'Aargh, avast, me lubber!' boomed Saliva.

'Aargh,' chimed in Bernard, unsheathing his sword and accidentally lopping off a part of Horatio's ear.

'Aarghoow,' belted out Horatio.

'What the fuck . . .' Ferret began, but he had no time to conclude before Saliva was upon him in a flurry of excitement and overtly feminine gesticulation.

'Oh my God!' he exclaimed. 'OMG. OMG. This is *so* exciting. Listen to this. And he began to rattle off: Serenely set against a picturesque mountain backdrop in an upmarket acreage estate, this sophisticated country style residence provides the perfect sanctuary for relaxed family living. Immersed in ...'

'Did you fucken' eat the manual?'

'We're all just so excited!'

'You're all just fucken' mad.'

'No it's alright, old boy,' Bernard interjected. 'Saliva explained it all to us and it makes perfect sense.'

'What?'

'The Tin Tin thing.'

'The..?'

'Look!' shouted Saliva with girlie glee. He pointed to a large sign above the front door, which read: Marlinspike Hall. 'It's just like I told you. Just like in Tin Tin. At the moment we haven't decided who'll be Captain Haddock but I think I should be. I think Bernard should be Jolyon Wagg, 'coz he's a real caution and with a bit of makeup Horatio could be Bianca Castafiore, the Milanese Nightingale. We'll have to buy a Milou, of course and Dirty Sanchez is to be Nestor, that's a given . . .'

'Dirty..?'

'Oh yes. He's already got the tea. See?'

Ferret looked over to one side of the house and there he was, Dirty Sanchez, in white tails, holding the silver service on a silver tray. Even at this distance he looked too greasy to be a servant.

'Oh Herge was such a genius!' Saliva sighed and swivelled on the spot.

'So who am I gunna be?' Ferret asked with half contempt, half interest.

'Why, silly boy,' yelped Saliva with delight, 'you're to be Tin Tin. Look – you've even got the little tuft of hair at the front and nothing behind. Oh isn't he adorable, boys?'

'Adorable,' echoed Bernard.

Horatio couldn't hear momentarily. He was trying to staunch the blood that spurted intermittently from his lower ear.

'Oh, it's going to be so exciting. We'll have adventures and . . .'

'So you want adventure, do yous?' Ferret interrupted with a sudden gusto of his own.

The three men nodded greedily. When Horatio nodded the bottom of his ear lobe fell off.

'Alright. Well fuck off those stupid pirate suits and come inside. I've got a proposal for yous.'

And ten minutes later they were seated inside a cool, tall room.

'Right. Now. Is everybody 'ere?'

'Jesus isn't,' Saliva replied. 'He's gone back into to the hills to see his friends and family.'

'How the fuck does he do that? Aren't they invisible too?'

'I can see him,' said Saliva.

Stay on track, Ferret thought to himself. 'Alright. Here it is . . . I intend to run for parliament.'

Silence.

'Did yous hear what I said?'

More silence.

'There's a by-election and I'm runnin' for Macquarie.'

Silence; followed by giggling; followed by minor chortling; followed by open guffawing; followed by back-slapping, voluminous hilarity and side-splitting, ground-rolling hysteria.

Ferret waited for the convulsions to cease before he said, 'What's so funny?' which began the process all over again. Bernard actually laughed so much he threw up on Horatio, who stopped laughing immediately.

'Alright. Alright. Knock it off!' shouted Ferret and normalcy was restored, though the occasional tear was swept from Saliva's eyes and Bernard sat for a good while with his head slightly lowered and his shoulders undulating silently up and down.

'Fucken' thanks for the vote of confidence,' said Ferret. 'What makes ya think I can't do it?'

Bernard answered that one. 'Not to be too unkind, Ferris, but you're a pugnacious, beer-swilling, hard-living, heavy swearing, western suburbs bogan.'

'Exactly,' countered Ferret. 'These are my people. They'll understand me.'

Bernard stopped smiling. 'You know, he may have a point. What do you think, Horatio?'

'No worries, the Bersun Burner,' he replied.

'Oh come now,' said Saliva, his laughter having subsided into concern. 'You can't be serious? You've got too many skeletons in the closet. They'll eat you alive.'

'I'll be honest.'

'Then you really *are* fucked.'

'No. I will. I'll tell 'em about everything except for the pheromones. I'll own up to the school bashin' incident and I'll admit that I've been a dole bludgin' loser but that I've made good and I wanna represent me fellow bogans.

What'd'ya think?'

Dirty Sanchez entered the room on the pretext of serving tea. 'Excuse me, Senor,' he whispered in his best obsequious Mexican voice. 'But I believe in you and I would like to 'elp – if possible?'

'There, ya see? A vote of confidence. Come on, boys. We can do this. You can be my campaign team. Saliva, you do the advertisin', Bernard you do the speech writin' and Horatio, you can be my bodyguard. I figure the only person who gets hurt when you're around is you. And Dirty, I may have a bit of dirty work for ya later on.'

'Oh, thank you, senor.'

Ferret paused for a moment. 'By the way, whatever happened to that floppy ranga, Pearl Necklace?'

'Alas, senor, It breaks my heart to say it but . . . .she died.'

'She died? How?'

'She ate pork.'

'I've eaten pork. How did that kill 'er?'

'When you eat a pig it is best to take more than one bite.'

'A variation on Mamma Cass,' added Bernard pensively.

'Ferret was about to ask more questions but he thought better of it. Instead he said, 'Okay. I have a plan.'

*

It was a week later. The writs had been issued. Ferret hadn't nominated yet but his campaign team was in full swing. Saliva was watching a rerun of Gilligan's Island, Dirty was skulking about the place without much purpose and Bernard was smiling and staring out of the window at Horatio who was kneeling beside what appeared to be some sort of ancient explosive device which he had found buried in the garden and which he was attempting to diffuse.

So far only the Liberal Party and The Labor Party had put up candidates for the vacant seat. That was predictable enough, but things were about to change.

Ferret said, 'Turn the channel would ya, Sal? I wanna watch the news.'

On it came. Ferret had missed the enticing bit at the beginning where the dynamic anchor-team duo foretells all the misery to come. He was greeted instead by a vision so awful and so surreal that he involuntarily dropped to his knees in front of the tele as he watched it.

It was a woman – kinda – holding a press conference. She was in a wheelchair; behind her stood several very serious-looking Japanese men in sunglasses. Her face bore a Frankensteinian checkerboard appearance, as though she had been pieced together by a mad butcher in a frenzied attack upon entropy. Her skin was multi-shaded; she had no hair at all, except for some thin wisps upon her chin; her bulk was gargantuan – had she appeared upon a beach she would have been put out to sea; she was a snarling, bitching advertisement for fast food; she was an angry aberration of a life form; she had steely, killer's eyes and perfect false teeth. She was speaking in a high-pitched, singsong honey-sweet voice that had to be put-on. When compared to the face it was too incongruous to be real. The strain of maintaining it was reddening her face and making even more pronounced the mottled continents drifting upon it. Ferret knew that face all too well. It was . . .

'Mumsy,' he whispered in disbelief.

'Yes, you're quite right,' she was saying to the bevy of press surrounding her, 'I am running for the seat of Macquarie because I want to represent all of the battlers out there in the Hawkesbury. As you can see, I myself have been physically disfigured and disabled ever since I was attacked and robbed by a group of school boys from an expensive private school. Apparently they needed the money.'

Sympathetic noises from the press.

'But I have forgiven them their trespasses for I am a good Christian woman, who also loves Muslims and embraces all world religions. I believe in tolerance and giving all battlers a fair go. If elected I will whole-heartedly represent the constituents of this great electorate and secure as many social security payment increases as possible, along with as many rises in the child welfare payments as I can achieve. I want a reduction on tobacco and alcohol taxes and I believe that every battler has a right not to work but to stay home and take money from the government. These battlers are the ones who contribute to our economy by spending all of their social welfare money. They, alas, have no disposable income. But they are none-the-less, the backbone of this great society and deserve cheap or free housing, free health care and a free education. I may be ugly to behold, ladies and gentlemen, but my heart is pure and beautiful.'

A few 'aaahs' from the female reporters.

'I am also one-eighth Aboriginal. I am descended from the Dharug people and feel great affinity with this - my land.'

'You're a fucken' Kiwi, ya fat cunt!' Ferret yelled at the screen as the story wrapped up. 'Fuck,' he muttered as he stood up and paced the floor. 'How do I fucken' counter that?'

'Something wrong, old boy?' asked Bernard.

'Fuck. Fuck,' Ferret repeated to himself and he continued pacing.

'Ferret, what's wrong?' asked Saliva.

'You remember I told you about Mumsy? Well the fucken' Yakuza must have some fucken' good surgeons is all I can say.'

'Did you say Mumsy, Ferris?' asked Bernard.

'Yeah. She's alive.'

'Excellent,' Bernard replied. He shouted through the window. 'Did you hear that, Horatio. Mumsy is alive!'

'Great!' Horatio shouted back.

'Alright,' said Ferret after some more perambulation. 'We'll nominate on the weekend. Bernard I need a shit-hot speech from you and Saliva get the campaign goin'. We begin our advertisin' campaign next week. Sue'll be back Saturday mornin'. If she stands beside me when I make the announcement she'll give me some cred. Boys, it's gunna be a tough battle. We'll have to stay focused and fit.'

Just then a tremendous explosion shook the foundations of the house.

'What the fuck was that?' blurted Ferret.

'Oh, it's okay,' replied Bernard, 'Horatio's just blown his leg off.'

*

The next morning, Ferret, resplendent in his 'Shakespeare was a Cunt' t-shirt, track pants and thongs, strutted into the Macquarie Electoral Office in High Street, Penrith. There was a solitary man behind the counter. Ferret approached. Ferret saw the man take quick inventory of him as he entered, so he was aware that the man knew he was there. The man was engaged in some paperwork and didn't look up again. Patiently, Ferret waited . . . and waited. After a few minutes he coughed. Still the man crouched over his paperwork and ignored him. Ferret coughed again. Finally, with a patronizing discharge of air from his lungs the man put down his pen in resignation and looked up.

'Yes?' he asked in a forerunner to the deep, pompous and manufactured voice that was to follow.

'I've come to nominate for the seat of Macquarie,'

Ferret responded, raising the edges of his lips in mock smile. The truth was he was very nervous and currently well out of his depth.

The man apparently thought so too, for he scanned Ferret up and down with his large nostrils twitching and flaring a little, as if contemplating a turd. He was a tall man, balding and big featured. He wore heavy-set glasses and Ferret thought that this counterbalance was the only thing that weighted down his nose sufficient to keep it from catching on the light fittings.

'The deposit is two thousand dollars,' stated the man, imperiously. He thought that that would be the end of proceedings but of course, he was wrong.

'There you go,' Ferret replied, and he dumped the cash on the table in front of the man. 'Sorry the last twenty bucks is in small change, but I miscounted when I left 'ome and had to scab it from a passersby. They recognized me, see, 'coz I'm in this band and . . .'

'I require a cheque,' the man replied curtly.

Ferret kept his cool. 'Most people prefer cash,' he retorted.

'Perhaps where you come from,' the man mumbled under his breath, just loud enough for Ferret to almost hear, but just quiet enough for him to be a little uncertain as to exactly what the man had said.

'What was that?' asked Ferret with a trace of aggression.

But the man ignored him. 'Are you an endorsed candidate?'

'eh?'

'Are you an endorsed candidate,' the man repeated with bureaucratic exasperation dripping from every syllable, 'or an Independent?'

'Oh,' Ferret replied. 'I'm an independent.'

'Show me the signatures.'

'eh?'

'Stop saying ''eh' and give me a copy of the one hundred signatures from legal voters in this constituency that you require if you are to run for office.'

'I never knew nuffin' 'bout that. But you can do me a favour and stop talking at me like I'm a dog.'

The man was unperturbed. In fact, he seemed to be enjoying Ferret's chagrin. 'I need a cheque for two thousand dollars,' he continued, 'a full disclosure of all donations made to you in the pursuance of your… attempt, and one hundred signatures from voters in this electorate before you can register.'

'But I never knew nuffin about it . . .'

'Yes, you've already said that.'

'And I can't drive, so I come by meself all the way from Kurrajong and it took two buses to get 'ere and . . .'

'Young man, my patience is wearing thin. If you do not know the rules I suggest you look up The Candidates Handbook. Here is a copy of the form you need for the minimum one hundred names, postal addresses and signatures of those endorsing you.'

With that he balanced himself once again upon the perilous point of his ballpoint and returned to the sedulous marking of his paperwork.

Ferret stood there for a moment or two, fuming. He imagined pulling the man's head down onto the pen like he saw Heath Ledger do once in a Batman movie, but instead, he controlled himself, and with the form, he left.

As he watched the Penrith Lakes pass by, he reflected upon the encounter and he realised something – the man was right. The man was a dickhead and a pencil pusher. He was a man who knew everything about nothing, but he was right. If Ferret wanted to contest this election, he would have to be more prepared.

So, he went to the pub.

'G'day, Steve.'

'G'Day, Ferret. When did ya get back?'

'Nearly a week. I been up in the hills plannin' me strategy. I'm runnin' for the by-election.'

'No shit? You still seein' that little filly I seen ya with a couple a month's back?'

'Sue? Yeah, she's back later on today as a matter of fact. I'm hopin' to see 'er too, if I can ever get this fucken' form signed for the fucken AEC or the EAC or whatever the fucken' thing is.'

'Whadaya need?'

'Right now, a hundred monikers from voters who say they endorse me.'

'Well, that shouldn't be too hard.' Steve shouted across the bar to the pool tables and the pokies. 'Eh Robbo, Billy, Cheryl, come 'n' sign this fucken' piece a paper!'

And they did. So did everyone else in the bar.

'That's twelve,' said Steve proudly. 'Come back later tonight and you'll get 'em easy. Frid'y night. There'll be heaps a people in.'

'Thanks anyway, mate, but I gotta get back there this arvo. I'm announcin' me candidacy to the press tomorra.'

'No shit?' said Steve. He thought for a second. 'I got an idea.'

At that moment, Steve's wife, Raylene, walked in. She looked a little sheepish to see Ferret. 'G'day,' she said and headed quickly past him.

Ferret shouted at her back, "Eh, Raylene!'

She stopped and turned. 'Yeah?'

'You still got that mole on the inside at the top of your leg?'

She screwed up her face like a surly schoolgirl, 'Ah fuck off, Ferret,' she said and disappeared around the corner.

Steve shouted after her, 'Hey! How's 'e know that?' He turned to Ferret. 'How'd you know that?'

'Settle down,' Ferret replied, laughing. 'I overheard her talkin' about it once. Relax.'

Steve shrugged. 'Oh well, fuck it anyway. She's had more mounts than Leister fucken' Piggott. Only difference is that Leister Piggott usually come first.'

She did for me, Ferret thought, but he said nothing.

'Listen, Ferret, back to my idea,' said Steve, real business-like. 'You're well known 'round these parts now. I reckon if ya just stood out the front and spruiked and told people what you were doin' you'd get those signatures easy.'

'Ya reckon?'

'No worries. I'd vote for ya.'

'Would ya?'

'No worries. A lot a people would, I reckon.'

'Gee, thanks, Steve. I might just do that.' Ferret got off his arse and headed for the front door and all the while he was thinking, 'Well, fuck me, Steve'd vote for me; would actually vote for me. What an honour. People would vote for me. Little Ferris Cutler – Windsor bludger.' He grew a little teary at the thought.

But as it turned out no one gave a rat's arse and he stood outside the pub wasting his time until he bribed eighty-eight people to sign the document.

Then he grabbed a cheque at the Commonwealth Bank and grabbed a bus back to Penrith to see his old mate behind the counter in Penrith Council and this time, he might not be quite so polite.

He wasn't.

'Here's your form, cunt. I got the signatures.'

The man opened his mouth to speak but no sound came out.

'I'm nominatin' for Macquarie, you condescendin', cock-sucking, arse lickin', festering cunt and if you say one fucken' word or look down your hairy fucken' nostrils at me again, I will kick you in the balls so fucken' hard you'll have to carry 'em round in an ice-bucket for a week! You'll have testicles for eyeballs!'

The man's hand trembled as he picked up the form and looked at it.

Somewhat hesitantly and with a slight stammer he replied, 'You need to fill out this other form. You need to disclose any person or establishment from whom you acquire funding.' He spoke quietly this time. He had lost all of his earlier bluster.

'I don't need it,' Ferret replied. 'I'm payin' for everyfink meself. I'm fucken' rich. Here's a cheque for two thousand dollars.'

The man took the cheque and looked at it.

'Let this be a lesson to you, baldy. I might look like a poor, useless loser and in some ways I am. But next time ya talk down your nose to someone who looks like me, remember this day, 'n' don't judge a book by its cover. Now deposit that fucken' cheque and register me name. I'm makin' a statement to the press tomorra morning.'

'I'll have it processed,' was all the man said.

*

When Sue arrived at her home in Carlingford in a shuttle bus from the airport later that evening, Ferret was already there. He wasn't sure what to expect but he was pleasantly surprised. She jumped out of the bus and wrapped her arms around him and when he told her he was running for Macquarie she doubled her intensity. She was so proud of him.

Needless to say, Ferret didn't need the pheromones that night. True love- making is a sacred act and certainly the intimate details of that night should not be publicly broadcast. However, it is fair to say that Ferret degraded Sue by making her dress up like a Japanese Elementary schoolgirl. He put her hair in pigtails and then he made her trowel makeup and lipstick on her face until she looked like a Roppongi hooker. Then he got her to bite his dick to point of pain while he fisted her. Then he fucked her up the arse and when he'd cum and couldn't get it up again straight away, he utilized a microphone stand for the intervening period while he recovered his stamina. Then he gave her the old two-fingered squirter and he followed that by pissing in her mouth and finally falling asleep with his nose in her twat.

But, as I say, these details are sacrosanct and will not be mentioned here.

*

The following morning there was a frenzied air of expectancy outside Blake's Music Tuition. On the steps, beside the main road, where Ferret chose to hold his press conference, stood Ferret in a tracksuit and beside him Sue, in a very becoming floral scarf and cream overcoat. It was a brisk morning. Horatio was rugged up and looked like an Ewok; Saliva wore a full-length trench coat that only reached his knees; Rusty and Felch turned up in sunglasses and cool rock star gear and froze their nuts off and Bernard wore a suit, as usual. He was also carrying a car horn of the early nineteenth century variety.

'What the fuck is that for and where did ya get it?' asked Ferret.

'In the marketplace and all will become clear,' Bernard replied cryptically.

And the press was at them.

'Mister Cutler,' began one pint-sized, ugly fat little fucker from Channel Ten, 'is it true that until fairly recently you were on the dole?'

Here we go, thought Ferret. 'Yes, that's quite true,' he replied, 'I, like you, and your fellow members of the media, was a parasite. I lived at the expense of others wifout adding anything to society. But I have changed.'

'How have you changed, Mister Cutler? I believe

that only a few months ago you illegally entered a school and assaulted a child. Is that true?'

'All true. Yes. I wanted to put something back into a society that has provided for me and in the process I was assaulted and publicly humiliated by a young man who got what he deserved.'

'Is it true that you made fun of the Christian faith at that time and was rude to Christians within the school?' asked an overly made-up woman from The Morning Show.

'Yeah, that's true.'

'Are you repentant?'

'No. Atheist.'

'A small, sweaty beer barrel of a bloke from Channel Seven asked, 'Is it true that you're in a punk band?'

'Yeah, I am.'

'Surely you don't expect the electorate to vote for a punk rocker?'

'Why not? They voted for Peter Parrot, or whatever his name was, from Midnight Boil and he can't sing neither.'

A woman in a head scarf from SBS asked, 'What are your policies?'

'Finally, a good question,' he replied. 'Thank (Hoot!) for that.'

Ferret turned to Bernard who had audio-censored him with the car horn.

'Don't worry, old boy.' He winked. 'I have you covered. If you're going to run for office, you can't swear publicly. It's against the law. Fire away.'

Ferret turned back to the microphones. 'Okay, here it is in a nutshell. Minimise censorship; make (Hoot! Hoot!) poker machines illegal; forbid any (Hoot! Hoot!) funding for (Hoot! Hoot!) private schools – if you wanna be (Hoot! Hoot!) elitist you can (Hoot! Hoot!) pay for it and so can the (Hoot! Hoot!) school; legalise mild hallucinogens; have a referendum to change the constitution so that dole recipients have to work sixteen hours a week community service to get it. I'm for euthanasia. I'm pro-abortion. I'm all about personal choice so long as you ain't (Hoot! Hoot!)'en up other people – your liberty ends where theirs begins and if ya come to our country you abide by our (Hoot! Hoot!)'en Laws and no (Hoot! Hoot!)'en exceptions. If ya don't, you get instantly deported. If you rape a woman you get thrown into a room with as many relatives or friends as she likes and they can't be charged wif nuffin' even if they (Hoot! Hoot! Hoot! Hoot!) ya up the (Hoot!). I wanna bring back public executions where there is absolutely no doubt of guilt but only after the killer has served a long jail sentence and I wanna save this beautiful park here across the road from being demolished unnecessarily.'

This stirred them up.

'Surely capital punishment is barbaric?' suggested one fiery red head. 'And it has proven not to be a deterrent.'

'It certainly deters *that* bloke but, don't it? And as far as barbaric goes - have some balls and draw a distinction between the initial act and retribution. The (Hoot!) who throws a girl in a (Hoot! Hoot!) dungeon for years and (Hoot!)s 'er mercilessly – now that's barbaric. Anyway, I ain't interested in deterrents or rehabilitation - I'm interested in justice. And before any of yous says any (Hoot! Hoot!) thing, in my world yous can forget about human (Hoot! Hoot!) rights in that situation. You intentionally (Hoot!) someone else up, your rights are forfeit. We don't need the people. If ya haven't noticed there's over seven thousand lots of a million people on this planet, folks, and the number's risin'. We can do wifout the scum.'

'In terms of private schools . . .' began the little fucker from earlier on, but Ferret held up his hand and stopped him cold.

'Listen,' he said. 'If I get elected I'll talk about all that shit later.' He turned to Bernard.

'Sorry. Missed that one.' Bernard smiled.

'In the meantime, I wanna draw your attention to the park behind yous.'

'Everyone turned, looked, and turned back.

'That park is the oldest park in Australia 'n' I'll be (Hoot!)ed if I'll stand by and see it destroyed. If it was an Aboriginal sacred site it'd be protected, so if elected I'm gunna oppose its destruction, hammer and tongs.' He yelled over his shoulder. 'Boys! Come out!'

Somewhat sheepishly four men came out of the doorway behind him. One was a medium-sized young man in his late twenties who had a guitar in his hand, was dark-haired and looked like every second presenter on television; the second was the owner of Blake's Tuition, a good-looking fellow in his thirties who carried a pen and booking pad; the third was a wiry haired man, also in his thirties who had recently had an operation to graft a bass guitar onto his upper-body and the last, was the mighty Jason Garwood himself. They stood on the steps behind Ferret and his entourage.

The members of the media where forced to avert their eyes temporarily while they adjusted to the effulgence emitted by Garwood.

'The men you see behind me, along with Peter Reynolds, of Reynold's Amp fame who works next door here in River Music, will be driven out of business if this new bridge is built. This can't happen. These men have dedicated their lives to teach the young people of the Hawkesbury how to play musical instruments. Their great work must continue. You can see the two guitarists Nick and Dave behind me, blinking. That is not only because of the light shed by Garwood but also because this is the first time in several years either of them has been allowed outside. And look at the owner, Mike. He carries his pen and booking pad everywhere. He is so poverty stricken that he can't afford a computer to record his bookings. We must protect our heritage.'

'Vote for Ferret and save the Windsor Bridge!' stated Garwood in a booming voice not unlike the deep, round, scary one they used to use in earlier ghost movies.

'Alright boys, you can go back in now,' said Ferret and the four men withdrew.

But the press gallery wasn't finished.

One thin piece of shit asked, 'Mister Cutler, what qualifications do you have to effectively govern this electorate?'

'I'm (Hoot! Hoot!)'en rich!' Ferret belted back at him. 'And if elected I'm pledging one thousand dollars to every member in this electorate enrolled to vote and there's about 90,000 of 'em. You do the maths. So if you're not enrolled yet, ya better get a move on.'

This really got them going. The pint-sized, ugly little fucker from Channel Ten happened to live in the Blue Mountains and he nearly shat himself. In fact, he did.

'That's a bribe!' yelled out one of the cameraman.

'Shut up! shouted the pint-sized, ugly little fucker from Channel Ten who had just shat himself.

But Ferret responded. 'It's not a bribe - it's a stimulus package for the economy. And finally,' he said, 'whatever you do don't vote for the other Independent candidate. She's a right (Hoot!).'

Even though the press was aroused and rampant, Ferret intended to end the interview right there. However, an unexpected and unwanted guest made a surprise visit.

'Speak of the Devil,' said Ferret.

It was Mumsy. She was in a wheelchair. A tattooed Japanese man in a suit and sunglasses pushed her through the media scrum.

'It's Mumsy,' Ferret whispered to Sue. 'They must've

put 'er back together somehow. But why would ya put somebody back together fat?'

'Who's Mumsy?' asked Sue.

'Mumsy!' cried Bernard.

'Mumsy!' cried Horatio.

And they both left the steps and hugged her.

'Get back 'ere, ya dickheads,' said Ferret.

'Boys!' she chirped in her fake falsetto voice.

As yet the media didn't know what to make of this, but they knew a story when they saw one unfolding and they weren't going anywhere.

'It's been so long. I missed you both so much,' cried Mumsy through her mock tears.

Bernard and Horatio blubbered like babies and Ferret was left standing there on the steps like a beer without a head.

When the hugs had finished, Mumsy's face grew pink with rage and she pointed an accusatory waggling finger in Ferret's direction. 'This man stole my money!' she bellowed.

All cameras back on Ferret.

'This woman tried to steal *my* money!'

All cameras back on Mumsy.

'He caused me to fall from the Kobe Tower!'

All cameras back on Ferret.

'She attacked her own men in a sexual frenzy!'

All cameras back on Mumsy.

'He has a magic potion that drives women wild!'

All cameras back on Ferret.

'Bullshit! She's connected to organised crime!'

'Bullshit! He's not even registered to vote!'

'Bullshit! I registered! She's not even from Australia! She's a Kiwi!'

'Bullshit! I got naturalised!'

'You should've got neutralised!'

'Get fucked!'

'No! You get fucked!'

'No! You!'

'No! You!'

Mumsy had dropped all pretense of her mock voice and now swung fully into her, 'Go and get fucked', Windsor voice – gruff and gravelly.

'I'll fucken' 'ave you, ya little cunt!' she screamed. And with that, she leapt out of her wheelchair. At the same moment, Ferret leapt from the steps. The two collided in midair and the thump and crunch could be heard as far as The Readers' Den, which is a bookshop that, like the Teachers' Federation, doesn't have an apostrophe. Unforgivable, really.

The media crews filmed the following interaction. The footage, with expletives 'beeped' out, was the lead news story later that night on every channel.

First, Mumsy bit Ferret on the ear. He screamed, fought off the attack and kicked her in the groin but got his foot stuck in her massive vagina. She moved towards him and his whole leg disappeared up there. Now Ferret was at a great disadvantage. He was hopping around with one leg completely up Mumsy and she was swinging wilding and punching him on both sides of the head. Sue tried to get involved but was held back by Felch but Rusty, who mistook Mumsy for a man, jumped into action, pulled down her stained witches' britches and started licking her arsehole. The tattooed Japanese guy waded in on Mumsy's side and started performing some weird martial arts shit on Rusty. He kicked Rusty's arse so hard that he completely lost his whole head up Mumsy's arse. Now Mumsy swung around in wide, frenzied circles with one leg in her cunt and a head up her arse. Everyone was screaming, except for Bernard and Horatio, who smiled affably throughout. Unfortunately, Horatio was too close to the fray and copped a stray punch in the throat, which closed up and he had to have an emergency tracheostomy on the spot. Finally, several of the braver journalists managed to break up the fight. Ferret's leg was eventually removed, but Rusty's head was a more delicate operation. So the whole circus moved to Hawkesbury Hospital where Rusty had to sit for two hours in Casualty with Mumsy on his head, six feet in the air calling everybody a 'Fucking Cunt!' When the doctor asked her what had happened she replied, 'What'd'ya think, you stupid cunt? It started off as a wart on me arse! Now get his fucken' melon outta there!'

And the journos all took off in helicopters.

When Rusty's head was finally extricated he had a sort of a brown tinge that he never really ever lost. Ferret reckoned he'd been permanently 'moon-tanned' and it must have infiltrated his immune system or his genetic structure or something because years later Rusty's kids were able to claim land rights down in the South Island of New Zealand.

Ferret and his gang finally made it back up into the hills by late afternoon to find Dirty Sanchez fucking a Shetland pony.

'Hey!' yelled Ferret. 'Get your cock out of there and come 'n' watch the news!'

Dirty yelled back, 'She doesn't mind, senor! Truly!'

'The pony's name is Billy, ya dickhead! It's a boy!'

'Oh no, senor! I am so embarrassed!'

'Just get up 'ere for Christ's sake!'

The news was predictably embarrassing for all involved and the anchor teams on every channel seemed caught somewhere between shaking their heads with the shame of it and biting their lips with laughter. Even the fact that the expletives had been beeped out somehow made the whole episode funnier, especially because even in the absence of swear words, it was completely obvious exactly what both Ferret and Mumsy were saying.

Ferret recorded as many snippets as he could

manage and at the end of it he said to Saliva, 'Right. Take all the bits where she swears and compile 'em. And take all the close ups of her fightin' where ya can't see me. Put the worst bits in a loop and I'll do a voice over for the T.V. ad. I'll record Lateline 'n' see what else I can get.'

But, unfortunately for Ferret, the commentary on that programme also homed in on the fistfight, highly ridiculing the two Independent candidates, but barely reporting a word about Ferret's political stance.

He had been upstaged.

'Fuck,' he muttered to himself. 'She's a smart cookie that one. She done that on purpose.' He walked around for a while considering his options. Finally, he said, 'Right the only way to get the message out among the people is to get out among the people. We'll fit out a car wif loudspeakers. It worked for The Blues Brothers. No, even better, we'll buy a Greyhound Bus. We'll drive the length and breadth of the electorate from Hume to The Hunter; from Chifley to Calare. We'll sock 'em in Singleton and Sackville; we'll blitz 'em in Bilpin and Bowen Mountain; we'll kill 'em in Kurrajong and Katoomba; we'll wow 'em in Woodford and Windsor. Folks,' he announced, 'we're hittin' the road. Now, can anybody drive a bus?'

Bernard said he could, though he'd never tried before and so by Monday morning they were ready roll. The bus was decked out with a dozen loudspeakers on the roof. Workmen had ripped out all but a few seats so Sue and Ferret could sit on the floor of the bus and plot their course with maps, and talk strategy, whilst Bernard more or less drove. Horatio was left at home, ostensibly to keep the fort, but really for his own safety. Saliva was hard at work editing the ads and Dirty was left to service the horses.

And off they went.

*

MONTAGE

Background music 'MILKIN' THE COW' by FERRET AND THE PHEROMONES

Ferret speaks into a microphone from inside the bus. People outside in the street turn to listen. Ferret gives them the thumbs up.

Sue smiling at people and handing out pamphlets.

CLOSE-UP of Ferret on the T.V. talking to a reporter. PAN BACK to reveal Mumsy sitting on a cushion of ice. We cannot hear her, but she is obviously screaming obscenities at the screen.

Ferret tries to kiss a baby, but it pisses on him. Ferret looks like he's about to hit the child, but Sue intervenes, and Ferret resists the temptation.

Mumsy in angry council with a conference table full of Yakuza. She looks far from happy.

Ferret knocks on a door and a guy who looks that guy in The Silence of the Lambs answers it. Ferret pisses off.

CLOSE UP of a man in a suit with a knife held to his neck. PULL BACK to reveal a tattooed man holding the knife and Mumsy hovering menacingly beside him. A poster in the background reads: The Liberal Party. We aren't Liberal at all.

Ferret addressing a public gathering. He is obviously swearing constantly and though we can't hear it, Bernard is standing beside him, smiling like an idiot and honking away on his car horn.

Ferret poses for photographs with a disabled Aboriginal Muslim girl with Leukemia.

A man in a suit holds his hands in the air. Mumsy holds a gun on him. Two Yakuza men stand menacingly behind. In the background a poster reads: The Labor Party - We spend beyond our means and the stingy Libs clean up.

DISSOLVE TO:

NEWSROOM

Good evening, even though you think you've seen me before, I'm actually the fifth female newsreader you've seen on this channel this week. We all have blonde hair and look the same. This just in - with only hours to go before the Macquarie Electorate goes to the polls in the by-election that will decide the balance of power in the Federal government – an incredible turn of events. Both Liberal and Labor candidates have stepped down, both citing ill health as the reason for their decision. At this late stage it is impossible for either party to enter another candidate, so it looks like an Independent will hold the balance of power come tomorrow night. We'll soon know whether that person will be Ferris Cutler or . . . (she pauses and squints at the teleprompt) Mumsy. (She shrugs) In other news sixty-eight million people died in a house fire in Pakistan this morning . . .

*

Saliva's television campaign was making quite an impression. Ferret had ploughed tens of millions into it and the main advertisement was shown in every primetime break on every commercial channel for the entire week leading up to the election. Ferret had become something of a celebrity because even though the ad was only applicable to, and aimed at, the electorate of Macquarie, still Saliva made sure that it was broadcast nationally.

It showed an angry Mumsy screaming, 'I'll fucken' 'ave you, ya little cunt!' jumping out of her wheelchair and attacking Ferret. The swearing was all beeped out, but the advertisement didn't lose its effect. This sequence was repeated behind Ferret as he addressed the camera and said: 'People of Australia, if elected to the House of Reps I will be a responsible member. Sorry I swear so much but I am a rock star. People of the Macquarie Electorate - Vote for me. I'll give each of you a thousand dollars if ya do.' Ferret didn't need to deride his opposition candidate - the background vision did that by itself. The ad trailed out with a Pheromone song about how poofters should be allowed to get married, which was currently charting, so Ferret figured that would assure him the young people's vote.

By contrast Mumsy's campaign was non-existent. She hadn't spent a cent. No one had heard from her, so the election result seemed a fait accompli. Until, late on the Friday night, on the eve of the election, there came a knock upon Ferret's door.

'Now who the fuck is that?' muttered Ferret as he went to answer it.

He had only pulled the door back a couple of centimetres when it was violently opened. Instinctively, he turned, and it hit him on the side of the head. He fell backwards onto the floor.

In the lounge room Sue screamed and Saliva stood

up. Bernard and Horatio kept watching 'Big Brother'. Dirty was out grooming the horses.

Three men with machine guns entered the hallway. They were all Japanese and they looked mean. With their guns they motioned everyone to sit. One henchman picked up Ferret, who was groggy, and threw him onto the lounge with the others. The men held their machine guns onto their captives as Mumsy rolled into the room behind them.

'Well well, fucken' well,' she said to Sue. 'What's a beautiful girl like you doin' hangin' out wif a loser like Ferret fucken' Cutler?'

'Is that your middle name?' asked Bernard, still watching his television show. 'You know, this show is so interesting. It's about a whole bunch of self-obsessed young people with absolutely nothing to say, talking about themselves and . . .

'Shut the fuck up, dick'ead.'

'Bernard turned around. 'Mumsy!' he squealed. But before he could stand up, one of the henchmen hit him on the back of the head with the butt of his gun and he was knocked out cold. He fell on Horatio and his weight pinned Horatio down onto the sofa, which suffocated and temporarily killed him.

'Fair dinkum that cunt wouldn't know it if 'is balls turned to butter.' She turned on Saliva. 'Who are you, ya tall cunt?'

'Absolutely nobody,' Saliva replied, with his hands still in the air.

'You're fucken' right,' Mumsy replied. She nodded to a guard who knocked him out. But as he hit Bernard the guard tripped and fell over hard on his face and knocked out a tooth.

'What the fuck are you doin', you clumsy fucken' Samurai? Get up!'

The man did, after he found his tooth.

'Now you,' she pointed at Sue. 'You're comin' wif me.'

One of the men grabbed Sue. She struggled but to no avail. 'Ferret!' she cried, but she was chloroformed and immediately out to it.

'Take 'er to the car,' Mumsy ordered. And the henchman obeyed. On the way out the door he tripped over and landed heavily onto the front porch. Fortunately for Sue she fell on top of him and not the other way around.

'What the fuck?' yelled Mumsy. 'I thought you fuckers were sure-footed and cat-like. You're fallin' over more often than a private school girl at the formal after-party.'

Ferret was still holding the side of his head and gradually returning to his senses. 'Wait,' he said quietly. 'What are ya doin'?'

'What does it look like I'm doin, fartface? I'm takin' a hostage to make sure you read this out on the news before the polls open tomorra mornin'.' She handed him a piece of paper, which he read.

'This says I'm withdrawin' from the contest.'

'Fucken' oath it does. And you are – unless ya want your pretty little friend to come back to ya in bite size pieces.'

'Look, what'd'ya want? Money? I'll give ya the fucken' money. Just don't hurt Sue.'

'Ooh. Sue, is it?' Mumsy replied, shifting her weight and holding her arse and wincing. 'Yeah, I seen 'er standin' beside ya on the tele and I thought ya might actually like this one. But no, Ferris, my boy, your fortune ain't enough to satisfy me no more. I got bigger fish t'fry.'

Ferret shook his head for clarity, 'What d'ya want?'

'Two fings,'she replied, 'One – I want the recipe to whatever the fuck it was that made me so randy I'd catapult meself off the Kobe Tower. The rights to that formula's gotta be worth the GDP of several countries; and two – I wanna win this by-election 'n' hold the balance of power in the government of this fine country of beer swillin' cunts.'

'You fucken' New Zealanders,' Ferret mumbled.

This seemed to rile Mumsy. 'Hey! Who bowled the fucken' underarm ball, you cunt!'

'Yeah yeah yeah.'

'Yeah yeah *fucken*' yeah! It was the fucken' Chappell boys, wasn't it?'

'Trevor bowled it. It was Greg's miscalculation. Let it go.'

'I will not let it fucken' go. Who was the greatest bowler from the southern hemisphere?'

'Thomo was the scariest, but it was either Lillee, McGrath or Warne. I know what you're gunna say.'

'Fucken' oath you know what I'm gunna fucken' say! Fuck Lillee up the arse wif a fucken' red-hot poker. It was fucken' Hadlee! *Sir* Richard Hadlee.'

'Bullshit!'

'Bullshit yourself.'

'We can't get knighted no more thanks to Gough Fucken Whitlam,' said Ferret. He held his head, and it was hurting horribly.

'Tell that to fucken' Tony Abbott.'

'Look what do ya fucken' want?'

'I told ya, schoolie-prawn dick, I want control of this country. You probably don't realise this, cockbreath, but this country's economy is pretty fucken' relevant in spite of the few people who live 'ere. These lucky fuckers have one of the largest capitalist economies in the world. Their fucken' total wealth is 6.4 trillion fucken' dollars! They own 1.7% of the world's economy! And that's wifout sellin' the uranium! Compared to that, your few billion bucks is chicken shit! I'm fucken' laughin'!'

'Are you fucken' mad? Who cares if you win the

seat? This is a democracy, ya fat cunt! They'll dissolve parliament if you win and fuck things up!'

Mumsy smiled. 'You know what, Ferris? You disappoint me. You just don't get the big picture, do ya? You've made some steps in the right direction, kid, but you still got a lot a growin' up t'do. Listen, peanut butter boy – less than a third of the world's governments are democracies. No one's gunna miss one more goin' AWOL. I got a shit load of organised crime money bettin' that I can swing this election 'n' when I do, it'll be - casinos you can smoke in, and trains that run on time. Face it, Ferris - you fuckers don't deserve this country. The Japs backed the wrong horse in the thirties but they're backin' me now. 'n' I'm gunna win this election 'n' turn this country around. So, you and the Chappells can go 'n' get fucked.'

Mumsy looked at the bodies slumped around the room. 'Look at 'em, Ferris,' she said, almost compassionately. 'You're hangin' about wif a tall poofta and two fucken' idiots. That pretty well sums up Australia.'

'I won't do it. I won't make the announcement. I'm fucken' runnin',' Ferret replied.

'Then you're gunna lose your girl 'n' it won't make no difference. I got this shit covered.'

Mumsy nodded and her henchmen withdrew, pointing their weapons at Ferret as they left. Mumsy rolled towards the door.

'Hey!' shouted Ferret.

Mumsy turned.

'There's a lot a decent people live in this country and I won't have ya fucken' it up for 'em. Not all of 'em are cunts like you 'n' me.'

'That's true,' she replied quietly, 'but in the end, money talks, don't it? Just ask the Yanks.'

And she was gone.

Ferret was about to phone the police but when he

tried to stand up, he couldn't manage it and he slumped back onto the couch. He had the worst headache he'd ever had in his life. It was even worse than the time he got pissed at the Tollgate in Parramatta and stacked his car and told his mum it got hit in the car park.

He thought he'd rest for a minute before he called the cops. He knew that in spite of his bravado, he was going to have to withdraw from the contest. He couldn't let Sue be murdered and he figured he could press charges against Mumsy later on when he got Sue back. Mumsy was obviously insane. The police would see that. There was no way she could get away with it. But he had to get Sue back first.

Unfortunately for Ferret he blanked out and didn't wake up until the next morning at ten o'clock. The polls were already open and the by-election was underway.

'Fuck!' he screamed as he looked at his watch. He grabbed a set of car keys, grabbed Bernard and reeled him out the door.

'Slow down,' said Ferret as they passed the Kurmond Public School Polling Booth. Ferret quickly scanned the crowd approaching the polling booth. As they turned up there were two people handing out 'How to Vote' cards: one was an employee of his; the other was a very angry looking Japanese man in sunglasses. 'Quick,' he ordered Bernard, 'swing past the North Richmond Booth.' They did and the story was the same. 'Now the Grose Vale Booth.' Once again, his man was there but so too was an angry looking, heavily tattooed Japanese man.

''Shit!' muttered Ferret.

'Everything alright, old man?' asked Bernard.

'They've got a man at every booth.' Ferret was more or less talking to himself. 'There's sixty-three polling booths in this electorate. I know - I had to pay sixty-three blokes to hand out 'How to Vote' cards. But that means that Mumsy's got at least sixty-three Yakuza workin' for 'er in this electorate alone. Fuck! How many's she got in the country? She might have a fucken' army. This could be an invasion!'

'At the time of the Rome, Berlin, Tokyo Axis the Japanese had a Blueprint for the Greater South-East Asia. Australia was to become part of their empire when they won the war but . . .'

'Will you shut the fuck up! I'm tryin' to think. Besides it's not the Japanese military, it's organised crime comin' in. We can do wifout that.'

'Wait 'ere!' said Ferret. He hopped out of the car and approached the Japanese man who was standing, momentarily, by himself.

The man attempted a smile and handed Ferret a piece of paper. Ferret looked at it. It read: 'Vote for Mumsy. You have a right not to work and be paid for it.' Ferret scrunched up the card. The man dropped his pretense of a smile.

'Hey, fuckface, what's your name?'

'Why you ask?' the man replied with an accompanying angry, suspicious squint.

''cos I got a message for Mumsy.'

'My name is Yamato,' he replied.

'Well, Yamato, you tell 'er this. I never intended to run today. I never woke up in time, thanks to that thump on the noggin'. Tell 'er if I win, I'll stand down after the poll. Just don't hurt the girl. Ya got it?'

Yamato sneered and grabbed for a mobile phone. He walked away from Ferret and had a conversation. Every so often he would look over at him. Eventually, he returned. 'Mumsy say you have 'til tomorrow. If you go to porice, she die. If you say anything to anyone, she die. If you win erection, you make excuse. You stand down.'

'I'll give you a fucken' erection if anyfing happens to . . .'

Yamato drew up close to Ferret and whispered with

menace, 'I repeat one more time for you, stupid man.' He stared into Ferret's eyes and emphasized every syllable. 'If you go to porice, she die. If you say anything to anyone, she die. If you win erection, you make excuse. You stand down. Girl be okay.'

'She fucken' better be.'

'Or what you do?' asked the man with a smug smirk.

'I'll shove a bento box up your arse!'

'I rike to see you tly.'

'I'll see you again, Shintaro,' replied Ferret dismissively. He jumped back into his car and Bernard took off.

Yamato gritted his teeth as he watched the car disappear down the long road and he imagined awful deaths for the scrawny little upstart: deaths that he himself would enjoy inflicting.

*

All that afternoon, Ferret was in a cold sweat. He had to wait for the election result before he could resign his position. On the one hand he hoped he would lose. That saved Sue and it was less embarrassing. But on the other that would mean Mumsy holding the balance of power in Australian politics with a view to corrupting the system.

Now it was nearing 8.30 pm. Ferret's friends and band members were all gathered together in the new house. Rusty and Felch were upstairs practising and Dirty was whacking off to one of the newsreaders.

The winner of the count was becoming clear. In reality, the winner had been clear for some time. It was informal votes, followed by donkey votes, followed by people who didn't bother voting at all. Many seemed to prefer being fined to wasting their time at the polling booths with an invidious choice. Of the two thirds, or sixty thousand people in the electorate who did bother voting, the vast majority wrote messages on the ballot paper like: 'We are not too happy with the candidates' and 'Would you kindly leave us alone?' but not exactly in those words. Of the few thousand votes that counted, Ferret easily won the majority. It didn't hurt that he got the donkey votes.

'Well done, Ferris,' Bernard congratulated him.

'Yes, good one, as ferris you go.'

Ferret hesitated. 'What did ya call me?'

'As ferris you go. That's what the man says at the fair when you get off the Ferris wheel. That's as ferris you go. Get it?'

'You're fucken' jokin'?' Ferret mumbled to himself and looked askance at Horatio. 'How can we be related?' He sat down and tapped anxiously on the coffee table. 'Now I gotta stand up and tell everyone I've wasted all that time and money. It's probably some sort of offence but I have to get Sue back in one piece.'

Saliva was standing by the front door peeking through the curtains. 'OMG!' he blurted. 'There's a lot of reporters outside. Ooh look. There's a pretty one.'

Dirty raced over with his lubricated cock still in his hand. 'Where, senor?' he asked in a wide-eyed Latin frenzy. He was disappointed when it turned out to be a strapping young lad of about twenty but then he shrugged, said, 'Oh well,' applied more lubricant and returned to pummeling his nodger.

'Dirty, could you put that fucken' thing away? You're gunna sprain it, for fuck's sake,' Ferret said, but his thoughts were totally occupied elsewhere. He was really dreading the announcement he knew he had to make. As far as he knew no one had ever won an election and immediately resigned. But those reporters were freezing out there and probably getting angrier by the minute and he had to save his girl. He kept imagining her suffering. 'Stuff it,' he decided, 'I'm not gunna wait 'til tomorra. I'll do it now.'

He opened the door. The blitz of photoflashes was blinding and the noise was tumultuous. He walked straight out into it and stood there for a good minute before the reporters shut up.

'Alright! Alright!' He quelled the noise with his hands in the air but the flashes kept coming for some time. 'I got an announcement to make!'

'How do you feel about winning the by-election?' asked the same little ugly fat fuck from Channel Ten who was at Ferret's first press conference.

'Oh, it's you again,' Ferret remarked. 'Doin' the night shift, 'eh? Try not to shit yourself this time.'

'Mister Cutler what do you think about . . .' began some other clown.

'Hang on! Hang on, will yous? I got somefin' else to announce. Somefin' important.'

Bernard grabbed his car horn.

'And I won't be needin' that either, Bernard.'

'But Ferris . . .'

'Nah, it won't be necessary. I looked it up. Ya get a maximum fine of about two hundred and fifty bucks for swearin' in public and offending the average citizen. I dunno if that's per word or by incident but either way, I don't fucken' care.'

Murmurs from the reporters.

'This is too fucken' important.'

More murmurs.

'Far too fucken' important.'

Murmurs.

'Will you stop fucken' murmurin'?'

'Good. Now. I know many of yous feel that I'm not fucken' fit to govern this electorate. And t'be fair to yous I ain't too fucken' sure about it meself. So that's why, as hard as it is for me to say it, I gotta say this . . .'

A voice rose up from behind the pack of reporters; a voice so angelic and sublime that it seemed to Ferret the world stopped for a moment, did a quick double-take, went back to spinning, stopped again and decided that the planet Venus right next door was indeed the most glorious thing in the Solar System, in spite of the fact that it has a retrograde motion, because that voice was (yes, you guessed it) the voice of Sue Hamilton. She was unscarred and as beautiful as ever. The reporters, who by now were getting used to it, parted like the Sea of Reeds for Moses and let Sue through.

'Ferret!' she cried. She threw her arms around him and wept.

'But how did you escape,' he whispered into her ear.

'Jesus saved me,' she replied.

'Hallelujah,' responded one doughy-eyed imbecile from the Telegraph.

'No, no,' Sue clarified. 'The invisible Jesus.'

'I understand,' replied the imbecile.

'Ferret's drummer.'

'We all march to his drum. Life is a miracle.'

'Fair dinkum,' Ferret replied, 'in the unlikely event that you cunts turn out to be right, I am gunna be so pissed off.'

'Jesus!' Saliva screamed and ran onto the porch. As far as the contingency of reporters was concerned, he embraced thin air and began hugging and kissing it. Then he started talking to it. 'What do you mean you were here the whole time? (pause) Well that was a mean trick. (pause) Oh, I see, you saw what was going to happen. (pause) Really. (pause) Really? And that was you? (pause) Oh, you are a cherub.'

'Who are you talking to?' asked a poker-faced, ashen-haired, spindly man with an American accent and broken veins in his nose.

'Ssh,' replied the doughy-eyed imbecile from the Telegraph, 'he's talking to Jesus.'

'It's alright everyone,' replied Saliva, 'everything's

under control. Jesus just told me that he tripped up a couple of Yakuza guys last night and jumped into their car and rescued Sue when she was kidnapped.'

The guy with the American accent shook his head in disbelief and said, 'Jesus talking to people. People being kidnapped. Swearing. What sort of a show are you runnin' here, Cutler? I'd like to have some faith in the newly elected member for Macquarie.'

The rest of the media pack agreed, and it took a while for Ferret to talk over them again. But finally, he said, 'I have a grave announcement to make!'

The reporters were listening. Ferret was standing very much a heroic figure beneath the outside porch light. The media's camera lights gave a stark solemnity to the occasion. There was a sense that a great patriotic speech was coming. Rusty and Felch, who had finished practising, grabbed their instruments once again and began to play the Star Spangled Banner behind Ferret, but they soon realised that it should be Advance Australia Fair, which they played, until everyone booed it down, on account of it being a shit tune. Finally, they settled for Waltzing Matilda and Ferret began.

'My fellow Australians - I stand before you, humbled and proud: humbled because I've been elected to public office and proud because Sue says my dick is bigger than her last boyfriend's, who dumped her. So if you're listen' dickwad - get a fucken' Easter Egg up ya! I swear that I will be a good representative of the people and since I have a casting vote in a hung Lower House, I intend to use my vote wisely in order to make it a well-hung Lower House. But my fellow Australians, I have dire news to impart. A grave and present danger lurks even now within our most cherished society and if it hadn't been for the love of Jesus and his strong left hook, that danger could have made it into that most holy of holies, the very parliament, the very government of this fair democracy. I think you would agree, good people, that in a world full of fuckwits we are less fuckwittish than many, especially those cunts who run around screamin' every time a fucken' bomb goes off. This, the very fabric of our society, is clandestinely being threatened right now. The enemy is wifin the walls, ladies and gentlemen. We are up against a formidable foe. For it is not the aforementioned fuckwits who threaten our status quo, but instead, a group of people who are in most ways superior to us. I am referring to – the Japanese! (pause) More specifically - Japanese organised crime! (pause) More specifically – the Yakuza! (pause) You can murmur now.'

Murmurs.

'Yes. That's right - a crime syndicate from Japan has infiltrated our country and is seeking to overthrow our democracy! And that syndicate is led by none other than my opposition candidate in this by-election – Mumsy!'

'These are slanderous allegations, Mister Cutler. I hope you can support them!' yelled out the guy who shat himself the first time but hasn't so far this time.

'Slanderous indeed!' came a thunderous voice from immediately behind him.

He shat himself.

Once again the scrum parted to reveal Mumsy. Behind her were half a dozen minders. She thrust forward through the reporters and stood in front of Ferret. 'And he *can't* substantiate 'em,' she whispered to him, 'can ya cockbreath?'

'Are you gunna turn up every time I make a speech, fatso?'

'Yous see?' Mumsy wheeled on the reporters. 'He can't prove nuffin'! Look at 'im people – look at 'is stupid little tuft of hair and 'is ferrety little fucked up face; look at his raggedy old jeans 'n' 'is Deep Purple t-shirt 'n' his stinkin' worn down fongs. 'e's a loser! 'e's a loser and 'e's a liar!

The ugly Channel Ten fat fuck whose stench had afforded him a lot of room down near the front yelled out, 'He just beat you in an election!'

Nice one, thought Ferret.

'Oh, so you like this turkey, do ya? Well what about the fact that 'es I liar? I can prove that!' She produced a document from her pocket and waved it in the air. 'This piece a paper proves that this man is not fit to be a member of your parliament. I introduce Carmel Milkshake, the Governor General of Australia.'

A stately, well-presented woman of middle age walked through the crowd and up onto the porch. She appeared to be greatly saddened.

'What are you up to?' Ferret whispered into Mumsy's ear.

'You're gunna love this one, ferret features,' she whispered back. To Carmel she said, 'Tell them the bad news, Ms Milkshake.'

Carmel took the document with trembling hand and held it up: 'I declare Ferret Cutler's election to the House of Representatives null and void. He has been imprisoned by the crown for a period of over one year for assault and theft and can therefore not be elected to office in this country.'

'I cite the precedent of 'Sue Versus Hill' in 1998 where the winnin' candidate was disqualified from office 'coz of a prior criminal record,' added Mumsy. 'In that instance the candidate comin' second was awarded the position. Old Ferret here served over a year in prison, so 'es disqualified 'n' I 'umbly accept my rightful position in the House of Representatives.'

The media pack gasped in unison and the photoflashes lighted the porch. The press launched into a thousand questions but before the Governor General could reply, a contingent of Japanese men escorted her away.

'That's not true!' screamed Ferret.

'Who are you gunna believe?' countered Mumsy, 'this loser, or the Governor General of Australia?'

'This is bullshit!' roared Ferret. 'It's just like I was sayin', we're bein' invaded!'

But those in the media pack not swarming around the Governor General's limousine were more interested in Mumsy's version of events than Ferris'. She'd handed around multiple copies of the document, which the journos clutched with glee. Most of them ran immediately for their cars grabbing at their precious IPhones. Before long, the only people left were Mumsy, Ferret and their retinues.

'It's not true is it, Ferret?' asked Sue. She blinked her crystal blue eyes, tilted her head to one side with the question and her dark wavy hair hung around her face like a glorious frame around a masterpiece.

'No. I swear to ya, Sue,' Ferret replied with a searching expression etched deep upon his face. He needed her to believe him. 'It's a lie.'

'Okay,' she replied, and she touched his cheek.

'Tell 'er it's a lie, you warthog.'

'Don't sweat it, spunkbubble,' replied Mumsy with a smile, '"course it's a lie. But Ferris, you gotta understand somefin' - I got so many people in me pocket, I could start a war if I emptied it.'

'You ain't getting' away wif this.'

'Oh, ain't I? Let me tell you somefin', short arse - the Yakuza spent millions and millions of yen to restore me into the beauty you see before you today. Now that's commitment. You saw what I looked like after that Kobe Tower fall. I was in more pieces than Buddy Rich's Big Band. They didn't invest that money for nuffin', kid. You're right, this is a fucken' invasion; it's an invasion by stealth. We'd been plannin' to infiltrate this fucken' hillbilly country for a decade. While you cunts've been watchin' the towel heads blowin' the fuck out of themselves and everybody else, I've been in the wings mastermindin' this whole takeover. They knew wifout me it wouldn't 'appen.'

'So you're the brains, Mumsy?' Bernard chipped in with a beaming smile.

'Fantastic,' echoed Horatio.

Yamato, who was standing nearby, punched Horatio in the face.

'As a matter of fact I am,' replied Mumsy proudly. 'You know fellas, people are interestin'. Some of 'em have no moral fibre at all. All you gotta do is bribe them blokes, 'n' trust e, that's a big proportion of 'em. Then there's people who need convincin'. You throw these blokes a few monetary bones and you justify their decision for 'em so they can justify it for 'emselves, 'n' ya got them. But then there's the troublesome lot, by far the minority, who actually hold to moral principles. These are the difficult bastards - but you know how you get 'em? You get 'em when they realise that the problem is bigger than any fucken' solution that might be possible. And when it dawns on 'em that you could fuck up their lives by, say, killin' their kids, or torturin' their wives, they pretty fucken' quickly get back into line. You know what I'm sayin, don'tcha, Ferret?' She grew dark, 'I'm tellin' ya, boy, 'n' I mean this - you're not gunna get in my way, 'n' if ya try, I'm gunna bring down such a planet of pain on you you'll wish your eyes had never seen the light a day.'

'You want me to kill them?' asked Yamato. He was staring directly at Ferret as he spoke. Ferret was aware that he was fingering some sort of weapon in his jacket.

'Not yet,' Mumsy replied. 'It'd create too much suspicion. Besides, I got what I want - for now. But let me remind you, bean dick, I'll be comin' back for that formula 'n' I suggest ya give it to me; ya can't watch your girl and your mates twenty-four seven.' She adjusted her bra and her right tit knocked out Horatio. 'Now, if you'll excuse me, me 'n' me boys need to catch a plane for Canberra. Parliament's sittin' tomorra. Ya might be interested to listen in, Ferret. It should be interestin.'

She turned and clomped away, lumbering from side to side like an ocean liner struggling through a heavy sea.

'You get any sleep last night, Saliva?' asked Ferret.

'You know I did. I was knocked out cold for most of it. I still have a low grade headache – thanks for asking.'

'Good. 'coz you 'n' me are gunna pull 'n' all-nighter. The rest of yous get some sleep. We're goin' to Canberra on the Greyhound at first light. Bernard, you're drivin'. Dirty, Rusty, Pierre 'n' Felch I got some work for yous. I'll tell yous tomorra. Jesus, I want you to stay behind and mind the fort. If anybody comes snoopin' around in our absence, you can fuck wif 'em. Sue, you ain't leavin' my side, darlin'.'

Ferret put his arm around his girl, and he guided her inside, but he stopped for a moment on the porch, now silent and juxtaposed with all the feverish activity of just moments ago. And he thought. Thinking was practice, he figured, 'coz he was definitely getting better at it. He thought, and he saw that these desperate times required desperate measures, but he wondered, silently to himself, whether the measures he had planned were desperate enough.

As he thought, he fiddled absent-mindedly with the Dictaphone that was still running in his top pocket.

*

It was almost two pm by the time the Greyhound pulled up in the car park outside Parliament House.

'Right,' said Ferret. He was in operations mode. 'Dirty, Felch, Pierre and Rusty, you know what to do. Give me three to five minutes.'

The three men nodded and dashed from the bus.

Ferret put on a pair of gloves and took a single sheet of paper out of a briefcase. He took a deep breath. 'The rest of yous, come wif me.'

Ferret and his friends approached Parliament House and at first no one challenged them.

'Cutbacks,' explained Bernard. 'The AFP were patrolling the perimeter but the contract ran out, you see. Now the DPS has hired other people as a cost cutting measure. Apparently we have nothing to fear from terrorists.'

'That's what they think,' Ferret replied.

It was only after they got right to the edge of the building that a very big man, with big hands, a big chest and probably a big schlong, showed up. He was speaking into a walkie-talkie as he approached them.

'State your business please, sir.'

'My name's Ferret Cutler and I'm here to take my seat in the House of Representatives.'

The man looked at his list. 'You don't appear to be on here, sir,' he replied.

'I got an important speech to make in the house.' He held up his single piece of paper. 'See?'

'I'll have to check, Mister Cutler. Wait here please.'

The guard was about to re-enter the building when he heard music. He looked out over the lawn and there, on the edge of it, was the strangest sight. A horn section comprising of three men, one playing the trombone, one playing the trumpet and one playing the saxophone, had struck up and a fourth man was dancing wildly around them. They were all naked. The man on the trombone began licking the arse of the trumpet player who responded by yelling out: 'I'm not gay!' while the third musician played a jazz version of Le Marseillaise on the saxophone. The fourth man dived frenetically about the lawn, rolling and cavorting like an epileptic on speed. He had an enormous hard on which he began rubbing on each of the musician's faces in time to the French National Anthem.

A crowd of Chinese elementary students was taking photographs. Their teacher was explaining to them that Australians are allowed great individual freedom. And they were certainly impressed.

'What the fuck,' the guard muttered and without a second's hesitation he ran in the direction of the demented horn section, raving into his walkie-talkie as he ran. Within seconds three other guards had raced past Ferret and the others in pursuit of the four naked men.

'Let's go,' said Ferret.

Once inside the building, the others went up to the viewing gallery. Ferret adjusted his flannelette shirt and smoothed back his tuft of hair. He adjusted his best denim jeans, momentarily felt the comfort of his brand new Ugg Boots and finally, tightened his gloves.

He entered the chamber and had a quick look around. The viewing gallery was full of Japanese men in suits and quite a large press contingent. Mumsy was up on her feet at the front of the house, about to make her maiden speech to the other one hundred and forty nine members. They were all there. Most of them were sober. The speech was being televised.

The Serjeant-at-Arms saw him and immediately approached. She carried the ceremonial mace. 'You can't come in here, sir,' she said.

'I hope you ain't gunna hit me with that,' he whispered to her and then in a very loud voice he announced, 'My name's Ferris Cutler and I've come to take me rightful place as member for Macquarie!'

The house erupted on cue and the speaker called for order.

When it was restored, he said, 'Mister Cutler. This is most irregular. You have no seat here. Your case is before the courts, I believe?'

'That's right 'n' I'm innocent until proven guilty.'

'The Governor General tells me that she is certain of your guilt, Mister Cutler. She has seen all the documents; spoken to the prison to which you were assigned; she has even spoken to the parole board. They all concur. We have records, Mister Cutler, proving that you were incarcerated for a period of thirteen months less than two years ago. These are undeniable facts. You may have your day in court, Mister Cutler, but you will not have your day in parliament.' Nicely put, thought the Speaker to himself.

'And I can prove that all of those people were coerced or bribed into saying that. I can prove I wasn't in jail when you say I was. Just ask Steve down at the Imperial.'

'Mister Cutler, you're wasting our time.'

'Hear me out for thirty seconds and I'll go.'

'Give him thirty seconds!' yelled out one backbencher.

'Seconded!' yelled out another.

It was as good as a circus. The house thundered with laughter and there was a general cry of 'Give 'im a go. What's the harm?' Everyone had seen the television footage and they wondered if Ferret and Mumsy could top their previous performance.

'Make it snappy,' snapped the Speaker.

Mumsy, who was still standing at the front of the house, shouted, 'I object!'

'This is not a court. I will determine who speaks. Continue,' replied the Speaker.

Up in the viewing gallery sixty-three Japanese men looked at one another and shifted in their seats. They also cast dark looks towards Horatio who had pushed his way through to the front row. He was leaning over the balcony to get a closer look.

Ferret began, 'I know I don't have time to disprove

the claims against me right now. But I can prove my innocence in due course. I've come here today for one reason and that's to reveal a *real* criminal. She's used illegal means to obtain a position of power within this chamber. She is not of sound mind. For these two reasons she is unfit to hold office.'

This caused a predictable ruckus.

'Really!' Mumsy belted out. 'I might be a little bit rough around the edges, but do I appear to be insane?' She laughed raucously at the idea.

One hundred and forty-nine pairs of eyes looked at Mumsy and thought 'Well . . .'

The house grew unsettled again.

'This piece of paper proves it!' Ferret shouted over the din.

This shut them up.

'Crap!' yelled Mumsy. 'Let me see that!'

'Mind your language or you'll be removed,' the Speaker responded.

'Sorry, your highness.'

'Mister Speaker, will do.'

'Show me that paper!' Mumsy commanded. She held out her hand with imperious disdain.

'Approach the front of the chamber, Mister Cutler. Present the document.'

Ferret moved forward among the watching eyes. Some of the sitting members thought the whole episode was hilarious, others found it demeaning to the parliamentary process. The Japanese contingent in the viewing balcony whispered in hushed tones.

'That's my brother down there, you know?' said Bernard to one very angry looking man with a deep scar riven across his neck.

'Isn't it exciting?' said Saliva, clutching his hands to his chest.

Sue looked from Bernard and Saliva to the

surrounding Japanese faces. 'I think we should go downstairs,' she whispered into Bernard's ear.

'Righty-ho,' Bernard responded cheerily and the three of them left. They had to leave Horatio because he was too far away to reach. Sue looked back and saw him chatting away affably to the man beside him. The man looked like he had just got on a twenty-hour flight to find that the person in the next seat weighs two hundred kilos and has a squalling baby.

Ferret reached Mumsy.

'Now what's this rubbish?' she asked, snatching away the piece of paper from Ferret, mindful of her Japanese 'investors' in the gallery above and mindful of the importance of her part in this theatre, before the real business of undermining the Australian way of life could get underway. All she had to do was remove this last speck from her path and she was home. What could this slip of paper possibly say that could prove her insane? There was nothing.

There was nothing. There was nothing on the page Ferret had given her.

She laughed, 'There's nothing on it!' she announced to the gallery. She waved it at the press. She waved it at her Japanese entourage, and she waved it at the sitting members. 'He's handed me a blank piece of paper. Must be a list of your policies, scumbag.' She roared with laughter right into Ferret's face. And the members of the house, the press and the greatly relieved Yakuza, joined in the hilarity.

Ferret placed his Dictaphone, upon which he had recorded Mumsy's unwitting confession, onto the Speaker's table, turned and, as if defeated, walked from the chamber to the strains of derisive laughter.

But after a short while the general laughter died a natural death. Ferris Cutler was gone, probably never to be seen again and it was time to listen to the member for

Macquarie begin her parliamentary career with the usual platitudes - the parliamentary equivalent of the beauty queen's 'world peace'.

The members had settled. The press had settled. The Japanese men in suits had settled. But Mumsy hadn't. She stood, wide-eyed and manic, shifting her gaze across the parliamentary floor. At last, the only noise in the chamber was a low gurgling sound that had replaced laughter in the throat of the massive woman.

'The Speaker grew uneasy. 'The Honourable Member for Macquarie?' he asked.

But the Frankensteinian vision continued to laugh. The patchwork of continents that made up the planet of her face became engorged with blood. It was as if some giant cork had stopped up an enormous geyser that must surely blow soon. Her self-control was slipping, slipping. The veins struck out upon her forehead like a twelve-year-old boy's dick when his twenty-two-year-old teacher bends over him to check his spelling and he sees a nipple, other than his mother's, for the first time. She noted that the Member for Hume was a fine-looking lad and that the Member for Lindsay was as sexy as hell in his new suit. Even the female members in the house, and there weren't many, all looked pretty fucken' good.

Mumsy began to tremble: a little at first and then a lot. She looked like she had an earthquake and wasn't prepared to share it. She shook upon the spot so violently that the prime minister's water went over, and several frontbenchers lost their pens to the floor. She began frothing lightly at the mouth and a low guttural sound began to emanate from deep within her. She appeared to be vertically defibrillating.

'Are you alright?' asked the Speaker.

And all hell broke loose.

First, Mumsy catapulted herself at the leader of the opposition and stuffed him, screaming, into her swollen vagina. Half of his front bench followed. It was later revealed that they had a spot of lunch and even a quick round of golf whilst in there. Next, not to be biased, she attacked the government benches. She ate the prime minister – actually, she sucked his dick so hard that the rest of him followed. It was a bit of a pisser for the government really because he was doing really well in the polls. Then Mumsy howled like a Baskervillian hound, looked up at the press gallery, scaled the balcony and began rubbing her genitalia upon all things moving. It was the sexual equivalent of a high school massacre. Even the Yakuza cowered and ran. 'Godzirra! Godzirra!' screamed one young newbie but even as he screamed, he looked up and screamed again as the giant shadow fell upon him. He raised his hands up to his fearful face, but it was to no avail. The ravenous vagina had seized and ingested him. While Mumsy screeched and moaned and attacked and the outside world went mad, inside her they were having a bit of a shindig. It turned out that Joan, who was Minister for Agriculture, knew Peter, the son of the shadow minister for Foreign Affairs. Having been usurped by Mumsy's engorged vaginal orifice they decided to make a holiday of it. Over time they fell in love and had an affair, which didn't end well – but that's another story.

For now, imagine this: Mumsy takes the mace from the Serjeant-at-arms - rams it completely up her own fat arse. The ministers gathered in her interior have to dodge it as it enters her vagina. She runs about the chamber with the tail end of the mace sticking out of her arse, swinging around wildly and knocking parliamentarians out with it. Screaming with hysteria all the while, she taunts the security guards who are trying to stop her. She laughs as she jabs, almost playfully, at them. She crashes through the doorway and runs out into the front courtyard of Parliament House. Two backbenchers are still hanging out of her rectum. One holds onto the mace, but the other doesn't make it. He is sucked into the vortex of her tornado-like twat suction. Screaming, he elongates as one would if approaching a black hole too closely. His dying howls are finally diminished by the sound of the suction created by the wind of her vacuumous orifice (which is not a bad name for a band).

Blasting through the front door of parliament house she runs out onto the front lawn where a helicopter lands and men with bazookas and hand grenades order her to be still.

But she is incensed. In spite of the cries for her to stop, she advances. Two grenades are thrown towards her. These, she eats. The helicopter crew is attacked. One good looking young man of about twenty-five will later tell doctors that he still has nightmares about the day a fifty pound vagina opened before his very eyes and took him in like one of those face-suckers in the major motion picture, 'Alien'. Mumsy commandeers the helicopter and although she has never flown one before, she manages to get it airborne but unfortunately, she stacks it into a crowd of Christians who are gathered for 'Life is a Miracle' week. She escapes the wreckage and rages into the streets of Canberra. But there's no one there and everything is clean but it's really boring, so she pulls a few frontbenchers from her arse and she has a couple of drinks with them before she throws up in Lake Burly Griffin and is finally captured by the combined forces of the Federal Police and Fire Service. She is taken to the local police station but, having thrust so many individuals into her body, she is too big for the cell, so they put her in an enclosed paddock, and she shits backbenchers for the next week.

As for the Yakuza? Well, they went home in defeat after toppling Horatio off the balcony of the viewing area. All except for Yamato, who, white with silent fury, waited behind for Ferret and his retinue as they walked triumphantly from Parliament House - just like in scary movies where you think all the bad stuff's over, but it isn't 'coz there's one more shock scary bit before the end.

'Oh my God, I just thought I would die!' Saliva screeched as they left the building. 'Well done, Ferris. Reversing the pheromone potion and soaking it into that paper was a stroke of genius!'

'Yes,' replied Bernard, 'it was very humorous. Pity Horatio broke his back.'

'I s'pose we'd better get Pierre and the boys outta jail,' said Ferret.

'I'm so proud of you,' whispered Sue, clinging to his arm and surreptitiously putting her finger up his arse.

Yamato stepped into their path like they do in one of those Clint Eastwood spaghetti westerns. 'Where you go?' he said.

Saliva replied, 'I was thinking pizza. What about you, Bernard? Anyone?'

'Shut up, stupid girly-man!' Yamato spat out with contempt.

'Oh, don't give me that girly-man bullshit. I've seen Jap porn.'

'You!' he screamed at Ferret. 'You have destroyed everything we plan for rast decade! Now you die!' He pulled out a nunchaka.

'Very clever,' said Ferret, 'wood and string – straight through the metal detectors.'

'Straight through your head!' replied Yamato, shedding his jacket and adopting a combative stance.

'Why don't ya drop them fings 'n' see if ya can beat me in a fair fight?' said Ferret.'

Yamato smiled evilly, 'It will be preasure,' he replied. He dropped his weapon. 'I called **Muramasa Sengo by my fliends.'**

'Yeah, well I say you're a pillow biter. Stand back,' Ferret said to the others, taking off his shirt. 'I'm gunna flatten this cunt.' To Yamato he said, 'Let me show ya how we do things in the Hawkesbury, shit'ead.'

Ferret came out with both fists blazing, but Yamato easily sidestepped him. Ferret came at him again. This time with more control. He attempted a quick jab or two, both missed. Then he went for a typical street fighter's round arm swing. That was his undoing. Within a second Yamato had hammered a rapid-fire barrage of direct punches to Ferret's face. He went down like a female Penrith sixth grader.

Yamato smiled as he watched Ferret get up upon his elbow. He was groggy and his mouth was bleeding. Sue attended him.

'You soft cock,' he taunted. 'Rook, your woman make you better.' He laughed and looked at Saliva. 'What about you, Girly-man? Tly your luck?'

'Don't look at me, pretty boy. I abhor violence - unless it's sexual, of course.'

He took stock of Bernard. 'What about you, big man? Or don't you have any honour?' Yamato was sure that Bernard would cower away, in spite of his bulk, but to his surprise Bernard said, 'Oh, what the hell. Why not? I'll give it a whirl.' And he took off his jacket. 'Marquis of Queensbury rules?' He struck a nineteenth century boxing pose.

Now Yamato was a strong man and a skilled fighter, but he was slight in build, and he wasn't much taller than Ferret. Bernard was ursine – six foot six and built like an Amish barn. So, when Yamato approached Bernard, who smiled back at him like an idiot on a village wall, and struck at the big man several times, he found only impenetrable arms. He tried again but with the same result. He was about to attempt a third volley when Bernard, quick as a flash, hit him with a pile driver: a straight left to the face. Years later Yamato would tell his children of the man-bear who showed him the galaxy.

Yamato saw stars. He knew no more.

'That was fun,' Bernard chortled as he looked down upon the deathly still body. 'Pity old Horatio didn't see it.'

The guards came running over and although Sue tried to explain, Bernard and Ferret were taken to the local police station where they caught up with Pierre and the others.

Eventually, they were all released.

Yamato was taken to hospital. He recovered but he never pressed charges.

A little less than a week later while Saliva was arguing with Jesus; while Bernard and Horatio were attempting to clean out the gutters above the concrete courtyard; while Dirty tended the horses; while the horn section practised and while Ferret was getting a head job from Sue, the phone rang.

Ferret answered. 'Yeah? (pause) You're kiddin'? (pause) Beauty. No worries.' He zipped up his fly and shouted, 'Hey! You lot! Come 'ere. I got somfin' to tell yous.'

Within minutes everyone was assembled.

'Great news! I've been reinstated to parliament!'

There was great joy at this. Sue gave him a kiss, but it tasted funny.

'They went through the Dictaphone and they followed a few leads and they believe me. Like I told yous I was never in jail. This calls for a drink. Let's go the Imperial.'

So they did.

'So what's in the capsule?' Steve asked as Ferret settled in for his first ale.

'What? In this thing?' asked Ferret as he patted the small cylinder he had placed on the bar. 'Oh, just a few bits 'n' pieces.'

'Like what?'

'A couple a pheromone wipes, the recipe for 'em and

a small booklet outlinin' me ideas for a Utopian society.'

'A what?'

'A perfect world. You know? I've outlined all me ideas, like the ones I told the press, plus heaps more. I've called it: The Book of Ferret. I've even added a dictionary of Windsor Speak and me own version of the Ten Commandments. *And* it's been touched by Garwood.'

'Fuck! What are ya gunna do with it?'

'I'm gunna bury it out the back of your pub, if that's okay?'

'Go for your life. I'd be honoured.'

'Thanks, Steve. That's a nice fing t'say.' Ferret looked at the capsule. 'Yeah, I'm takin' me ideas to the House a Reps but I don't reckon they'll take me too seriously. I guess I'm just ahead of me time.'

'Could be,' replied Steve.

'Maybe someday,' said Ferret wistfully, staring for a moment or two at the time capsule. 'Oh, and did I tell ya I'm getting' cryogenically frozen? Me 'n' me mates. It's fucken' expensive.'

'Yeah? Why?'

'I dunno. I wouldn't mind havin' another go, I suppose. I wonder if I'd make the same mistakes again?'

'I reckon you done real well, Ferret. I'm proud of ya.'

'Thanks again, Steve. But I gotta ask ya, did ya ever use the money I gave ya to get out of the Hawkesbury and have a look at the world?'

'Nah, I didn't, but before ya say anything, we've had a bit of an unexpected setback. Well, it's not really a setback.'

'What? Everyfin' okay?'

'Oh yeah. She's sweet. Nuffin' like that. It's just that, you wouldn't believe it, but Raylene's pregnant.'

Ferret was caught mid swill and he coughed up beer everywhere. It even went up his nose.

'Yeah, I was surprised too,' Steve replied with a

smile. 'I 'aven't fucked 'er for two years. Anyway, off ya go. Bury your hidden treasure. There's a shovel out the back.'

So Ferret buried his time capsule deep in the backyard of the Imperial Hotel in Windsor, where it remained for many years.

The Pheromones toured without Ferret for the next three years. He made a few guest appearances but he was too busy in parliament to do much more. And as it turned out, Ferret was right - his ideas did fall largely on deaf ears. No one seemed to have a taste for public hangings, even if it would help by removing some of the filth from the community. He couldn't work out whether he was behind the times or ahead of the times. Eventually he consoled himself by thinking that they were pretty well the same thing. And even though he had a powerful position in the Reps, the Senate was hostile and he wasn't about to cause a double dissolution. He figured he'd caused enough trouble already. So he worked hard and he did what he could for the Hawkesbury. He tried hard to get the bridge stopped and to save the park but in the end he lost. He figured Mumsy was right about that one – money talks and as for corruption? Well, who knows?

Saliva and Jesus got married in New Zealand, 'coz they don't have limitations on love over there. They're happily arguing to this day. Dirty, Felch, Rusty and Pierre merrily humped their away around the world several times over. Felch wasn't gay on many occasions and Dirty became the group's manager. He said he enjoyed sorting through the shit. Bernard and Horatio were as happy as two poofs in a soccer change room and they were ever so proud of Ferret. Horatio was run over by a high-speed train whilst touring in France, but he was fine. Sue and Ferret were married that summer. Steve and Raylene had a little boy they called Oscar. His first words were, 'Get fucked cunt!' and Steve was mighty proud. Ferret swore that he'd always see Oscar right and he ploughed a small fortune into the Imperial to help out Steve and Raylene.

Ferret was leaving the pub early one summer evening, but before he left he gave everyone a pheromone wipe. 'I got a trick for yous,' he said with a wink. 'It's a hot night. When I count to three apply the wipe to your neck. It's very refreshin'. One. Two. Three. See yous.'

Ferret smiled to himself as he walked down George Street, Windsor. He remembered three years ago, or more, when he'd stumbled in the gutter after picking a fight with Steve. God, was that over three years ago? It was. It was the night before he met his brothers. So much had changed in that time and yet so much had remained the same. He was a happier man now. He had a lovely wife and some good friends and . . .

But his thoughts were interrupted and he stopped to listen.

By Christ they were makin' a lotta noise up at the Imperial.

Episode Four

The Water Wars

'Get your fucken' hand of me Jatz crackers!' yelped Ferret. 'What the fuck do you think you're doin'?'

'Sorry, my Lord,' replied the man who had manipulated Ferret's testicles. He was small and thin, had a gaunt face, beady eyes and a strained, high-pitched voice. He was wearing black jeans and a black Led Zeppelin T-shirt. He backed away into a group of other men. 'I was inquisitive.'

'Yeah, well your arse'll be inquisitive if you touch 'em again,' replied Ferret. He looked around. 'Where am I?'

'You're home,' replied another man. He was small and thin, had a gaunt face and a strained high-pitched voice. He was wearing black jeans and a black Led Zeppelin T-shirt.

Ferret was still fuzzy in the head. He sat up. 'Fuck me,' he croaked. 'I'm in Windsor Hospital.'

'It's good to have you back, my Lord,' said another man. He was small and thin, had a gaunt face and a strained high-pitched voice. He was wearing black jeans and a black Led Zeppelin T-shirt. 'Based on the Scriptures.'

Ferret stood up. 'Scriptures? What Scriptures? What the fuck are you talkin' about?'

Instantly the men bowed.

'And what the fuck are you callin' me 'my Lord' for? 'I 'ain't nobody's Lord.'

'Only the true Messiah denies his own authenticity,' commented one man who was small and thin, had a gaunt face and a strained high-pitched voice and was wearing black jeans and a black Led Zeppelin T-shirt to the man beside him who was small and thin, had a gaunt face and a strained high-pitched voice. He was wearing black jeans and a black Led Zeppelin T-shirt.

Ferret shook his head and cleared the muck out of his eyes. He looked upon the gathering of perhaps a dozen men, all wearing black jeans and black Led Zeppelin T-shirts and then into a mirror that hung on the wall beside his bed. He was small and thin, had a gaunt face and a strained high-pitched voice and was wearing black jeans and a black Led Zeppelin T-shirt.

'Shit!' he exclaimed as he remembered that these were the clothes that he had been wearing when he had been cryogenically frozen. 'It worked. I've come back to life. Hey. How come all you blokes are dressed just like me?'

'We are your disciples, oh Lord.'

With this, all the men began to prostrate themselves and chant solemnly, 'Praise be to He, the Lord Ferret, for He is the only true God. Praise be to He, the Lord Ferret, for He is the light, for He is the only true God.'

'Sounds like another bloke I've heard of. Sure you blokes ain't mixed up?'

'Oh no, my Lord. We extirpated your capsule . . .'

'Sounds painful.'

'. . . and found that you were right. In this world of wild antithetic chaos, we realised that you were right.'

'Anti – what?'

'You are the saviour.'

'What am I savin' you from?'

'Political Correctness and the drought!'

'Have you blokes been wandering through the herb garden or somefin'? Get off the fucking floor and answer me some questions!'

The men obeyed.

What year is it?'

'2050,' replied another of the men who was small

and thin and . . .'

'Seventeen years,' mused Ferret, pulling at his jeans, which had crawled up his arse. 'What happened?'

'One of us found your time capsule and your scriptures and your writings,' said the man who was small and thin, had a gaunt face and a strained high-pitched voice, wearing black jeans and a black Led Zeppelin T-shirt, who had said earlier, 'We are your disciples, oh Lord.'

Ferret stopped him with a wave of his hands. 'Hold on, mate. I'm not your fucking Lord. Ok?''

The man immediately dropped to his knees and yelped in extravagant falsetto, 'Oh do not smite me, Holy One.'

'Get up, dickhead,' replied Ferret. 'I 'ain't smitin' no-one. When I was frozen things were goin' to shit. Sydney was still tryin' to recover from the economic cost of the 2020 fires and then the last thing I remember was an uprising in the city.'

'That was 2033 – the year The Great PC Cull began,' said a man who was small and thin, had a gaunt face and a strained high-pitched voice, wearing black jeans and a black Led Zeppelin T-shirt, who hadn't said anything before.

'Did Australia recover? 'Cos the right wingers were dying like female stand-ups when they tucked me to bed.'

'It turned out, that apart from the brainwashed Millennials, most people were secretly politically *incorrect* but were too afraid to say so. So the politicians rounded up and shot the free thinkers and libertines who opposed high censorship,' replied the same guy who hadn't said anything before, again.

'They killed nearly everyone who wasn't politically correct,' added the first guy who was looking at Ferret's balls at the intro. 'Only a few of us unenlightened, intolerant individuals survived. And our balls have shrivelled to nothing since the Great Tolerant Culls of the 30s. We believe it was a literal manifestation based upon a metaphor. That's why I was admiring your Jatz crackers at the intro.'

'Did they get the Abos?'

'Yes. It turns out they weren't politically correct. They were just in it for the fringe benefits. They do keep a few for special occasions.'

'Please tell me it got the Muzzos?'

'No,' replied a man who was small and thin, had a gaunt face and a strained high-pitched voice, wearing black jeans and a black Led Zeppelin T-shirt, who hadn't said anything yet either, 'They were defended by the PCs, because they dominated their women and didn't believe in homosexuality, which suited most of the Christian politicians.'

'For the women it was a case of conflicting ideologies,' added another. 'The PC women had to decide which they loved more: feminism or censorship and mistreatment of women. In the end they decided that censoring everything was more important than women's rights. They convinced themselves that having their clitorises hacked off and wearing a hessian cloth in public wasn't blatant socialisation and male domination, but was what Muslim women wanted, so they justified it as women's rights, and they went with the Muzzos.'

'Fuck!' bellowed Ferret.

'Not only that, but religious groups were largely spared the cull because they were no threat to the PCs. They and their forefathers hadn't thought for centuries, so the PCs figured they weren't going to start now. Besides, many of the PCs are religious. I guess those two stupidities go hand in hand.'

'Fuck!' bellowed Ferret.

'But that's not the worst of it. What with climate change and the drought . . .'

'Oh yeah,' Ferret interrupted. 'What happened with that? Was it bullshit or what?'

'No,' continued the man, 'it was real. The Earth's temperature rose by four degrees in less time than was expected. Parts of Sydney are underwater, including the airport, so we're very isolated. It's the same in many major capital cities across the world. Chaos reigns.'

'Not only that,' added another man who looked identical to everyone else, except that he had glasses, 'but the constant fires and the drought have divided the city dwellers from the country folk even more. The city dwellers won't allow back burning because the smoke makes them cough in winter, so the country folk have to put up with endless fires and damage to the destruction of many of their homes both in Summer when fires never stop and all through winter as well.'

'Hold on. Slow down,' mused Ferret. 'Let me get this straight. Sydney is isolated, smoky, partly underwater and ruled by a bunch of cunts?'

'Yes, my Lord,' interjected a man who (take it as read) was small and thin, had a gaunt face etcetera. 'And that's without the water war.'

'Water war?' Ferret parroted.

'Yes, my Lord. Because of the drought, water is scarce and it's become the new currency. The City dwellers are dependent on the weather because no state government had ever had the foresight to insist that all city dwellings had water tanks. But out here in the outer west and in the country we have tanks and access to the old water truck outlets. Sometimes the city dwellers attack us and we have to protect our stocks.'

'Sydney has become a violent city, divided into several camps: the PCs in the CBD - they control the military and uphold Political Correctness with an iron fist – they call themselves The Tolerant Ones and kill anyone who disagrees with them; many of them are also

Christians; they claim they don't have opinions, they know the facts, but everyone else has opinions; the Jehovah's Witnesses have allied with the Pentecostals, who have a small enclave at Bowen Mountain; the Muzzos - have seized Parramatta and the South West – they are great water wasters but welcomed, none the less, by the PCs because they control Warragamba Dam and therefore Sydney's main water supply; there are some inbred Orthodox Jews in the Eastern Suburbs and then there's us - the Ball-less Atheists and our allies, the Angry Icers in Richmond and Windsor. They are paid with Ice to guard the precious river water and water outlets for us. But a drought is once again upon us and our rivers and tanks are running dry. The Tolerant Ones will happily let us die of thirst. They know our time is limited. We have no balls, so we can't reproduce. But the PCs are breeding like rabbits. So, it's a PC future, I'm afraid.'

'God, help us,' muttered Ferret. 'That's a shitload of exposition.'

With this, all the men who were small and thin, had gaunt faces and strained high-pitched voices, were wearing black jeans and a black Led Zeppelin T-shirts, bowed low.

'Hang on. Hang on,' replied Ferret, quietening the rabble with his downward palms. 'The way you're behavin' 'ain't exactly atheistic.'

'We were atheists, until we found your capsule, my Lord, but now we have found you, we have finally something to believe in; something tangible, returned from the grave. Please tell us what to do.'

'Well the first thing yous can do is stop callin' me your Lord. And the second thing is - stick to your guns. For fuck's sake! You were atheists before and yous were spared, so I'd stay on that horse if I was you. How many fucken' times do you hear about Mosques buryin' people alive? Or gunmen runnin' riot in churches? I'd say that's pretty clear evidence there 'ain't no loving God worth a fuck and if he does exist at all, he's a right cunt. Now stop grovellin' and explain what happened.'

'We found your Scriptures and realised that you were the truth, the light and the way.'

'That's a load of shit,' retorted Ferret. 'And if ya keep sayin' shit like that I'll make yous all drink Kool Aid.

'Only the true Messiah denies his authenticity!' chanted the men.

'Please save us from the tyranny of this tolerant world. We shall take you to the Church Bar where The Doctor lives.'

This was said by the man who was small and thin, had a gaunt face and a strained high-pitched voice, wearing black jeans and a black Led Zeppelin T-shirt, who said earlier. . . Listen – although when I started writing this, it seemed like a funny idea to have all of these characters looking identical, I think you would have to agree that it's already becoming a pain in the arse. So, if you don't mind, I might change that, so everyone looks different. If that's okay? But I'd rather not rewrite the first couple of pages, and it was kinda funny for a little bit there – did you think? Maybe not. Anyway, if it's okay with you guys I'll just keep going from here and these other characters will all look different in scene two. Look, thinking about it, it doesn't really matter because these guys in the Led Zeppelin T-shirts are only in the next scene, then they're gone. But even so it'll add a bit more colour to scene two if they don't all look and sound the same. Thanks for understanding . . . Oh, there is just one more thing. Sorry about this. I forgot to put in one detail about the men who were small and thin, had gaunt faces, strained high-pitched voices and were all wearing black jeans and black Led Zeppelin T-shirts. Each of them had shaved and cut their hair so that they were bald, except for a small tuft of yellow hair at the front. And if you were one of the few people who read the first Ferret book, you'll know that Ferret has that same shock of hair. So, rather than going back and adding that, which is really boring for me, I thought I might just tell you that now. Not that it really matters because, as I said before, these characters are only in the book for one more scene . . . unless of course . . . no, I won't bother saying it . . . Oh, fuck it, yes I will. Sorry to take up so much narrative time. I know it's unprofessional to be so visible in the narrative, but listen . . . I might change my mind and have them come back later. It is always possible, you know, because I make this shit up as I go along and, as you can probably tell, I don't edit much, except to correct typos. So, let's take all that as read and get on with the story. Shall we? Cheers. Sorry.

'Let's get outta here,' replied Ferret.

*

'One thing,' asked Ferret as he was led out of the hospital by the men, 'if you guys survived, then that means there must be some anti-PC survivors all over the world.'

'We don't know,' replied one of the men who had a beautiful mellifluous voice, dark, swarthy looks and sported a bright green Kaftan.

'We have no access to the technology,' added the man beside him. He had a fake tan and was completely naked, except for flippers. 'And The Tolerant Ones censor everything.'

'This may even be a purely Australian phenomenon. Although many world governments were headed in the same direction in the 10s and 20s,' interjected another man who wore a light summer frock, emerald earrings and black fishnet stockings.

'Don't let Saliva catch you in that rigout pal,' said

Ferret, 'or he'll be up you quicker than a wog concretes his yard.'

'Another thing,' continued a seven-foot-tall black man in a jester's costume, 'This may even be a purely Australian phenomenon.'

'He just said that,' retorted a spastic midget.

'You're just jealous because his dick is bigger than you,' suggested a box of tissues that had already been opened.

'Enough!' yelled Ferret. 'This is fucken' stupid and it's not advancing the story. So yous can all piss off.'

And they did. And they never came back. Probably.

*

Ferret walked cautiously down the main street of Windsor. It appeared to be deserted. He turned up a side street and came upon a small, shabby building. Years of neglect had defiled it. The courtyard was filthy and there was rubbish scattered everywhere. It sported a sign proclaiming it: The Church Bar.

'I'm not sure whether that sounds welcoming or not,' he mumbled. 'Jesus. These Icers 'ain't too keen on house keepin'.'

Ferret had mumbled to himself, but his comment received a response.

'Pssst,' whispered a voice from the interior of the building.

Ferret was alarmed. 'Who's there?'

'Quickly. Come inside. It's not safe,' replied the voice.

Ferret did a quick scan and saw nothing but decided that the voice sounded educated, so he entered.

When Ferret's eyes adjusted to the sudden gloom, he saw a small man, wearing taped up spectacles. He wore a white coat and had a stethoscope around his neck.

Judging by his facial creases Ferret reckoned him to be at least seventy.

'Sorry to alarm you, Mister Cutler.'

'Who are you?'

'I am Doctor Campbell, the man replied. 'I unfroze you. Call me Doc. How do you do?'

Ferret shook his hand. 'Well until yesterday . . . I mean, until seventeen years ago I was doin' alright; right up until the PC Revolution. Now I find out I'm a fucken' Messiah in a PC world full of Icers, Muzzos and assorted shitheads.'

'Alas, true, Mr Cutler. Shall we?' He began walking down a foetid corridor and Ferret followed. 'The world has gone quite mad, you see.' Doctor Campbell opened a trapdoor and he and Ferret descended into the clean sterility of an operating room. 'Here are my living quarters and my operating room,' he explained. 'My hide-out, if you prefer.'

The two men sat down at a bare wooden table on two wooden chairs in the old man's austere living area. 'Now, what do you wish to know?' he asked.

So, Ferret repeated what he had heard.

'I see,' said the Doc, thoughtfully adjusting his permanently askew glasses. 'That is basically right, but I'm afraid there are two or three other salient points to be ma de.'

'More fucken' exposition,' mumbled Ferret.

'You see,' he hesitated, 'before I reanimated you, I had already brought two others back to life.'

'Two others?'

'Yes. One young male and a rather revolting older woman I found alongside you in the cryogenic chamber beneath Hawkesbury Hospital. I reanimated them about a year ago. After their aggression I was reluctant to reanimate you.'

'Do you know who they were?'

'I have no idea. I was hoping that you could tell me.'

'As far as I remember I was frozen alone. I paid for a few of me mates to be frozen too but when the time come, things were such a rush, I dunno what happened to 'em. The last thing I remember is me lawyer bustin' into me mansion mumblin' somefin' about freezin' me and some bloke wif a syringe pokin' me in the arse. I dunno who the other two characters in the hospital were. Did they say anything?'

'Sort of. As soon as they came to life the young boy punched me, and the rather flaccid women told me to . . . um, 'Fuck off, cunt', I believe were the words she used. Then they left. Together.'

'Them silly Zeppelin disciple fuckers told me they found me capsule. Have you got it?'

'Yes. It's here.' And he produced the time capsule that Ferret had buried at the back of Steve's pub, just in case there was a sequel. 'But some of the contents were a mystery to me, I must say.'

Ferret fumbled through his capsule. In it, on a flash drive, were all of his writings and his ideas for a perfect new world – ideas that weren't going to be too welcome in the current milicu, some of the files were encrypted; the formula for his pheromone wipes and a few other assorted files that he had figured might come in handy.

'Hey, Doc,' said Ferret,' if I gave you a formula, could you make it up for me? A prescription, kinda.'

'Yes.'

'Alright,' nodded Ferret thoughtfully,' It's about time someone stirred up the shit around here. Are you wif me, Doc?'

Doctor Campbell looked around his tiny underground apartment. 'I have nothing much to lose,' he replied. He grabbed a plastic bag from a draw beside him. 'There you are.'

'What's that?' asked Ferret,

'Your pheromone wipes.'

'Fuck. That was quick.'

'I have an old computer. I read your files before I re-awaked you. I knew you'd want them when you came-to.'

'Do they work?'

'Well, let's put it this way – I fucked my cat, which was lucky.'

'Not for the cat.'

'No. True. But I'm probably the only person with a cat in these parts. The rest have been eaten.'

'Bit rough on the pussy.'

'Yes, but it was either that or bonking the toaster. Those wipes are dynamite. I've never been so aroused.'

'Hey. Hang on. That was the second formula: The reverse pheromone wipe. The original pheromone wipes made women to want to fuck you.'

'Oh yes, I made those up as well.' And he retrieved another bag from the draw. 'You might notice the two different colours. The original wipes, the ones that make you irresistible, are blue, while the reverse wipes are red: that turn you into an aggressive sexual predator. Just so you don't get confused.'

'You're a genius. Do they work too?'

'Yes. Snuggles was raped by a pack of field mice after I wiped her down with one. Come to think of it, Snuggles had a rough day.'

'Great. Okay. So, we're in business. You know the lie of the land better than me, Doc. Where do you think we should go first?'

'Well, it's dangerous, but I suggest we see The Icers. They're basically on our side. I'm the chief cook for their Ice, so they need me. But be careful. They mainly come out at night and they are remarkably unpredictable. And we don't need to go anywhere to find them. The bar above us will be full of them later this evening.'

'No worries,' replied Ferret, thoughtfully nodding

his head. 'And bring that bag of tricks wif ya, Doc? And a few bucks might come in handy as well if you've got it? I'll pay ya back. Oh, and hide this for me would ya?'

And Ferret handed the Doc the flash drive.

*

After dark, Ferret and the Doc quietly emerged from their hiding place. To avoid being seen, they made their way around the back of the bar and onto the road outside. There, sitting in the gutter, in front of the noisy bar, was a sandy-haired young man, smoking a glass pipe. His hair was like straw, he was emaciated, and his skin was irrevocably ravaged by cavities. His sunken cheeks drew in the white smoke, which he exhaled prodigiously.

'G'day,' said Ferret.

The man did not reply but instead handed the pipe to a child waiting patiently beside him. The boy had short blonde hair, was baby-faced and was no more than twelve or thirteen. He was handsome, in a young boy, feminine sort of way, but he looked like he had been neglected. He took the pipe with uncertainty.

'Go on,' the thin man encouraged. 'Take a hit.'

'I don't wanna,' replied the boy.

'I said fucken' smoke it. Drag hard and hurry up; it's burnin'. You're fucken' wastin' it.'

'No. I don't wanna,' the boy repeated, but these words had hardly left his lips before the wiry, sandy-straw-haired man smacked him in the back of the head. The boy fell forward onto the bitumen. The man couldn't save the boy from falling, but he managed to save the pipe, which he finished with an exuberant exhalation.

He turned to Ferret. 'He won't fucken' smoke, silly prick. Don't know what's good for 'im. You wanna be in the tribe, you gotta follow the tribe's rules, eh?'

'Fucken' 'A',' replied Ferret in his best bogan.

'The man reclined, to suggest his high status. He eyed Ferret with interest. 'So, who the fuck are you?' He nodded towards the Doc. 'I know that old cunt, but I 'ain't never seen you.'

'I'm from just around the corner,' Ferret replied, 'but I been gone for a while.'

'I been livin' in these parts for the last ten years,' questioned the man, 'How come I never seen you?'

'I just got back.'

'Where you been?'

'Frozen. I was frozen in 2033 at the age of 33. The Doc here brought me back to life.' Ferret smiled.

For a moment, the man hesitated, as if a cloud had momentarily crossed the sun. Then he began laughing. He laughed and he laughed and he hit the ground with glee and he lay back and laughed some more. When at last his mirth had waned, he wiped a tear from his eye, and he sat up. 'I like you, ya cunt,' he said. 'I'm Parrot. Come and meet the boys. And you,' he turned on the young man, 'next time I tell ya to take a drag, you fucken' take a drag. Ya got me?'

But the boy did not reply. He looked glum and cast an embarrassed glance from the gutter towards Ferret.

'Little dickhead,' Parrot mumbled. 'He's already two years past his rights of passage and the little cunt still won't smoke. Come on.'

Ferret and the Doc followed Parrot into the bar.

Inside, the smoke haze was as thick as John Holm's cock. Moving inside the haze were perhaps fifty skinny, sickly-looking people of various ages. Some were twitching and scratching themselves like flea ridden dogs; others were in an extreme state of agitation; still others were effusively happy about nothing in particular and all about the room were couples fucking: mainly men and women but none of them seemed to be too fussy.

'Fuck me!' exclaimed Ferret. 'These cunts don't need

no pheromone wipes.'

'Excessive sex drive,' whispered the Doc. 'The males will be beating the females up later.'

'The Australian way,' replied Ferret.

'Listen up!' exclaimed Parrot and everybody did, except for the fuckers and the fuckees. 'This blokes alright wif me. So I don't want no cunt pickin' on 'im. Got it?

The inhabitants nodded and murmured and went back to their previous activities.

'Hey, Parrot, can a fella get a meal 'ere? I'm hungrier than a middle-aged man for a teenage twat.'

Parrot laughed. 'You won't find no food in 'ere, mate. None of us eat. We Ice 'til we die.'

'Ice 'til we die,' several nearby Icers replied by rote.

'Well, do you know where a bloke could get a feed?'

'Up at the Imperial they still got food. Steve won't have Ice on the premises. I reckon he's misguided but we respect 'im 'cos he makes the best beer in the Hawkesbury.'

'Steve?' mused Ferret. 'Well I'll be fucked. Come on Doc. Let's go grab a beer. And Parrot, can I borrow your boy for a few hours, to give me the low down on the low down?'

'He 'ain't my boy,' replied Parrot. 'And you can fuck 'im up the arse for all I care.'

'Thanks, but I don't reckon that'll be necessary. And, Parrot, you're obviously the boss around here. Do you reckon you could rally your troops if I tried to make a few changes to the way things run in Sydney town?'

'Like what?'

'I dunno yet, but I hate censorship and I hate political correctness, I'm not too keen on religion and I believe in making intelligent choices that don't hurt otters. So somethin' in that general direction.'

'Why are you so keen on otters?'

'I 'ain't. That was a typo. It shoulda been 'others', but

I kinda liked it.'

'Oh. Right. Ok. Sounds good, Ferret. I like your style. If you come up with a plan, get back to me.'

'Cheers,' replied Ferret. I'll cop ya later.'

Ferret and the Doc left the bar, spoke to the boy, and the three of them wandered up the road towards the Corso.

'What's your name, son?' asked Ferret as the boy walked dejectedly beside him.

'Billy,' he replied, still looking at the ground.

'Well, I'm Ferret, and this here is the Doc. You're not too keen on the old Ice, eh?'

'That stuff'll kill ya,' mumbled Billy.

'Good for you.'

'Don't you use it?'

'No fucken' way. That stuff'll kill ya.' Ferret smiled at Billy and Billy smiled back.

The Doc chipped in. 'That's very true. Did you know that if you lock two male Ice addicts in a room for long enough they'll have sexual intercourse so vigorously and for so long that eventually one of them will die?'

Ferret raised his eyebrows. 'Puts a new spin on 'Fuck me dead', don't it?'

Billy laughed.

Shortly after, the three entered the empty bar and there was Steve. He was still recognisable, but he was a lot older.

'Steve!' yelled Ferret. 'You old cunt! How the fuck are ya?'

Steve looked up from behind the bar as if he had heard the echo of a dream. 'Ferret?' he asked. 'Ferret Cutler?'

'The same,' replied Ferret with a rakish smile. 'Fuck me. You look like a week-old turd!'

'Fuck you too!' replied Steve, coming out from behind the bar and shaking hands with Ferret. 'How are you, old mate? You don't look a day older.'

'I'm not,' said Ferret. 'This is the Doc and this is Billy.'

'G'day,' said Steve shaking hands with each.

'I don't believe it. The cyrogenic thing worked.'

'Cryogenic,' Ferret corrected, 'and yeah it did. I told you it would. You shoulda listened to me, you old prick. How old are ya now?

'I lost count,' replied Steve. 'About sixty I reckon.'

'Shit. You look at least seventy.'

Steve shook his head with a smile. 'Fuck off,' he replied.

'Nice come back,' said Ferret. 'Hey, listen, you wouldn't know where a fella could get a beer and steak 'round here would ya? I nearly been asleep as long as Rip Van fucken' Winkle.'

'Yeah. Shit. Of course. Sit down boys. I'll get Tom to rustle 'em up.'

'Bring a beer for Billy too and I'll 'ave his.' Ferret smiled.

'You haven't changed,' laughed Steve. 'I'll get him a lemonade.'

Soon Ferret was stuffing his face and slurping away. When he finished, he pushed the plate away and sat back with a satisfied grunt. 'Thanks, old man. That was fucking delicious. So, tell me, where's Rayleen?'

Steve let out a sigh. 'Ah, she left me Ferris. Years ago.'

'Fuck. That's no good. How come?'

'A Jehovah's Witness come by and she ran off with 'im.'

'Fuck me. He showed her The Truth, eh?'

'I reckon he showed her more than that.'

'Jesus.'

'She divorced me, ya know?'

'Well, she had ta, didn't she? All them Christians

have gotta get married to root. And to the same person.'

'Yeah. And she did marry 'im too.'

'Mate, that's rough. I'm sorry to hear that.' Ferret paused. 'Hey wait a minute. What happened to your boy? What happened to Oscar?'

'I got no idea. She never took 'im, I know that.'

'No fucken' way!'

'Just as long as he never became a Witness.'

'Yeah, or the poor little bastard'd be trottin' 'round knockin' on doors and hasslin' people and ridin' around in a horse and cart.'

'That's the Amish, isn't it?'

'Same fucken' thing.'

'And he wouldn't be a little cunt anymore. He'd be almost as old as you.'

'Yeah, shit, that's right,' mused Ferret. 'I forgot. I been asleep for a long time, eh? Well, listen, I gotta go. I don't like the way things are goin' 'round 'ere. I'm gunna do somefink about it.'

'What?' asked Steve.

'I dunno,' Ferret replied. 'I gotta check out the scene first. The Doc's gunna come wif me. What about you, Billy?'

Billy perked up. 'Yeah Sure.'

'You don't have to ask your mum, or nothin'?'

Billy just laughed.

'I'll be back, Steve.'

'Yeah. No worries. It was good to see you, Ferris.

'You too.'

'Come back when you can, and we'll talk about old times.'

Ferret shook Steve's hand. 'And don't worry. I'm gunna do my best to shake up this town.'

The three of them said goodbye to Steve and left him looking sadly out of the window.

'So where can I bloke score a taxi 'round these parts?'

asked Ferret.

'There are no taxis,' replied the Doc.

'Uber?'

'There are no cars at all.'

'How does a fella get around?' asked Ferret.

'Horse,' said Billy.

'Horse?' Ferret squinted. 'I can't ride no horse.'

'We could walk,' the Doc suggested.

'I know where there's pushbikes,' added Billy.

'Where are we headed?' asked the Doc.

'Bankstown,' sighed Ferret. 'Take me to the horses.'

*

Soon the three were trotting down the Parramatta Road. Ferret's riding style was like a beauty pageant – arse all over the place. When he finally dismounted on the outskirts of Bankstown, his arse was as sore as a dry root.

'Fuck me!' he exclaimed as he dismounted. 'I can't believe that people used to ride these things everywhere.'

The Doc interjected. 'Until the internal combustion engine they were the fastest means of transportation.'

'Don't forget the steam engine,' Billy suggested.

'Oh yes. Good point,' replied the Doc. 'You like to read, do you?'

'I love it. I read all the time.'

'Good for you. Most people can't read at all these days. First the Internet eroded reading . . .'

'. . . and then after the PCs came to power . . .'

'Look, excuse me,' Ferret interrupted, 'but could we save this character development for later? I finally managed to lose a bunch of cunts from the last book who couldn't stay focused. Now, let's water the horses, tie 'em up in the shade and see what's goin' on in Bankstown. And Doc, keep your little black medical case handy. I intend to make good use of those pheromone wipes.'

On the outskirts of Bankstown Ferret produced two burqas and a false beard. 'There you go.' He handed the burqas to Billy and the Doc and put on the false beard.

'Where did you get these?' the Doc queried.

'Listen,' replied Ferret, 'Don't ask difficult questions. Just go with the flow.'

The Doc didn't argue. He and Billy donned the burqas. The doc looked passable, but Billy's burqa was too long, and he looked like a bedraggled grim reaper.

'Okay,' said Ferret as he adjusted his moustache-less beard. Now listen. Neither of you two says a word. Got it?'

Neither the Doc nor Billy said a word.

'Got it?'

Again, silence.

'Listen, dickheads, this is not a vaudeville routine. Just nod your head if you're reading me.'

They nodded.

'Good. Now stay that way. I'll do all the talkin.'

The three of them walked slowly into Bankstown centre, past a large park, along a mall. They didn't attract much attention. In front of the shops, women stood in the heat, wearing burqas, and the men sat, in their jeans and casual attire, smoking hookahs. Every man sported a moustache-less beard.

Beside a fountain two women in burqas took a selfie.

'Now there's the definition of irony,' whispered Ferret.

Another woman passed by a group of men who seemed excited as they watched her pass. She was wearing a niqab.

'Nice eyes,' said one of the men.

Another shouted out rudely, 'Show us your face!'

That's an old one,' said another.

Through the bustle of the mall the trio wended quietly and cautiously until, at length, they came upon a large man, resplendent in Arab robes and a taqiyah. Around the man sat several fully covered women. A bare-chested slave stood behind him, waving a large palm frond to keep him cool.

Ferret approached him, followed by Billy and the Doc. He bowed slightly and placed his fingers to his forehead. 'Er, salami,' he said. 'Peace be up you.'

The imposing man looked sternly at him. 'Salaam,' he replied, 'and with you.'

'You look like the head cheese around here, what with the harem and all.'

The man did not reply.

'So, I was wonderin' if you could help me and . . . ,' he looked around towards the rather comic appearance of his two companions, 'er . . . me girls out?'

The man sat up straight and pointed towards Billy. 'Show me the little one's face.'

'Is that allowed?' asked Ferret, somewhat alarmed.

'It is if I decree it,' replied the man. 'Show me.'

There was no way out. 'Take off your invisibility cloak, Billy . . . ah, I mean, Shazam.'

Billy was hesitant but he complied. He shook his blonde hair and looked at the man.

'By the beard of the Prophet,' he exclaimed. 'She has the look of a young boy. I must have her. Is she your sister?'

Ferret had to think quickly. 'Um, no, no, this is Shazam, my wife.'

The man sat back with disappointment. 'Then it is forbidden, but I warn you young one,' he pointed a wagging finger towards Billy, 'if any harm should befall your master, I shall find you, and you shall be mine.'

Billy gulped and quickly refitted his invisibility mask.

The man returned to business. 'My name is Mustafa Khan. I have risen like a star above this stormy sea upon which we now sail. I am the master of two thousand horsemen. Who are you and what do you wish of me?'

'The name's Ferret. G'day. I'm a convert from the Hawkesbury. Too many derros out there.'

Ferret laughed nervously but the man did not respond.

'So, I, er, heard that you fellas controlled the water out of Warragamba Dam, and I was wonderin' if we could make a deal?'

Mustafa looked suspicious. 'The water is precious and the Dam is three quarters dry. What sort of a deal could you offer?'

'I have a sort of potion that makes men irresistible to women that I thought I could trade for some of me tribe's access to the dam. We're runnin' out of water out west, ya see.'

'I have heard of such potions,' replied Mustafa quietly, 'but I would have to see proof before I would enter into any such bargain.'

'No worries,' Ferret replied. 'Hey Doc, I mean, Fatima, grab one of them original blue wipes, will ya?'

The Doc did so, and Ferret handed it to Mustafa. 'Now, find an unlikely bloke, wipe it on 'im and stand back.'

Mustafa turned the sachet quizzically in his hand then stopped suddenly and turned his head, as if he had had an idea. He spoke to his slave. 'Abdul, wipe this on your arm.'

Abdul did so, as Mustafa explained, 'Abdul is a eunuch and, as you can see, is a very ugly man. If women find him sexually attractive, this potion must indeed be strong.'

As he spoke, there was a general rustle in the marketplace. Every woman, up to fifty metres, turned suddenly to look at Abdul, even though he had not even completed wiping on the pheromones. He looked up.

Though he could not see their eyes, he became aware that at least seventy or eighty women were staring at him. For an instant, all was calm until . . .

From a rumble to a howl, to a cacophonous shriek, the street turned to chaos. Burqas and niqabs flew into the air like policeman's hats at graduation. Poor old Abdul was quickly surrounded by women, including Mustafa's wives. They ripped and tore at his clothes and he was soon denuded. Mustafa was pulled aside and out of the melee. Women punched and smashed each other for ascendancy. Several reached Abdul's cock only to be ripped away by others. Soon there was a howl of despair as the women realised that Abdul had no balls. 'Grab a splint!' one cried, and it was soon applied. Screams followed as women frantically gyrated upon the wooden stick, which held Abdul's cock rigid. 'Splinters! Splinters!' cried another and a plastic splint was quickly applied.

'Talk about all dressed up and nowhere to go,' whispered Ferret to his companions.

At last, the women's lust was sated and in one baffled wave they came-to from the frenzy. In distress and ashamed, they collected their garments and withdrew. Husbands chastised them as they dressed. Abdul was scratched and badly injured and was carried away in a horse drawn cart.

Mustafa was greatly impressed. 'I am astounded,' he proclaimed. 'How many in your tribe?'

'A couple of hundred,' Ferret replied.

'Very well. I will allow you and your tribe to dwell by the dam and draw water from it for the time being. In return I want thirty of your wipes. We can renegotiate in four weeks.'

'Done,' replied Ferret. And the transaction was completed.

'But tell me,' Mustafa asked,' why did your wives not succumb to the love potion?'

Ferret replied, without a beat, "Cos I'm such a good root.'

Mustafa thought for a moment and then he began to laugh. 'He patted Ferret on the back. I will see you back here in four weeks,' he said. 'In the meantime, my wives have several nieces I must visit.'

Ferret and his companions left.

As they mounted their horses on the outskirts of Bankstown, Ferret said, 'Okay. Now, you two, go back to Windsor and grab a couple of hundred of those Icers and take 'em across to Warragamba. Set up camp there and I'll come back as soon as I can.'

'How long will you be?' asked the Doc.

'I dunno but it's gotta be less than four weeks or the Muzzos'll kill all of yous. And Doc, make up as many pheromone wipes as you can, both types.'

'Right,' he replied.

'And cook up heaps of Ice for the Icers. Try and keep 'em happy 'til I get back.'

'Do we need food supplies?'

'No. I wouldn't worry about it. Those fuckers don't eat.'

'What's the plan?' asked Billy.

'I still dunno,' Ferret replied. 'I gotta see what happens in the CBD first. Doc, give us a few wipes - both types, and I'll see yous soon. Oh, and Doc, I'm keepin' me beard, but you can lose the burqa now.'

'I actually thought it was quite becoming.'

'Well, it's an improvement. See yous soon. Wish me luck.'

And Ferret rode towards the city.

*

He arrived as the autumn sun was setting. He tethered his horse in Pitt Street and entered a bar. Inside there were only a few people, so Ferret bought a beer and sat near two men, so that he could eavesdrop.

'Oh yes. You're absolutely right, Christopher,' one was saying. 'One must always defer to another culture, even if it's contra to your own culture's wellbeing. It goes without saying.'

Ferret thought this fella sounded pompous but then again, he was used to the Hawkesbury; anything sounded cultivated compared to that.

'That's so true, Neville,' stated Christopher, 'any other opinion is heresy.'

'Can you believe,' returned Neville, 'that in the McCarthy Period in America they actually dismissed the arguments of the left?'

'Yes. Imperialist, capitalist thugs. Things generally go so well in Socialist countries like the Soviet Union and Venezuela.'

'Thank God we are all equal here.'

'Absolutely. In Sydney today you can hold any opinion that you want, so long as it's the right one.'

'And of course, it always is, isn't it?'

And the two men laughed.

Ferret interrupted. 'Excuse me fellas but who's the honcho around here?'

The two men cast such a look of disdain towards him that for a moment Ferret thought that he had farted without realising it.

'Don't talk to him, Neville,' said Christopher. 'He's one of those heathens from the west. Look at that Led Zeppelin t-shirt.'

'There's no need to be rude,' Ferret replied. 'For your information, mate, they were the best rock band of all time and as for me bein' a heathen, 'ain't you PC blokes supposed to be The Tolerant Ones?'

'Oh, my God. Probably from fire country,' added Neville. 'Probably from one of those areas where the fires start and affect my sinuses every summer.'

'Hey, listen, mate,' Ferret replied angrily, 'fuck your sinuses. There's people dyin' out there each year tryin' to stop them fires. Not just for country folk; for everybody.'

'Make yourself scarce,' replied Christopher, making a shoo motion with his hands, 'or we shall call the police.'

'Hey. Hang on,' said Ferret, 'I 'ain't done nuffin' wrong.'

'Oh my God, listen to how he talks,' stated Neville, and then to Ferret he said, 'Now listen here, little fellow, we are good, tolerant people but we won't tolerate bigots like you. Your type is prejudiced against other cultures. You are racist and wrong.'

'You don't even know me, cockbreath. And what if I do think differently to you? Whatever happened to democracy?'

'Well that just shows how little you know,' replied Neville, smiling smugly, 'because Sydney is no longer a democracy.'

'Since when?'

'Since the recent arrival of The Mother and The Son: The Enlightened Ones. They rule Sydney now and it won't be long before people like you are eradicated.'

'So much for tolerance,' Ferret quipped as he stood and prepared to leave.

Just then a huge female police officer entered. Raised voices are a rarity when everyone agrees all the time and she had come to investigate. She was over six feet tall and weighed about two hundred and fifty pounds. She had a face like a gorilla biscuit.

'What's going on here,' she asked with a voice that sounded like the dark low drawl you get when a person's voice is disguised on television.

'This country man is insulting us,' bleated Christopher, pointing an accusatory finger at Ferret. 'And he shouldn't even be allowed in the city.'

'Now hang on,' Ferret protested, but it became instantly obvious that this policewoman was not in a conciliatory mood.

'Right,' she bellowed, moving purposely towards Ferret with a pair of handcuffs.

But, quick as a flash, before the officer could apply the manacles, Ferret had jumped aside, applied a reverse pheromone wipe on her arm as she passed, and raced out the door.

'Aren't you going to go after him?' asked Neville.

But the officer stared back at him and Christopher with the strangest expression that either of them had ever encountered. Her silence was unnerving. She appeared to be experiencing some sort of internal combustion that was rising through her body and engorging her face with an increasingly ruddy hue. As the men watched on with mounting horror, the female behemoth began to shudder like a 1970 Valiant in severe need of a tyre balance. To add to the growing panic rising within the two men, she screamed like a Baskervillian hound, and began tearing at her clothes, whilst advancing upon them. They backed up, knocking over their martinis, and she cornered them against the far end of the bar.

A bartender casually wiped the bar and looked on with interest.

Then it began. It was *Heart of Darkness* all over again: 'The horror. The horror.' As she grabbed Neville by the head and thrust his face mercilessly into her massively lubricated vagina. 'I'm drown . . ing! I'm drow . . ning!' Neville screamed as his face appeared and reappeared from the swollen orifice.

The bartender looked on with interest.

With her other hand she tugged like a maniac at Christopher's cock and balls and held him by them up above her head swinging him about like a lasso. He screamed until he was hoarse and eventually fell mercifully unconscious.

The bartender looked on with interest.

Then she shoved Neville's entire head up her arse. Then she sucked Christopher's left testicle right through his scrotum. Then she paraded about with Christopher trailing behind and kicking his legs like an epileptic. Then she chewed on Christopher's knacker, blood streaming down her cheeks, her vaginal juices awash upon the pub lino floor. Then she pierced Christopher's rectum repeatedly with her six-inch distended clitoris.

The bartender looked on with interest.

Then, she saw the bartender . . .

*

As Ferret walked cautiously up Pitt Street, he noticed that apart from the many businessmen leaving work for the day, there were also many Muslim men. He decided to don his beard and to turn his Led Zep t-shirt inside out, so he didn't look too incongruous.

He passed the old cinemas and was pleased to see that projectors still existed. He cast a quick glance to see what was playing. In Cinema One was a PC thriller called: *Other Cultures are Always Right*; in Cinema Two was a comedy called: *I Hope I haven't Offended Anyone*, and there was a documentary in Cinema Three called: *I Choose to be Invisible – A Feminist's Support of the Burqa*. There was also a poster advertising an upcoming action flick called *The Vaginal Nicker v's the Rabbi*. The slogan was: *Their genitals were butchered but they were grateful.*

'Fuck me,' thought Ferret, 'Goebbels has got nothin' on these cunts.'

He finally made it down to the old Circular Quay, which was partially under water, and he looked over towards The Opera House, which had a large wall around it to protect it from the risen harbour beside.

A tall man, who had glasses and a face, stopped him. 'Peace be with you, my Muslim brother. How can I be as obsequious as possible?'

'Take me to the honcho,' Ferret replied, in an attempted Arab voice that came out sounding like a mix between South African and Leb.

'And whom shall I say is calling?'

'Um, just tell her that there's a Muzzo who has come to see her about a water allocation in Warragamba.'

'And your name?'

'Um, oh shit, um Mustafa: Mustafa Root.'

'One moment, sir,' said the man and he disappeared into the Opera House.

While Ferret waited, he looked around. Bearded Muzzo men in jeans and t-shirts and white businessmen in suits, were all around. There were a few women in burqas but not a dress in sight.

'Jesus, what happened to the eye candy? Sydney sheilas used to be hot.'

Just then, the man with the face returned, and took Ferret into the Opera House Foyer. Ferret waited for a few minutes before a young boy of thirteen or fourteen appeared. The boy was dressed in the full Arab clothing of The Gulf. As he approached, Ferret noted that the boy wore a ghutra tied on with an aghal, which Ferret thought looked strange (a) because the boy had no visible hair except for a little yellow tuft above his forehead and (b) because Ferret didn't know what any of those words meant. He also admired the boy's dishdasha, worn as it was with a pair of long sirwal. (see (b)) above.

The boy strode up to Ferret. 'Whatta you, fucken' want?' he bellowed.

'Peace be somewhere near you,' said Ferret with a bow.

'Listen fuckface, if you're an Arab, I'm in the fucken' Saudi Family!' shouted the boy as he ripped the fake beard from Ferret's chin. 'And I know who you fucken' are. I went back to wake you up, but you'd been moved.'

'What?' replied Ferret. 'What do ya mean? Who are you?'

'Take one guess, shithead.' The boy removed his headgear.

'You're not . . .' Ferret stammered.

'Yes, I fucken' am. I'm Oscar. Your boy.'

Ferret was gobsmacked.

'Follow me and I'll tell you a little story.'

So, in a bewildered state, Ferret followed the boy into the building.

'I had no say so in any fucken' thing,' Oscar grumbled as he stormed quietly through the interior rooms. 'Rayleen sold me off into slavery when I was just a kid. I don't fucken' know: I'm seven years old, Mum's divorced Steve, who at that time I still believe is me real Dad, I'm livin' the dream (cough, cough - bullshit) up at Bowen Mountain, knockin' on doors and tellin' people what The Truth is when - could things get any worse? You bet they fucken' could. What happens? Fucken' Rayleen, me, own fucken' Mum, goes and sells me off to some twat who's just outta jail, is fucken' crazier than a turd in a tornado and is uglier than a middle-aged botoxed bitch admirin' herself in a mirror maze. And where does that leave me? I'll tell ya where it fucken' leaves me – here talkin' to you, because you, me real Dad, rooted me real Mum, once only, accordin' to her. And just lookin' at ya I can believe that. Then, just to top things off, this bitch tells me she's got a plan to rule Sydney. 'Yeah, right,' I say, and she punches me in the face for bein' rude and then every mornin' first time I see 'er she does the same, so I don't forget it. And the worst of it is, she fucken' done what she said she would – she's the fucken' dictator of Sydney and she makes me wear this shit every day.'

'So why did you go back to wake me up?' Ferret

asked, having regained some composure.

Oscar stopped at a doorway and turned to Ferret. 'I'd be easier to ask her. Good luck.' He pushed open the door and motioned for Ferret to walk in, which he did, followed by Oscar.

There, on the stage of the Drama Theatre, backlighted for effect, in silhouette, was the frame of an enormous female, seated upon a throne. As Ferret entered, light erupted all around in a brilliant blaze that momentarily blinded him. When his eyes adjusted, he saw a gross approximation of a human form, irredeemably obese, a sprawling city of flaccidity, lounging upon the throne like a puddle of mercury in the palm of a madman's hand. She wore a bikini and a Carmen Miranda headdress of tropical fruit. She stood with difficulty and her belly hung below her knees, but her belly was eclipsed by her tits, whose massive single nipple hung pendulously, centimetres above the fearful stage floor. Her skin was dappled and patched. She was a violence of physical graffiti. She was . . .

'Mumsy,' whispered Ferret.

'You betta fucken' believe it, fuckface!' she bellowed. 'Hit it!' The auditorium lights dropped again as the stage lights came on. The music struck up and she did three numbers from the popular musical *Oklahoma*, finishing with *'I'm Just a Girl who can't say No'*.

When the auditorium lights rose again, Ferret's mouth was open, and his eyes were wide like some old cunt on pension day in the queue at Aldi.

'Fuck me,' he muttered.

'No thanks,' Mumsy replied. I got me own root. 'Sambo! Get over 'ere!'

A tall, handsome, well-built black man entered, wearing nothing but a G-string and a codpiece, and judging by the strain on the codpiece it had some work to do. He handed her a robe.

'Thanks, Sambo,' said Mumsy with a quick tug at the codpiece. 'Now go backstage and fashion that thing into somefin' angry, and Oscar, take fuckface down to my office. Give us two minutes. I wanna fuck Sambo.' And she went.

'Come on,' sighed Oscar.

'So, you're doin' it tough are ya, son?' asked Ferret as they walked.

'Don't fucken' call me son and yes, I am doin' it fucken' tough.'

'She's not . . . interferin' wif ya, is she?'

'Fuck off,' retorted Oscar. 'I can't get away from the bitch, but I'd rather slash me own throat than hammer that. And besides, she's got Sambo.'

'But why would a good lookin' fella like that . . .'

'Because he's 'er slave. Catch up wif the program will ya? She paid some Arab bloke to organise it. These Arabs 'ave got more contacts than a spitfire. Harems, money, wives, slaves, the lot.'

'Because of the oil?'

'No, dickhead. That's the old currency. It's because they control the water. Here. This door.' And Oscar ushered Ferret into a backstage room.

As he entered, followed by Oscar, Mumsy was drying her hair. She wore Arab robes and a headscarf and was making up in front a mirror.

'That was quick,' said Ferret.

'Sambo's got two organs in one - his cock is a foot.'

'And I wouldn't bother with the makeup: there's not enough on the planet.'

'Fuck off.'

'And what the fuck are you dressed like that for?'

'Just playin' the game, Ferris. Just playin' the game. I got a meetin' shortly wif the real Mustafa.'

'And how the fuck did you get 'ere?'

'Easy,' Mumsy replied, turning towards him. 'Before

I got thrown into jail for fucken' all them backbenchers, I liberated a few Australian Government assets in the form of gold bars, which are comin' in very handy now. When I found out you'd been frozen, I figured I'd find your doctor and pay him to have me frozen too. After all, I know you rich fuckers are 'in the know' and always stick together. You were already frozen by then, so me and Lawrence of Arabia here,' she motioned towards Oscar, 'were frozen beside ya wif a note to wake us up before you, which that doctor done.'

'Yeah, and you punched 'im in the face.'

'But it done the job, didn't it? I knew he'd think twice before he reanimated anyone again. It's been over a year since then and it's given me time to knock this pack of drongos into shape. I'm tellin' ya Ferret, these PC cunts are straighter than Sambo's dick and they wouldn't know shit from shampoo.'

'Hang on,' replied Ferret, 'so why did you send Oscar back to unfreeze me?'

'Well, I knew you'd be woken up eventually and I'm on top of the situation here, so I figured I'd bring ya back for the competition. I'm tellin' ya Ferris, there's not one PC with a brain worf keepin' in a jar.'

'Hey, I fucked you up last time – twice, so what makes you think I can't do it again?'

'Because, dicknose, this time I'm already the king: She who controls the water, controls the world. And I've got a more auspicious sendin' off for you next weekend. I'm gunna make you pay for what you done to me. See if ya can get out of that one.'

'What sort of sending off?'

'I don't wanna spoil the surprise.'

'I'm sure I can trust you to cook up something spiteful, thundergut.'

'Look whose talkin' about trust?' replied Mumsy, as she shifted forward, stood up and cracked a few tiles. 'We might ask old Steve at the Imperial about trust, 'eh Oscar?'

Oscar, who had stood glumly beside Ferret during the whole conversation, did not reply.

Mumsy adjusted her headscarf as she started to leave the room.

'Don't embarrass the boy,' replied Ferret to her back.

Mumsy turned on him. 'What the fuck? Listen, limpdick, you're a cunt just like me and just like your boy and just like every other fucker on the planet, and don't you fucken' deny it. I just got the brains to get what I want. Oscar, take this little pipsqueak up top and lock 'im in. He can look out over the harbour for a few nights and work out how he's gunna get outta here.' She made for the door, but she turned when she got there. 'Oh, and Ferret, ya might notice that clown's face on the other side of the harbour? Just down from North Sydney? Well, he'll be smilin' at you on Saturday mornin' at about nine am, but I tell you, old son, you won't be smilin' back. Oscar, take away them sexy wipe things he's no doubt got in 'is pocket and bring 'em to me.'

She laughed as she slammed the door behind her.

In a futile attempt at a comeback Ferret yelled, 'Yeah? Well, I'd reconsider the headscarf and go wif the full burqa!' But she was gone, and Ferret knew that this time, he was in real trouble.

'Come on,' said Oscar, 'I'll take you up.'

A short while later, Ferret stood looking out over Sydney Harbour at Luna Park on the other side, thinking about what Mumsy had in store for him on Saturday morning.

'Empty your pockets,' Oscar mumbled.

Ferret didn't argue. He handed him a small handful of pheromone wipes.

'What do they do?' asked Oscar.

'The blue ones are the original wipes. They make you irresistible to women. And the red ones are the newer ones. They make you wanna fuck everything.'

Oscar looked at the wipes with interest. 'I don't need the red ones, that's for sure.'

'That's my boy,' said Ferret.

'But I could sure use the blue ones.'

'No skirt about?'

'You're jokin'? What wif ten-ton Tessie watchin' over me every move? I'm lucky if I can fit in a wank.'

'Yeah, well don't wipe on a blue one and wank: you might pull yourself off – literally.'

Oscar was about to leave when Ferret said, 'Hey, Oscar.'

Oscar stopped.

'I'm really sorry about what happened to ya, son. I hope I can explain it to ya someday.'

Oscar hesitated for a moment but said nothing; then locked the door.

*

The twilight was upon the Sydney foreshore as Mumsy made her way out into the courtyard of the Opera House. She was on her best behaviour. She was preceded by a half a dozen Aborigines dressed in native loincloths, who shook sticks and leaves about, and blew smoke everywhere, and gave Mumsy a coughing fit.

When she reached Mustafa, who stood in the courtyard, his dishdasha ruffled by a zephyr, looking romantic under the fading light, a retinue of faceless women behind him, she recovered from the coughing fit sufficiently to say to the token Aborigines, 'Alright, yous can fuck off now.' And they did.

'Sorry about that, your highness,' said Mumsy with an attempted curtsy that almost toppled her face first into the courtyard. She regained her balance just in time. 'Peace be wif you.'

'As-Salam-u-Alikum,' he replied.

'We only bring the Abos out for special occasions.' She held out her hand for Mustafa to kiss it, but he decorously declined and had his attendant do the honours.

'Where's your usual attendant?' asked Mumsy.

'He had an unfortunate accident,' replied the Sheik. He half turned to his wives who all looked down ashamedly at their invisibility sacks.

Mumsy motioned towards the harbour. 'Shall we walk?' she suggested.

Mustafa nodded and together they took a stroll beside the water, followed by the faceless women.

'You look beautiful in your abaya,' lied Mustafa.

'Thanks. You too,' she replied.

Mustafa smiled like a grimace and closed his eyes momentarily but did not correct her.

'Can we speak in private,' she asked.

Mustafa snapped his fingers and his wives retreated to an appropriate distance.

'I thought you could only take four wives?' Mumsy questioned.

'I am in control of South-Western Sydney. I am in control of the dam. I am the master of my domain. Mohammed made up rules that suited him. I do the same.'

'No worries,' Mumsy replied. Then she lowered her voice. 'So, er, how's the dam level lookin'?'

Mustafa also lowered his. 'The official word is that the dam is twenty-five per cent full, but the truth is much worse.'

'How bad?'

'Warragamba has under fifteen percent capacity and it is dwindling quickly. And it will continue to do so. However, be aware that I have allowed a tribe of western suburbs Icers to camp beside the dam with impunity, for the time being.'

'What the fuck did ya . . . I mean. Why is that, oh Jewel of the firmament?'

'I would rather keep them where I can keep an eye on them. I have plans for them I will divulge to you later. But in the meantime, I have a task, which I wish for you to perform and in return I shall shower you with gold and precious water. It will greatly increase your power base.'

'I would love to be showered by you, oh munificent one.'

Mustafa let that one through to the keeper.

'What would you have me do?'

'I want you to reduce the population of Sydney by twenty percent to save on water usage and I want you to start by killing all of the Jews in the Eastern Suburbs.'

'I beg your pardon?'

'You heard me. Kill them all.'

'Um, right. Listen, that may be a little more difficult than it sounds. You see they're still getting mileage out of that holocaust thing and I've only just got them to accept me as their leader.'

'They will respect you for your strength and resolve.'

'Um, I'm not so sure that's how it works, oh controller of the orbs.'

'Did Mohammed shirk from his duty to Allah when he re-entered Medina and slew all the Jews – every man, woman and child?'

'I'm guessing not?'

'No, he did not. And neither shall you if you wish to remain alive.' Mustafa was raising his voice in Arab bravado. 'You have a police force. You have a military. Use them! Destroy the Jews! They are insular and of no practical use. Destroy them! You have four weeks. After that time, if you have not acted, I will cut off all water to the CBD. Then, I will come for you.'

Mustafa bowed slightly and exited with a flourish, followed by his black clad wives, who swarmed behind him like a pack of bloated blowflies.

'Fuck,' muttered Mumsy. 'And I thought I was a cunt.'

*

Back in Windsor, night was just falling and the Icers were just rising. A few shuffling, sniffing, skinny Icers were already in the Church Bar being incredibly enthusiastic about nothing in particular. They laughed as they heaved the corpse of a fellow Icer, who had been fucked to death the night before by one of his mates, out into the garbage bin.

Beneath the floor of the Church Bar, Billy watched the Doc finish preparing a batch of pheromone and reverse pheromone wipes. As the two sat there in silence, they could hear a rapidly escalating argument in the bar above, between one Icer couple.

'I never fucken' done that!' shouted a male voice.

'You fucken' did!' a rough female voice shouted back.

'I fucken' neva!'

'And I'm tellin' ya, ya fucken' did!'

'When?'

'Last night. Right where you're fucken' standin'!'

'Bullshit!'

'You fucken' did!'

'What? Fucked 'er?'

'Yeah! Ya fucken' grabbed her by the cunt and told 'er you wanted to fuck 'er.'

There was a brief hesitation.

'Oh, yeah, I might remember that, but I never fucked her.'

'Then you fucked 'er. You fucken' did. Ask Chardonnay. Hey Chards, did my fucken' husband fuck you last night or what?'

'Yeah,' replied Chardonnay.

'See?'

'I fucken' neva!'

'No. You did,' replied Chardonnay in a remarkably matter-of-fact voice. 'Remember? You started to cum inside me right away and I pulled your cock out just in time. Then you came in me eye and it fucken' hurt.'

'See?'

'Ah, it's all fucken' bullshit.'

And so it continued.

The Doc cast a glance at Billy and tried to smile but his smile fell well short. It was a smile full of pity and Billy knew it.

'I know,' he replied, to the Doc's silent affirmation of a truth he understood too well. 'I gotta get out of this place or it'll kill me.'

'Don't worry,' replied the Doc. 'Let's get as many of these people out to Warragamba as we can and hope that Ferret has concocted a plan. Come on, young man.'

And the two of them were soon out on the street addressing Parrot and explaining the situation to him, as far as they understood it.

'And all I know,' said the Doc, 'is that Ferret has gained the sheik's assurance of impunity for four weeks, and unlimited access to the drinking water for that same period.'

'Assurance of what?' asked Parrot, inhaling on a pipe.

'Impunity,' added Billy. 'It means we'll be safe for the time being.'

'What've you got to do wif this, ya little cunt?'

'Look, please,' Mister Parrot,' the Doc interrupted, 'we must trust Ferret. He appears to have a plan and surely you can see that Windsor is rapidly running out of water? This way we can have as much water as we want in the short term and hope that the rains come soon to fill our tanks.'

Parrot sat in silence for some time before he scared the hell out of Billy and the Doc by shouting out loudly, 'Hey, you cunts! We're goin' on a campin' trip!'

*

Later that night, the bulky, shadowy figure of Mumsy clumped its way down the stairs of The Opera House. She carried a large sack with her and under the silvery moonlight, looked like a bloated Santa Clause. Looking about furtively, she entered the Drama Room. Once beside the stage, she opened a trapdoor and descended into the bowels of the building. Hauling her heavy hessian bag behind her, she entered a room full of Aborigines. Several were asleep but two were playing cards.

'What d'ya want, missus?' asked a flat-nosed, skinny elder, without bothering to look up.

'I brought you some gifts,' she replied, with a disingenuous smile. She placed the bag on the floor.

'Not more fucken' roo meat?' he asked, as he threw down a card and went to grab the pile of coins in the centre of the table.

'Hey. Fuck off!' replied a smaller man on the far side of the table. 'You 'ain't seen me yet.'

'I seen your hand, brudder,' replied the first. 'You've had your finger up your bum all mornin.'

'Ah, fuck off, boss,' replied the smaller fellow, but he relented and the elder took the haul.

'As a matter of fact, no. I need a favour and I've brought you a few treats,' replied Mumsy and she withdrew from the bag four cartons of cigarettes. 'Marlboro, Winfield, Benson and Hedges and Camel filter less.'

'You fucken' beauty,' said the elder, standing up

with enthusiasm.

The supine natives suddenly came-to.

'I thought that that might interest you.'

She threw the cartons onto the table.

'Where' did ya get 'em?' asked one of the extras, who was the envy of his friends because he'd been given a fifty-worder.

'I have my sources,' replied Mumsy. 'But don't smoke 'em all at once. They're a thousand dollars a packet on the black market.'

But the cellophane was already on the floor and the congregation was puffing away like an old man on an eighteen-year-old hooker.

'And not only that,' added Mumsy, 'but . . .,' and she produced two flagons of port.

An exclamation of collective joy reverberated around the enclosure. Before the second bottle hit the table, the first was opened and well towards drunk. Soon both were depleted and the men, replete.

'And there's more where that came from,' Mumsy assured them.

At length, the elder, wiping the alcohol away from his mouth and lighting a second cigarette, settled back into his chair and with a satisfied exhalation asked, 'So, sister. What's the deal?'

Mumsy smiled and produced two bags from the larger sack. One bag was apparently very light because Mumsy held it outward with ease. 'In this bag,' she said, 'I have twenty pairs of sanitary gloves, 'and in this one,' and she dropped a second larger bag to the floor with a loud 'clang', 'I have a few hundred dollars in twenty cent pieces. Your job, if you wish to have as many cigarettes as you can smoke and as much port as you can drink, is to scatter these coins randomly in the Eastern suburbs of Sydney from Watson's Bay, to Bondi, to La Perouse.'

'Home come?' asked the elder.

'I want you to wipe out the population of the Eastern Suburbs of Sydney.'

'You want us to hit 'em all with that sack of coins?'

No, you fu . . .' started Mumsy before quickly biting off her annoyance with a grimace masquerading as a smile. 'I have dipped each one in paramyxovirus. Whoever touches them will die but not before they pass on the virus to their families and friends.'

'What does it do?'

'I don't know. I found it in the medical supplies, but I'm assured by my son that it's very, very potent. So make sure that you all wear the gloves.'

'We'll do it on one condition, sister.'

'And what's that?'

'We want Queensland.'

There was a silence.

'What?'

'We want Queensland. Me and the boys are sick of your white capitalistic ways, eh? We're sick of you forcin' alcohol down our throats and throwin' us in jail for no reason. We're sick of you owning the land, when the land should own you. So, we wanna own Queensland.'

'I can give you Brisbane to Cairns.'

'Done,' replied the elder. 'We're goin' back to our roots, boys. Back to our traditional ways.'

'Distribute the coins tomorrow,' stated Mumsy and she left with the hilarious mirth of the natives diminishing behind her.

*

The next afternoon in Bondi:

'Oi. Solly. Look. On the ground. Is that a ten-cent piece?'

'No, Rachael. It's a twenty-cent piece. And look there's another one!'

'Quick. Quick, Solly. Let's lend it to someone.'
'I won't take less than ten percent.'

*

The next evening outside the Opera House:

'Good work, boys,' said Mumsy to the Abos. 'We'll give it a few days and they'll be droppin' like a shit in a Matzo ball soup.'

*

Ferret had wracked his brain on how to escape from his gilded cell, but there was no way out. It was Friday night and although food had been pushed under the door every day, he was locked up tight and hadn't seen anyone for two days.

As he sat, looking over the harbour, wishing like hell he had a beer - with a surprising 'click' the door opened and Oscar poked his head around the corner. He glanced about furtively and motioned for Ferret to come to him, which Ferret did.

Oscar did not enter the room but gave Ferret a red, reverse pheromone wipe from the doorway. He whispered, 'Keep that for tomorrow. I gave the rest to the fat fuck, but I never told 'er that I reserved these for you. She'd fucken' kill me if she found out.'

'Thanks, son,' Ferret replied.

'Look, don't . . .' Oscar began, but for some reason didn't finish his sentence. 'Just have 'em handy tomorra.'

He was about to leave when Ferret lightly took his arm. 'Is that a black eye?'

'Yeah. I told ya – every mornin' she hits me.'

'There's a group of us headin' for Warragamba Dam,' Ferret whispered. 'If you can get away, meet us there. If I don't make it, tell the Doc I sent ya.'

Oscar nodded. 'And if I was you, I'd stay away from the Eastern Suburbs for a few weeks, or so.' And with a brief smile, he was gone.

'The Eastern Suburbs?' thought Ferret. 'I wouldn't go near the fucken' place. What's Frankenstein's monster up to now? And what's gunna happen tomorra?'

*

The following morning Ferret was bustled from the Opera House and pushed into the courtyard. Upon regaining his balance, he raised his eyes to find a massive crowd assembled. They cheered, but he had the distinct feeling that they weren't exactly cheering *for* him. Casually attired Arab men jeered and jostled in a sea of colour, whilst up the back, the black berobed women kept their proper place.

Mumsy appeared on the steps beside Ferret. She whispered in his ear. 'G'day, cunt.' And then to the crowd she stated in a loud, authoritative voice. 'This man is to be executed today for Fasaasd Fi al- Ardh, for 'Spreading mischief throughout the land' to de-stabilise our well-balanced society. You all saw what happened down in Bankstown as a result of his magic potion and now he has unleashed terror into the hearts of our Jewish friends in The Eastern Suburbs.'

The crowd remained silent at this. Arab men looked towards each other, raised their shoulders and tilted their hands. 'So, what's the problem?'

Mumsy continued, 'As a result we will first behead him, and then will we hang him!'

At this point a small man, in robes, shuffled quickly towards Mumsy and whispered in her ear.

'Oh, right,' she mumbled. 'A technical difficulty.' She continued, 'Not only has he sought to de-stabilise our society, but he was also caught raping a young man. He was engaging in homosexual behaviour!'

This brought forth stifled giggles from the females up the back and fierce yelling from nine out of the ten male members of the crowd. One in ten remained relatively quiet.

'Fuck off!' shouted Ferret over the melee. 'I 'ain't no stool stabber!'

'Bring out the executioner!' pronounced Mumsy.

A huge man dressed in a black mask; black boots with spurs; black jeans and an open black jacket with adorning chains, and massive tattooed arms, walked up from behind Ferret, with an enormous axe in one hand and with the other, pushed Ferret towards a chopping block.

Ferret looked at him. 'Fuck me. It's one of the Village People.'

The man was not amused and looked like he was going to shove Ferret once again when suddenly, Mumsy held up he hand to quieten the crowd. 'Wait!' she cried.

The crowd settled.

'Due to a technical hitch, we have not yet built the gallows.

There was a collective sigh from the crowd. The day was hot and there was no shade. The men sat down and began to smoke and gossip. The woman had to stand.

'I'm enjoyin' this, Ferret features,' whispered Mumsy. She had a divan brought out upon which she lounged, shaded by palm leaves held by two men: Sambo and Mustafa's eunuch. The eunuch stood directly beside Ferret.

Ferret looked up and did a double take. 'Abdul?' he whispered.

Abdul looked down at Ferret and then immediately straight ahead again.

'Abdul. It's me. Remember?'

Abdul certainly remembered but he didn't respond.

'Listen, sorry about what happened back in Bankstown. What are you doin' here? Did Mustafa rent you out or somefin'? Do you freelance?'

'Silence!' shouted the executioner. He shoved Ferret for effect.

There were a few desultory noises from the crowd. It was hot and sweaty, and they were growing restless as the gallows were being erected.

'Hey, Abdul,' whispered Ferret. 'You seem like a good bloke. In a minute I'm gunna give this big heap of shit behind me somefin', and when I do, don't ask any questions, just run. Okay?'

Abdul said nothing but ever so slightly, nodded his head.

'Good man. There's a meeting at Warragamba later on today, if you can make it.'

Ferret turned to the executioner.

'It must be hot in all that clobber, mate.'

No reply.

'I've got a nice cool wipe in me pocket. Here.'

Ferret handed the executioner a red wipe and the man snatched it without a word. Ferret turned back to the crowd. No one was paying much attention.

Another ten minutes and the heat was oppressive. The crowd was becoming angry, and some were now standing. Mumsy could see that she had played her hand to its natural end. She rose from the divan and addressed the throng.

'We are ready!' she announced with a flourish and the crowd regained its feet and its full voice.

Ferret whispered to the executioner, 'She'll crap on for another ten minutes; then it'll take another ten to get me up there and settled under the noose; then they'll have to cut me down before you can cut off me head. Why not use that nice cool wipe. I won't tell no-one.'

Multiple beads of sweat traced their journeys down the side of the executioner's neck. He was sweltering under his full-face mask. He felt the wipe in his hand and clandestinely tore it out of its paper cover. Then he quietly applied it to the back of his neck, just as Mumsy was saying:

'Yes. We are a unified people! United against everyone else. That's what unity means . . .' when a primordial groan rent the air.

The crowd, as one, watched as the executioner ripped off his mask revealing his huge Mardi-Gras horseshoe moustache. His Ginsbergian howl reverberated through the courtyard and immediately Ferret took off like a poofter at a Trump rally. Abdul was not far behind.

Mumsy was about to command that he stop, when the executioner approached her from behind. She got as far as 'Seize hi . . .' when the huge man porked her up the clacker.

This caught the crowd's attention.

Ferret and Abdul escaped.

There were 'oohs' and 'aahs' from the `mass as the black-clothed man rode Mumsy from behind and dug his spurs into her sides. She screamed and the two of them rolled down the steps and through the crowd with the executioner still attached. He detached when he reached the bottom and stared, wide-eyed, around at the berobbed men. Then, following his distended penis where it would wander, he began ravaging any arse within range.

The men dispersed in wild abandon, treading all over each other in the chaos – or, at least, nine tenths of them did. The other one tenth thought they might hang around just to see what happened.

What happened was physical carnage the likes of which have not been seen since the Khans sacked Europe in the thirteenth century.

Strangely enough the women at the back all stayed

behind as their husbands scattered.

After the maniacal scene quietened and a hundred men and several hundred women lay gently tossing upon the steps in satisfied spam, Mumsy sat upon her toilet. A soothing lotion was rubbed all over a small boy, whom she applied to her ravaged clacker.

'I'll get you, Ferret, you fucker,' she cursed, as she rubbed and dabbed the boy upon her mauled undercarriage.

He later died. There are some experiences that no-one can endure and live.

*

Meanwhile, in Bondi:

'What's that?'
'What's what?'
'What's that under your pecker?'
'What are you talkin . . .?'
'Under your pecker.'
'Oh my God! My testicle is enormous.'
'Go to the doctor.'
'I'm not goin' to the doctor.'
'*Go* to the doctor.'
'Rachael, I'm not goin' to the doctor.'
'Solly, listen to me. Your left ball is enormous. Go to the God damn doctor!'
'Ok. I will. One condition.'
'And what's that?'
'You ask him why your jowls are hanging on your chest.'

*

Ferret and Abdul rode cross country on Ferret's

steed. Abdul sat behind Ferret, but Ferret reckoned he was safe on account of Abdul had no balls and was highly unlikely to get a massive stiffy en route (so to speak).

It was middle day and quite hot by the time they arrived at the dam. As they approached, they could see a large group of people camped beside it. In fact, they heard the noise of the group before they saw it. It sounded like some sort of argument had erupted.

'Please. Please,' the Doc was saying as he stood between two aggressive men. He got clobbered for his trouble by one of them who looked like he was over one hundred years old and had only three teeth in his head. The other, who looked like he was over one hundred years old and had only four teeth in his head, took advantage of this, to punch the man with three teeth in the face. The Doc crawled away to one side, aided by Billy, who was also screaming at the men to stop, but his shrill request was drowned out by the volume of the excited men and women who crowded in a circle around the pugilists like a group of adolescent high school students.

Then it was on.

The man with three teeth grappled with the man with four teeth and the man with four teeth bit the man with three teeth. The man with four teeth lost a tooth as he did do, so now both men had three teeth, which makes this fight difficult to describe because . . . anyway . . . the man with three teeth, who had just been bitten, by the other man with three teeth and also lost a tooth (that's good 'cos it makes it much easier). Then they both bit each other and lost all their remaining teeth (shit). Now both men gummed each other until one man got the better of the other, knocked him out, turned him over, and fucked him up the arse until he was dead, but I'm not sure which man won and which man lost, but let's for argument's sake say that it was the man with three teeth at the start of the fight. He packed his pecker away and held his arms up in triumph to the cheering crowd. One man offered him a pipe which he inhaled upon furiously, before king hitting his corporeally corrupted concubine, to the hilarious glee of the multitude.

Ferret turned up as the dead man was tossed aside into the bushes with his arse up in the air.

'At least that'll give me some place to park me bike,' crowed the victor and he left in another haze of smoke.

'Are you alright?' asked Ferret as the Doc recovered.

'Yes. Yes. I'm fine,' he replied. He dusted himself off and Billy helped him to his feet.

'What the fuck was that all about?' asked Ferret.

'Well, I'm not absolutely certain,' replied the Doc.

'I can tell yous,' chimed in Parrot. 'The good lookin' fella stole the other fella's stash.'

'Which was the good lookin' fella?' asked Ferret.

'The bloke wif the extra toof. He got what he deserved.'

'I'm not sure the punishment was commensurate with the crime,' the Doc interjected.

'Huh?' replied Parrot.

'He means that the punishment didn't fit the crime,' Billy explained.

Parrot turned on Billy, 'Hey, listen, you, don't talk about what you don't understand. We've got a strict code of conduct in our community. The law of the jungle, eh?'

'Yeah, right,' Billy replied with some venom. 'A man steals some of that shit that rots your teeth out, so he deserves to be fucked up the arse, murdered and thrown into bushes for a burial. I hate you.' He stormed off.

'Hey, dickhead!' yelled Parrot in response.

'Leave 'im be. He'll calm down,' said Ferret. Then changing the subject, he asked. 'So how are things goin' down here? Plenty of water. Plenty of shade.'

'Yeah. Alright,' replied Parrot. 'So long as the Doc here keeps up his supply of the meth, everyone's happy.'

'I wouldn't call what I just saw – happy,' countered the Doc.

'Ah, just a friendly difference of opinion.'

The Doc looked at Ferret; Ferret shrugged; the Doc shook his head; Parrot walked away.

'Doc,' said Ferret, 'how is the supply of Ice holding out?'

'Well, I've made pounds of the stuff, so enough for the next couple of weeks at least.'

'Good work.' Ferret fidgeted about a bit. Then said: 'Look, I'm sorry to keep asking you for favours, but I'm gunna need another big one.'

'Go on.'

'Can you make LSD in liquid form?'

The Doc was unfazed, 'Yes. I think so. I'll have to locate the chemicals. How much of it do you need?'

'A big bucket full should do it.'

'Ferris, what on earth for?'

'Just trust me. I got a plan.'

'Very well,' replied the Doc but he sounded less than convinced. 'You know how strong that stuff is though, don't you?'

'That's what I'm banking on. And at the risk of strainin' the friendship . . .'

'Ferret,' replied the Doc, 'there's no need to apologise. I haven't had this much fun since humour was disallowed in Sydney.'

'Thanks, Doc. I need you to make a shitload more wipes: both kinds. Take Billy too. If he hangs around here for too long Parrot will find a reason to kill 'im.'

'Very well.'

'How long will you be?'

'Give me a couple of days.'

'Okay. Thanks, Doc. Tomorrow Abdul and me will pay a little visit to me old mate, Mustafa.'

'But master . . .,' started Abdul.

'I'll explain it all to you, Abdul. And don't call me master. The name's Ferret. Jesus, you're as bad as them Ball less Atheists.'

''That is because, Master Ferret, we have the same thing in common.'

'And what's that?'

Abdul looked down at his groin. 'Nothing,' he replied with a smile.

Ferret laughed. 'That's actually pretty good, Abdul. And don't worry about Mustafa. I've got it covered.'

A movement behind a nearby tree caught Ferret's attention.

'Who goes there!' he yelled on impulse.

Oscar popped his head out from behind the tree.

'Oscar! Come on over, son.' shouted Ferret. He added proudly, 'This is me boy.'

Oscar looked over with concern at the Icers camped along the side of the dam.

'It's okay, mate,' shouted Ferret. 'They won't hurt ya. What are you doin' here?'

'I escaped when you did.'

'Good boy. Tether your horse and tomorrow you can come wif me and Abdul to see Mustafa. It's good to see you, son.'

'Thanks . . .,' replied Oscar, . . . dad.'

And Ferret was a proud as a post prostatectomy patient with a hard on.

*

Back in Bondi:

'Dr Goldstein, I'm here for a very embarrassing reason.'

'Don't tell, Heimi, I already know.'

'You do?'

'Yes. You have one swollen testicle.'

'How did you know?'

'I've been looking at nothing but balls for the last day and a half.'

'How come?'

'There's an outbreak of mumps.'

'Mumps? How come?'

'I don't know exactly, but since so many people around here choose not to get vaccinated it's spreading like a nineteen-year-old Madonna.'

'I never saw that issue.'

'The issue we need to talk about is not 'Penthouse' – it's vaccination.'

'Is it fatal, doc?'

'Vaccination isn't, not getting vaccinated can be.'

'That's not what a past Australian of the Year told my son.'

'Yeah? Well, she's wrong. If she thinks that, she's batty. The trouble is none of us leave the Eastern Suburbs enough. We don't always see the big picture. Too much Shabbos and not enough site seeing. My eight-year-old son went to Katoomba on a camp last month. Until then he thought everyone in the world was Jewish.'

'They're not?'

'See?'

*

While the Icers were beating the shit out of each other at Warragamba, a very irate Mustafa was visiting Mumsy in The Opera House. Word had reached him that no one was dying in the Eastern Suburbs.

He ranted, 'They are not dying, you fool! All they have is the mumps! Who told you that paramyxovirus was lethal?'

'A boy.'

'Your son?'

'He's not my son.'

'I don't care who he is. I will kill him. Hand him over to me.'

'I can't. He pissed off.'

'You have failed to remove the Jews from Sydney. They continue to use the water supply.'

Mumsy was beginning to tire of Mustafa's attitude, but having been publicly humiliated by Ferret, she was out for revenge, and she needed Mustafa's compliance for a while, so she remained as polite as she could.

'Yes, your golden-ness. But tell me, what is it with you Muzzos and the Jews anyway? All you ever do is fight.'

'Because Islam has precedence over Judaism. They stole our prophets and claimed them as their own!'

'Sorry, oh scintillating star, but unless my memory is faulty didn't your religion come six or seven hundred years after Jesus? And didn't you guys rip off ideas from the Jews - including Jesus?'

'Silence!' boomed Mustafa. 'Jerusalem belongs to us! And if you say another word,' he placed his right hand on the hilt of his scimitar, 'I will silence you, myself.'

Mumsy was internally furious but externally calm. 'I am sorry to offend you, munificent one. I'll see what I can do about the Jews.'

Mustafa's eyes were ablaze, but he removed his hand from his sword. 'While those bogan white men are camped at Warragamba, I shall take my men and take control of the western water supplies. If you wish to join in the spoils, you must eradicate the Jews. You have two days. Slaughter them.' He turned sharply and his robes licked the floor. He left.

Mumsy watched him go and let go the fart she had been harbouring. 'I'll get you, you big-headed cunt. Just you wait.'

*

The next morning Ferret, Abdul and Oscar set off for Bankstown.

'Rightio, boys,' said Ferret. It's seventeen K's to Bankstown, cross country. We should be there by midday at a canter.'

But as they mounted their steeds, something was obviously troubling Abdul. 'Master Ferret,' he said.

'Yes Abdul,' Ferret replied patiently. He had given up on Abdul losing the 'master' bit.

'Mustafa will kill me for running away.'

'No, he won't,' Ferret replied with certainty.' He gently slapped the two bags, one attached to each side of his saddle. 'I got some magic potion here that I'll barter in return for you.'

'Oh, Master Ferret,' sighed Abdul, 'you would do this for me?'

'Abdul, I'd do it for a white man. I 'ain't too keen on slavery. But I warn ya, there may be a price tag attached to your freedom.'

'Whatever it is, I shall welcome it,' Abdul replied.'

'Good on ya, dad,' said Oscar. 'I wish I'd been brought up by you and not a Foc.'

'What's a Foc?'

'A fat old cunt,' replied Oscar. 'Speakin' of which, I never told ya what I told Mumsy.'

'Yeah? What's that?'

'Mustafa told her to kill all the Jews. So, I told her she could do it by spreadin' paramyxovirus.'

'Sounds dangerous,' replied Ferret.

'That's what I thought, and so did she, and she believed me.'

'What is it?'

'The mumps. They must be wonderin' where it come from.'

Ferret laughed. 'I might tell 'em.'

'I'm just glad you turned up 'n' rescued me. I couldn't stand another day with that fat shit.'

'Well, now that I've found ya, I'll be lookin' after ya. And someday soon, when this shit is over and done wif, I'll tell you a story and introduce you to a bloke you are really gunna love.'

They took off at a gallop and at around lunch time they reached the outskirts of Bankstown. Oscar and Abdul left their horses to graze under a tree and followed Ferret and his laden steed into town.

Mustafa was couched in the main square, as usual, surrounded by his wives, but on this occasion, he was also flanked by a dozen burly men with scimitars. As the three approached, several of the large men looked towards Mustafa for orders. He held up two fingers and they stood down.

'I see ya brung in the cavalry,' said Ferret, nodding towards the large men.

'In these troubling times,' replied Mustafa, 'such are the requirements of a leader.'

Ferret didn't buy that for a second. He had kept his eyes open as he, Oscar and Abdul had walked the final leg into Bankstown. He had seen the hundreds of tethered horses and the excess of men in the city centre. He knew that something was afoot, but he said, 'Yeah. No worries.'

'I believe that you, yourself, narrowly escaped at the hands of that gargantuan in the city.'

'We have a long history.'

'I do not trust her.'

'Good thinkin'.'

'So, you see? We are natural allies, you and I.'

Ferret smiled but both men knew that they could trust one another as much as a frog could trust a hungry taipan.

'I see you have brought my slave back to me, but who is this young man with the lonely tuft of hair?'

'This is me son, Oscar.'

'I thought as much. He is the splitting image. And what a poetic name,' Mustafa stifled a smile.

'Yeah. It was either that or Mahammad,' retorted Oscar.

For a moment Mustafa paused, and for that moment, Ferret thought that Mustafa might be angry, but instead, he let out a hearty laugh. 'I see that the fig does not fall far from the tree.' He motioned towards the two bags swinging upon the horse's sides. 'But what surprise do you have for me this time?'

'I'm gunna make Mumsy pay for what she done to me, but I need some help.'

'Go on,' replied Mustafa, sitting further back on his divan.

'You heard about how I escaped? How that executioner fella lost the plot and went crazy?'

'The women likened him to a wild escaped bear in heat.' He cast a glance towards his wives. 'But a male bear, which they apparently entertained for some time.'

The women shuffled in their burqas.

'I sent him into that rage by getting' 'im to dab another secret potion of mine onto his neck. And in these saddle bags here I've got hundreds of 'em I'm willin' to give ya.'

Mustafa sized up Ferret for a moment and stared upward for some time. At last he said, 'Two questions. How do I know that you are telling the truth about the magic potion? And why would you supply them to me?'

'To answer the second question,' Ferret replied, 'I want you to give them to your troops when you attack Sydney, as you soon plan to do.'

Mustafa did not contest this.

'Because I want to defeat Mumsy as much as you do, and I want my share of power when that happens.'

'And why should I invest you with power when we

are successful?'

''Cos I've got two hundred maniacs without a brain between 'em smokin' Ice by Warragamba Dam, just itchin' to hit or fuck somfin.'

'Very well. It will be done,' Mustafa said, but he was lying.

'It'll be my pleasure,' Ferret replied, and so was he.

'And the first question?' enquired Mustafa. 'The story of men going wild is as old as history itself. For the main part it *is* history.'

'Yeah, but one bloke rapin' a few hundred men and women at a time 'ain't exactly routine. And you saw me last magic potion work on Abdul. And I bet you managed to find time to pay at least one of them nieces of yours a visit?'

Now it was Mustafa's turn to shuffle uneasily. He thought for a moment. 'What you say is true. But if I am to combine forces with you, I will need more solid proof.'

'That's why I brung Abdul,' Ferret replied.

'What?' whispered Abdul.

Ferret approached his horse and withdrew a single wipe. As he did so, he was turned momentarily from Mustafa. 'This is the price of freedom,' he whispered back.

Concern ran across Abdul's face like a startled teenage boy whose been caught wanking over his sister's best friend.

Ferret turned to Mustafa. 'I suggest that you and your wives stand behind your guards.'

Mustafa replied, 'Your potion may be strong, but I doubt Abdul will have the strength to overpower this entire crowd.'

'I wouldn't bet on it,' Ferret replied.

'Enough!' commanded Mustafa. 'The tales that have reached me from Sydney were surely exaggerated. And look at Abdul. He is weak and pathetic, and he has no balls.'

This was said very loudly and many of the men in the crowd laughed, except for a few who had witnessed the chaos at The Opera House. They gathered up their wives and left. Strangely enough, many of the women who had also been there preferred to hang around.

'Get on with the demonstration!' commanded Mustafa.

'Give me that wipe, Master Ferret,' said Abdul through gritted teeth. 'We'll see who's laughing then.'

'Good lad,' Ferret replied, and he handed Abdul the red wipe.

The guards looked on sternly, and Mustafa and the crowd watched silently, as Abdul opened the single packet and slowly wiped the small moist cloth on his neck.

For a moment there was silence. Enough time passed for some doubt to rustle through the crowd. The first small catcall of derision began to break through the silence when Abdul began to tremble fiercely. The silence returned. Abdul's face began to redden, and a low-pitched rumble began to emanate from his lower torso. It grew in intensity. Simultaneously, a huge erection thrust erratically from his loin cloth and seemingly began to look around its environment for victims.

Mustafa stood up on impulse. 'It is impossible!' he bellowed.

But it was possible, and as the oversized organ cast its single eye about like a submarine's periscope, both men and women stepped back in awful anticipation. The guards unsheathed their scimitars and stood in a line in front of Mustafa.

It began. Abdul screamed at the top of his lungs and lunged into the crowd. Burqas, thobes and sirwals crowded the sky. Abdul was cracking heads together at the rate of a pair per second as he advanced through the multitude, whilst simultaneously porking multiple orifices, regardless of whether they were covered or exposed. His python penetrated cloth and tore into vagina and arsehole alike. His cock spat out its fury: one quick thrust at a time; one quick load at a time; into one distraught cavity at a time. At one point he turned in wild circles driven by his penis' machine gun rapidity. His engorged genitalia struck forward like an enraged cobra attacking all in its path. Men and women scrambled about like wounded crabs evading the unexpected tide. Abdul screamed and rose his fists into the air. Upon those fists writhed wretched men, impaled, wild-eyed and crying for mercy. He clapped his hands and the men cracked heads and fell unconscious behind him. He ran at full pace through the melee impaling all and sundry. At one point he collected six people upon his glorious phallus and, as he passed, swiped away bystanders with his flailing, maniacal cock.

At length, the market square resembled a battlefield shortly after the slaughter. Abdul stood among the carnage, breathing heavily, his semi-flaccid appendage trembling and twitching with the exertion of combat. It was only at this time, when the furore of his temper and passion had dissipated, that the guards felt brave enough to approach him and bring him before Mustafa.

The sheik appeared sheepishly from behind several guards, recomposed himself, adjusted his robe, resat and tried to look leader-like, but it was clear to Ferret that he was both massively impressed and disturbed by the display.

'So, what'd'ya think?' asked Ferret.

It took Mustafa a moment or two to regain his voice, but when he did, it cracked a brief falsetto as he replied, 'This is indeed powerful magic.' He cleared his throat. 'With only one wipe for each of my men I can easily conquer Sydney.'

'Then we have a deal?' Ferret asked.

'I want to trust you,' replied Mustafa pensively, 'but you must understand it is against my usual instincts. However, if you are prepared to leave your son behind as insurance until after we have taken Sydney, then yes, we have a deal.'

Ferret was about to protest when Oscar stopped him.

'Dad,' Oscar interjected, 'I'll be alright. I've survived so far.'

'I warn you no harm will come to him,' pronounced Mustafa.

Abdul added, between heavy breaths, 'I will stay with him, master Ferret.'

Mustafa looked quizzically at Abdul. 'You were staying anyway, slave. Or have you forgotten who your master is?'

'Part of my deal was gunna be Abdul's freedom,' Ferret replied, 'and it still is. But I can hold off until we defeat Mumsy, so long as my boy is safe. Abdul and Oscar can stay here, and you can have all the wipes.'

'Very well,' replied Mustafa. 'Let it be so.'

With a click of his fingers the guards approached Oscar and Abdul.

'Make sure no harm comes to him Mustafa or . . .'

But Oscar stopped him, 'Dad. Trust me. We'll be okay.'

'I will keep to my word,' said Mustafa, 'but there is one last thing I am keen to know.'

'And what's that?' asked Ferret.

'Where is the young girl with the short hair and the boyish looks?

'Shazam's back at Warragamba,' Ferret replied. 'Why?'

'Oh, no reason. Give her my regards.'

'Yeah. Sure,' Ferret replied, but he remembered Mustafa's previous interest in Billy.

'Randy old cunt,' he thought to himself.

Then the two men mock-smiled. Ferret handed over the bags of pheromones and walked away with a heart filled with trepidation. Mustafa knew something he didn't. He could hear it in the tone of his voice.

*

Back in Windsor, the Doc was down below The Church Bar, cooking up his brews for Ferret, when he heard a loud scuffle above him. He climbed the stairs and opened the hatch long enough to hear Billy's screams for help, and to see several large Arab men roughly bustling him out of the door. He followed as far as the door, keeping well out of sight.

Through the window, he saw thirty or forty men in robes, on horses, guns in holsters and swords in sheathes. Two men were tying up Billy. Then, one threw him across the saddle of a riderless horse, jumped upon his own stallion and rode off at speed.

A large, muscular man, who was obviously the commander of the platoon, spoke to the rest.

'Go to the sites to which you have been designated. Take possession of the water outlets and all houses with large water tanks.'

'Shall we imprison anyone protecting them?' asked one of his men.

'No,' replied their leader. 'Kill them. Kill anyone you find.'

The horsemen dispersed.

The Doc turned away from the door and rested his back against the wall in thought. 'I must warn Ferret,' he said aloud, and he ran downstairs to collect the bottles of Lysergic Acid.

*

Half a dozen senior policemen and several generals in full regalia stood to attention in The Opera House courtyard.

Mumsy addressed them.

'Right, you cunts!' she shouted. 'Listen up. I'm sick of kowtowing to that Muzzo fuckwit. The time has come to regain our supremacy. As you all know, I am a lying, deceptive bitch, but I get things done. And no, I'm not politically correct, as the more astute of you may have noticed. That's why ya love me. That's why you elected me dictator. Because I was the only one who understood that people 'ain't really politically correct. They just got scared of speakin' their minds from the nineties 'coz of a few noisy fucken' minority groups. Never give people a right, boys 'n' girls, 'coz you'll have a cunt of a time if you ever wanna revoke it. So, I am telling you now, without reservation, that I know what Sinbad is up to. According to my spies, he has amassed an army and intends to attack Sydney. And I'm guessing that he intends to use the Icers as part of his attack force.'

A small wave of disquiet ruffled the ranks of the listening men.

'But don't worry,' she continued, 'we still have time to prepare. Coppers and generals get your men and your horses ready. We're gunna lure 'em in and kill the fucken' lot of 'em, 'coz that's what tolerant people do. Dismissed.'

The men dispersed and Mumsy farted again, because it's always nice to end a scene with some sort of tag.

*

By the time Ferret got back to Warragamba the Doc was already there. He told Ferret what had happened.

'That treacherous bastard,' said Ferret. 'I knew he was up to no good. So he wants to control all the water, does 'e? Next thing it'll be fucking Sharia Law.'

'What shall we do about Billy?' asked the Doc.

'We can't do nuffin' for the time bein', unfortunately. Poor old Billy'll have to fend for himself. Or fend *off* for himself, more like it. But we're gunna have to move fast to save him. Did ya make up that LSD, Doc?'

He pulled a dozen old beer bottles out of hessian bag. 'I did. It's right here. But I hope you know what you're doing, Ferris. This stuff is dynamite. I hope you're not planning on giving it to these Icer barbarians.'

'No,' Ferret replied. 'I'm goin' over to the Eastern Suburbs, hopefully to get us some new allies. But I want you to do one thing for me later on this arvo.'

'And what's that?'

'I want you to take them bottles further downstream and tip 'em all in the dam. I'll warn the Jews. You make sure these Icer fuckers stay in this vicinity.'

'But that will pollute the water supply within a day or so.'

'That's the idea. I'll be back later tonight.'

Ferret jumped onto his horse. He swivelled around as he was leaving. 'And Doc, I'm plannin' on movin' camp tomorra.'

Then he rode off to the northeast.

*

On Bankstown Oval, where the Waugh brothers used to score a lot of runs, Mustafa had set up his huge tent and a host of smaller ones for his guards, his wives and their attendants. There were no fires. It was unusually warm for early April, but there was a full moon and a silvery hue was shed upon the encampment.

Mustafa entered the tent and two guards stood aside to reveal his captives: Oscar, Abdul and Billy. Mustafa approached Billy.

'Ah, little one,' he purred licentiously, 'I see by your

apparel that you are a young boy and not the maiden you professed to be.'

He touched Billy's cheek and Billy pushed his hand away.

Mustafa laughed, 'No matter. Why make a fuss over such a small thing?'

'Leave 'im alone, you sleazy prick,' countered Oscar.

Mustafa looked Oscar up and down as if he was a rotten piece of meat. 'I have seen you before, you uncouth turd. Now, where might that be?' He studied the boy for a moment. 'No matter. It will come to me. Guards, take the pretty one to my tent.'

Billy screamed and flailed as he was muscled out and Oscar had to be restrained, but it was useless. Soon Billy's protestations diminished into the twilight.

Mustafa laughed and turned on Oscar, 'And you, son of Ferret, if you deceive me, I will kill you.' He peered closely at Oscar's face. 'I know I have seen you before,' he mused. 'And you, Abdul, you ungrateful pig, I will execute you in two days, when the west is secured, and my troops are ready to attack. Guards! Wrap him in chains. Deny him food and water.'

Mustafa exited as Abdul felt the blunt end of a scimitar.

*

A little earlier that evening, Ferret had reached Bondi and knocked on the door of the first house he came to. It happened to be Solly and Rachael's house. I know it's unlikely, but it saves me from creating more characters.

'Who is it?' asked Solly, without opening the door.

'My name's Ferret!' shouted Ferret.

Ferret heard Rachael shout to Solly, 'Who is it?'

'I think he's selling ferrets!' shouted Solly.

'Tell 'im we don't want any!' Rachael shouted back.

'We don't want any!' shouted Solly.

'No mate. Me name's Ferret!' shouted Ferret.

'His name's Ferret!' Solly shouted to Rachael.

'Well open the door!' shouted Rachael to Solly.

'He could be anybody!' shouted Solly to Rachael.

'Of course he's somebody, you schlemiel! He spoke to you didn't he?'

'Yeah!'

'So he couldn't be a ferret! Open the God damn door!'

'Okay! I'll open the door!'

And he did.

'Can I help you?'

'My name's Ferret.'

'What'd he say?' shouted Rachael.

'His name's Ferret!' shouted Solly to Rachael.

'Now, let's not start that again!' shouted Rachael to Solly. 'So let 'im in!'

'Come in. Come in,' said Solly.

So Ferret did. He followed Solly's limping figure and found himself in a cosy ground floor apartment.

'Please sit. You look cold. Would you like some coffee?'

'No thanks,' replied Ferret.

'Maybe some soup?'

'No thanks. I'll be right.'

Rachael entered. She was middle aged, like her husband, but while he was skinny and bald, she was matronly and had hair. She also had the most pendulous jowls that Ferret had ever seen.

'Hello. I'm Rachael and this is my husband, Solly. Did you offer him some coffee?'

'Of course I offered him coffee.'

'It's cold. Would you like some soup?'

'I offered him some soup.'

'Please excuse my husband. He has no manners.'

'I have manners.'

'He only thinks about himself.'

'You should talk. Last night she ate the last of the biscuits. Didn't even ask me. And I'm selfish?'

'And right now he's even worse. He has the mumps and he's become a kvetcher.'

'I'm a kvetcher? She has mumps too. All she does is complain. Oy, these jowls, they hurt.'

'Listen, with these jowls I could mop the floor. All you have is one enlarged ball.'

'Just because you can't see it, doesn't mean it isn't significant.'

'I don't wanna see it.'

'It's givin' me hell.'

'I told ya. I don't wanna see it. Would you like a roll mop, mister ferret?'

'Listen I need to talk to the local honcho.'

'The head honcho?' asked Solly.

'That's a tautology,' retorted Rachael.

'What's a tautology?'

'A tautology is when you repeat . . .'

'Rachael, I know what a tautology is. What's the tautology?'

'Head honcho. Honcho means head man. So head honcho is like saying head head man.'

'Excuse me. I should slit my throat and become a Muslim. God forbid.'

'That's what I'm here about,' said Ferret.

'You want I should become a Muslim?'

'Is this some kind of witness protection thing?'

'You mean - Jehovah Witness thing.'

'Sydney needs your help. We'll soon be under attack.'

'Sydney needs our help?'

'He just said that. We'll soon be under attack?'

'He just said that too.''

'So who's the honcho in the Eastern Suburbs? Someone who people would follow in a crisis?'

'There's Wally Silvermire,' offered Solly.

'Wally Silvermire? You're joking. He's a schmuck,' countered Rachael.

'You should know. You went out with him.'

'One time; one time years ago before I even met Solly, I went out with Wally Silvermire. That's how I know that's he's a schmuck.'

'What about David Cohen?'

'I never went out with David Cohen.'

'I never said you did?'

'David Cohen is a schlimazel. Put him in charge of an army and he'd jinx it. They'd kill themselves before they got to the enemy.'

'Please,' interrupted Ferret, 'Who would you say is the strongest public figure around?

'There's Rabbi Abelman.'

'Are you kiddin' me? All he ever does is talk to that shikse in the delicatessen?'

'The man shouldn't eat?'

'It's not the eating that's the problem. The man should look for God above his navel is all I'm sayin'. Perhaps you'd like some gefilte fish, mister ferret?'

'Is there anyone else yous could think of that people around here would listen to?'

'There's Doctor Goldstein.'

'He's a mensch.'

'I can't believe it Rachael. You agreed with me on something.'

'What d'ya mean? I always agree with you.'

'Could you take me to see him?' asked Ferret.

'Of course. He lives down by the beach.'

'He has money. He's a doctor.'

'I coulda been a doctor.'

'I coulda been a doctor, he says.'

'I coulda.'

'So why did you go into the rag trade?'

''Cos I'm Jewish.'

'So is Doctor Goldstein.'

'Let's go,' said Ferret, standing abruptly. 'I'm in a hurry.'

'I'm with you,' said Solly and followed him.

'Don't be too long. Your matzo balls will get cold.'

'Everything's balls these days,' said Solly.

Minutes later, Ferret and Solly were in Doctor Goldstein's clinic.

'Hey, Doctor Goldstein why you workin' so late?' asked Solly.

'Why do think, Solly? Every man from here to La Perouse has aggravated balls.' He pointed at Ferret. 'Who are you?'

'The name's Ferret.'

'Ferret? This is a name?'

'My real name's Ferris but everyone calls me Ferret.'

'My real name's Leon but everybody calls me Leon. How do you do?'

They shook hands.

'You don't look Jewish.'

'I'm not.'

'Thank God for that. I thought for a minute the distended balls had caused an abnormality. No offence.'

'None taken.'

'We spend so much time protecting our gene pool we're seeing more inbred deformities these days. So, how can I help?'

So Ferret told Doctor Goldstein the whole story, which starts on page one, if you're not sure. And at the end of that, the Doctor sat back pensively into his chair and ruminated for a considerable time. Eventually he sat forward with urgency and said quietly, but intensely, 'Sorry. I was thinking about something else. Could you say that again?' So Ferret did.

At length, the doctor said the same thing again. No he didn't. This time he said, 'Mister Ferret, I am greatly disturbed by what you have just told me. I have been worried for some time that Mustafa Khan would make such a move. It was only a matter of time before he mobilised. We have been too ensconced here, in our tiny world. He, like his predecessor, Mustafa Shit, has always had designs on our sandy beaches. It's in their genes.'

'They have sand in their jeans? asked Solly.

'I will mobilise as many of the East as I can. We shall meet you on the battlefield for deadly combat. Where will that be?'

Ferret replied heroically and, for no apparent reason, spoke like a Cavalier in the English Civil War, 'We meet at dawn in Victoria Park, there to defeat the Muslim threat and protect our Australian way of life.'

'Dawn?' interjected Solly. 'Could we make it a little later? Tomorrow night I'm playin' cards with Walter and Heimi. I won't get home 'til midnight.'

'Very well,' Mister Ferret, replied Doctor Goldstein. He raised his glass. 'L' Chaim.'

'Here's lookin' at ya,' replied Ferret.

They drank.

Solly added, 'You're lucky they didn't decide to attack on Saturday.'

*

At about that same time, Mumsy was in her bedroom masturbating. She had acquired an epileptic and waited for him to fit before she had inserted him in her muck hole. She pushed him up a bit too far and he slipped in completely. The poor man's arms and legs protruded outward from her skin like a woman in the last days of pregnancy, or even better imagery, like the guy in Alien.

His manic, squirming panic only increased her pleasure, so that when she came, she spat him into the far wall with such velocity, that he cracked his skull against it, and mercifully knew no more.

Then there was a knock at the door.

'What the fuck do you want?' she bellowed, as she mopped up her cunt with a dwarf.

'Excuse me, Mm'am,' a small voice stuttered, 'but there is wword from the Mmuslim camp.'

'Well come in, you snivelling cocksucker.'

A tiny, bespectacled man tremulously opened the door and entered. He looked like . . . you know the guy in the original Lost in Space who plays the Space Trader? Well, him, except that he was a lot smaller and was really scared looking and he was Asian, whereas the other guy wasn't and, oh yeah, the other guy who played the Space Trader didn't have spectacles either, so, on reflection, he didn't look anything like that other guy. But anyway, this little guy came in and said, 'Um.'

'Well spit it out Jinping, or I'll shit on ya.'

This didn't increase the man's confidence. He began to stammer. 'Thethe spy ssssaid that Mmmmustafafa . . .'

'Oh for fucks, sake!' she shouted, jumped from the bed and shat on him. As she slammed the door, his muffled cries for help from within the massive upside-down cone of faeces, diminished behind her.

'What the fuck's goin' on?' she asked an astrologer she kept handy in the foyer, because she had heard that Hitler had one . . . an astrologer, not a foyer, although he probably had one of those as well.

The astrologer was wearing an outfit like Jimmy Pages' in 'The Song Remains the Same' but he also had a turban with stars on it and those gold Genie shoes that curl backwards at the front (if that makes sense).

He looked into his crystal ball and said, 'Mustafa Khan intends to attack you with a complement of two thousand men at Victoria Park, tomorrow.'

'Fuck,' replied Mumsy, 'You can tell all that from that crystal ball?'

'No,' replied the man, 'That little cunt who just come through told me.'

*

The next morning, Ferret rode into camp just before sunup. He went to see Parrot. 'Hey, Parrot,' he whispered. 'Wake up.'

'What d'ya want?' mumbled Parrot, rolling over onto his side on his grassy bed.

'We gotta move, mate. The Muzzos are comin'.'

'What?' replied Parrot, rubbing his rheumy eyes.

'We gotta get to Victoria Park by nightfall. It's a day's walk.'

'Hang on,' Parrot replied and he picked up a full pipe that was in readiness beside him and dragged it dry.

'That shows forethought, mate. Good work.'

'That's why I'm the boss,' Parrot stated, his wits now alive with adrenaline, but even so, he hadn't picked up on Ferret's sarcasm. 'Now, what's this about Muzzos?'

So Ferret told Parrot about the impending battle and Parrot told the Icers and the Icers complained that sixteen kilometres is a long way to walk, so Ferret told them that he would not ride his horse but would walk with them to show leadership. They still weren't convinced, until Ferret lied that there was a land of milk and honey in Victoria Park, where little children handed out bags of cocaine and MDMA grew on trees and ice-cream was made of Ice and besides, they were running low on meth and so this was the only option.

An hour later, not long after sunrise, grudgingly they set out from Warragamba Dam. They stopped off for a quick smoke at the Warragamba Recreation Area, then headed up Farnsworth Road until they got to the old Caltex Station in Wallacia. It took ages to get served because the place had been destroyed years before during the plague, so they made their way across the Nepean River on the Silverdale Road and took the second exit onto Park Road. However, several Icers accidentally took the first exit and they kept going until they reached the land of their ancestors in South Windsor, where they discovered a rich vein of naturally occurring meth and lived happily ever after. The main contingent beat the shit out of some old guy in Luddenham because he had teeth, and filled up on Ice at Kemp's Creek and ran at top speed until they reached Cabramatta, forcing Ferret to ride to keep up with them. They slowed down at Bass Hill, where some of them wanted to see the drive-in but Ferret explained that (a) it was daytime and (b) it had closed seventeen years before. They were stealthy as they passed Bankstown and Lakemba, they were paranoid by the time they got to Ashfield, so they had another smoke. They all stopped for sex on the Parramatta Road at Annandale while Ferret watched the sun starting to set, and they finally made it to Victoria Park, Ultimo. It was after dark by the time they set up camp, or rather, lay on the ground, and the Icers were all so tired that they went to sleep straight away.

Ferret and the Doc talked for a while. They looked up at the Southern Cross and wondered what the new day would bring. Ferret cast his eye over Victoria Park and envisaged the carnage of the morrow. Then he, too, fell into a dead slumber.

A short time before Ferret and the Icers reached Victoria Park, Mustafa and the Muzzos had reached Warragamba Dam to parley with Ferret, where they discovered that he and the Icers were gone.

Mustafa was angry that Ferret had betrayed him. He looked out, over the dam, and skipped a stone angrily across its surface. He stared across the water, a slight zephyr ruffled his robes romantically, as it always did, regardless of whether there was a zephyr or not. The sun set behind him and its rays flooded around him in glorious Lawrence of Arabia splendour.

To himself he whispered, 'We shall see you on the battlefield tomorrow, Ferret Cutler,' then to an attendant standing behind him he commanded, 'Bring Shazam to my tent.'

Later that evening, Doctor Goldstein was addressing a bunch of Jews on Bondi Beach. They all wore white socks and shoes and complained about the sand. Both Orthodox and non-traditional Jews were gathered in their hundreds, arguing about the Talmud, so they missed what was being said, but pledged to turn up to Victoria park early the next morning, so long as there were bagels.

At the same time, Mumsy was oiling her bath. She had to lubricate it because once she forgot and had to walk nude, in search of a hammer, carrying the bath on her back.

She had been in there for half an hour when there was a knock at the door.

'What the fuck is it, you turd!' she bellowed.

Sambo entered with his enormous appendage slapping against his left knee.

'Oh, it's you,' she said. 'Prime that thing so I've got something to hang onto while I get out of this tub.'

*

The following morning was crisp. A fine mist hung over Victoria Park. Ferret gathered up the Icers and he spake unto them thus:

'Alright, listen up, druggos. Today we strike a blow for democracy and your right to fuck yourselves up however you want and whenever you want!'

There was no applause because everyone was toking on ice pipes.

'In a short while, the Muzzos will attack. I seen 'em smokin' hash behind The Seymour Centre. Now, I know yous are fearless and fucken' strong when you're on that shit, but I'm gunna give yous all somfin' what'll make the difference in the battle to come.' He began handing out red reverse pheromones, which the excited mass grabbed greedily. 'Don't use 'em 'til I tell yous. We'll hold our ground here at Lake Northam until I get word from the Jews that there in position in Sydney University. My guess is the Muzzos will attack front-on and Mumsy and the Politically Correct will assail us from our left flank from somewhere in the vicinity of Toby's Estate Coffee Roasters. Good fortune, Icers.'

But no one heard him say this because some of them were punching one another; some were fucking, and some were doing both.

'Morning rituals,' thought Ferret. 'Everybody likes routine.'

And he waited for the onslaught.

On their Eastern flank, in Chippendale, behind Angry Tony's Pizza and Liquor Delivery, Mumsy was preparing for battle with her Politically Correct troops. Full of nerves before the battle, they were hydrating with copious quantities of water.

'Oh Christopher,' said Neville (remember him) passing on the water jug, 'I do hope we don't have to kill anyone from a minority group.'

'Don't worry,' replied Christopher, 'they're all white, so we can kill whomever we want.'

'That's the great thing about political correctness,' added Neville, 'White is Never Right, as the saying goes.'

'Right! Listen up!' boomed Mumsy, so loudly that Neville followed through, but just a little bit. He'd been doing that ever since he was buggered by the female copper's six-inch clitoris. 'When we get the signal from Mustafa, we attack Ferret and the Fuckwits. When we finish with them, we double cross the Muzzos and Warragamba is ours!'

'Who will we attack then?' asked a voice from the crowd.

'Ourselves, off course. We're just a bunch of miserable, whingeing cunts and we have to get offended by someone!'

And everyone cheered.

'Now, give me that jug. I'm fucken' thirsty.' And she drained the jug in one steady gulp, before picking a clinker the size of a tombola from her arse, flicking it and knocking out the drummer boy.

Behind The Seymour Centre Mustafa was handing out the blue, original pheromone wipes that Ferret had given him. Beside him stood Oscar, Abdul and Billy, who had a pillow tied to his arse.

'Prepare for battle, men!,' Mustafa commanded. 'Your horses have been well watered. When I give the signal, use your pheromone wipes and charge upon your steeds like you have never charged before. The fate of Sydney is in your hands!'

'Allah Akbar!' rose from the throats of the Muzzo horsemen like a light turd in a toilet bowl.

All was now in readiness. The tension was as thick as a poofter's hymen. When . . . Sorry but it's late and I'll just have time to have a wank before the news. See you tomorrow.

But wait. The news is being taped and I can see it later. Cool.

No, not really. It's the next day. Here we go:

The first thing that happened was that the Muzzo horses began to make odd murmuring sounds. Several of the Muzzos could have sworn that they heard the horse they spurred whisper back, 'Hey. That hurts,' as they galloped off, across City Road and towards Victoria Park. Some of the riders couldn't seem to get anywhere: their sound and vision appeared to be growing evermore towards slow motion. Others shook their heads as the advancing park revealed itself as a slideshow narrated by Charlton Heston.

Mumsy, lumbering at the rear of her foot-soldiers, conceived their thundering feet and running bodies before her as a boiling cauldron of tar and could have sworn that she heard a mammoth trumpet in the distance - 'Fuck the La Brea Tar Pits,' in a ghostly whisper. All the stranger because she had never heard a mammoth trumpet before.

At that same moment, Doctor Goldstein and the Jews (which was not a bad name for a band before political correctness) were in readiness in the University of Sydney Law School, discussing the degree to which Einstein had been involved in the creation of Palestine, when Doctor Goldstein gave the signal to Ferret that he and his swollen-balled men were ready to attack the left flank of the advancing horsemen.

Ferret stood beside the Doc and gave the order for the Icers to apply the red Pheromones.

'I hope that LSD's had time to work, Doc,' he said.

'I think we may be in luck,' he replied. 'Look.'

And as they did, three things happened.

One, Mustafa's Muzzo army and Mumsy's PC Army, both of which had advanced into the heart of the park, were anything but two unified attack units. Muzzo horses were swerving about like Asian drivers and the berobbed men were screaming - Allah McDonalds! and Valhalla Snack Bar! and Vanhallen Rock Star! Some of the men had dismounted and were running about in mindless circles menacing invisible demons. Mumsy's men were laughing uproariously at this, had dropped their guns and were rolling gently on the grass, holding their sides in exploding mirth. Mumsy was shaking her head, as if to dislodge the pictures that had begun appearing in her mind. Buddy Rich was playing a drum solo on Abraham Lincoln's tummy and he was farting out maths formulas.

Two, the Icers began screaming like the hounds of hell and ran at the flailing Muzzos like over-sexed middle-aged men who have just been shown a flash of panties or a nip slip from . . . well . . . anyone really.

And three, the Jews attacked from the right flank, swinging their massive balls around like neutron stars, screaming: 'Oi! Vey! Such a day I'm having!' and 'Oh goy, oh goy! How did I get myself into this mess?'

And, just for the record, Heimi didn't make it. He came home late from cards and his wife wouldn't let him.

Within seconds, the armies met near the swimming pool, lake and café, and the carnage began. The Icers attacked with a screaming ferocity, matched by the screaming horror of the Muzzos, many of whom tried to tunnel away from the advancing phalluses and distended clitorises, but to no avail. The Icer women, enraged by Ice and pheromones ensnared each Muzzo head with their swollen vulvas, while the Icer men porked the Muzzo arses with pulsating penises, balls and all.

Then the Jews arrived, pounding Muzzo ribs with their enlarged testicles. The orthodox Jews dovened at them aggressively and cracked their skulls. One wise guy cracked: 'Curls just wanna have fun.'

In the melee, Mustafa scurried back to The Seymour Centre, disoriented by fear, followed by a slow-motion tyrannosaurus. Mumsy, trod on and squashed most of her army, who were still laughing riotously, until she trod on them.

It was later revealed that they were laughing so hard because, being politically correct, they had never understood the nature of humour until they took drugs. Those who survived Mumsy's reckless trample were soon cured of this sudden revelation when the Icers reached them and fucked them so hard, that many lost teeth. Later, the Icers would collect these and try to superglue them on so that they could eat meat again.

'They're getting away!' Ferret yelled and he and the Doc took up the chase.

The cacophony abated behind them as they finally reached the front courtyard of the Seymour Centre, where they found Mumsy and Mustafa standing beside Oscar, Billy and Abdul who were tied to a poster of an upcoming Aboriginal play called: *It's All Your Fault That We're in Jail.*

Billy still had the pillow tied to his arse.

'I don't know what you have done to us, infidel, but this will not end well for you,' cried Mustafa as he took out his scimitar and held it to Oscar's throat.

'Hold on a second,' replied Ferret. 'Take me, but let the boy go. He's done nothin' wrong.'

'It's too late, Ferret,' replied Mumsy. I told him Oscar was the cunt what give mumps to the Yids.'

'Yes,' added Mustafa, 'and for that, and for being your son, he will die.'

As Mustafa was about to slice Oscar's throat, Ferret yelled out, 'Shit! Look out! The Abo in the poster's after ya! He's breakin' outta jail!'

'You can't fool me!' Mustafa shouted back.

'Shit!' yelled Mumsy, reeling back in horror.

'Shit!' cried Mustafa looking up with equal alarm.

The twelve-foot Aborigine had broken through the bars of the poster and snarled at them like a Newborn Feminist.

Mustafa began to shake so badly that he dropped his scimitar and ran as fast as his legs could carry him up City Road towards Newtown.

'I'll be back in the sequel!' screamed Mumsy as she waddled after him, pursued, in her enlivened mind, by the twelve-foot Aborigine.

'Well done, Ferret,' said the Doc, placing a friendly

hand upon Ferret's back.

'No. Thank you,' Ferret replied. 'You're responsible for the victory, Doc, not me.'

They untied the three captives. Oscar gave Ferret a hug, so did Billy.

Abdul prostrated and humbled himself before Ferret.

'Knock it off, will ya Abdul. 'You're a free man.'

'I cannot leave you, master,' Abdul replied. 'I am forever in your debt.'

'Yeah, well, everybody wants to be in the sequel. C'mon, let's see how things turned out on the battlefield.'

They walked across to Victoria Park to a scene of devastation.

Disengaged arses and penises were a feature of the landscape. So too were writhing, nerve-tortured torsos. The Jews wandered through this garden of genitalia admiring the foreskins complaining that although it wasn't Kosha, it was a shame that they had been denied the extra pleasure of it rubbing on the underside of their sexual organs.

The Icers had run out of living things to fuck, so they turned upon each other in frenetic, uncontained lust. The Jews sat and watched and commented on this spectacle with interest.

Doctor Goldstein said, 'I wish Mrs Goldstein had such enthusiasm.'

Icer engagement was gladiatorial in nature. When any two Icers met in a flurry and blur of crazed, libidinous combat, one would eventually fuck the other to death and move on to another who had achieved the same feat. In this manner the Icers were finally reduced to two heavily breathing and exhausted contestants – Parrot and a ferocious, emaciated Windsor woman, who had yellow straw hair and a face like a cunt that a fox had gnawed at. They circled each other warily, Parrot taunting the woman by suggesting that it was lucky she didn't have any teeth because no one wanted a cunt with teeth, except for really kinky people. She was in deep consultation with her clitoris, which whispered instructions into her left ear as she circled. Parrot made the first move. His engorged organ thrust forward like a horizontal sledgehammer and knocked the woman off her feet. He sought to gain advantage by attacking her prostrate body, but she rolled away and avoided his lunge. As a result, he impaled his penis into the upturned earth and ended up looking like a street sign under a heavy wind. She took advantage of his struggling form and dived at him from behind with her angry clitoris rigid and uncompromising. She penetrated his rectum and pierced his heart, killing him instantly. Then she turned on the Jews, but they were having none of it. As a group, they surrounded her and while two or three of them felt the wrath of her sex organ, she was soon beaten to death by their massive wrecking-ball balls.

When at last her withering clitoris wilted, cursing the Jews as it drooped, only then did they celebrate their victory. They held up Ferret, the Doc and Doctor Goldstein upon their shoulders and paraded them through the streets of Sydney. Down towards The Opera House they celebrated, ticker tape falling upon them from the buildings, merrily thrown by the ninety five percent of the city's citizens who secretly hated political correctness but were too scared to speak out, lest they be called an 'ist' of some description.

As they reached the courtyard, an awesome sight greeted the eyes of Jews and goys alike. Massive lightning and dark ominous, angry clouds had suddenly appeared in the west and were tumbling furiously across the sky in black and green consternation. As they watched, a luminous cloud began to form a solid shape across the harbour at Luna Park. In breathless anticipation they waited, as tense as a poofter's first penetration, until, at length, the cloud assembled itself into a human form.

'Garwood,' Ferret whispered in quiet rapture.

The rain clouds were now fully behind the spectre as it parted the waters of Sydney harbour and floated through the tunnel of air, which was miraculously holding the surrounding water on each side. If you ever saw that movie, *The Ten Commandments* - well, like that. Behind him straggled a tribe of Aborigines and the Ball-less Atheists. (Sorry about that, but I thought I'd better round it all off.)

Garwood floated up onto the courtyard and raised his arms to the heavens and lo, it began to pour with rain. The Abos gathered behind him. The Ball-less Atheists mingled with the Jews. The Jews complained about the weather.

Thus spake Garwood: The drought is over!' he boomed. 'It will rain for forty days and nights.'

One of the Jews spoke out, 'Excuse me, but I have a bar mitzva in two weeks for my son, Leon. Could we have a rest day?'

'Oh, you are a stiff-necked people,' replied Garwood. 'If that's the 15th, I can't do it.'

'At least put in a good word for me,' added the man.

Garwood continued: 'The dams will be full and the land plentiful. The poles will reassemble, and the waters of the oceans will retreat. Jews you are cured. Look down and see that the engorgement of your testes is no more. And Ball-less Atheists, your testes have returned now that the blight of political correctness has been banished from the land. And Abdul, you can have your balls back too for fighting for the cause of freedom of speech.'

And there was great rejoicing.

'But Jews, hear this. Next time, get vaccinated.' And he disappeared in a silvery miasma of sparkling mist.

'Why are you back?' Ferret asked the Aborigines.

'They give us half of Queensland,' replied the boss of the mob, 'but we couldn't get no mobile reception out there in the rainforest.'

'And their 'ain't no electricity, or Netflix,' added another.

'Or dole,' chimed in a third.

Then all, except Ferret, the Doc, Oscar, Abdul and Billy, who still had a pillow on his arse, left.

'Thanks to you, Doc,' said Ferret, 'we've won the day.

'Any time, Ferret,' the Doc replied.

'I am forever your servant,' said Abdul with a generous bow.

'No worries, Abdul,' replied Ferret. 'You're a free man now. You can do as you wish. And what about you, Billy. How's your arse?'

'As fucked as Hong Kong,' he replied.

And they all had a merry chuckle.

'Well done, dad,' Oscar congratulated Ferret.

'It was my pleasure, son,' he replied. 'Now let's get out of this rain.

*

The next day Ferret and Oscar rode back out to Windsor. They stopped in at the Imperial Hotel.

'G'day, Ferret,' Steve greeted them. 'It's good to see ya. It's been quieter than a married fuck since you and the Icers left. And who's this young bloke?'

'This is Oscar,' replied Ferret.

'He's a good-lookin' young fella. How are ya, son?'

'Good thanks,' replied Oscar with a handshake.

'Where'd you come from? I 'ain't never seen you before.'

'To tell you truth, Steve,' said Ferret, 'he only just found out the whole truth of the matter. I explained it to him on the way here.'

'And what's that?' asked Steve.

'I'm your boy, Steve. Your long-lost son. Ferret

rescued me.'

'Holy shit,' murmured Steve. He sat on a bar stool to steady himself. 'Yeah, I can see a bit of Rayleen in ya, but he also looks like . . .'

'I guess I got two dads,' interjected Oscar. 'That alright with you, Steve? I mean, dad?'

Steve was lost in thought for a moment, then a tear welled up in his eye. 'Fuck it. It's great to have you back son. Come 'ere.'

Oscar and Steve embraced, but Ferret didn't, 'cos he thought that was a bit poofy, until Oscar said, 'Come on dad,' and he joined in too.

After the hugs were all done Ferret said, 'Well boys, looks like we got a lot of work to do.'

'What are we gunna do?' asked Steve.

'Mate,' Ferret replied, 'when this rain stops, we're gunna knock this town and country back into shape, or my name 'ain't Ferris Cutler.

'If anyone can do it you can, dad,' replied Oscar.

'Thanks, boy,' he replied. 'Now let's get outta these clothes. I'm wetter than a virgin at a stag party.

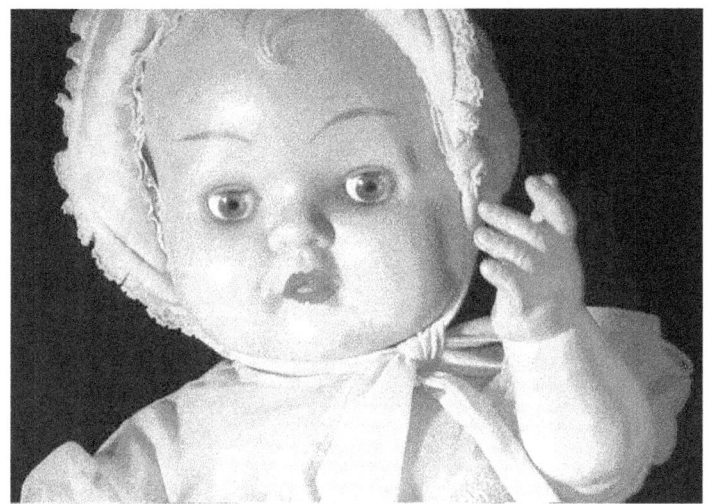

Madison Doll is a prolific writer of children's books. She has written such classics as: 'Paedophiles Have to be in Bed by 6pm' and 'Christopher Robin Rims Tigger'.

Her non-fiction works include: 'Christianity Versus Evolution – An Apes Perspective' and 'The Funny Side of Genital Mutilation'. As band manager she has also produced two albums of offensive songs by 'Ferret and the Pheromones'.

She lives alone in Windsor N.S.W. and has no friends.

www.ingramcontent.com/pod-product-compliance
Lightning Source LLC
Chambersburg PA
CBHW071059250626
47159CB00002B/528